Ghost Stories

Ghost Stories

Edited by
Deborah Shine

Illustrated by
Reg Gray

CONTENTS

First published 1980 by
Octopus Books Limited
59 Grosvenor Street
London W1
Reprinted 1981, 1982, 1983, 1984

ISBN 0 7064 1158 7

Printed in Czechoslovakia

50 394/6

THE RIDDLE

Walter de la Mare

So these seven children, Ann and Matilda, James, William and Henry, Harriet and Dorothea, came to live with their grandmother. The house in which their grandmother had lived since her childhood was built in the time of the Georges. It was not a pretty house, but roomy, substantial, and square; and a great cedar tree outstretched its branches almost to the windows.

When the children were come out of the cab (five sitting inside and two beside the driver), they were shown into their grandmother's presence. They stood in a little black group before the old lady, seated in her bow-window. And she asked them each their names, and repeated each name in her kind, quavering voice. Then to one she gave a work-box, to William a jack-knife, to Dorothea a painted ball; to each a present according to age. And she kissed all her grand-children to the youngest.

'My dears,' she said, 'I wish to see all of you bright and gay in my house. I am an old woman, so that I cannot romp with you; but Ann must look to you, and Mrs Fenn too. And every morning and every evening you must all come in to see your granny; and bring me smiling faces, that call back to my mind my own son Harry. But all the rest of the day, when school is done, you shall do just as you please, my dears. And there is only one thing, just one, I would have you remember. In the large spare bedroom that looks out on the slate roof there stands in the corner an old oak chest; aye, older than I, my dears, a great deal older; older than my grandmother. Play anywhere else in the house, but not there.' She spoke kindly to them all, smiling at them; but she was very old, and her eyes seemed to see nothing of this world.

And the seven children, though at first they were gloomy and strange, soon began to be happy and at home in the great house. There was much to interest and to amuse them there; all was new to them. Twice every day, morning and evening, they came in to see their grandmother, who every day seemed more feeble; and she spoke pleasantly to them of her mother, and her childhood, but never forgetting to visit her store of sugar-plums. And so the weeks passed by. . . .

It was evening twilight when Henry went upstairs from the nursery by himself to look at the oak chest. He pressed his fingers into the carved fruit and flowers, and spoke to the dark-smiling heads at the corners; and then, with a glance over his shoulder, he opened the lid and looked in. But the chest concealed no treasure, neither gold nor baubles, nor was there anything to alarm the eye. The chest was empty, except that it was lined with silk of old-rose, seeming darker in the dusk, and smelling sweet of pot-pourri. And while Henry was looking in, he heard the softened laughter and the clinking of the cups downstairs in the nursery; and out at the window he saw the day darkening. These things brought strangely to his memory his mother who in her glimmering white dress used to read to him in the dusk; and he climbed into the chest; and the lid closed gently down over him.

When the other six children were tired with their playing, they filed into their grandmother's room for her goodnight and her sugar-plums. She looked out between the candles at them as if she were uncertain of something in her thoughts. The next day Ann told her grandmother that Henry was not anywhere to be found.

'Dearie me, child. Then he must be gone away for a time,' said the old lady. She paused. 'But remember, all of you, do not meddle with the oak chest.'

But Matilda could not forget her brother Henry, finding no pleasure

The seven children soon began to be happy in the great house.

in playing without him. So she would loiter in the house thinking where he might be. And she carried her wooden doll in her bare arms, singing under her breath all she could make up about it. And when one bright morning she peeped in on the chest, so sweet-scented and secret it seemed that she took her doll with her into it—just as Henry himself had done.

So Ann, and James, and William, Harriet and Dorothea were left at home to play together. 'Some day maybe they will come back to you, my dears,' said their grandmother, 'or maybe you will go to them. Heed my warning as best you may.'

Now Harriet and William were friends together, pretending to be sweethearts; while James and Dorothea liked wild games of hunting, and fishing, and battles.

On a silent afternoon in October, Harriet and William were talking softly together, looking out over the slate roof at the green fields, and they heard the squeak and frisking of a mouse behind them in the room. They went together and searched for the small, dark hole from whence it had come out. But finding no hole, they began to finger the carving of the chest, and to give names to the dark-smiling heads, just as Henry had done. '*I* know! let's pretend you are Sleeping Beauty, Harriet,' said William, 'and I'll be the Prince that squeezes through the thorns and comes in.' Harriet looked gently and strangely at her brother but she got into the box and lay down, pretending to be fast asleep, and on tiptoe William leaned over, and seeing how how big was the chest, he stepped in to kiss the Sleeping Beauty and to wake her from her quiet sleep. Slowly the carved lid turned on its noiseless hinges. And only the clatter of James and Dorothea came in sometimes to recall Ann from her book.

But their old grandmother was very feeble, and her sight dim, and her hearing extremely difficult.

Snow was falling through the still air upon the roof; and Dorothea was a fish in the oak chest, and James stood over the hole in the ice, brandishing a walking-stick for a harpoon, pretending to be an Esquimau. Dorothea's face was red, and her wild eyes sparkled through her tousled hair. And James had a crooked scratch upon his cheek. 'You must struggle, Dorothea, and then I shall swim back and drag you out. Be quick now!' He shouted with laughter as he was drawn into the open chest. And the lid closed softly and gently down as before.

Ann, left to herself, was too old to care overmuch for sugar-plums, but she would go solitary to bid her grandmother goodnight; and the old lady looked wistfully at her over her spectacles. 'Well, my dear,' she said with trembling head; and she squeezed Ann's fingers between her own knuckled finger and thumb. 'What lonely old people we two are, to be sure!' Ann kissed her grandmother's soft, loose cheek. She left the old lady sitting in her easy chair, her hands upon her knees, and her head turned sidelong towards her.

When Ann was gone to bed she used to sit reading her book by candlelight. She drew up her knees under the sheets resting her book upon them. Her story was about fairies and gnomes, and the gently-flowing moonlight of the narrative seemed to illumine the white pages, and she could hear in fancy fairy voices, so silent was the great many-roomed house, and so mellifluent were the words of the story. Presently she put out her candle, and, with a confused babel of voices close to her ear, and faint swift pictures before her eyes, she fell alseep.

And in the dead of night she rose out of her bed in dream, and with eyes wide open yet seeing nothing of reality, moved silently through the vacant house. Past the room where her grandmother was snoring in brief, heavy slumber, she stepped lightly and surely, and down the wide staircase. And Vega the far-shining stood over against the window above the slate roof. Ann walked into the strange room beneath as if she were being guided by the hand towards the oak chest. There, just as if she were dreaming it was her bed, she laid herself down in the old rose silk, in the fragrant place. But it was so dark in the room that the movement of the lid was indistinguishable.

Through the long day, the grandmother sat in her bow-window. Her lips were pursed, and she looked with dim, inquisitive scrutiny upon the street where people passed to and fro, and vehicles rolled by. At evening she climbed the stair and stood in the doorway of the large spare bedroom. The ascent had shortened her breath. Her magnifying spectacles rested upon her nose. Leaning her hand on the door post she peered in towards the glimmering square of window in the quiet gloom. But she could not see far, because her sight was dim and the light of day feeble. Nor could she detect the faint fragrance as of autumnal leaves But in her mind was a tangled skein of memories

—laughter and tears, and children long ago become old-fashioned, and the advent of friends, and last farewells. And gossiping fitfully, inarticulately, with herself, the old lady went down again to her window-seat.

THE SYBARITE

Stanley W. Fisher

Nothing could have been cosier. Dr Gordon's housekeeper had cleared away the debris of an excellent dinner, and the four doctors, for once each able to anticipate an evening free from interruptions, sat in deep, leather-covered club armchairs before a blazing fire.

Gerald Gordon, MD, FRCP frankly owned to being a sybarite. It was well-known in the profession that he scorned any form of exercise (to which his portly form was witness enough), preferring to spend his considerable income upon the rare and beautiful antiques which crowded his spacious sitting-room, upon which he was content to gloat during those hours of leisure when other lesser and (in his opinion) less cultured men wasted their time and energies playing golf and other childish games.

It was entirely in character that as he sat sipping his brandy his gaze wandered idly and obviously proudly round the contents of his room. A Hepplewhite mahogany break-front bookcase filled with mostly first editions bound in red, brown and green Morocco leather, early Sèvres porcelain vases converted to electric table-lamps with red and green silk shades, Sheraton mahogany and satin-wood Pembroke and Sofa Tables intricately inlaid or painted, Chelsea and Bow figures and groups upon the mantlepiece, early English watercolours upon the

He would gloat upon the rare and beautiful antiques.

walls, and silk Bokhara rugs on the polished oak floor. All these, and much more.

If he had been alone it would have been his pleasure, as usual, to re-examine every piece, to build up in his mind its possible past history, to revise his meticulously kept records—in fact, to indulge in all those delights which all collectors know so well. But of course he was not alone, and with some reluctance he remembered his duties as host and made some attempt to join in the conversation passing between his three colleagues.

As might be expected, all were members of the jealously exclusive Harley Street fraternity. Gordon had doubts about the eligibility of Brian Mansen, who after all was a mere MBChB, a rather non-descript, self-affacing little man, though none could question his growing repute as an unusually brilliant anaesthetist.

On the other hand, Jasper Benson, FRCS was the surgeon to whom he referred many of his own patients, and who had his full approval and confidence. A tall man, stern-faced with steel-grey hair. A man to give his patients confidence as the piercing blue eyes twinkled reassurance, though as Gordon knew full well they had already learned much concerning their condition even before he had shaken them firmly by the hand and seated them comfortably in the chair facing his desk.

Gordon had his reservations regarding the fourth member of the party. Roger Hawkins was a neurological surgeon who had taken his Birmingham MD before coming to London, where he had gained his Fellowship, and already he had well earned a growing reputation though there were rumours that his technique was perhaps more revolutionary, even at times reckless, than might be expected of one of comparatively short experience. Nevertheless, there he was, a short, lean man, with a sallow complexion and lead-coloured eyes set rather too close together for Gordon's liking. The good doctor disliked also the young man's thin-lipped mouth, which curled in ill-concealed contempt when his theories or opinions were contradicted.

The truth was, as Gordon admitted to himself, was that at heart he mistrusted all surgeons, though he had to use them. It was this professional snobbery, if such it might be termed, that had been the topic of conversation before dinner. He had made it clear (and immediately regretted his outspokenness) that in his opinion a surgeon was little more than a carpenter, and that any operation, however skilfully performed, was a mutilation of the human body. The argument had become heated when it was interrupted by dinner. Hawkins in particular had been angrily vehement in his rebuttal of what he clearly considered to be a slur on his recently acquired qualification.

Gordon had done his best to soothe the man. After all he had on several occasions found it necessary to call upon his special skills, and would doubtless need to do so again. Besides, though he would never have openly admitted to being a snob (which at heart he knew he was) what else but uncouth behaviour could one expect from a Midlander? Especially one, he suspected, of humble origin. However, the man was a close friend of Benson, which was why he had been invited to dinner, and it was politic to ignore his shortcomings.

As he feared, when he reluctantly rejoined the shop talk, the two surgeons held the fort, while Mansen said nothing, being obviously content to look from one to the other with something close to hero-worship in his eyes.

The subject appeared to be the vexed one of the transplanting of hearts and other vital organs. It was therefore unfortunate that Gordon held opinions directly opposite to those held by the surgeons, which he had no hesitation in expressing.

Gordon remained adamant in his opinion that the saving of a very few lives by transplantation, for example, was no legitimate excuse for what he suspected was reckless experimentation carried out in operating theatres, which all too often resulted only in failure or in prolonged and unnecessary suffering.

He refused to be persuaded by any argument, and was uncomfortably aware that perhaps he would have been wiser to have restrained his tongue. He could see that Benson was eying him coldly and objectively as if were making a reappraisal of a man who had been his friend for many years. He did not like it, and would have made some attempt to bridge the gulf which was so clearly widening between them, had not Hawkins stepped in.

The neurologist had been steadily growing angrier during the exchanges of opinion. And now, unable any longer to restrain himself, he burst in. . . .

'Look, Gordon! You've been talking a lot of rubbish for the past half hour! I'll put one question to you, and I want a straight answer! If you had the choice of living on with some crippling disease which left your brain fully active, or of undergoing an operation of the kind we have been discussing which would cure you, what would be your choice?'

Gordon saw too late the difficult position in which he had put himself. He hesitated, but Hawkins gave him no time to think how best he could escape from it without eating his words.

'Surely you can have no doubt if you have the courage of your convictions?' Then twisting the knife in the wound. . . . 'Or perhaps your fine words were nothing but wind?'

There was a long silence as Gordon gathered his thoughts, while the eyes of his companions were fixed upon him, as if daring him to retract. He was damned if he would! What he had said was what he believed. And he would stick to it!

'A hypothetical question, Hawkins, and you know it! And the way in which you put it is unpardonable since you are a guest in my house! My answer is such that even you may understand. I'll keep it short. I'd say be damned to your operation!'

Then—and he could not resist it—'And be damned to you, Sir!'

It was not surprising that after this exchange the party broke up.

Gordon was disturbed and angry, not so much with Hawkins as with himself. He could not but feel that he had impulsively let himself be placed in a ridiculous position, simply because he had allowed his dislike of the other man to overcome his discretion.

However, he consoled himself with the conviction that he had been in the right, and his anger slowly passed. He helped himself to a night-cap and went to his bed determined to forget the whole disagreeable affair.

To do this proved to be easier said than done. Over the next few months his relations with Benson, both friendly and professionally gradually deteriorated, though on rare occasions the two found it advantageous to call each other into consultation. He avoided Hawkins deliberately. Mansen seemed anxious to be friendly, and obviously went out of his way to avoid any reference to the disastrous dinner party.

Two years passed. Hawkins had left London, and had opened a private nursing-home in Kent, where he gained a growing reputation for successful inplant operations, in which he was assisted occasionally by Benson who however remained in Harley Street.

It was towards the end of that time that he first felt a certain stomach discomfort which, despite careful dieting and medication developed into actual bouts of pain. He suspected an ulcer. He lost weight, and his sunken cheeks and general feeling of debility made it increasingly obvious that much against his will he should lose no time in seeking surgical advice. After all, he thought, an operation for ulcer was not very serious.

Following the advice he always gave to his patients in such cases, which as a doctor he could not cure, he made an appointment to see Jasper Benson, as being the best man available.

The surgeon received him amicably enough. Why should he not, when the two men had never completely severed their professional relations. He asked the usual questions. When did the pain begin and where exactly? What was it like? Was it persistent or intermittent? And so forth.

When Gordon lay on the examination couch Benson's immaculately manicured, slender yet strong fingers pressed and probed, his eyes fixed on Gordon's face as he did so.

The examination over, the surgeon gave the verdict that Gordon had steeled himself to suspect might be a possibility.

'I can definitely feel something there, but we'll have to have a set of X-rays before I can advise you further. I would suggest that you get Ames to see to them for you—and that you waste no time.'

Ames was one of the half dozen doctors and surgeons who shared Gordon's Harley Street rooms, and the following day, for the first time in his life, in middle age, a now very anxious doctor underwent the nauseous business of forcing down in stages the Barium Meal which he had so often described to his patients as 'a pleasant drink of Horlicks. Nothing to it!'

He saw Benson the same afternoon. The two men examined the plates together, and Gordon's heart sank as the surgeon's finger traced the lights and shadows which represented his own blood-filled organs. The picture was all too clear.

'I'm more sorry than I can say,' said Benson, 'but you can see the extent of your trouble as well as I. Of course, you have a carcinoma, but it is not certain to what extent it has spread. Your only course is to undergo a laparotomy.'

Now that he knew the worst, at least for the moment, Gordon felt resigned. He nodded. Benson went on. . . .

'I will of course be willing to perform the operation, if you agree. Yes? Then the next thing to decide is where you would prefer it to take place? The choice is of course yours. But may I make a suggestion? As you know, I have for some time worked with Hawkins at his clinic. His theatre is excellently equipped and the man is really a brilliant surgeon. I feel sure that he would fit you in, and would be most willing to assist me.'

Gordon's heart sank. Benson, yes. But Hawkins? He was about to refuse angrily when the surgeon raised a restraining hand.

'Please, don't be hasty! I know how much you dislike Hawkins, but this is no time to be swayed by personal feelings. Your condition is serious, my friend, and as I have heard you say so often the only wise course is to put yourself in the hands of only the best.' He shrugged, smiling grimly. 'I would be the last to boast of my own skill. You have known me and my work for too long for that to be necessary. And of course you may well feel that Hawkins has a reputation for, shall we say, unorthodox techniques. Nevertheless, I can assure you that whatever new and perhaps revolutionary methods he has perfected have my entire approval. Take my word for it, Gordon! Or perhaps you would prefer to consult another surgeon?'

The tone in which Benson made this suggestion was such that his patient understood very clearly that in effect it was an ultimatum. He persuaded himself that his dislike of Hawkins should not be allowed to relate to his professional skill, as it was so glowingly praised by Benson. And certainly he wanted Benson.

He agreed.

★   ★   ★   ★

A week later the two men drove down together into Kent in the surgeon's Rolls Royce. Conversation lagged, but just as they drove through the stone-pillared entrance to the drive leading to the nursing home, Benson remarked, casually, that Mansen had agreed to act as anaesthetist. Gordon merely nodded agreement. His companion said no more, though he too nodded his satisfaction, but slowly, and with a little smile lingering on his lips.

To Gordon's surprise (for he had not looked forward to the meeting) Hawkins greeted them cordially at the door of his sizeable, stone-built Georgian house, which had clearly recently been enlarged by the addition of a single storeyed wing containing perhaps half a dozen rooms, judging by the number of windows.

Hawkins glanced at his wrist-watch.

'I see we have an hour or so before dinner. I'll get your bags taken up to your room, and perhaps you would care to take a look round?'

This question was of course evidently addressed mainly to Gordon, but both the surgeon and his patient did as Hawkins suggested. Gordon was certainly impressed by the operating theatre, which more than lived up to Benson's description. There was no doubt about its up-to-date nature, for much of its equipment was entirely new to him. Though admittedly he was not a surgeon.

They passed what was clearly the entrance to the new wing. To Gordon's enquiries as to its purpose Hawkins merely remarked that its rooms were occupied by post-operatives and convalescent patients.

'You will be in one of them, of course. But now we must not over-tire you. Let me take you up to your room for a rest before dinner. I can promise you that I have an excellent cook. And I want you to enjoy your meal.'

He smiled.

'It is the last you will have for some time, you know!'

The meal was indeed extremely good, though Gordon was unable to do justice to it, being anxious and beginning to suffer from one of the attacks of pain which during the past weeks had attacked him ever more often.

Hawkins, observing his discomfort, suggested that he retire to bed. He accompanied his patient, and seemed anxious to ensure that everything had been provided that he might need.

As he was leaving he paused in the doorway.

'Benson and I will be discussing what we shall do with you before we come up to bed. He told you, I suppose, that our friend Mansen will be along to put you to sleep? Good man, Mansen. Very cooperative. Sleep well!'

Strangely enough he did, having taken two tablets of pethidine.

The next day followed the usual pattern which precedes a major operation, and Brian Mansen duly arrived during the evening. He was almost sickeningly apologetic in his tapping, sounding and blood-pressure testing, but had little to say apart from the necessary questioning. He did not linger. On leaving he declared himself satisfied, from his own point of view, with the patient's condition, and assured him that he anticipated no problems 'at his end.'

★   ★   ★   ★

Gordon's recovery from the anaesthetic followed the usual pattern. A drowsy, comfortable state of half sleeping, half waking, which his subconscious was loth to leave. The sound of faraway, dulled voices which meant nothing. Then, a sudden awakening to life and to an awareness of his surroundings.

'Ah, Gordon! So you are back with us again! All snug and comfortable in your room!'

The voice was that of Hawkins.

But it was not his room. At least, not the comfortably furnished one from which he had been taken earlier in the day.

The two surgeons were standing before him, smiling benevolently, in their white jackets.

And everything else was white.

The walls facing him, the ceiling, and the enamel of the glass-fronted cupboard, its shelves carrying an assortment of bottles and gleaming steel instruments. He tried to turn his head but found he could not do so. Neither could he look up or down. It was as though from the neck upwards he was held in a vice.

Surely by now the effects of the anaesthetic should have worn off? He felt no pain. He felt nothing.

What was even more strange was that he realized that his head was not resting on a pillow. It was upright. Resting, then, on what?

By now thoroughly alarmed he opened his mouth to speak.

And could make no sound.

Of course, this was a nightmare! But who in a nightmare could so fully comprehend the meaning of what Benson (who had been watching his efforts closely) then said, clearly and deliberately?

'You are awake, Gordon. And you are of course alive according to the concensus of modern medical opinion. Hawkins and I, with Mansen's invaluable assistance, have carried out what I may say without conceit has been a most successful operation.

'We were just in time, my dear fellow! Your carcinoma, I regret to say, was in the usually accepted sense quite inoperable, since it had spread to your liver.'

He turned to Hawkins. 'Perhaps you had better continue? It is due to your skill and not mine that our friend here is not, shall we say, a doomed man?'

So addressed, Hawkins stepped forwards and began to speak in a half sneering, half mocking voice very different from that which he had used to his patient the previous day.

'Do you remember, Dr Gordon, our conversation two years ago? Perhaps you do not. Permit me to remind you. Somewhat offensively you expressed the opinion that you would be content with a life of complete immobility provided that your mental powers were unimpaired. Or words to that effect.

'You are indeed fortunate. The "carpenter", as you so charmingly expressed yourself, has saved your life, and your brain is as active as it has ever been. How have I worked this miracle you ask yourself, since I fear you cannot ask me? I will be brief.

'I have removed your arms and legs and, of course, your diseased body.

'Below your head is a somewhat complicated cabinet of my own design, which I regret you will never be able to examine. It contains only your heart, the beating of which will, I trust, may be audible companionship for you in the hours of darkness. You retain your own blood in sufficient quantity to nourish your brain, and which is automatically supplied with nourishment and air. You have no need for excretory organs. I could of course have preserved your lungs, had I not decided to avoid being wearied by the inevitable but quite unreasonable insults which doubtless are even now—er—on the tip of your tongue.'

Gordon closed his eyes, longing for oblivion. No memories, no awareness, only everlasting, unwaking oblivion. He was denied even the relief of a scream, though his terror was in his head one long, unending scream.

Benson spoke.

'Your official funeral has of course been arranged, and your next of kin informed. An aunt, I understand, living in Australia? She will of course inherit your possessions in due course. I could wish that some of your treasures might have been removed and brought here to furnish what must as time passes become a somewhat boring apartment, but you will of course understand that such a course might have given rise to suspicion in less enlightened minds.'

Gordon's tormentors turned to leave.

As they reached the door. . . .

'For how long can our friend be kept alive? asked Benson.

'Oh, I should say indefinitely,' replied Hawkins.

ECHOES IN THE SAND

Roger F. Dunkley

'Matt's scared!'

Matt paused at the entrance to the cave.

Outside, the sun spilled down on the beach, topping the break-ing waves with white fire. Inside was a twilight world, curving upwards into moist, rocky blackness. A seagull wailed mournfully overhead.

'He *is*! He's scared!' shouted Ben. He called to their sister, who was hesitantly teasing a crab in a nearby rock pool. 'Look, Maggie. Matt doesn't want to come into the cave.' Ben strode boldly into the dark mouth gashed in the cliff. His scornful laugh took on a hollow ring as the mouth swallowed him.

He took several more steps and the darkness wrapped round him. He disappeared from view.

Matt hesitated. It was hard being the elder brother. You felt so responsible all the time. The cave might be dangerous; there could be rock falls and so on. And they were a long way from the village. What if anything happened to them? He looked back across the stretch of shining sand which formed the floor of the cove and saw the sharp, towering rocks over which they'd climbed to get here. They began to look like a wall which had shut them in.

Maggie, small and insistent, was tugging at his hand. 'Come on, Matt, let's explore,' she said, and ran off into the cave mouth.

'No!' shouted Matt suddenly, and surprised himself by the sharpness of his voice. 'Come back.'

'Coward!' boomed Ben's voice out of the darkness, followed by a hollow giggle from Maggie.

Matt stepped reluctantly out of the sunlight into the instant gloom of the cave. He shivered. It had a wet, cold smell. He waited for a moment, then groped a little further and stumbled against a rock. He put out a hand to support himself. He felt something warm, something that moved. His heart raced.

'Ouch!' said the something.

'Maggie!' Matt's voice betrayed his relief. '*There* you are!'

'There's no need to pinch,' said his sister, rubbing her arm in the gloom. 'Spooky, isn't it?' She shuddered, only half pretending.

'I *told* you to stay outside,' said Matt.

'Just because I'm younger than you. . . .'

'No. . . . But if you're frightened. . . .'

'*I'm* not frightened.'

'All right. Let's go and find Ben.'

Maggie hesitated. 'No,' she said uneasily.

'Well, go *back*, then,' said Matt, exasperated.

'Shan't.'

Then she screamed. From the depths of the cave bubbled a dreadful laugh. Its echoes danced on the invisible surfaces around them.

'I'm going,' wailed Maggie.

She went.

Matt laughed. 'Ben!' he called, you shouldn't tease her like that. Where are you?

'Here,' said the distant voice not very helpfully. 'It comes into a sort of cavern. But the tunnel gets jolly narrow first.'

Matt slithered forward with his head down, groping from sand to stones, from stones to rocks, until he felt the roof of the tunnel rising and found he could stand up again in safety.

He looked round. The darkness had been replaced by a grey light which hung in the cavernous space. Walls arched up and up like those of a cathedral. A thin beam of sunlight had found its way through a cleft in the rocks and kindled the white stalactites which dripped glittering from the roof.

'Wow!' said Matt, awed. A little booming 'Wow' came back from the surrounding walls.

Ben clambered off a nearby rock. 'Let's go,' he said, sounding less cheerful than before.

'Hang on,' said Matt. He put his head on one side. 'Can you hear anything?'

Ben shivered slightly and tried to disguise it by jumping up and down and rubbing his arms.

'*Now* who's scared?' said Matt, unable to resist the taunt.

'Oh, come *on,*' said Ben.

'O-o-n. O-o-n,' sounded the cave on a curious booming note.

'No, wait a minute,' said Matt. 'It reminds me of something.'

Wasn't there some story. . . .? he thought, and then remembered. An old saint. . . . Yes. St Nestan. Hundreds of years ago. People said he used to ring a bell when ships got too near the coast—or something like that. But what had it got to do with the cave?

'Hallo,' said Matt experimentally.

'Lo . . .. Lo . . .. Lo . . ..' murmured the cave.

'Oh, Matt,' said Ben, beginning to sound really frightened, 'you're not going to do your werewolf thing? Not here?'

Matt was tempted, but thought better of it. 'I just thought I'd heard a sort of . . . bell,' he said.

'Bell?' said Ben uneasily.

'Yes, bell. You know. A thing that goes ding–dong in a belfry.'

Ben saw that Matt was making a joke of it and felt better. 'Bats in the belfry!' he shouted. 'Matt's bats!' He laughed.

The sound broke the spell. Matt chased Ben cautiously back the way they had come, slithering and scrambling together, until they emerged again into the dazzling roar of surf and sunshine. He gave his younger brother a friendly thump.

Maggie was making letters in the sand just outside the cave. Ben, not looking where he was going, trod on them. Maggie howled. He dropped to his heels beside Maggie. 'The sea would have spoiled them anyway,' he said. 'Look. The tide's nearly up to us.' He quickly scrawled letters in the sand: THIS IS MAGGIE NEWPORT'S BEACH. SEA, KEEP OFF.

In a moment water swirled round his ankles and then retreated, leaving a large blob and the words, THIS IS MAGGIE. Maggie giggled.

Ben joined in the game and scrawled, BEN WAS HERE, with a stick.

'Typical!' thought Matt. 'No imagination.' He remembered the cave again and wondered whether his own imagination had led him astray. There had seemed to be a sound. . . . Like a bell.

Waves came up the beach and obliterated BEN. The three retreated.

'Are these yours?' said Matt presently, pointing to three crosses firmly etched in the sand.

'No,' said Maggie.

'Of course not,' said Ben scornfully, scrawling BEN IS STILL HERE with his finger. 'Catch *me* drawing kisses!'

Water washed away BEN for the second time and then retreated, leaving the sand fresh and bare—except for three crosses.

'Well, look at that,' said Ben indignantly.

Water washed round his ankles again, and again fell back. Three crosses remained.

'That's odd,' said Matt. He knelt down and swept the crosses away with his hand.

Again the tide swirled round their feet and ran back down the beach. Three crosses had reappeared.

Matt saw that Maggie was delighted and Ben merely puzzled, but the hairs on the back of his neck felt ruffled as though someone was watching him. He glanced over his shoulder at the mouth of the cave, but it was black and empty.

'I expect there are some rocks or something underneath the sand,' he said. 'Maybe they make the water run like that.'

But as though to disprove him, the crosses had disappeared when the next wave swept their feet.

★　　★　　★　　★

'Ding-dong,' said Ben, looking up from the tea-table with his mouth full of bread and butter. 'Matt's going mental, you know.'

'Serviette, dear,' said Mrs Newport absently.

'He's hearing things. *And* seeing crosses in the sand.'

Matt kept a dignified silence.

'I saw them, too,' said Maggie, spraying crumbs. 'Kisses. Crosses.'

'We *all* saw them,' said Matt quietly.

'We didn't all hear your ding-dong in the belfrey.'

'I can't think what you're talking about, dear,' said Mrs Newport.

'Matt,' said Ben. 'He's bats in the belfrey. Batty Matty. Matty batty.'

'For goodness sake, Ben,' said Mrs Newport, watching Matt scowl and feeling some sympathy, 'do be your age. Thank heaven your father's coming down.'

The remark was well-judged. Matt beamed with satisfaction at the thought that somebody else could now take 'those kids' in hand. Maggie yelled. Ben shouted, 'When?'

'On Friday, dear. Don't shout. He 'phoned this afternoon. 'He's coming for the last weekend of the holiday.'

'The boat!' squeaked Maggie. 'Did Daddy say he'd take us out? In the new boat?'

'"Cruiser",' said Ben, 'not "boat". Mum, it's not fair. It's been tied up there by the jetty all holiday. *I* could have navigated. Dad said so. It's not fair.'

'No, yes, no, no,' said Mrs Newport, trying to answer everybody's questions at once. 'I mean, I'm sure he'll take you out. If,' she added with quite unconvincing cunning, 'you behave very nicely for the rest of the week.'

Matt smiled quietly to himself. He knew that nothing would stop dad from showing off the new motor-vessel to the family as soon as he could.

Ben let out a noisy whoop of joy and skated about on the polished stone floor.

'Can Carrin come, too?' asked Maggie.

'Of course,' said Mrs Newport. 'Who's Carrin?'

'His dad's a fisherman,' said Ben. 'Grumpy old bloke. They live in those cottages at the end of the harbour.'

'They're lovely cottages,' said Mrs Newport. 'A bit pokey, though.'

'I think they're rather poor,' said Matt. 'We met Carrin down the harbour.'

'You should've seen his jersey!' said Maggie. 'All holes. I don't think he's got a mum.'

'He was sitting staring at Dad's new boat. You could see he was dying for a ride in it. We couldn't see the harm in offering.'

'Of course not, dear.'

'But you should have seen his old man!' said Ben.

Matt nodded and raised his eyebrows. 'He growled something about flashy boats and rich trippers. Us, trippers!'

'Ah well,' said Mrs Newport gently, 'anybody who comes down just for the summer must look like trippers to hard-working fishermen.'

Later, when Ben and Maggie had gone off to play smugglers and wreckers in the garden, she turned unexpectedly serious. 'What's this cave they're talking about?' she asked.

Matt explained. 'It's just up the coast,' he said. 'About a mile north of the village.'

'Near Trebarwitt?'

'Yes.'

Mrs Newport stood looking out of the kitchen window for a few moments.

'Matt,' she said presently, 'I don't want to be a spoil-sport or anything, but. . . .'

'But what, Mum?'

'I think I'd rather you didn't all go back there again.'

'You're going to tell me it's haunted!' said Matt, managing to sound scornful but finding that his neck was prickling a little.

'Oh, that. Yes. Practically everything's haunted round here—you know what Cornish people are like! First of all there's that legend of St Nestan, saving ships with a bell or something. Then—if I've got the right cave—there are stories of terrible wails on stormy nights; shadowy shapes; a madman with eyes of fire prowling through the tunnels; and all that sort of thing.'

'Do you believe that, Mum?'

'No,' said Mrs Newport firmly.

'Well, then. . . .?'

'There's something else,' she said, closing the kitchen door. 'Don't talk about it to the younger ones, but there's some story of a murder there. Something to do with wreckers and a man called Jack Fairmill.'

'*Wreckers*, Mum?' said Matt scornfully. 'There haven't been any wreckers since. . . . Oh, I don't know. At least a hundred years.'

Through the window they could see Ben standing on a little mound, waving a bicycle lamp. Maggie, a sailing-ship in distress, ran to and fro with terrible moans. Presently, like a moth drawn to a candle, she stumbled against the mound and fell at Ben's feet, looking up at the lamp. 'I'm wrecked! I'm wrecked!' she wailed. 'I've lured her to your doom!' shouted Ben.

'He's lured her to her doom!' said Matt. 'Honestly! Where does he get it from?'

'Late Night Horror Movie, I should think,' said Mrs Newport. 'But I'm not sure the wreckers have gone, you know,' she went on. 'Remember that mysterious shipwreck up near Trebarwitt last year? Not far from that cave of yours. I'd much rather you didn't take Ben and Mags back there.'

'OK, Mum. But who's Jack Fairmill?'

'I don't know, darling. Something to do with a murder, though. Perhaps he was a wrecker. You could ask that funny old Mr Oakes up at the Rectory. He's writing a book about the village.'

★   ★   ★   ★

'You'll have to come back this afternoon,' said Mr Oakes' housekeeper suspiciously. 'And *only* this afternoon, mind. He's away up to Truro tomorrow. What'll I say you'm wanting?'

Matt hesitated. He had too many questions. He thought for a moment. 'I'd like to ask him about Jack Fairmill,' he said.

'Jack the Killer?' said the old woman with a harsh laugh. That's a big question, my son.'

Matt was told to come back at four that afternoon. 'Sharp, mind. He's a busy old owl, is the master.' She shut the door firmly.

The Rectory lay on the north side of the village. It was half way to the cave. . . .

'Jack the Killer,' said Matt to himself with a shudder. 'Wreckers. Murder.' What business was it of his? he wondered. Why not go straight home? But he found his feet turning towards the north.

Twenty minutes later he had scrambled down the cliff path into the hidden cove.

Near the cave entrance Matt found what he was looking for and then wished that he hadn't.

The tide had been in twice since he was last here. Twice. It should have washed the beach quite clean. And yet. . . .

He looked again to make sure.

In the smooth sand at the foot of the cave entrance there were the faint outlines of three crosses.

Matt lifted his foot, meaning to wipe them away but was stopped by a shrill laugh from somewhere above his head. He looked up, his heart pounding. A seagull swooped away.

He began to walk slowly backwards down the beach, not liking to turn his back on the cave, and then stumbled on a rock and fell. A clammy tentacle of seaweed slithered across his cheek. Matt turned and ran.

'You're scared!' he said to himself five minutes later, standing on the cliff top. 'Just plain scared!' Nothing, he felt, would make him go back to that little cove again. Nothing.

Perhaps not scared, he thought presently, walking back to the village. Perhaps just sensible. Perhaps it was only commonsense to keep away from a place like that; there might be rock falls or something.

But he knew that something important had happened. The crosses said so. He felt they were meant for him. He *had* to find out whatever Mr Oakes could tell him. It suddenly seemed urgent.

★   ★   ★   ★

Mr Newport arrived at lunchtime, a day earlier than expected. Matt could see from the gleam in his eye that nothing would keep him off the water for very long. 'Oh, dear,' he thought, 'I'm going to have to choose between Dad and Mr Oakes. Why is everything so complicated?'

The lunchtime dishes were still on the table when Ben and Maggie started their war-dance round Father's chair.

'The boat! The boat!' chanted Maggie.

'The *cruiser*!' shouted Ben.

'Don't shout,' shouted Father.

'What on earth's all this shouting?' bellowed Mother.

'You promised,' wailed Maggie, 'And we promised Carrin.'

'Please! You've deafened the goldfish,' said Father.

'We haven't got any goldfish,' objected Maggie.

'I expect they left because of the noise,' said Father.

Silence arrived abruptly.

'Well, you might have the decency to laugh at my jokes if you want me to do you a favour,' said Mr Newport.

'What jokes?' said Ben, and ducked.

His father cuffed him playfully. 'When do we set sail, bo's'n?' he asked. 'Any objections to this afternoon?'

'Wowee!' said Ben.

'I suppose . . .' said Matt hesitantly, and then thought better of it.

'What?'

'Dad, I don't think I can come with you this afternoon.'

'Why on earth not?' said Mr Newport. 'I don't see much of you, Matt. . . . And I thought you were pleased about the new boat.'

'Oh, I am, Dad,' said Matt. 'It's just that. . . .'

Mr Newport shrugged and tried not to look put out. 'If you've something better to do, of course.'

'I'm sorry, Dad.'

Ben and Maggie rushed away to put their sea-clothes on. 'Poor old Matt,' shouted Ben over his shoulder. 'Afraid of being seasick, I expect. Batty Matty. Seasick Matty.'

Matt remained, staring gloomily out of the window.

'You've really disappointed your father,' said Mrs Newport in a cross whisper.

'Damn!' said Matt miserably. 'Damn! Damn!' He went out, giving the door a little slam.

'Well, really,' said Mr Newport, raising his eyebrows. 'How long has he been like this?'

'It's his age, I expect,' said Mrs Newport. 'You know how they get.'

★　　　★　　　★　　　★

Outside, the Rectory was smothered with ivy; inside, it was smothered with books and papers.

'Well, now. Well, now. What now?' hooted Mr Oakes, perching his small, grey-flannel body on the edge of the desk. He peered at Matt through large, bright eyes which were magnified by thick glasses. He looked a little owl which had accidentally grown a moustache.

'We've done old St Nestan, boy. What do you want to know now?'

There had not been much more to learn about St Nestan. Matt was almost disappointed. Centuries ago, Mr Oakes had said, some old hermit had lived in a cave or a hole in this part of Cornwall. People called him St Nestan. He had spent his life, when he wasn't fasting or praying, trying to stop shipwrecks. 'Walked about on the beach with a lamp and a big bell,' said Mr Oakes. 'Must have looked a proper sight, ho, ho! Just like a little lighthouse!'

'What about the bell?' asked Matt.

'Never been seen, boy. But they say it used to ring sometimes. In the days of the wreckers. Must have had a guardian angel. Or some old madman. Ho, ho!'

'When did the wreckers stop?' said Matt.

Mr Oakes turned solemn. His eyes grew wide and owlish. 'That's a *history* question, boy. I'm only writing legends, you know. Ask me something else.'

Matt had the feeling that Mr Oakes was not telling him all he knew. He thought about the crosses in the sand. 'What do three X's mean?' he asked, feeling rather foolish.

Mr Oakes looked quite excited. 'Wha—a—at a good question!' he hooted, flapping his arms. 'Sounds like folklore. Or a secret code. Or an ancient language. Could be children being naughty, of course.'

'No,' said Matt.

'Let me see, now. Kisses?'

'No.'

'A winning line in a football pool?'

'No.'

'Hmmmm!' said Mr Oakes. 'Haaaa! What about a Roman thirty? XXX, you know.'

'Oh,' said Matt. 'Thirty what?'

'Ho—o—ow should I know?' hooted Mr Oakes indignantly. 'That's your problem, boy.' He waved his arms about, scattering papers like feathers. 'Any *more* questions?' he added.

33

Matt had a question but was nervous about asking it. Looking out of the study window, he was surprised to see that the afternoon had turned windy and overcast. Low clouds were scudding across the sky.

'Well, now. What now?' prompted Mr Oakes.

'Jack the Killer . . .' began Matt hesitantly, listening to a mutter of thunder in the distance.

'Who—o—o—o?' screeched Mr Oakes, jumping up from the desk. A little burst of wind hurled raindrops against the study windows.

'Jack Fairmill,' said Matt. 'Why do they call him "Jack the Killer"?'

Suddenly Mr Oakes seemed large and angry. He puffed up his chest and widened his eyes until they seemed enormous. 'Whooooo's been telling you tales, boy? Who—o—o? Who—o—o?' For a moment the moustache looked like a little beak.

'I'm sorry sir,' said Matt, leaning back from Mr Oakes's wagging forefinger and slipping in 'sir' as a precaution.

Mr Oakes relented a little. His ruffled feathers began to subside. 'I'm writing a chapter about Jack Fairmill,' he hooted, flapping an arm at the desk and sending papers scurrying. 'You'll have to wait for my book, boy. But I'll tell you this . . .'

'Yes?' said Matt uneasily.

'Jack Fairmill lived about a hundred and fifty years ago. When the wreckers were at their worst. And he was quite mad, you know. Ma—a—a—ad!'

'Yes, sir,' said Matt meekly.

'But he *disappeared*! said Mr Oakes with a chirping shriek. 'There isn't a trace of him after 1840. Not a gravestone, not a cross, not even a line in the parish register.'

'But . . . what did he kill?'

'Aaaa—a—ah! That's a question! What indeed, boy?' Mr Oakes settled his head between his shoulders with a hunched look. The eyes blinked. 'You'll have to wait for that book of mine,' he said. 'But I'll tell you two things more. Some of the villagers know more than they like to tell. And. . . .'

'And. . . .?'

'There's still a Fairmill or two living in these parts.'

'But. . . .'

'But you ask too many questions, boy. You'll have to buy my book.

34

And now you'd better fly home. There's quite a storm coming. I can feel a storm from ten miles away, you know.'

As Matt left, Mr Oakes was ruffling through his papers again. One or two drifted idly to the floor, like leaves or feathers in the first, small eddies of an approaching gale.

★   ★   ★   ★

Matt ran home through the gathering dusk. It was now far too stormy to go down to the jetty to meet Dad, as he had thought of doing.

From the lane which led down to the cottage he was surprised to see three figures silhoutted against the sky on the coast road further up the hill. They were trudging north, heavily clad in waterproofs. One of them seemed to have a large, unlighted lantern. He looked a little like Carrin's father, though it was impossible to be sure in the bad light.

As Matt came into the kitchen he could hear his mother talking on the telephone. She sounded anxious. 'Yes . . .,' she was saying. 'Yes. . . . But I want to be there to meet them. . . . Yes, I *know* it could be a long wait. . . .'

Matt put his head round the door.

'Oh, darling,' said Mrs Newport, putting the 'phone down, 'I'm just going down to the harbour. Dad's a bit late back with the boat. They think he's held up by the storm.'

'I'll come, too, Mum.'

'I'd rather you stayed here, darling. In case there's a 'phone message —from up the coast, or something. You can ring me at the jetty if you hear. . . .'

'It's OK, Mum,' said Matt firmly. 'I'm sure it's OK. I'll bake some spuds in their jackets for when you all get home.'

'Oh, Matt,' said Mrs Newport, kissing him lightly on the forehead, 'you're so like Dad sometimes.'

She went out, and he presently heard the car drive away into the wind and the rain.

Looking out of the window, Matt saw that the storm was worsening. It was driving hard towards the north—towards Trebarwitt, towards. . . . An image of the cave rose to his mind. He thought of

35

Dad's cruiser, perhaps also drifting towards the north. He thought of three men, silhouetted against the skyline, trudging north. . . . Carrying a lantern. . . .

He wandered about the living-room, restless and uneasy. Everything seemed to be happening at once—today. He suddenly caught his breath as the calendar on Mum's writing-table leapt to his eye.

It was the thirtieth of August.

The thirtieth.

Thirty.

XXX.

Three crosses in the sand.

Someone or something had given him a message. It meant, 'Now! Today!'

'Oh, no!' said Matt out loud. 'Oh, please, not me.'

But already he was pulling on the great, thick sweater and the heavy oilskin which Dad had bought him at the beginning of the summer, when anything so thick and heavy seemed absurd, and the sunshine looked as if it would last forever.

★　　★　　★　　★

Carrin stood next to Mr Newport in the wheelhouse of the cruiser. Spray lashed against the glass enclosure and the boat rocked and plunged alarmingly, in the heavy sea. They had been out of sight of land for nearly three hours.

'Where do you reckon we are?' said Mr Newport. He was a good navigator, but the freak storm had thrown them far off course. It was a comfort to have a local fisherman's son with him.

Carrin peered into the cloudy seascape ahead, but for the moment said nothing.

'Dad!' shouted Ben excitedly from behind Carrin's shoulder, 'there's a light! Look. Can't you see it?'

A tiny flicker was visible from dead ahead.

'It's land all right,' said Mr Newport. 'Could be the jetty beacon.'

Carrin narrowed his brown eyes with an uncertain expression. 'Reckon it's too far north,' he said. 'There's terrible rocks round Trebarwitt. Reckon you'd better go south a while.'

'But the *light*,' said Ben. 'It must be the harbour or something.'

Carrin shrugged, dropping his eyes. 'Can't be sure of nothing,' he said.

'Well,' said Mr Newport, 'I think we'd better head for the light for a while. It's the only thing I've got to steer by.'

★　　★　　★　　★

Matt's heart was pounding as he stumbled down the last few yards of the cliff path towards the cove. Coming out from behind a rocky shoulder, he stopped dead and held his breath. Barely twenty feet away, with their backs turned to him, were three men clad in heavy oilskins. One of them was holding a lighted lantern on a tall pole. It carried a large reflector, pointing out to sea. Though the wind was howling, snatches of the men's rapid talk gusted back to where Matt stood.

'Rich all right. . . .' The voice was that of Carrin's father's. 'That good-for-nothing lad of mine. . . . I've made him keep an eye on 'em. . . . There's rich pickings there. . . .'

'. . . that lad o' yours?' said another voice with an unpleasant laugh. 'Needs a thrashing, that one. . . . Proper little softie. . . . got it from his mother, I wouldn't wonder. . . .'

'. . . you can lay off that kind o' talk. . . .' Carrin's father again, loud and angry.

'She were a Fairmill, weren't she?' A third voice this time, high-pitched and sneering.

The lantern swayed as Carrin's father swung round and shook his fist. 'Never you mind what she were!' he shouted. 'She were a good wife till she died.' The rest was swept away by the wind.

The four men fell silent.

Four men?

Matt counted them again. Carrin's father, holding the lantern. Two companions to the left of him. But now—a few paces behind them stood another figure. A ragged and shadowy man with a tattered shirt and torn breeches.

Matt's teeth began to chatter. He had a violent impulse to turn tail and run. But he knew what he must now do. With his heart racing and his stomach muscles knotted, he began to creep slowly forward. To his right, the mouth of the cave had now come into view.

The four men were still in view: three wreckers and one, silent and apart.

'We'd better keep going,' said Mr Newport, holding his voice steady and staring straight ahead.

He saw suddenly with shock that tears were running down Carrin's face. 'What is it?' he said angrily. It was bad enough trying to keep Mags and Ben cheerful without having to cope with a fisherman's son who ought to know better than to start crying at a little wind and rain.

'Da' couldn't have known,' said Carrin in a choked voice. 'He couldn't have known.'

'Known what?'

'That his own son. . . . That I . . . was on this boat. That's a wrecker's light, Mr Newport! Mr Newport, please save us! Turn back!'

'For heaven's sake, boy,' said Mr Newport angrily. 'Stop talking nonsense and pull yourself together. Fine fisherman's lad *you* are! You're frightening the younger ones.'

There *was* something wrong with that light, though. And there were some rocks to starboard which shouldn't have been there.

But they'd better keep going, thought Mr Newport. What else was there to do in the stormy darkness, with fuel running low and little to be seen except that flickering beacon?

Mr Newport steered ahead.

★   ★   ★   ★

The mouth of the cave yawned and swallowed Matt alive. The back of his neck was prickly with risen hairs.

The four men were still in view: three wreckers and one, silent and apart.

Behind him the cave moaned and boomed as a gust of wind swept into it. Further back, the main cavern reverberated with a deep, ominous note.

Matt knew that the time had come. He dared not wait any longer. He took a deep breath and then shouted with all his might.

'The curse of St Nestan!' he screamed into the wind. 'The curse of St Nestan be upon you!' His words were magnified by the rocky tunnel. Their echoes were taken up by the great cavern behind him.

'Nestan! Nestan! Nestan!' shrieked the cave like a giant in agony.

The three wreckers spun round. They seemed to look right through the fourth man without seeing him. Carrin's father stood stock still, holding the lantern. The other two began to run towards the mouth of the cave.

'Jack Fairmill!' shouted Matt on a sudden impulse. 'Behind you. Look. Jack Fairmill. Jack the Killer!'

The two men stopped; turned; looked about them; began to retreat. Matt could have sworn that one of them stumbled through the strange fourth figure.

'Where? Where?' shouted one.

'What in God's name?' came the high-pitched voice of the other.

'Superstitious fools!' yelled Carrin's father. 'It's only some filthy brat. Look. Up there. In Nestan's Hole. Drag the little devil out!' But his companions had already vanished into the blackness like snuffed candles, their voices dying on the wind.

Carrin's father, lantern held aloft, began to tread menacingly up the beach. 'I'll see for you, my sonny!' he roared.

'Carrin! Carrin! Carrin!' shrieked Matt.

Carrin's father halted, peering uncertainly ahead.

'Carrin. He's on that boat. Carrin. Your son. He's on my father's boat!'

Carrin's father gave a terrible groan. 'God save us!' he said, dropping the lantern. He fell to his knees in the sand. 'God spare us! For the lad's mother.'

In the lampless gloom it seemed to Matt that the fourth figure was now standing over Carrin's father where he knelt weeping on the beach.

From somewhere out at sea the faint chug-chug of a motor-vessel could now be heard, faint or loud as the wind caught the distant sound and gusted it shorewards.

'Go back! Go back!' howled Matt uselessly against the wind. He began to scramble down from the cave-mouth. . . . but a dark figure was now approaching. It came swiftly forward, no more than a shadow against the blackness—until, with the suddenness of a lightning flash, moonlight broke through the scudding sea-wreck. For a moment it cast the beach into glittering relief: Carrin's father lying on the sand, weeping; the doused lantern; the gaunt figure of a man, clad in unfamiliar clothes and striding swiftly towards the cave, towards *him*, his eyeballs catching the moon-flash like cold fire.

Matt gave a moan of terror and fled, stumbling, into the cave—back along the narrow tunnel, over the dank rocks and shifting sand, into the central cavern. Something brushed past him in the darkness like an icy wind.

Matt shrieked. The cavern resounded. Words seemed to form themselves in the choking blackness.

'Kill . . .' resounded the rocks. 'I'll kill. . . . Let Fairmill kill. . . . Oh, sweet Nestan! . . . Help Fairmill kill . . . their devilish trade. . . . Before they kill . . . so many souls. Before they kill . . . poor Jack . . . poor Jack.'

Falling forward into a merciful unconsciousness, Matt heard the first, deep, tolling notes of a great bell. In the echo-chamber of the cavern they thundered upon him, driving him down into oblivion with hammer-blows of unbearable sound.

★   ★   ★   ★

'The bell!' Carrin pointed urgently towards the shore. The wind tore at the notes calling into the night. 'Turn back!' he yelled. 'Listen! We *must* turn back.'

Suddenly, to starboard, a dark rock loomed from the water where no rock should have been. Waves pounded against it, lashing spray into the wind.

'Dear God!' exclaimed Mr Newport. On every side black shapes thrust out of the sea, teeth bared, ancient, hungry.

He struggled with the controls. The engine throbbed and protested; spray crashed against the wheelhouse; Maggie screamed as a rock lurched towards them out of the blackness. With a final heave, the wallowing vessel began to reverse towards the open sea.

Carrin shivered. 'That was St Nestan's bell,' he said.

★   ★   ★   ★

At the end of the garden Ben and Maggie played at shipwrecks with Carrin in the September sunlight. 'Ding-dong! Ding-dong!' chanted Maggie, pretending to be a marker-buoy with a sea-bell. Ben glanced in Matt's direction, where he lay at ease in the deckchair, resting a bandaged leg. 'How d'you feel?' he asked.

'Sound,' said Matt, grinning, 'as a bell.'

'I still don't know how you had the strength to ring that thing,' said Mr Newport.

'But I didn't,' said Matt. 'I keep telling you.' He shook his head. How could he explain the inexplicable? An icy wind rushing past him in a dark cave.

'Jack the Killer!' he said with a little laugh. 'But all he tried to kill was the work of the wreckers. So I suppose that's why they killed *him*. Jack the Killed, really. Murdered—not a murderer. No wonder he haunted that cave!'

Mrs Newport shuddered. 'That's enough, Matt. No more hauntings, now.'

Matt looked thoughtful. 'D'you know, Mum? I think you're right: no more hauntings . . . now.'

He lay back, closing his eyes against the sun. He remembered one final incident from that strange night which he had not mentioned to anyone—and never would. Lying on the beach after Carrin's father had carried him from the cave, Matt had noticed something in the sand, now lit by peaceful moonlight. Three marks. Faint but unmistakable. They had seemed to appear one after the other. The first was a cross, but the others were letters: a P and an A.

XAP, they seemed to read, until one remembered what they would look like from the other side—from the direction of the cave.

PAX.

The Latin for 'Peace'.

THE MORTAL

Oliver Onions

'Oh, Egbert,' the White Lady implored, 'let me beg of you to abandon this mad, wicked idea!'

Sir Egbert the Dauntless was in the act of passing himself through the wainscot of the North Gallery; he turned, half on this side of the panel, half already in the Priest's Hole in the thickness of the wall.

'No, Rowena,' he replied firmly. 'You saw fit to cast doubts upon my courage before all the Family Ancestors, and now I intend to do it. If anything happens to me my essence will be upon your head.'

The Lady Rowena wailed. In her agitation she clasped her hands awry, so that they interpenetrated.

'Nay, Egbert, I did but jest! On earth you were known as the Dauntless; our descendants are proud of you; cannot you forget my foolish words?'

'No,' replied Sir Egbert sternly. 'Though it cost me my Non-existence I will spend the night in a Human Chamber!'

'Egbert—Egbert—stay—not *that* one—*not* the Parson's! Think—should he exorcise you—!'

'Too late; I have spoken!' said Sir Egbert, with an abrupt wave of his hand. He vanished into the Fifth Dimension. No sooner had he done so then the general lamentation broke out.

His horrible embodied eyes were on the poor harmless Spectre.

'Oh, he'll Be, he'll Be, I *know* he'll Be! the White Lady sobbed.

To be re-confined in Matter, so that there is no speech save with a tongue and no motion save with limbs—to be once more subject to the Three Dimensions of the grosser life—is the final menace to the spectral Condition.

'Poor chap—I fancied I detected a trace of Visibility about him already,' grim Sir Hugo muttered.

'Oh, it's playing with Flesh!' another cried, with a shiver.

'Almost Human folly!'

'Already his guide isn't what it was,' said the melancholy Lady Annice, who on Earth had been a famous attender at funerals.

'I shall never behold his dear Aura again,' moaned the White Lady, already half opaque herself. 'It will be the Existence of me!'

'If only it had not been a Parson's Chamber,' said the Lady Annice, with mournful relish.

'Here—catch her quick—she's solidifying!' half a dozen of them cried at once.

It was with difficulty that they brought the White Lady even to a state of semi-evaporation again.

★   ★   ★   ★

It was midnight, and the Parson snored. He turned uneasily in his sleep. Perhaps already he was conscious of Sir Egbert's presence.

Sir Egbert himself dared approach no nearer to the Mortal Bed than the lattice. Fear had given him the pink gossamer look that is the perilous symptom of veins and blood, and he knew that he received faintly the criss-crossed shadow of the lattice. To save his Nonentity he could not have glided up the shaft of moonlight that streamed in at the window.

Suddenly a violent Hertzian Wave passed through Sir Egbert's ether. He jumped almost clear out of his Dimension. The Parson had opened his eyes. To Be or not to Be? Had he seen him?

He had. His horrible embodied eyes were on the poor harmless Spectre. The two looked at one another, the one quailing in the moonlight, the other sitting in all the horror of Solidity bolt upright in bed.

Then the Mortal began to practise his fearsome devices.

First he gave the hoarse cry that all ghosts dread, and Sir Egbert felt himself suddenly heavier by a pound. But he remembered his name—the Dauntless. He would not yield.

Then the Parson's teeth began to chatter. He gibbered, and Sir Egbert wondered whether this was the beginning of the Exorcism. If it was, he would never see the happy old Ancestral Gallery again, never hold his dear Rowena in perfect interpermeation again—never pass himself through a Solid again—never know again the jolly old lark of being nowhere and everywhere at once.

'Mercy, mercy!' he tried to cry; and indeed his voice all but stirred the palpable air.

But there was no mercy in that grisly Parson. His only reply was to shoot the hair up on his head, straight on end.

Then he protruded his eyes.

Then he grinned.

And then he began to talk, as it were, the deaf and dumb alphabet on his fingers.

Sir Egbert's semi-Substance was like reddish ground glass; it was the beginning of the agony. How near to the Mortal Precipitation he was he knew when suddenly he found himself thinking, almost with fright, of his own dear White Lady. *She was a Ghost.*

Then the Mortal began to gabble words. It was the Exorcism.

Oh, why, why, why had Sir Egbert not chosen a Layman?

The gabbling continued. Colour—warmth—weight—these settled down on Sir Egbert the Dauntless. He half was. And as he continued steadily to Become, the words increased in speed. Sir Egbert's feet felt the floor; he cried; a faint windy moan came. The Parson bounded a foot up on the bed and tossed his pillow into the air.

Could nothing save Sir Egbert?

Ah yes. They that lead a meek and blameless Non-existence shall not be cast down; they shall not be given over at last to the terrors of the Solid and Known. From somewhere outside in the moonlight there came a shrill sound.

It was the crowing of a Cock.

The Parson had the pillow over his face. It fell, and he looked again. Nothing was there.

Sir Egbert, back in his comfortable Fourth Dimension, was of the loved indivisible texture of his dear White Lady again.

FAME

Michelle Maurois

Théodore Norély was dead. They carried him out of the house, with a great pile of flowers on top of him. Gladys followed, her tears and her grief-ravaged face hidden by a heavy black veil.

The great man was no more. Never again would he be seen stepping forth from his house in the morning with his cloak billowing from his shoulders, walking with his nonchalant, leisurely gait along that street in which he had lived for thirty years, the Rue des Fleurs.

He had died at the height of his fame, or rather a little past it. A minister, three academicians and a general had come for the funeral; but Gladys had an uncomfortable feeling that the painter would very soon be forgotten. She realized that his art, which belonged to its epoch, would quickly become outmoded. Already the younger generation was unfamiliar with his paintings, or considered him an old fogy. In ten years' time, perhaps, people would laugh at him, or, worse, they might not even know his name. Gladys could not bear the thought of that. She who, as a girl, had loved Théodore Norély in the first blaze of his fame, she who had shone with his reflected glory, would sink with him into oblivion! She had no illusions about it; she was known only because she bore the Master's name, because he had loved her and painted her in every sort of mood and attitude.

His portraits were already dated. They had been chiefly remarkable as likenesses, and now that most of the models were dead this quality carried no weight.

As the coffin was carried through the gates Gladys felt a painful conviction that soon nothing would be left to remind the world of the painter's existence. The procession moved up the street and passers-by bared their heads respectfully. She remembered that, a year ago, her husband had said to her: 'One day this street will be called Rue Théodore Norély, and part of my spirit will go on dwelling here.'

The idea inspired Gladys with sudden courage and she raised her head proudly. She knew her duty now, she recognized her aim in life; the street must bear the name of the great man who had lived there; that, better than any museum, would ensure the survival of his fame. The street might be widened, might even become an avenue. . . .

And she would live on in the same house until her death. When they saw her garden, people would say: 'That's where Théodore Norély lived. A plaque at the street-corner would commemorate the painter's fame, and that fame would be reflected on Gladys. From one generation to the next the Master's name would be repeated. In the churchyard, while she threw a handful of soil onto the coffin, Gladys made him a silent vow: 'You shall have your street!' And this thought saved her from giving way to despair.

That evening Gladys wandered about the studio, which was decorated in the style of an exhibition of contemporary furniture; she considered, one after the other, the canvasses hanging on the walls and the unfinished ones which were stacked untidily on the floor. She made her plan. Théodore Norély had made a bequest of several paintings to the Louvre. She would take advantage of this to insinuate the idea of giving his name to the street where he had lived.

She composed a letter which seemed to her subtle and appropriate, and sent it off next morning to the Directors of the National Museums.

Their reply was non-committal. Naturally, the bequest was accepted and greatly appreciated; but the hanging of the pictures would have to depend on the space available. As for the street, that must be referred to a special commission of the Ministry of Fine Arts.

48

Gladys wrote to the Ministry of Fine Arts; she was informed that such matters were the province of the Prefecture.

The Prefecture, in turn, had to consult the Ministry of Education.

Months passed. Gladys's grief at her irreparable loss was undiminished, but she had recovered her zest for life. She tried another method. She started entertaining again, invited official personages, pestered them, rang them up. They occasionally came to her receptions, but their promises remained vague. She was well aware that the people who came to see her only did so out of respect for the Master's memory. She must at all costs consolidate her own reputation, and for that purpose bolster up that of her husband, which was gradually weakening.

The street, once so quiet, had grown noisier; there had been a good deal of building in the neighbourhood. A bus now passed in front of the house.

It happened finally that an old friend of Théodore Norélys, whose portrait the artist had painted in his youth, became Minister of Fine Arts. Gladys promised to make him a present of the painting if he agreed to take up her case, and so one day she received an official communication informing her that her wish was to be granted; the street would shortly be renamed Rue Théodore Norély.

She stayed at home for several weeks in order to prepare for the ceremony and draw up a list of the people whom she wished to invite.

The day of the inauguration came at last and the ceremony, a very touching one, was performed. A few old friends were present, less numerous than at the funeral, but full of affection and reverence. It was a lovely spring day and Gladys, dressed all in white, felt like a bride. Speeches were made and the plaque was unveiled. Now Théodore Norély was assured of immortality, thanks not to his own talent but to the pertinacity of his wife.

She spent all the rest of the day pacing up and down the street and looking up to stare at the plaque. She heard a schoolboy ask: 'Who was Théodore Norély?' and a lady remark to her husband: 'What a nuisance! We shall have to change the address on our visiting-cards. What tiresome thing will they think up next?'

A few days later Gladys went into the town centre and then took a bus home. When they drew near the stop she was preparing to alight

She spent the day pacing up and down and looking up at the plaque.

when she heard a stentorian voice bellow: 'Théodore Norély!'

She gave a start. But the conductor was not speaking to her.

'Hullo,' a lady said, 'so they've got a new name for the Rue des Fleurs. Whoever was Théodore Norély?'

'He must have been a mayor,' said a young man. 'When it's somebody you don't know it's sure to be a mayor.'

Gladys had never envisaged a bus stop. She could not bear to hear them yell out that beloved name. Never again would she travel by bus; it was intolerable.

Next day, however, she could not resist the urge to see what would happen. She took the bus two stages from her home.

A small boy offered his fare to the conductor: 'How much to Théodore Norély?'

Then an old lady asked: 'Is Théodore Norély the end of a fare-stage?'

And once again the conductor bellowed: 'Théodore Norély!'

So this was fame! People said his name mechanically; nobody knew who Théodore Norély was! The Master would not have liked that. As for herself, hearing the name shouted in this way made her feel as if she had been the wife of Victor Hugo or General Marceau; she felt no longer alive.

She wrote to the Transport authorities to ask for the street to be unchristened. Her request met with polite amazement. She appealed to the Minister of Fine Arts. They told her she should make up her mind what she wanted.

But she was too miserable. Even in the privacy of her garden she heard them shouting every five minutes: 'Théodore Norély! Théodore Norély!'

The only solution was to move out of the district, which she did without delay.

GIOVANNI PAOLO'S LAND

Hesbia Brinsmead-Hungerford

Bill said, 'It must be on a river.'

So I was looking for land with a river frontage, where you could grow things.

'And of course, Pip,' Bill added, 'it must be out of the rat race.'

So I was looking for land with a river front and out of the rat race.

'It must be reasonably large, nothing poky,' said Bill. So I was looking. . . .

'But not expensive.'

As usual Bill wanted the impossible. Which takes longer.

I lived with a 'Land for Sale' section of the newspaper in my hand. Of an evening I studied 'Land for Sale' advertisements. After a while I began to dream land.

Anyway, I must have dreamed the man with the broadarrows on his clothes.

Mind you, I felt awake. First I seemed to feel a presence one early morning. I turned, and there he was. Ragged, dark. He wore, as I say, shapeless trousers and shirt with broadarrows stamped on them. Then, dimly, I saw that I was in a different place—not even in the flat, much less in my bed. There was grass under my feet. I sensed, rather than saw, great trees close by. His hand rested on a pile of stones. He spoke. There was an accent on his tongue.

'Mio son, he planta trees. When he is young I tell him this—to planta the trees. For the old land of his Papa—and for the new land, that is his-a land. But it is not here. . . .'

That was all. I blinked—and I was in the flat, after all; in my bed, and it was a new day. . . .

All that morning I kept hearing that sad, lilting voice. I kept sensing trees; above all, I smelled wild lemons. . . .

It was quite soon after that dream—daydream or nightdream, whichever it was—that our friend Jim called at the flat.

'You're looking for land?' he said. 'I believe Bob Turner wants to sell his orchard, on the Colo River. He's had a bit of a heart scare. Reckons he can't take it with him, and he's sick of a farmer's worries. So he's prepared to let it go cheap.'

'Where is the orchard?'

'Oh, way out beyond.'

'Beyond what?'

'Everything. I'll take you, if you like.'

Next day we drove along the crest of a ridge of foothills and down the zig-zag gravel road that leads into the Colo Valley. However many centuries, I wondered, did the river take to cut this deep incision through the sandstone mountains, to hack its way to the Hawkesbury and so at last the sea? Far below us was a rift of brilliant green. That was the river bottom. To either side were sandstone cliffs and bouldered crags. In the shallow, sandy soil wild flowers throve. There were drifts of flannel flowers like snow patches: the gold of native gorse, purple-flowering vines and many kinds of boronia that scented the wind; and often, the blood-red splash of waratahs. The valley was laid out below us like an aerial map. There was the rich green and gold of orange orchards; the Kelly green of water meadows and great sweeps of brilliant mauve where water hyacinths filled old meanders of the river. You could see by the hyacinth billabongs and reedy pathways where old river beds had run. You could see how, over the long years, the great floods that sweep down from the watershed mountains had forced new channels for the river, slashed away sandbars and heaped new banks and bars in new places. It must have been going on from the Dreamtime, surely. They say the Colo is a dangerous river. The wild floods scoop great holes from the unfathomed sand beds, and fill them with quicksand. The Colo claims many lives.

Then the dizzy, plunging road levelled out on the valley bottom, and Jim drove downstream for a mile or so. A steep, sandy track led left over a wooden bridge. We saw the water flowing beneath us, through the cracks in the bridge, as we rattled over. Then the track reversed the steep side of the bank, and turned back the way we'd come. Then sharp left again—God rest the suspension—into what seemed nothing but thickly-timbered mountainside.

'Where are we?'

Yet to my surprise there was a road beneath our wheels. It was carved into the mountainside. To the left was a sheer drop to the water meadows, the side built up with drystone work. It was a wall of beautifully squared blocks of sandstone, fitted together. No one would care to build that way, not any more.

'What road is this, ever?'

'It's part of the old convict-built road that used to go North, through to Cessnock. Lower down along the Hawkesbury it's called the Old North Road. But few people realize that this stretch of it still exists.'

'Look down there, Pip. That's the orchard.'

Through gaps in the dense bushland there was a glimpse below of orange trees, laden with ripe fruit, standing out against well-tilled loam. Beyond the orchard a crop of young maize was greening. Then we turned sharply around an overhanging cornice, and the glimpse was gone. The road became a dark and ferny tunnel, until again it turned—plunged sharply downwards—and suddenly we came into open sunshine, our way marked by a rusty gate. It stood open.

'The sharefarmer's expecting us,' said Jim. 'Tom Bostow is his name. He lives a few kilometres downstream and comes every day to tend his maize and melons.'

Beyond the gate the car skidded in a damp hollow, then the ground rose into a grassy knoll where a she oak stood, and a young peppermint gum. The fine-dust track skirted the orchard, turned back downstream —though the river was out of sight below high, terraced banks—and we pulled up near a utility on a grassy, sunlit space.

I felt, somehow, that I knew it; especially the trees. A stone-pine tree and a kurrajong had long ago been planted close enough that now their boughs mingled. An Australian tree—and a Mediterranean exotic; how long had they grown here, mingling their shade? Together they made a sheltered place; shaded from the hot sun, shielded from storm, on high, safe ground above the rogue river, Beneath the boughs an old horse wagon stood mellowing, the grass high about its wheels. Towards the back of the grassy circle was wild peach underbush, flurrying pink. There was another great tree partly in ruins, yet with leaves and blossoms springing from gnarled boughs.

'That's an apricot,' said Jim. 'It's as big as an oak could grow. Must be a hundred years old or more.'

'And—smell the wild lemon.'

There was a tree of what the folk call 'wild lemon', or 'bush lemon'.

It was burdened with a crop of rough, pungent fruit of almost luminous pale gold.

Tom, the sharefarmer, said, 'Most of this orchard here was grafted onto stock from that tree.'

Then I saw the ruined fireplace, with part of the chimney still standing. It was half hidden by the peach trees.

'There's the old baker's oven, too,' Tom told us. 'Now it's just a hump under the grass, but she's there all right. Just needs someone to clear away the weeds.'

'Who came here first?' I asked. 'Who owned this land?'

'I told you—it belongs to this chap I know with the dicky heart.'

'But before him?'

'That I wouldn't know.'

'Tom?'

'Can't rightly remember. All under this grass there's great blocks of squared sandstone. Beautiful hand-shaped stuff.'

I hardly listened while they talked. I seemed to feel—a welcome. . . .

It was after I had told Bill about the orchard on the Old Road that I met the Broadarrow Man again. Yet looking back I could not place the time or occasion. Waking or sleeping, in daydream or night-dream, I could never remember. This time the dark man was leaning wearily on some tool and wiping sweat from his eyes. I glimpsed also another figure—springing away across high boulders, climbing quickly, to disappear among thick timber. There was a mountebank look to it; young, jaunty—but evil perhaps. The Broadarrow Man spoke to me.

'It is here,' he said. 'Somewhere it is—but never will I find it. *Per favore,* I ask you that you find. . . .'

In midsentence—the time, the place, the dark-visaged man were gone. . . .

We bought the orchard in the river bottom below the Old Convict Road. At any rate, we put down a first payment and set legal wheels turning to that end. The orchard was ours.

'It's an odd turn, finding that orchard,' Bill said. 'For you, anyway.'

'Oh, I don't know. People are drawn to their roots. Nobody seems to know who the first settler was in such a remote spot.'

Yet, after all, Bill never really took to the place. He said the great cliffs made him feel shut in. The day came late and ended early. The sun was switched suddenly on and off by the ramparts of the gorge. Yet to me there was magic in this sudden transformation of dark to glowing light; of bright to starry dusk. The brief days had a special sun-glitter to them, for the valley could capture and reflect back from the cliffs each scrap of light from the sun. Those many-hued boulders would be warmed through and through, as long as the sun was imprisoned between them, and for hours after. While Bill worked in his office, I spent much time in the valley, supervising the building of a shack on great timber pylons—a loft, I called it. From its tiny balcony one saw out above the orange trees and above the wild-grass terraces to the river itself. It snaked like a golden dragon along its bed of gold sand; twisting between beaches and small golden islands, washed down from the watershed crags and now with bleached grass and river oaks posturing on them. It looked such a gentle river; one would never think of its reputation for treachery. One would forget how floods could come rampaging down the rift-valley, all under a blue sky, if it had deluged beyond the crags. Flotsam clung, however, in the top branches of the river oaks along the lower terrace, and even to the orchard fence.

'Do floods ever come as high as my loft?' I asked Tom.

'Only once in my time. They come as high as the old chimney

once in fifty years. It was in '39 that the water came up; so you're safe until '89.'

'Still, I'm glad we built the loft high. We still haven't discovered the name of the original owner.'

Yet not long after this our solicitor rang me.

'At last,' she said, 'the deeds for your orchard have come through. They're very interesting. Do you want to come to the office and see them?'

Indeed I did. An hour later I was being shown into her sanctum. Already a large sheet of paper was spread out on her desk. It was the strangest paper I had ever seen. It was thick, and brittle with age. The solicitor pointed out the copperplate handwriting in faded ink that headed the document.

'In this Year of Our Lord, 1824,' it read, 'Governor Sir Thomas Brisbane does cede to Giovanni Paolo eleven acres of land beneath Colo Mountain.'

'Well! 1824!' I breathed.

'It's the oldest deed I've ever seen. Now—lower down—it becomes very strange. It appears that this man, Giovanni Paolo, owned his land for about fifteen years. Then it seems to have belonged to a Benjamin Mason Paolo. Surely Giovanni's son, though it doesn't say so. But this time the document is speaking of "twenty acres of land". There seems no record of how the Paolos acquired the extra land. Then—down here—in 1843 it speaks of the land being returned to the Crown. Then—here—we have record that a George Giles took up "the twenty-four acres of land beneath Colo Mountain". What I can't understand is where the extra land keeps coming from. There's never the name of the person from whom it must have been brought. Even way down here—down in time, and down on the paper—is the record of the previous owner to yourselves. "Robert Turner". It shows him to have purchased "thirty-four acres of land" from Gregory Thomkins. This is the area that you have acquired, of course. Well, we don't need to bother our heads over it. It's just odd, that's all.'

Yet. . . .

Of course it was just a fancy—but afterwards I could have sworn that around a bend in the homeward road I met the Broadarrow Man. But it was a different road. A different time. You could feel it.

The dark-haired man was weary. He sat with his head in his hands. He sat on a block of squared stone. I saw now that it was the Old Convict Road. But where was the orchard? The field of corn? Things looked different. The Broadarrow Man looked up and spoke to me.

'A man's life for a man's land,' he said. 'Is this then the good bargain? Land and life, they are the same. Is his life—or my life. . . .'

He closed his eyes and passed a hand across his face in a gesture infinitely weary. 'His life—or my life. . . .'

I blinked—and he was gone. The road was gone. There was only the busy highway with its afternoon traffic, its bright hoardings, its car sales yards. Surely the dark man had never been. . . .

'How do you look up parish records?' I asked Bill.

'Search me. You're not still on about Giovanni Paolo's land? On things that happened a hundred and fifty years ago?'

'Well—the past is parent to the present, and all that. I just feel there's something I should know about our river orchard.'

The parish records, I discovered, were housed in the old building at Wilberforce, where the local council was centred. But the shire clerk shook his head over my questions.

'You're talking about a time before there *was* a parish.'

I asked, 'How would one find the names of the convicts who worked on the Old North Road?'

'You think your Giovanni Paolo was a convict? Why?'

It did not seem acceptable to reply 'Because I've met him'. So I said, 'It's such a small grant of land. And in such a strange place. Surely, no free settler would *want* "eleven acres of land under Colo Mountain". I just feel that he must have been a convict who worked on the road in that place. Were freed convicts given land grants?'

'I believe they were, in special circumstances.'

'Such as?'

'Such as if they'd done some service to the Crown. Helped to catch a bushranger was the usual thing. You'd better try State Records.'

It was autumn now. From Paolo Loft—as I'd christened the shack on the orchard—daylight brightened over skeins of white vapours, following the river and billabongs, and curving and twining above the hollow between the orchard gate and the knoll of the peppermint gum, and along between the orchard and the Old Road, looping back to the river. I liked to watch the sudden blaze of eastern sunlight that would turn it to silver and pink before it was suddenly gone. Now, driving from the village on the Hawkesbury floodplans, I remembered the Broadarrow Man, weary and confused, as a mountebank figure leaped away towards the timbered steeps of Colo Mountain. . . .

I wrote letters, followed elusive trails that were themselves like the Old Road—overgrown, crumbled beyond hope, all but obliterated. Bill thought I was crazy. At last my efforts turned up a list of names in a dusty corner of the State Archives. It was the names of convicts who had worked on the Old Road. 'Ted Miller, transported for sheep stealing; Jacob Cohen, twelve years for robbery, Giovanni Paolo, twelve years for political rioting. . . .'

So. It was little enough. Could he, then, never return to any other land? 'His life—or my life,' he'd said. 'Land and life, they are the same.'

It was no use; records would never tell me more. They would never tell me of the man to whom life and land were the same. Records were like our own yellowed parchment; they left too much unsaid. I'd not learn about the man from them. But how else?

The land? The land itself? 'Eleven acres of land under Colo Mountain. . . .'

So I would sit on the miniature balcony of Paolo Loft, and stare at the river and its dramatic valley—willing it to tell me who, then, had first set foot here, and why.

It was a day when the next spring was beginning. Bill was there, and Tom, the sharefarmer. It was Tom who triggered the answer.

'I must plant a grape-vine,' I said.

'You've got one!' cried Tom.

'A grape-vine here, on the orchard? Where?'

'Over there in the top corner, just below the road. On a bit of a shelf, half-way up the steep pinch to the roadwork. I've never had the time to go right up, but I see it every time the leaves unfurl. The birds get all the fruit.'

A grape-vine is what every Italian plants by his house. His house. . . . But the house was here. It's tumbled under the grass, all but the fireplace. Which I use as a barbecue. So why did a vine grow on a sunny shelf above the hollow? In Italian the word for 'vine' is almost the same as the word for 'life'. His land. . . his home . . . his vine . . . his life. . . .

'But of course!' suddenly I exclaimed. '*That's* where the river ran! What was the year of Giovanni Paolo? When was the last big flood, Tom? What year? Did you say '39? Go back fifty years from that. . . .'

'What are you on about now?' said Bill patiently.

But I was counting backwards on my fingers, and already down the wooden stairs and scuffing through the ploughed orchard, making for that shelf below the drystone roadwall. . . .

Of course. Now suddenly I saw. The dip in our track near the gate before the hillock of the peppermint gum. That had once been the river bed! From our balcony I could easily trace the old river course. It must have flowed close by the gate. Then there was the marshy spot where no oranges grew but two willows instead—and Tom said there had once been a dam there, but it had silted up. The hollow led all the way through to the boundary fence where it ended in a reedbed that joined the present river. The arable land plus the steep slope that was contained between the road and the long hollow would come to about eleven acres.

'There must have been a big flood in about 1839,' I was even talking to myself. 'Another about 1889 . . . and the last in 1939. . . .'

There were three terraces between our loft and the river. Surely, each terrace would represent where the river had once flowed—before its next great flood.

I came to the corner of the fence that shut the steep hillside away from the reedy swamp and from Tom's pumpkin and melon vines. I could see the grape-vine now—bursting into new leaf. Giovanni Paolo's vine. I climbed through the fence and fought my way towards it through the thick and prickly underbrush. Again there were wild peach scrub and quince trees gone wild. But someone must once have planted them. How lush was every kind of growth!

Scratched, twigs in my hair, I came to the vine. No wonder Tom had never tried to reach it. He was always too busy growing things to want to hack his way to an old grape-vine. But I could see among its tangle of dead wood and new growth another heap of dressed stones. Another fireplace. I stood still, taking stock of it all.

'It was a very small house.'

The stone slowly pivoted and turned.

I ventured closer. The fireplace. The hearth stone. It was a great, flat slab, tilted. If I lifted it—if I *could* lift it—there would quite likely be a snake underneath. I looked for a strong, wooden haft; but everything was rotten and crumbling. Snake or no. I'd try with my hands. I was able to get a good purchase on the top-tilted corner. I heaved. The stone slowly pivoted and turned. It was not beyond my power, thanks to the shifting soil beneath. With a last shove I threw it on its back, clear of the space where it had rested for many a year. Underneath was another stone. The stonemason, who had learned his trade breaking his back over the Old Road, had fashioned this stone beautifully for himself. He had carved a small crypt in it, with a bevelled channel to keep away the damp. In the hollow was a lead box.

'May I, Signore Paolo?' I whispered, lifting it out.

Sitting beneath his vine, I opened it. There were two folded sheets of paper. I opened out the first.

'Oh, yes, Signore. It's your pardon. You'd need to keep it safe.'

'Governor Bourke does hereby grant pardon to Giovanni Paolo, the convict, inasmuch as he gave information which led to the capture in Singleton of the bushranger, Patrick Dolley.'

'But,' I murmured, 'you never forgave yourself, did you, Signore?'

I opened the larger sheet of paper. I suppose you would call it the last will and testament of Giovanni Paolo.

'The great flood comes. They cannot take away my land, for I have given it to my son. He is safe, and his mother is safe. For he is also the son of Jemima Mason of The Ferry. I have tell Jemima that when he is grown he must build again a house upon this land, and plant again the vine. He must also plant a tree for my old country and also a tree for this new country. When again the vine is planted, then will I rest. The great water does come. The river roars like many mad beasts. I sign—Giovanni Paolo.'

'He built the house, Signore,' I said, 'with the stone you and your fellows had shaped. He planted the trees. It was only the vine that he forgot.'

I put away the documents and took up the box. It was heavy. I was glad to see Bill coming through the orchard. He picked his way among the pumpkin vines, and looked up to wave. I joined him at the fence.

'Walk softly through the reeds,' I called down. 'Giovanni Paolo lies there.'

He took the box from my hands. 'Does he now, Philippa Jemima Mason Jones of the Old Ferry?' He added, 'For the love of your dark eyes, what's in this?'

'My birthright, I think. Tomorrow I will plant the grapevine.'

I did. Much to Bill's annoyance, for he had to spade up the soil and move many dressed stones.

I never saw the Broadarrow Man again. I think of him when the grape burgeons into leaf. I think he sleeps well at last.

THE RED ROOM

H.G. Wells

'I can assure you,' said I, 'that it will take a very tangible ghost to frighten me.' And I stood up before the fire with my glass in my hand.

'It is your own choosing,' said the man with the withered arm and glanced at me askance.

'Eight-and-twenty years,' said I, 'I have lived, and never a ghost have I seen as yet.'

The old woman sat staring hard into the fire, her pale eyes wide open. 'Ay,' she broke in; 'and eight-and-twenty years you have lived and never seen the likes of this house, I reckon. There's a many things to see, when one's still but eight-and-twenty.' She swayed her head slowly from side to side. 'A many things to see and sorrow for.'

I half suspected the old people were trying to enhance the spiritual terrors of their house by their droning insistence. I put down my empty glass on the table and looked about the room, and caught a glimpse of myself, abbreviated and broadened to an impossible stoutness, in the queer old mirror at the end of the room. 'Well,' I said, 'if I see anything tonight, I shall be so much the wiser. For I come to the business with an open mind.'

'It's your own choosing,' said the man with the withered arm once more.

I heard the sound of a stick and a shambling step on the flags in the passage outside, and the door creaked on its hinges as a second old man entered, more bent, more wrinkled, more aged even than the first. He supported himself by a single crutch, his eyes were covered by a shade, and his lower lip, half-averted, hung pale and pink from his decaying yellow teeth. He made straight for an arm-chair on the opposite side of the table, sat down clumsily, and began to cough. The man with the withered arm gave this newcomer a short glance of positive dislike, the old woman took no notice of his arrival, but remained with her eyes fixed steadily on the fire.

'I said—it's your own choosing,' said the man with the withered arm, when the coughing had ceased for a while.

'It's my own choosing,' I answered.

The man with the shade became aware of my presence for the first time, and threw his head back for a moment and sideways, to see me. I caught a momentary glimpse of his eyes, small and bright and inflamed. Then he began to cough and splutter again.

'Why don't you drink?' said the man with the withered arm, pushing the beer towards him. The man with the shade poured out a glassful with a shaky arm that splashed half as much again on the deal table. A monstrous shadow of him crouched upon the wall and mocked his action as he poured and drank. I must confess I had scarce expected these grotesque custodians. There is to my mind something inhuman in senility, something crouching and atavistic; the human qualities seem to drop from old people insensibly day by day. The three of them made me feel uncomfortable, with their gaunt silences, their bent carriage, their evident unfriendliness to me and to one another.

'If,' said I, 'you will show me to this haunted room of yours, I will make myself comfortable there.'

The old man with the cough jerked his head back so suddenly that it startled me, and shot another glance of his red eyes at me from under the shade; but no one answered me. I waited a minute, glancing from one to the other.

'If,' I said a little louder, 'if you will show me to this haunted room of yours, I will relieve you from the task of entertaining me.'

'There's a candle on the slab outside the door,' said the man with the withered arm, looking at my feet as he addressed me. 'But if you go to the red room tonight'—

('This night of all nights!' said the old woman.)

'You go alone.'

'Very well,' I answered. 'And which way do I go?'

'You go along the passage for a bit,' said he, 'until you come to a door, and through that is a spiral staircase, and halfway up that is a landing and another door covered with baize. Go through that and down the long corridor to the end, and the red room is on your left up the steps.'

'Have I got that right?' I said, and repeated his directions. He corrected me in one particular.

'And are you really going?' said the man with the shade, looking at me again for the third time, with that queer, unnatural tilting of the face.

('This night of all nights!' said the old woman.)

'It is what I came for,' I said, and moved towards the door. As I did so, the old man with the shade rose and staggered round the table, so as to be closer to the others and to the fire. At the door I turned and looked at them, and saw they were all close together, dark against the firelight, staring at me over their shoulders, with an intent expression on their ancient faces.

'Goodnight,' I said, setting the door open.

'It's your own choosing,' said the man with the withered arm.

I left the door wide open until the candle was well alight, and then I shut them in and walked down the chilly, echoing passage.

I must confess that the oddness of these three old pensioners in whose charge her ladyship had left the castle, and the deep-toned, old fashioned furniture of the housekeeper's room in which they fore-gathered, affected me in spite of my efforts to keep myself at a matter-of-fact phase. They seemed to belong to another age, an older age, an age when things spiritual were different from this of ours, less certain; an age when omens and witches were credible, and ghosts beyond denying. Their very existence was spectral; the cut of their clothing, fashions born in dead brains. The ornaments and conveniences of the room about them were ghostly—the thoughts of vanished men, which still haunted rather than participated in the world of today. But with an effort I sent such thoughts to the right-about. The long, draughty subterranean passage was chilly and dusty, and my candle flared and made the shadows cower and quiver. The echoes rang up and down the spiral staircase, and a shadow came sweeping up after me, and one fled before me into the darkness overhead. I came to the landing and stopped there for a moment, listening to a rustling that I fancied I heard; then, satisfied of the absolute silence, I pushed open the baize-covered door and stood in the corridor.

The effect was scarcely what I expected, for the moonlight, coming in by the great window on the grand staircase, picked out everything in vivid black shadow or silvery illumination. Everything was in its place: the house might have been deserted on the yesterday instead of eighteen months ago. There were candles in the sockets of the sconces, and whatever dust had gathered on the carpets or upon the polished flooring was distributed so evenly as to be invisible in the moonlight. I was about to advance, and stopped abruptly. A bronze group stood upon the landing, hidden from me by the corner of the wall, but its shadow fell with marvellous distinctness upon the white panelling, and gave me the impression of someone crouching to waylay me. I stood rigid for half a minute perhaps. Then, with my hand in the pocket that held my revolver, I advanced, only to discover a Ganymede and Eagle glistening in the moonlight. That incident for a time restored my nerve, and a porcelain Chinaman on a buhl table, whose head rocked silently as I passed him, scarcely startled me.

The door to the red room and the steps up to it were in a shadowy corner. I moved my candle from side to side, in order to see clearly the nature of the recess in which I stood before opening the door. Here it was, thought I, that my predecessor was found, and the memory of that story gave me a sudden twinge of apprehension. I glanced over my shoulder at the Ganymede in the moonlight, and opened the door of the red room rather hastily, with my face half turned to the pallid silence of the landing.

I entered, closed the door behind me at once, turned the key I found in the lock within, and stood with the candle held aloft, surveying the scene of my vigil, the great red room of Lorraine Castle, in which the young duke had died. Or rather, in which he had begun his dying, for he had opened the door and fallen headlong down the steps I had just ascended. That had been the end of his vigil, of his gallant attempt to conquor the ghostly tradition of the place; and never, I thought, had apoplexy better served the ends of superstition. And there were other and older stories that clung to the room, back to the half-credible beginnings of it all, the tale of a timid wife and the tragic end that came to her husband's jest of frightening her. And looking around that large shadowy room, with its shadowy window bays, its recesses and alcoves, one could well understand the legends that had sprouted in its black corners, its germinating darkness. My candle was a little tongue of flame in its vastness, that failed to pierce the opposite end of the room, and left an ocean of mystery and suggestion beyond its island of light.

I resolved to make a systematic examination of the place at once, and dispel the fanciful suggestions of its obscurity before they obtained a hold upon me. After satisfying myself of the fastening of the door, I began to walk about the room, peering round each article of furniture, tucking up the valances of the bed, and opening its curtains wide, I pulled up the blinds and examined the fastenings of the windows, leant forward and looked up the blackness of the wide chimney, and tapped the dark oak panelling for any secret opening. There were two big mirrors in the room, each with a pair of sconces bearing candles, and on the mantleshelf, too, were more candles in china candlesticks. All these I lit one after the other. The fire was laid,—an unexpected consideration from the old housekeeper,—and I lit it, to keep down any disposition to shiver, and when it was burning well, I stood round with my back to it and regarded the room again. I had pulled up a chintz-covered arm-chair and a table, to form a kind of barricade before me, and on this lay my revolver ready to hand. My precise examination had done me good, but I still found the remoter darkness of the place, and its perfect stillness, too stimulating for the imagination. The echoing of the stir and crackling of the fire was no sort of comfort to me. The shadow in the alcove, at the end in particular, had that undefinable quality of a presence, that odd suggestion of a lurking living thing, that comes so easily in silence and solitude. At last, to reassure myself, I walked with a candle into it, and satisfied myself that there was nothing tangible there. I stood that candle upon the floor of the alcove, and left it in that position.

By this time I was in a state of considerable nervous tension, although to my reason there was no adequate cause for the condition. My mind, however, was perfectly clear. I postulated quite unreservedly that nothing supernatural could happen, and to pass the time I began to string some rhymes together, Ingoldsby fashion, of the original legend of the place. A few I spoke aloud, but the echoes were not pleasant. For the same reason I also abandoned, after a time, a conversation with myself upon the impossibility of ghosts and haunting. My mind reverted to the three old and distorted people downstairs, and I tried to keep it upon that topic. The sombre reds and blacks of the room troubled me; even with seven candles the place was merely dim. The one in the alcove flared in a draught, and the fire-flickering kept the shadows and penumbra perpetually shifting and stirring. Casting about for a remedy, I recalled the candles I had seen in the passage, and, with a slight effort, walked out into the moonlight, carrying a candle and leaving the door open, and presently returned with as many as ten. These I put in various knick-knacks of china with which the room was sparsely adorned, lit and placed where the shadows had lain deepest, some on the floor, some in the window recesses, until at last my seventeen candles were so arranged that not an inch of the room but had the direct light of at least one of them. It occurred to me that when the ghost came, I could warn him not to trip over them. The room was now quite brightly illuminated. There was something very cheery and reassuring in these little streaming flames, and snuffing them gave me an occupation, and afforded a reassuring sense of the passage of time.

Even with that, however, the brooding expectations of the vigil weighed heavily upon me. It was after midnight that the candle in the alcove suddenly went out, and the black shadow sprang back to its place. I did not see the candle go out; I simply turned and saw the darkness was there, as one might expect and see the unexpected presence of a stranger. 'By Jove!' said I aloud; 'that draught's a strong one!' and, taking the matches from the table, I walked across the room in a leisurely manner to relight the corner again. My first match would not strike, and as I succeeded with the second, something seemed to blink on the wall before me. I turned my head involuntarily, and saw that the two candles on the little table by the fireplace were extinguished. I rose at once to my feet.

'Odd!' I said. 'Did I do that myself in a flash of absent-mindedness?'

I walked back, relit one, and as I did so, I saw the candle in the right of one of the mirrors wink and go right out, and almost immediately its companion followed it. There was no mistake about it. The flame vanished, as if the wicks had been suddenly nipped between a finger and a thumb, leaving the wick neither glowing nor smoking, but black. While I stood gaping, the candle at the foot of the bed went out, and the shadows seemed to take another step towards me.

'This won't do!' said I, and first one and then another candle on the mantleshelf followed.

'What's up?' I cried, with a queer high note getting into my voice somehow. At that the candle on the wardrobe went out, and the one I had relit in the alcove followed.

'Steady on!' I said. 'These candles are wanted,' speaking with a half-hysterical facetiousness, and scratching away at a match the while for the mantle candlesticks. My hands trembled so much that twice I missed the rough paper of the matchbox. As the mantel emerged from darkness again, two candles in the remoter end of the window were eclipsed. But with the same match I also relit the larger mirror candles, and those on the floor near the doorway, so that for the moment I seemed to gain on the extinctions. But then in a volley there vanished four lights at once in different corners of the room, and I struck another match in quivering haste, and stood hesitating whither to take it.

As I stood undecided, an invisible hand seemed to sweep out the two candles on the table. With a cry of terror, I dashed at the alcove, then into the corner, and then into the window, relighting three, as two more vanished by the fireplace; then, perceiving a better way, dropped the matches on the iron-bound deed-box in the corner, and caught up the bedroom candlestick. With this I avoided the delay of striking matches, but for all that the steady process of extinction went on, and the shadows I feared and fought against returned, and crept in upon me, first a step gained on this side of me and then on that. It was like a ragged storm-cloud sweeping out the stars. Now and then one returned for a minute, and was lost again. I was now almost frantic with the horror of coming darkness, and my self-possession deserted me. I leaped panting and dishevelled from candle to candle, in a vain struggle against that remorseless advance.

I bruised myself on the thigh against the table, I sent a chair headlong,

'What's up?' I cried, with a queer high note getting into my voice.

I stumbled and fell and whisked the cloth from the table in my fall. My candle rolled away from me, and I snatched another as I rose. Abruptly this was blown out, as I swung it off the table, by the wind of my sudden movement, and immediately the two remaining candles followed. But there was light still in the room, a red light that stayed off the shadows from me. The fire! Of course, I could thrust my candle between the bars and relight it!

I turned to where the flames were dancing between the glowing coals, and splashing red reflections upon the furniture, made two steps towards the grate, and incontinently the flames dwindled and vanished, the glow vanished, the reflections rushed together and vanished, and as I thrust the candle between the bars, darkness closed upon me like the shutting of an eye, wrapped about me in a stifling embrace, sealed my vision, and crushed the last vestiges of reason from my brain. The candle fell from my hand. I flung out my arms in a vain effort to thrust that ponderous blackness away from me, and, lifting up my voice, screamed with all my might—once, twice, thrice. Then I think I must have staggered to my feet. I know I thought suddenly of the moonlit corridor, and, with my head bowed and my arms over my face, made a run for the door.

But I had forgotten the exact position of the door, and struck myself heavily against the corner of the bed. I staggered back, turned, and was either struck or struck myself against some other bulky furniture. I have a vague memory of battering myself thus, to and fro in the darkness, of a cramped struggle, and of my own wild crying as I darted to and fro, of a heavy blow at last upon my forehead, a horrible sensation of falling that lasted an age, of my last frantic effort to keep my footing, and then I remember no more.

★   ★   ★   ★

I opened my eyes in daylight. My head was roughly bandaged, and the man with the withered arm was watching my face. I looked about me, trying to remember what had happened, and for a space I could not recollect. I turned to the corner, and saw the old woman, no longer abstracted, pouring out some drops of medicine from a little blue phial into a glass. 'Where am I?' I asked. 'I seem to remember you, and yet I cannot remember who you are.'

They told me then, and I heard of the haunted Red Room as one who hears a tale. 'We found you at dawn,' said he, 'and there was blood on your forehead and lips.'

It was very slowly I recovered my memory of my experience. 'You believe now,' said the old man, 'that the room is haunted?' He spoke no longer as one who greets an intruder, but as one who grieves for a broken friend.

'Yes,' said I; 'the room is haunted.'

'And you have seen it. And we, who have lived here all our lives, have never set eyes upon it. Because we have never dared. . . . Tell us, is it truly the old earl who—'

'No,' said I; 'it is not.'

'I told you so,' said the old lady, with the glass in her hand. 'It is his poor young countess who was frightened—'

'It is not,' I said. 'There is neither ghost of earl nor ghost of countess in that room, there is no ghost there at all; but worse, far worse—'

'Well?' they said.

'The worst of all the things that haunt poor mortal man,' said I; 'and that is, in all its nakedness—*Fear!* Fear that will not have light nor sound, that will not bear with reason, that deafens and darkens and overwhelms. It followed me through the corridor, it fought against me in the room—'

I stopped abruptly. There was an interval of silence. My hand went up to my bandages.

Then the man with the shade sighed and spoke. 'That is it,' said he. 'I knew that was it. A Power of Darkness. To put such a curse upon a woman! It lurks there always. You can feel it even in the daytime, even of a bright summer's day, in the hangings, in the curtains, keeping behind you however you face about. In the dusk it creeps along the corridor and follows you, so that you dare not turn. There is fear in that room of hers—black Fear, and there will be—so long as this house of sin endures.'

LONELY BOY

Paul Dorrell

Jimmie Edmonds wandered across the school courtyard and made his way to the green where the other boys were playing football. He hoped that today they might let him join in the game. Especially as he had a brand new ball, one of the very best.

What in fact happened was that Nick Clark, the form bully, snatched the ball from under his arm and knocked Jimmie over in the mud. Then they all ran off, laughing and calling him 'teacher's pet'. This was most unfair, because, although he *was* clever and *did* work hard, he had never, at least not often, tried to 'suck up' to any of the teachers. It just happened that they liked his serious approach to school, wanted to encourage him; and they all felt a special sympathy with this shy boy who had lost his mother so recently. However hard he tried, Jimmie could not be as outgoing and carefree as the others of his age. But at thirteen most boys still have a great deal to learn about how other people think and feel. Jimmie's trouble was partly that he was just a bit more adult in his approach to life, this due largely to his recent bereavement and the amount of time which his father had always spent with him, encouraging him to be interested in all manner of serious subjects. And Mr Edmonds had instilled in his son a spirit of inquiry, made him challenge the ideas which he received from others and sought to make him understand why people acted as they did.

The mud clung to his hands and his clothes too hard for him to brush it off. He would have to take a bath when he arrived home, and wash his trousers. It was while he stood there, at the edge of the green, struggling to overcome the feeling of utter loneliness which seemed to engulf him, that he became aware of the curious gaze of another boy. He had not seen him approach, nor heard him, but now only a few feet separated them. There could not have been more than a few months difference in age either way between them. More than that, Jimmie felt some strange affinity with this newcomer, even though he had no idea who he was, had never seen him in town before. Ah! He looked as lonely as Jimmie himself was.

'Hello,' said the new boy, timidly.

It was a little while before Jimmie could answer. They both stood staring at one another, totally oblivious of the others who were now at the far end of the green. There was something strange about the clothes and the haircut, decided Jimmie. Perhaps he was a foreigner. There were so many in England now, with the world in such a state. His father talked about politics sometimes, and, although he could not always seize the exact meaning of it all, he was no longer surprised at the strange people one saw.

'Hello. I'm Jimmie,' he said, suddenly finding a new self-confidence which was born partly of sympathy for the stranger. He held out his hand, and it was only then that he realized how withered and small was the arm which he had expected to see extended to him. He blushed at his clumsiness; he should have noticed!

'I'm sorry,' said the other. 'Something went wrong when I was born. They don't quite know what.' He smiled wanly. 'I don't get to play very much. Other boys say they don't want a cripple in their crowd.'

'They don't seem to like me much either,' replied Jimmie. 'Perhaps we'd better form our own team. Except I don't have my own ball any more.' He pointed to the players in the distance.

'We could go for a walk. I've got strong legs,' said the . . .

No, not a foreigner, decided Jimmie. At least, not judging from his accent. But what was it about him that was so strange? Apart from his clothes and haircut, there was nothing definite, just a . . . difference? Why worry about it? He had someone to spend time with now, and he need not be alone. And the other boy obviously felt the same way about Jimmie.

'Oh yes! My name's Tom Nicholson. My father's just taken over as manager at Simmonds' factory. . . .' Obviously he had expected Jimmie to show some sign of recognition, but he did not push the point when he saw that this information meant nothing.

'Where would you like to go?' Jimmie asked.

'We could go up to the top of Reacher's Hill. They say there are the remains of an old Roman fort there.'

'So they say, but I've never been able to find anything. Still, it's a good walk—if that's really all right with you.' Jimmie looked at Tom with concern.

'As I said, I've got strong legs,' said Tom. 'You can always give me a hand—if you don't mind.' He laughed as he realized the irony of what he had just said, and this was so easy and natural to him that Jimmie was able to laugh too. When you're lonely and you find someone who doesn't reject you, you can afford to laugh at misfortunes more easily.

The sun was still pale, and the wind was rather biting, but although Jimmie shivered, the January weather did not seem to trouble his companion who trudged up the hill so fast that Jimmie could hardly keep up with him.

At last they were at the top. Below them they could see the town spread out along the banks of the wide river. Suddenly it became quiet. Too quiet. Jimmie turned to speak to Tom. Tom was not there. He spun round, looking down the side of the hill, but still he could not see him. A thought almost crept into his mind as he called out.

'I'm here,' said Tom. He stood not more than two feet from where he had last been. 'Where did you go?'

Jimmie did not answer. Instead, he suggested that they look for the traces of the Roman fort. They found nothing at all. Eventually they sat down on the grass and looked over the town once more. As they did so, it seemed as if a slight mist passed around them, momentarily, hiding all the surrounding area.

'That's Simmonds' . . . over there,' said Tom, pointing. Jimmie did not remember having seen the building before. In fact, the whole town looked . . . wrong. He began to be afraid and he turned to look at Tom, to see if he was still there.

He was. He had not moved, and the expression in his eyes convinced Jimmie that he had nothing to fear from his friend. He even began to doubt the conviction which was growing ever stronger. But then . . . those clothes, that haircut, that otherness. He thought that Tom understood what he was thinking.

'It's so good to find a *friend* at last,' said Tom.

Jimmie shivered once more. He could not understand why Tom did not wear a sweater, but then . . . probably he didn't wear one, didn't feel the cold. The strange mist seemed to pass around them once more. The town resumed its customary look. Down on the green, the other boys were still playing. Their cries drifted up on the wind. And what unease had remained left Jimmie. Now he was glad that he had not given way to his fears and run away. That would have been unkind. Obviously Tom needed his help. He must find what it was that kept him here.

'I'll race you to the bottom of the hill,' said Tom.

'Fine,' said Jimmie as he scrambled to his feet. 'But then,' looking at that frail arm, 'what if you fall down?'

'I'll be all right,' replied Tom.

'Of course.' Of course he would be all right. A fall would not hurt *him*.

When they had reached the green once more, Jimmie was almost laughing at himself. Fancy imagining such things! One day he might tell Tom about what he had thought. All those other things he had seen had been tricks of the light, illusions strengthened by the train of his thoughts. The other boys were now coming back towards him, Nick Clark at their head, bouncing Jimmie's ball along the ground as ostentatiously as possible, trying to anger him.

'Where've you been then, Swat-spot?' demanded the bully.

'With a friend,' replied Jimmie.

'What friend?'

When Jimmie turned towards Tom, there was no one there. Perhaps he could see a vague, vague outline of someone, someone desperately trying to cross back into this other world, other time. Nick and his friends only sniggered; they, of course, could not see anything at all, and this was grand fun as far as they were concerned. More ammunition to use against the boy who they already tormented so mercilessly.

'Been seeing ghosts, have you?' jeered Nigel Fleming.

'Yes, actually.' So unexpected was this reply, that the aggressive group immediately drew away from him, looked afraid. If Jimmie were mad, who knew what he would do?

The next day, it was Jimmie's turn to be afraid, and for no reason which he could identify. He was not afraid of Tom now, even if he were a ghost. Oh yes! He had really accepted that fact now. Tom was a ghost, and, if he could, Jimmie would help him. But he felt that something dreadful was going to happen. He did not want to go to school at all. But he could not persuade his father to let him stay at home. Reluctantly, he opened the front door and stood on the step. When he tried to turn back and run inside, the door was firmly shut. And painted a different colour! Nevertheless, he hammered on it, hoping that whoever were the ghosts in there, they might be friendly and help him back to the world of the living. His pounding fists made no sound. Of course. It was a ghost door.

The town around him now, so unfamiliar except from that brief moment's view from the hilltop, this was a ghost town. The people who passed in the streets were as unaware of him as if he did not exist.

Overhead, a plane passed. For some reason this frightened Jimmie more than anything else in this awful experience. Why?

Now, he wished that he could see at least one familiar face, even Nick Clark. But the pale-visaged inhabitants of this town had obviously been dead long since. They would not know of Nick Clark, nor of Jimmie; *they* were yet to come, yet to be born. And, when it should have been mid-January, it was high summer. For a moment, it seemed that a rag-and-bone man's horse had sensed his presence, lifting its head in his direction and seeming to stare as hard as an animal could. But this was only for the briefest span.

Jimmie screamed. But no sound came. He could not tell whether this was because his throat was paralysed, or because, in this other world, he could not make any physical impression.

Perhaps, if he went back inside the house. . . . Surely, he would be able to pass through the insubstantial walls. But this was too

He realized that he had passed right through her.

upsetting an idea for him. What might he find in there? Nothing familiar. Not his father. He ran down the strange street, his feet as soundless as though they were striking on air.

As he came to a corner, he saw a woman in his path, laden with groceries, and he tried to stop, to avoid her. But it was too late. Then he realized that he had passed right through her, and she had been totally unconscious of his presence. He was trapped in a world of ghosts!

He ran on, ran on towards where he guessed he must find the green. Perhaps there he might find some of the other boys whom he knew, from his own time. That was where he had met Tom. Tom! He had forgotten about him in his terror. If he had met the strange boy there, it might be that that was the true crossing place between the two times. If Tom were a ghost, as surely he was, then perhaps he would hold the key to the mystery, would be able to tell him how to reach the Present.

He reached the green, and yes! There was Tom, standing near the edge, where they had first met. Waiting for him. Jimmie had no doubt of that. He ran on towards his ghost friend who looked up, obviously relieved and happy that he had not been abandoned. Then, as the world shifted again, Tom was gone, and the strange town. The school bell was tolling and all the boys who Jimmie knew were hurrying towards it, crossing the playground.

He could not wait now, to find the ghost boy. He must not be late for school. He was only just in time for assembly. Cold and shaking with fear, he took his place in the hall, relieved to be back in the Present, the world of the living. Yet he was pained at having been unable to reach his friend, the only friend he had truly known in years.

Overhead, a plane passed. Nick Clark looked up.

He was standing on the green once more, in that other-time place, with Tom still on the same spot. Both boys looked at one another. They knew for certain now what had been in their minds from the very beginning.

'Come on, Jimmie, I'll show you what it's all about,' said Tom.

'About you being a . . . ghost?' asked Jimmie.

Tom nodded. In his eyes was the strangest expression of something like sympathy, but even stronger. He beckoned once more, and they crossed the school courtyard which was surrounded by buildings which Jimmie could not recognize.

They stopped in front of one of the unfamiliar buildings, and Tom raised his hand, pointing at a plaque in the wall. He opened his mouth to speak. Jimmie knew now what he was going to say, and started to protest, but the light shifted once more; the world slipped round a little, and he knew.

He was once more in the assembly hall. Nick Clark was still looking up in the direction of the plane, his face fixed in an expression of terror. The bomb struck so quickly that there was no hope of anyone's escaping. Jimmie was lifted off his feet as the flames leapt up round the headmaster's table. Screams tore through the air. Then the second and third bombs fell. And the World went black.

He read the plaque in the wall now:

'ON THIS SITE STOOD THE ORIGINAL BUILDINGS OF THE CAWLEY SCHOOL FOR BOYS, FOUNDED IN 1912, AND DESTROYED BY ENEMY ACTION ON JANUARY 23RD 1941, WITH ALL PUPILS AND MEMBERS OF STAFF.'

'And I thought *you* were the ghost,' said Jimmie. 'But . . . if I died in Nineteen-Forty-one, what year is this?'

'Nineteen-Seventy-nine,' said Tom.

'And I've been a ghost for thirty-eight years!' Jimmie was so overwhelmed by this, that he could not prevent the tears from welling up. And they burnt on his cheeks! Somehow, he took this as a sign that soon he would be free.

Tom managed to raise his withered arm just enough to touch Jimmie's elbow. 'But you can still be my friend, can't you?'

'Of course I can. That's why I was made to stay here . . . because I died unhappy, not having anyone to play with.'

A terrible thought struck the other boy. 'But what will happen to you when I'm grown up? I shan't be able to play with you then.'

'By then I'll be free to sleep,' said Jimmie. 'I won't be looking any more. I'll have known what it is to have a friend.'

He smiled as he had not smiled before; and the two boys, revenant and living, ran off in the August sunshine.

THE PHANTOM HORSES

Colin Thiele

It was hot. The turkeys were all sitting behind the fence posts at midday with their beaks open and their wattles drooping down in folds like melting pink wax—and that, Uncle Gus said, was a sure sign that summer was really cracking its whip.

The Nagala Creek stopped running and the two big dams on the farm went dry. February bushfires raged along the Ranges. So Uncle Gus turned all the stock into the far paddock where there was a big waterhole in the bed of the creek—all except two trolley horses that he used for fetching and carrying about the homestead. These he shut in a tiny paddock near the house and fed by hand with sheaves and oaten straw from the barn; and because they had no water he set up a fat tub as big as a double hogs-head by the back door and filled it with rainwater which he carried in handbuckets from the underground kitchen tank. On the sixth day of the heat wave Uncle Gus was starting to get tetchy. Benny was helping him carry water from the pump near the underground tank to the tub at the back door so that the two horses in the house-paddock would have enough to drink.

'Dey must have a terrible t'irst, dese two,' he grumbled. 'Soon d'tank empty vill be. Und still no rain komming.'

Benny was tired too. The bucket kept clipping his right ankle and peeling back the skin like bark from a sapling branch. The weeping pink blood smeared the bruises and the pain was hot, like a tiny branding iron pressed against the skin. Luckily the jolting of the bucket spilt some of the water, and it ran down his leg over the bruises in a cool trickle. But Uncle Gus was grumpy. *'Nach! Nach!'* he said. 'Must you be spilling d'water yet; now d'tank vill be dry before long, certainly.'

He was in an even worse mood the next morning when he found that the tub at the back door was empty for the second night in succession. He looked angrily at the two house-yard horses for a long time, and then decided that they could not possibly have drunk all that water during the night. His eyes narrowed. 'Py golly, Bert'a,' he said to Benny's mother, 'I t'ink d' udder beasts in d' house-yard are in d' middle of d' night komming. Vell, ve pretty soon put a stop to dat.' So he wired up the gates into the house-paddock and reinforced the fencing so that nothing but a snake or an owl would have had the slightest hope of getting at the water tub.

'Now in peace ve can sleep und about time,' he said when it was finished. 'Und dese two horses only one bucket vill be drinking to-night, you vill see.'

But the next morning the tub was empty again *'Donnerwetter!'* Uncle Gus said. 'Dis is too much!' He fumed up and down on the verandah for a while, and then his face broke into a cunning smile. 'Someone dis vorter from our noses is taking,' he announced. 'It is a t'ief. Someone no vorter has got left for d'kitchen in d' drought so in d' night he comes sneaking mit kegs and mine takes. Haha! Vell, ve see! Ve see!'

Benny's mother was much more matter-of-fact. 'A hole I suppose the tub has got in it somewhere. It is leaking perhaps.'

Uncle Gus didn't waste time on nonsense of that sort. 'Would ve not d' water see on the ground, den, und d' mud? No hole dere is, Bert'a. *Quatsch! Quatsch!'*

It was a German word that sounded as if Uncle Gus had landed someone in the face with a handful of mashed potatoes. 'No! No! I vill tonight dis cheeky beggar a lesson learn; he vill t'ink a t'underclap has him by d' t'roat got.' And he walked heavily out of the kitchen, his great blucher boots clumping on the concrete floor like the steps of doom.

All the morning he worked in the blacksmith's forge near the barn, inventing the sort of hideous contraption that only Uncle Gus could invent. At lunch time he said very little, although the children were bursting to know what he was up to. Even little Freddie got nothing but a black look and a short answer when he asked.

After lunch, however, everything became clear. Uncle Gus had made an alarm, a clever Heath Robinson invention that looked like a cross between a time bomb and a remote-controlled artillery piece. He had taken the ballcock from one of the old water troughs near the well and fixed it to a long metal arm with a hinge on it. Then he screwed the free end of the arm to the side of the water tub.

Benny, Emma, and Freddie watched, fascinated. 'You'll catch them robbers, Uncle Gus,' Freddie said. 'You'll catch them tonight, for sure.'

Uncle Gus's mood was getting better and better as his invention took shape. He chuckled with delight. 'Dey'll t'ink d' end of the vorld has komm,' he said gleefully. 'It vill be more dan salt on dere tails dey vill dis time be getting.' And he laughed a sly guttural laugh full of craftiness and triumph.

When he screwed the contraption to the tub he moved the ball up and down quickly a number of times to make sure that the hinge was working freely. The brass ball was a big one, about twenty centimetres in diameter, and it clunked down heavily when he let it go.

'Goot! Goot!' he said. There was pride and satisfaction in his voice. 'Now d' tub ve must fill mit vorter full up,' he went on. 'Benny, d' buckets! Und Emma and Freddie too—all can help. *Schnell! Schnell!*'

So they all carried and splashed, and splashed and carried, with straining arms and stuttering feet like the Sorcerer's Apprentice, until the big tub was brimming and the brass ball was buoyed up strongly and straining to rise even higher near the surface of the water.

'Aha! Aha!' said Uncle Gus expressively. 'It is all ready except for d' last t'ing.' He turned to the three children. 'Und now you must neffer komm here till I say, must neffer touch nuttings.' And he banished them sternly through the back door into the house.

Benny knew that it was useless to argue with Uncle Gus. So he ran quickly through the house, slipped out through the front door, and scuttled along on all fours behind the wood heap until he could sidle up to the big pepper-tree by the kitchen. There, hidden away in the huge fork of the trunk behind a screen of leaves he had a good view of Uncle Gus at work on the last stages of his invention.

As soon as he was settled Benny took his first peep—and almost fell out of the tree. For Uncle Gus was attaching his double-barrelled blunderbuss to the bargeboard of the house right above the tub of water. He was chuckling now and then and humming snatches from a German hunting song. When the shotgun had been fixed firmly to the side of the house he took a long piece of thin wire, tied it to the triggers, passed it over a hook near by, and then ran it straight down to the metal arm that held the ball. There he stretched the wire until it was taut, and wound the end tightly around the arm.

Benny saw at once what he was up to. It was an automatic alarm system that would simultaneously wake the household and scare the daylights out of the thief. A Gus Geister patent warning device—the Blunderbuss Broadside! For as soon as the water level in the tub dropped, the heavy ball would drop with it, putting more and more tension on the wire that was tied to the triggers. Then it was just a matter of time before the hammers fell.

When he had tested everything to his satisfaction, Uncle Gus climbed up to the gun for the last time, slipped a heavy cartridge into each chamber, and slowly locked the breech. Then he adjusted the position of the triggers and carefully, very carefully, started to pull back the hammers.

Benny saw what he was doing and hastily scrabbled out of the pepper-tree because the long black barrels were pointing straight at him. If one of them had accidentally discharged—which was very likely with an Uncle Gus invention—he would almost certain have been the first victim. Fortunately all went well, and the infernal device was left there at last, poised like a guardian harpy above the water tub.

Uncle Gus was in such great good spirits at the tea table that Mutter Eisenstein muttered a gruff warning about over-confidence. But it ran off Uncle Gus's back.

'It is time for d' vorter t'ieves to learn a lesson,' he said cheer-fully, 'mit two barrels in d' earhole.' And that was that.

By bedtime he had everyone in such a state that they were

afraid to go out to the dunny by the woodheap, so they had to use chamber pots instead—all except Uncle Gus and Benny who, being manly, were not easily frightened by perils and shadows, and were not in need of dunnies anyway.

Benny went to bed resolved that he would lie awake all night, waiting for the warning. But gradually the labours and the excitements of the day began to weigh on his eyelids and he slipped off into slumber. Outside, the stillness held the house close, like a hug. The moonlight lay over the farmyard as white as frost. The pine ceilings creaked in the cooling air after the day's heat. Somebody snored.

Even Uncle Gus must have dozed off because when the cannonade started he didn't react as quickly as Mutter Eisenstein or even Bertha. The two thunderous explosions came close together, the sound roaring in under the eaves and reverberating between the roof and ceiling. Benny awoke to shouts and cries all over the house, and the sounds of padding footsteps and keys rattling in doors.

'*Gott im Himmell!*' It was Mutter Eisenstein's voice—a cry full of anguish and the wringing of hands.

'What have you done, Gustav?' Benny's mother shouted. 'For God's sake, are the children safe?'

Uncle Gus heard none of these things because he was wrenching open the door and hurtling along the enclosed verandah like a demon in a nightshirt, his moustache fairly bristling and the pom-pom on the end of his nightcap bouncing against his shoulders. He reached the back door, flung it open, and rushed out into the moonlight.

'*Verdammten Dieben!* Dis time ve haff you got!' he shouted to the night, and spun round, sparring, ready to seize the first thief he could lay his hands on and twist out his Adam's Apple.

But there was nobody there. Benny came catapulting out, and even Bertha and Mutter Eisenstein ventured to the back door, peering about fearfully. There was nothing. The acrid reek of gunpowder hung in the air, the pepper-tree stirred imperceptibly. In all the wide silence there was no sound of footfalls, no movement of animals, no human speech.

Uncle Gus stood out in the moonlight turning this way and that, nonplussed. Benny's mother gazed beyond him even to the horizon's line, imagining silhouettes and shadowy figures; Granny cocked up

Uncle Gus was nonplussed.

her wrinkled face and listened as blind-people listen. Nothing. Then Benny looked at the water tub and let out a yell.

'Uncle Gus! Look!' He stood pointing.

Uncle Gus came over quickly and stopped short.

The tub was empty. The damp mark on the staves still showed up darkly where the water level had been, but now there was barely a drop in the bottom. The brass ball of Uncle Gus's invention hung far down, straining desperately on the tripwire that was as taut as fiddle-string. It had done its job just as Uncle Gus had planned, but it hadn't led to the arrest of the thieves. It hadn't even given a clue to show who they were.

'*Ganz Grässlich*,' muttered Mutter Eisenstein. 'Vot next vill be happening yet; murdered in our beds ve vill all be mit shotguns in d' night.' Despite her gloomy predictions she was the first one to go back to bed, and the others slowly followed.

'How did dey do it, den, I like to know,' Uncle Gus kept muttering. 'How?'

'You can look in the morning,' Benny's mother said. 'So stop playing with guns like a silly boy, and go to sleep.' But neither Uncle Gus nor Benny slept much after that. They were thinking too hard about the riddle of the tub.

At breakfast the next morning Uncle Gus had time for only three cups of tea and four fried eggs because he was in such a hurry to investigate. Benny was flattered when he was asked to help, but Emma and Freddie were ordered to stay inside.

'Everyt'ing went just like I said,' Uncle Gus repeated several times. It was clear that he was very proud of his invention and the way it had worked, and so he was all the more frustrated to find that it hadn't really helped at all. 'How so quick did dey get away den, dese t'ieves. Pretty clever dey must be.'

He stalked all around the back door, peering minutely at the hoops and staves of the tub for signs of bucket marks or bruises, and finally ranged out wide into the house-paddock. The two trolley horses were standing in the furthermost corner, fidgeting and watching.

'It must be dese two, surely,' Uncle Gus said at last, pointing at them.

'*Drachen!*' Dey must have fire in dere t'roats. How else could dey a whole tub of vorter empty?'

'It couldn't have been these two.' Benny said it with such certainty that Uncle Gus stopped short.

'Und vy not couldn't it be?'

'Because there are no hoof-marks near the tub.'

'Hoch!' Uncle Gus exclaimed, alarmed and excited. 'No marks?'

'None at all. No horseshoe marks. Nothing.'

Uncle Gus glanced at Benny in admiration. 'A policemans you vill be yet,' he said, 'to notice such t'ings so quick.'

Having satisfied himself about the truth of it all, he sat on the end of the tub, pursing his lips and sucking the air between his teeth in a sort of Stonehenge whistle.

'It is t'ieves sure enough,' he concluded at last. 'Very clever t'ieves at dat. Dey must fresh vorter need very bad.' He cogitated and whistled a little longer. 'Und I t'ink I know how dey play d' trick.' He looked at Benny craftily. 'Dey use d' zifen.'

'A siphon?' Benny looked astonished.

'Dat's right. A zifen, a zifen.'

'What siphon? Where from?'

'D' hose! Dey bring d' long hose like a snake to drain the vorter somewhere far away to drums, perhaps, and trolleys.'

'I think we'd see the hose marks in the dust,' Benny said, 'and the trail of water when they pulled it back.'

Uncle Gus was getting fed up with Benny. 'Den dere only von t'ing left to do is,' he said angrily. 'Vonce more ve vill d' tub to the top full make and den tonight I vill mineself vatch mit d' old *Donner und Blitzen.*'

And so it was. Through the afternoon heat they struggled yet again to fill the tub with buckets and billies. Then, as soon as it was dark, everyone else was shepherded off to bed so that Uncle Gus could arrange himself in silent ambush on the back verandah with the loaded shotgun resting across his knees. He had left the back door slightly ajar so that he could get a good view of most of the tub. The water lay mirror-still, silvered by the moon, reflecting a pepper-tree branch deep below.

Uncle Gus was not good at ambushes. His legs were stiff and creaky, so that he had to keep moving them all the time, and the double-barrelled blunderbuss was as heavy as a cannon. Nine o'clock went by, ten o'clock, eleven. Uncle Gus lifted the shotgun from his lap and stood it against the wall. He stretched himself and settled down more comfortably. From time to time he dozed, snapped back into alertness, and dozed again. A movement as soft as a sigh passed through the pepper-tree, and died away. The moon shone bright and full. The house creaked and was still. Uncle Gus dozed more deeply. In the whole wide landscape of farms and valleys and hills not a rooster crowed, not a cricket stirred. Silence. Stillness. Breathlessness.

Uncle Gus awoke suddenly to an uneasy feeling of company. The windlessness and moonlight—even the silence—were there as before, but something had changed. There was a Presence now, an over-powering sense that he was being watched. Little uncontrollable goose pimples prickled his neck. He got up carefully and stood there unmoving, testing the silence. He turned his head imperceptibly and moved his eyes to take in as much of his surroundings as he could without betraying himself. He could see nothing unusual, yet, he had an absolute conviction that something was very close to him. It was the same uneasy feeling he had experienced on that first night when his jinker had been stopped by something unseen.

His gun was just out of reach near the wall. In a manoeuvre to reach it he pivoted his whole body, plaiting his legs into a kind of corkscrew and almost over-balancing. He flung out his arms to brace himself against the window-frame of the enclosed verandah, and as he did so his gaze fell full on the house-paddock—its trees and fences standing out as clearly as dark cutouts on white cloth. At the same instant he saw the two trolley horses standing no more than twenty paces away, and recoiled so sharply at the sight of them that his body jolted back and his legs unwound. For the horses were staring at a spot near the back door in a fixed, trance-like way.

They were arched back in the same way, their heads held up and their bodies tensed in terror. Almost involuntarily, he followed their gaze. For a moment nothing registered. Then he jolted with fright more sharply than ever. The water level in the tub had fallen by almost half, leaving a dark ring of damp wood on the inner side: but, more unbelievably, it was still falling as he watched.

His scalp crawled and a chill passed over him. Though all was utter silence there was an uncanny sense of motion outside. The water level continued to fall. Uncle Gus stared at it, bulbous-eyed. His chest hurt and he felt faintly sick. The tub was barely a quarter full now. The air breathed and the night grew colder.

A sudden sense of outrage swept Uncle Gus, and the spell broke. The picture of the siphon snapped back into his mind, the thought of a long garden hose laid cunningly somewhere to drain the tub. He took a step forward and reached nervously for the blunderbuss. But in the shadow of the verandah his trembling hand knocked it forward and sent it crashing to the floor with an uncontrollable clatter.

At once there was a bat-like stirring in the air, a rush and eddy of movement in the stillness. There were currents in the pepper-tree and a soughing in the eaves. The echoes of the falling blunderbuss clanging in the enclosed space were still reverberating up and down when Uncle Gus dashed aside the half-open door and rushed outside.

At the same time the trance that had held the trolley horses seemed to break; they sprang back, snorting, and stampeded off in a fury of fear straight for the far corner of the little paddock. They didn't pause, didn't seem to see the fence, but crashed blindly into it, through, it, over it, the wires twanging and bursting like torn strings, the fence and animals flung together in a terrible turmoil of legs, necks, posts, manes, wires, and rumps, until the horses picked themselves up at last and went plunging off madly into the moonlight.

The noise on the verandah and the pandemonium in the paddock, unnerved Uncle Gus for a second and he was flung about rudderless. Vaguely he became aware that there were no horses in the tub, no siphons, no thieves. The falling water level had stopped abruptly where it was, the surface rocking imperceptibly as if it had just been touched by a moth-wing or brushed by a lifting muzzle. And above the racket of echoes he thought he caught the thud of other hooves, an unbodied sound of horses in air, and the faint turning of urgent wheels—a team in a buggy perhaps, or a hurrying hearse—from the skyline over the ridge.

Uncle Gus stood trembling. He blinked his eyes hard and peered through the gloom of the pepper-tree, seeing shapes and shadows, the quaint forms of limbs and light, the hints of manes and galloping feet, pricked ears and thrustforward heads that seemed suddenly to be swept out over the airy spaces beyond the tree into the infinite reaches of moonlight, starlight, and sky.

The early clatter and stomp around him died away at last, and the strange airy swirl died with it. The Presence seemed to fall away, the chill lifted. The moonlight burned intense and still again, the silence settled back like a solid thing.

The gooseflesh on the nape of Uncle Gus's neck began to subside, but he still stared about him like someone stupified, until the glint of the water in the bottom of the tub roused him to reality. Then he glanced round fearfully, hastened back into the enclosed verandah, and picked up his gun. But he had lost the lust for combat. Instead of staying to challenge the water thieves further, he went inside quickly, locked the door in dread and hurried back to bed.

Uncle Gus had had his first encounter with the phantom horses.

THE YELLOW CAT

Michael Joseph

It all began when Grey was followed home, inexplicably enough, by the strange, famished yellow cat. The cat was thin with large, intense eyes which gleamed amber in the forlorn light of the lamp on the street corner. It was standing there as Grey passed, whistling dejectedly, for he had had a depressing run of luck at Grannie's tables, and it made a slight piteous noise as it looked up at him. Then it followed at his heels, creeping along as though it expected to be kicked unceremoniously out of the way.

Grey did, indeed, make a sort of half-threatening gesture when, looking over his shoulder, he saw the yellow cat behind.

'If you were a black cat,' he muttered, 'I'd welcome you—but get out!'

The cat's melancholy amber eyes gleamed up at him, but it made no sign and continued to follow. This would have annoyed Grey in his already impatient humour, but he seemed to find a kind of savage satisfaction in the fact that he was denied even the trifling consolation of a good omen. Like all gamblers, he was intensely superstitious, although he had had experience in full measure of the futility of all supposedly luck-bringing mascots. He carried a monkey's claw sewn in the lining of his waitcoat pocket, not having the courage to throw it away. But this wretched yellow cat that ought to have been black did not irritate him as might have been expected.

He laughed softly; the restrained, unpleasant laugh of a man fighting against misfortune.

'Come on, then, you yellow devil; we'll sup together.'

He took his gloveless hand from his coat pocket and beckoned to the animal at his heels; but it took as little notice of his gesture of invitation as it had of his menacing foot a moment before. It just slid along the greasy pavement, covering the ground noiselessly, not deviating in the slightest from the invisible path it followed, without hesitation.

It was a bitterly cold, misty night, raw and damp. Grey shivered as he thrust his hand back into the shelter of his pocket and hunched his shoulders together underneath the thin coat that afforded but little protection against the cold.

With a shudder of relief he turned into the shelter of the courtyard which lay between the icy street and the flight of stairs which led to his room. As he stumbled numbly over the rough cobblestones of the yard he suddenly noticed that the yellow cat had disappeared.

He was not surprised and gave no thought whatever to the incident until, a few minutes later, at the top of the ramshackle stairs, the feeble light of a hurricane lamp revealed the creature sitting, or rather lying, across the threshold of his door.

He took an uncertain step backwards. He said to himself: 'That's odd.' The cat looked up at him impassively with brooding, sullen eyes. He opened the door, stretching over the animal to turn the crazy handle.

Silently the yellow cat rose and entered the shadowy room. There was something uncanny, almost sinister in its smooth noiseless movements. With fingers that shook slightly, Grey fumbled for matches, struck a light and, closing the door behind him, lit the solitary candle.

He lived in this one room, over a mews which had become almost fashionable since various poverty-stricken people, whose names still carried some weight with the bourgeois tradesmen of this Mayfair backwater, had triumphantly installed themselves; and Grey turned it skilfully to account when he spoke with casual indifference of 'the flat' he occupied, 'next to Lady Susan Tyrrell's'.

Grey, although he would never have admitted it, was a cardsharper and professional gambler. But even a cardsharper needs a little ordinary luck. Night after night he watched money pass into the hands of 'the pigeons', ignorant, reckless youngsters, and foolish old women who, having money to burn, ought by all the rules of the game to have lost. Yet when playing with him, Grey, a man respected even among the shabby fraternity of those who live by their wits, they won. He had turned to roulette, but even with a surreptitious percentage interest in the bank he had lost. His credit was exhausted. Grannie herself had told him he was a regular Jonah. He was cold, hungry and desperate. Presently his clothes, the last possession, would betray him, and no longer would he be able to borrow the casual trifle that started him nightly in his desperate bout with fortune.

His room contained a wooden bed and a chair. A rickety table separated them. The chair served Grey as a wardrobe; on the table stood a candle with a few used matches which he used to light the cheap cigarettes he smoked in bed; the grease had a habit of adhering to the tobacco when the candle was used, and Grey was fastidious. The walls were bare save for a cupboard, a pinned-up *Sporting Life* Racing Calendar and two cheap reproductions of Kirchner's midinettes. There was no carpet on the floor. A piece of linoleum stretched from the empty grate to the side of the bed.

At first Grey could not see the cat, but the candle, gathering strength, outlined its shadow grotesquely against the wall. It was crouched on the end of the bed.

He lighted one of the used matches and lit the small gas ring which was the room's sole luxury. Gas was included in the few shillings he paid weekly for rent; consequently Grey used it for warmth. He seldom used it to cook anything, as neither whisky (which he got by arrangement with one of Grannie's waiters), bread nor cheese, which formed his usual diet, require much cooking.

The cat moved and, jumping noiselessly on to the floor, cautiously approached the gas ring, by the side of which it stretched its lean yellowish body. Very softly but plaintively it began to mew.

Grey cursed it. Then he turned to the cupboard and took out a cracked jug. He moved the bread onto his own plate and poured out the little milk it contained in the shallow bread plate.

The cat drank not greedily but with the fierce rapidity which betokens hunger and thirst. Grey watched it idly as he poured whisky into a cup. He drank, and refilled the cup. He then began to undress, carefully, in order to prolong the life of his worn dinner-jacket.

The cat looked up. Grey, taking off his shirt, beneath which, having no vest, he wore another woollen shirt, became uncomfortably aware of its staring yellow eyes. Seized with a crazy impulse, he poured the whisky from his cup into the remainder of the milk in the plate.

'Share and share alike,' he cried. 'Drink, you. . . .'

Then the yellow cat snarled at him; the vilest loathsome sound; and Grey for a moment was afraid. Then he laughed, as if at himself for allowing control to slip, and finished undressing, folding the garments carefully, and hanging them on the chair.

The cat went back to its place at the foot of the bed, its eyes gleaming warily in Grey's direction. He restrained his impulse to throw it out of the room and clambered between the rough blankets without molesting it.

By daylight the cat was an ugly misshapen creature. It had not moved from the bed. Grey regarded it with amused contempt.

Usually the morning found him profoundly depressed and irritable. For some unaccountable reason he felt now almost light-hearted.

He dressed, counted his money and decided to permit himself the luxury of some meagre shopping in the adjacent Warwick Market, which supplied the most expensive restaurant proprietors with the cheapest food. Nevertheless, it was an accommodating spot for knowledgeable individuals like Grey.

The cat, still crouching on the bed, made no attempt to follow him, and he closed the door as softly as its erratic hinges would allow, aware that the cat's eyes still gazed steadily in his direction.

In the market, he obeyed an impulse to buy food for the cat, and at the cost of a few pence added a portion of raw fish to his purchases. On the way home he cursed himself for fool, and would have thrown the fish away, the clumsy paper wrapping having become sodden with moisture, when he was hailed by a voice he had almost forgotten.

'Grey! Just the man I want to see!'

Grey greeted him with a fair show of amiability, although, if appearance were any indication, the other was even less prosperous than himself. He, too, had been an *habitué* of Grannie's in the old days, but had long since drifted out on the sea of misfortune. Despite his shabby appearance, he turned to Grey and said:

'You'll have a drink?' Then, noting Grey's dubious glance, he laughed and added: 'It's on me all right. I've just touched lucky.'

A little later Grey emerged from the public house on the corner the richer by five pounds, which the other had insisted on lending him in return for past favours. What exactly the past favours had been, Grey was too dazed to inquire; as far as he could recollect he had always treated the man with scant courtesy. He did not even remember his name.

He was still trying to remember who the man was when he climbed the stairs. He knew him well enough, for Grey was the type who never forgot a face. It was when his eyes alighted on the yellow cat that he suddenly remembered.

The man was Felix Mortimer. And Felix Mortimer had shot himself during the summer!

At first Grey tried to assure himself that he had made a mistake. Against his better judgement he tried to convince himself that the man merely bore a strong resemblance to Felix Mortimer. But at the back of his mind *he knew*.

Anyway, the five-pound note was real enough.

He methodically placed the fish in a saucepan and lit the gas ring.

Presently the cat was eating, in that curious, deliberate way it had drunk the milk the night before. Its emaciated appearance plainly revealed that it was starving; yet it devoured the fish methodically, as though now assured of a regular supply.

Grey, turning the five-pound note in his hand, wondered whether the cat had after all changed his luck. But his thoughts kept reverting to Felix Mortimer. . . .

The next few days left him in no doubt. At Grannie's that night fortune's pendulum swung back unmistakably. He won steadily. From roulette he turned to *chemin de fer,* elated to find that his luck held good.

'Your luck's changed—with a vengeance!' said one of the 'regulars' of the shabby genteel saloon.

'With a vengeance,' echoed Grey, and paused; wondering with the

97

superstition of the born gambler if there were significance in the phrase.

He left Grannie's the richer by two hundred odd pounds.

His success was the prelude to the biggest slice of luck, to use his own phrase, that he had ever known. He gambled scientifically, not losing his head, methodically banking a proportion of his gains each morning; planning, scheming, striving to reach that high water mark at which, so he told himself with the gambler's time-worn futility, he would stop and never gamble again.

Somehow he could not make up his mind to leave the poverty-stricken room in the fashionable mews. He was terribly afraid it would spell a change of luck. He tried to improve it, increase its comfort, but it was significant that he bought first a basket and a cushion for the yellow cat.

For there was no doubt in his mind that the cat was the cause of his sudden transition from poverty to prosperity. In his queer, intensely superstitious mind, the yellow cat was firmly established as his mascot.

He fed it regularly, waiting on it himself as though he were its willing servant. He made a spasmodic attempt to caress it, but the cat snarled savagely at him and, frightened, he left it alone. If the cat ever moved from the room he never saw it go; whenever he went in or came out the cat was there, watching him with its gleaming amber eyes.

He accepted the situation philosophically enough. He would talk to the cat of himself, his plans for the future, the new people he met—for money had speedily unlocked more exalted doors than Grannie's—all this in the eloquence derived from wine and solitude, he would pour out into the unmoved ears of the cat, crouching at the foot of the bed. And then, without daring to speak of it, he would think of Felix Mortimer and the gift that had proved the turning-point of his fortunes.

The creature watched him impassively, contemptuously indifferent to his raving or his silence. But the weird *ménage* continued, and Grey's luck held good.

The days passed and he became ambitious. He was now within reach of that figure he fondly imagined would enable him to forsake his precarious existence. He told himself that he was now, to all intents and purposes, safe. And he decided to move into more civilized and appropriate surroundings.

Nevertheless, he himself procured an expensive wicker contraption to convey the yellow cat from the garret to his newly acquired and, by contrast, luxurious maisonette. It was furnished in abominable taste, but the reaction from sheer poverty had its effect. And then he had begun to drink more than was good for a man who acquired a cool head and a steady nerve for at least part of a day which was really night.

One day he had cause to congratulate himself on his new home. For he met, for the first time in his thirty odd years of life, a woman. Now Grey divided women into two classes. There were 'the regulars'—soulless creatures with the gambler's fever and crook's alphabet—and 'pigeons', foolish women, some young, most of them old, who flourished their silly but valuable plumage to be plucked by such as he.

But Elise Dyer was different. She stirred his pulses with a strange, exquisite sensation. Her incredibly fair hair, flaxen as waving corn, her fair skin, her deep violet eyes and her delicate carmine mouth provoked him into a state of unaccustomed bewilderment.

They talked one night of mascots. Grey, who had never mentioned the yellow cat to a soul, whispered that he would, if she cared, show her the mascot which had brought him his now proverbial good luck. The girl agreed, with eager enthusiasm, to his diffident suggestion to go with him to his flat; and he, in his strange simplicity, stammered that she would do him honour. He had forgotten that Elise Dyer knew him for a rich man.

Elated by his triumph, he paid her losses and called for champagne. The girl plied him skilfully with wine, and presently he was more drunk than he had been since the beginning of his era of prosperity.

They took a cab to the flat. Grey felt that he had reached the pinnacle of triumph. Life was wonderful, glorious! What did anything matter now?

He switched on the light and the girl crossed his threshold. The room which they entered was lavishly illuminated, the lights shaded into moderation by costly fabrics. The room, ornate and over-furnished, reflected money. The girl gave a gasp of delight.

For the first time the cat seemed aware of something unusual. It stretched itself slowly and stood up, regarding them with a fierce light in its eyes.

The girl screamed.

'For God's sake take it away!' she cried.

'For God's sake take it away!' she cried. 'I can't bear it! I can't be near it. Take that damned cat away!' And she began to sob wildly, piteously, retreating towards the door.

At this Grey lost all control and, cursing wildly, shouting bestial things at the oncoming animal, seized it by the throat.

'Don't—don't cry, dearie,' panted Grey, holding the cat; 'I'll settle this swine soon enough. Wait for me!' And he staggered through the open door.

Grey ran through the deserted streets. The cat had subsided under the clutch of his fingers and lay inert, its yellowish fur throbbing. He scarcely knew where he was going. All he realized was an overwhelming desire to be rid of the tyranny of this wretched creature he held by the throat.

At last he knew where he was going. Not far from Grey's new establishment ran the Prince's canal, that dark, sluggish stream that threads its way across the fashionable residential district of the outlying west. To the canal he ran; and without hesitation he threw the yellow cat into the water.

★　★　★　★　★

The next day he realized what he had done. At first he was afraid, half hoping that the superstitious spasm of fear would pass. But a vivid picture swam before his eyes, the broken surface of a sluggish dream. . . .

'You're a coward,' she taunted him. 'Why don't you act like a man? Go to the tables and see for yourself that you can still win in spite of your crazy cat notions!'

At first he refused, vehemently; but it gradually dawned on him that therein lay his chance of salvation. Once let him throw down the gauntlet *and win* and his peace of mind would be assured.

That night he received a vociferous welcome on his return to the Green Baize Club.

It was as he feared. He lost steadily.

Then suddenly an idea came to him. Supposing the cat were still alive? Why hadn't he thought of that before? Why, there was a saying that every cat had nine lives! For all he knew it might have swum safely to the bank and got away.

His feverish impulse crystallized into action. He hurriedly left the club and beckoned urgently to a passing taxicab.

After what seemed interminable delay he reached the spot where he had madly flung the cat away from him. The stillness of the water brought home to him the futility of searching for the animal here. This was not the way to set to work.

The thing preyed on his mind in the days that followed. Exhaustive inquiries failed to discover the least trace of the yellow cat.

Night after night he went to the tables, lured there by the maddening thought that if only he could win he would drug the torment and be at peace. But he lost. . . .

And then a strange thing happened.

One night, returning home across a deserted stretch of the park, he experienced a queer, irresistible impulse to lift his feet from the grass and make for the gravel path. He resented the impulse, fought against it; he was cold and worn out, and by cutting across the grass he would save many minutes of weary tramping. But the thing—like a mysterious blind instinct—persisted, and in the end he found himself running, treading gingerly on the sodden grass.

He did not understand why this had happened to him.

The next day Grey did not get out of his bed until late in the afternoon.

He crossed the room in search of his dressing-gown and caught sight of himself in the glass of his wardrobe. Only then did he realize that he was clambering over the floor with his head near the carpet, his hands outstretched in front of him. He stood upright with difficulty and reached a shaking hand for brandy.

It took him two hours to struggle into his clothes, and by the time he was ready to go out it was nearly dark. He crept along the street. The shops were closing. He saw nothing of them until he reached the corner where he halted abruptly, with a queer sensation of intense hunger. On the cold marble before him lay unappetizing slabs of raw fish. His body began to quiver with suppressed desire. Another moment and nothing could have prevented him seizing the fish in his bare hands, when the shutters of the shop dropped noisily across the front of the sloping marble surface.

Grey knew that something had happened, that he was very ill. Now that he could not see the vision of the yellow cat, his mind was a blank. Somehow he retraced his footsteps and got back to his room.

The bottle of brandy stood where he had left it. He had not turned on the light, but he could see it plainly. He dragged it to his lips.

With a crash it went to the floor, while Grey leapt into the air, savage with nausea. He felt he was choking. With an effort he pulled himself together, to find that it was beyond his power to stop the ghastly whining sound that issued from his lips. He tried to lift himself onto the bed, but in sheer exhaustion collapsed on the floor, where he lay still in an attitude not human.

The room lightened with the dawn and a new day passed before the thing on the floor moved. Something of the clarity of vision which comes to starving men now possessed him. He stared at his hands.

The fingers seemed to have withered; the nails had almost disappeared, leaving a narrow streak of hornish substance forming in their place. He tore himself frantically towards the window. In the fading light he saw that the backs of his hands were covered with a thin, almost invisible surface of coarse, yellowish fur.

Unimaginable horrors seized him. He knew now that the scarlet thread of his brain was being stretched to breaking-point. Presently it would snap. . . .

Unless—unless. The yellow cat alone could save him. To this last human thought he clung, in an agony of terror.

Unconscious of movement, he crept swiftly into the street, his shapeless eyes peering in the darkness which surrounded him. He groped his way stealthily towards the one place which the last remnant of his brain told him might yield the secret of his agony.

Down the silent bank he scrambled headlong, towards the still water. The dawn's pale radiance threw his shadow into a grotesque pattern. On the edge of the canal he halted, his hands embedded in the sticky crumbling earth, his head shaking, his eyes searching in agonized appeal, into the depths of the motionless water.

There he crouched, searching, searching. . . .

And there in the water he saw the yellow cat.

He stretched out the things that were his arms, while the yellow cat stretched out its claws to enfold him in the broken mirror of the water.

A LITTLE HOUSE OF THEIR OWN

Stanley W. Fisher

When you are alone at night, perhaps reading or looking at television, do you ever fancy you see something move, out of the corner of your eye? Perhaps you turn your head, slowly to make quite sure it is really only a fancy?

Perhaps you own a dog or a cat? Particularly a cat. Have you seen it wake suddenly from deep sleep to lift its head and follow the movements of something or someone you cannot see? A fly, or a spider, of course. But are you really sure?

Of course you do not believe in ghosts. And in any case you live in a brand new house. Who ever saw ghosts in a new house?

Jim Boone did, and it happened like this.

★　　　★　　　★　　　★

He and his new young wife Jessie were both out at work, he as an accountant and she as a teacher. They had been married a year and lived with his parents, who had lived in the village all their lives, and their ancestors before them. The young couple had their own sitting-room and bedroom, for the house was large, but though it was a comfortable enough arrangement for the most part, occasional friction cannot be avoided when two women share the same kitchen.

The problem of finding a house was not a financial one, for Jim had a tidy sum in the Building Society, and could afford to build if only a suitable plot of ground could be found within easy travelling distance of their work, which was in the cathedral city some six miles distant from the village.

It was a large hamlet rather than a village, with no church but boasting of no less than five inns fairly equally spaced among the cottages and half-timbered houses which straggled along the road. It was on one of these inns that Jim kept a careful eye, because belonging to it was a small piece of land, long disused and overgrown with brambles and thorn. The inn was his father's 'local'; he was on friendly terms with the landlord with whom he had gone to school, and it was understood that if ever the land was sold, Jim should have it.

To cut a long story short, for he took a great deal of persuading over many months, the landlord at last agreed to sell his plot, which was long but narrow, about twenty-five yards by ten. Just big enough in fact to take a house provided it were built close to the road. Plans were drawn up and passed, and the bulldozers moved in.

It seemed likely when the work began that given fine autumn weather the house would be ready for Jim and Jessie to move in before Christmas, but there was immediately an unforeseen delay. When the bricklayers began to dig out the foundations it was found that concealed by the thick undergrowth were the levelled remains of a much older house, which neither the innkeeper nor the villagers had known about. These had to be dug out and removed, and after this had been done work went on apace, though it was early in the New Year before the house was ready, and the Boones moved in.

It was an attractive little place, double fronted with bay windows, a large labour-saving kitchen, and three bedrooms.

During the spring and summer months Jim and Jessica worked like slaves to make a garden. Except when they they took an evening off to visit the local tennis club or to visit friends, they grudged every hour away from it, but the hard toil was a pleasure because at last they had a place of their own all to themselves.

It was when the days began to shorten and the children were hard put to reach their homes before dark that the first little crack appeared in their happiness.

Quite simply, Jessica was afraid of her house.

Several weeks elapsed, in fact, before she plucked up the courage to tell her husband. It often happened that she reached home first of an evening, and it was not long before she realized, much to her self-disgust, that she was terrified to enter the house alone. She could give no reason for her fear; she knew it was foolish and unreasonable, but there it was. She was not of a nervous disposition, but she had a dread that something was waiting for her in the darkness. She confessed that for some time she had made excuses to walk down the road to call on Jim's parents, so that he might reach home before her. To give him credit, he listened patiently and consoled her with his reassurance that all would be well when she had grown accustomed to the place. In the meantime, it was easy to arrange that they arrived home together, or that he arrived first.

With the new arrangement the subject was tacitly avoided, though it was obvious to both that their nerves were on edge. The slightest sound in the house, when the curtains were drawn and the night shut out, made them start and look furtively at each other. And it could not be denied that there were certain curious sounds, or that each began to make a habit of switching on unnecessary lights as they went about the house.

The noises usually began late at night, when only an occasional all-night lorry rumbled through the village, and the last maudlin song from some rustic turned out from the inn at closing time had faded away in the distance. They found themselves sitting tense and expectant for the first quiet, stealthy tread in the corridor outside the sitting-room door or in the bedroom above, for the soft closing of a door and, worst of all, for what was surely a muffled groan. Neither would speak of their fears to the other, but on some pretext or other Jim would leave the room and go upstairs, only to find nothing that was not ordinary and normal.

Both were at breaking point one night soon after they had gone to bed.

For the first time—since their rest had up to then been undisturbed—slow, deliberate footsteps could be heard mounting the stairs, to halt outside the bedroom door. A pause, and a groping as of searching fingers which was followed by a thunderous tattoo which seemed to shake the house.

Jessie shrieked and flung her arms round her husband. He tore him-

Jessie shrieked and flung her arms round her husband.

self free, rushed to the door and flung it open. There was nothing to be seen or heard, and he returned to his almost hysterical wife.

'What's the use?' she managed to sob. 'You know as well as I that there's something wrong with this house! It's haunted, Jim, and I can't stand it any longer! We shall have to sell it. I'm so unhappy!'

The two clung together in misery until at length they fell into uneasy sleep, for there was no further disturbance. The next morning they were recovered enough to talk reasonably and to try to decide what was best to do. Jim was most reluctant to be hasty, but what was the alternative to selling the house and trying to find somewhere else? Certainly things could not go on as they were if Jessie was to remain sane.

At length it was agreed that she should go to stay for a week or so with her sister in the city, while Jim stayed on in the house, in an attempt to get to the bottom of their troubles. At heart he dreaded the thought of what he had rashly suggested, but he put on a brave front for his wife's benefit. He blustered—'I'll be damned if I'll be driven out of my own house by noises!,' and he argued, 'After all, my dear, neither of us was actually harmed! You just go and have a good rest, and everything will be all right when you get back home.'

Much against her will off went a tearful, clinging Jessie, and Jim came home to an empty house at the end of the day.

★   ★   ★   ★

As Boone performed his necessary chores, lighting a fire, preparing and eating a high tea, washing up and clearing the kitchen, he fought against an increasing feeling of depression, almost of despair for which he could not altogether account. That he should be apprehensive was to be expected, he knew that he ought to be terrified, but he was not. Instead, he realized with a kind of resigned fatalism that as every moment passed it became more and more difficult for him to remember that he was James Boone, an accountant, with a wife named Jessie. And with that remorseless near loss of his identity the knowledge grew that some ordeal lay before him which he could not escape.

Moving as in a dream he sat down in his chair before the open door to wait for what was to come.

The night was still and through the window at his side he saw the lights of the houses opposite go out one by one. The pool of yellow light from a street lamp outside yielded to the cold silver and the black shadows of a rising moon. The room was warm. Against his will Jim began to nod, and was soon asleep.

He woke with a start. The room seemed strangely dark. He looked round him at the rough, lime-washed walls and up at the low, raftered ceiling. The pewter plates and mugs on the rickety old dresser gleamed dully in the flickering light of the candle which stood on the scrubbed pine table. The dirty platters and scraps of uneaten food spoke of a neglect which was also evident in the pile of cold wood ash on the stone hearth and the dust and filth which lay everywhere.

How long had he sat? Why? Even, where? For a while to half his mind everything around him was long familiar; even now, surely awake, some memory of other things half forgotten caused him to gasp and struggle as if to burst from nightmare.

He sank back exhausted, only to struggle to his feet as the outer door was flung open with a crash. Terrified but incapable of further movement he watched the two cowled and menacing figures emerge from the darkness of the passage to stand in the open doorway before him. Motionless. Their hands hanging at their sides. Waiting.

Memory flooded back. With a dreadful cry the unhappy man found strength to stagger towards them. He thrust them aside, evading somehow their clutching hands, and clambered desperately up the steep and narrow stairs to the room above. His fingers scrabbled on the closed door before he found the latch. On the threshold he paused and stood to listen, but no sound came from the darkness below.

Then he heard the sound of the bell. Faintly at first, but ever nearer, the mournful sound of a passing bell, and with it the clapping of hooves and the rumbling of iron-shod wheels over the uneven cobbles.

He stumbled to the window. The full moon rode high in the sky and by its light he saw the horse and cart which had drawn up at his door. Its driver stood beside it, his silent bell in his hand, looking up at him expectantly. As if impatient at the waiting he again swung the bell, and as its clanging note died away his cry rang out . . .

'Bring out your dead! Bring out your dead!'

Boone reeled back, his hands pressed tightly against his ears to shut out the dreadful sound, until he was brought up sharply against the truckle bed which lay against the opposite wall. He groped behind him and with a shrinking compulsion forced his fingers to trace the sharpened features of the sheeted form which lay stiff and cold upon the bed.

Sinking to his knees, he felt rather than heard the approach of the eager ghouls who pushed him roughly aside, and who lifted up his dead wife in their arms, one at the head and the other at the feet.

As they left the room, one of them turned his head. . . .

'We'll be back anon,' he said.

★ ★ ★ ★

Sobbing, with tears streaming down his face, Jim Boone found himself awake in his armchair, cold, and stiff in every joint. Bewildered, he looked around him. The fire was almost out, and he rose to poke it into a blaze. He shut the door. His nightmare, if indeed it were, was fresh in his mind in every ghastly detail, and it was only after he had visited every room in the little house that he was entirely reassured.

Jim spent what remained of the night in urgent thought—for he knew it was useless to try to sleep—and by morning he had decided what had to be done. He went to the office as usual, whence he telephoned Jessie. He said nothing about his experiences of the previous night, only that he had decided that she was right and that the house had to be sold. She said she would meet him for lunch.

This done, he walked to the old building near the cathedral where the Registrar for Births and Deaths had his office. Vague memories of what little history he had learnt at school prompted him to ask the official whether any records were available which dated back as far as the late seventeenth century? The registrar pursed his lips and shook his head doubtfully. Was it any particular parish that was in question? Jim named it, whereupon after a great deal of clambering on library steps amid clouds of dust, a tattered old leather-bound volume was produced and laid upon a table.

Eagerly, Jim turned the discoloured pages. He had no doubt, somehow, about what he would find.

At length, among the entries for the year 1667. . . .

'16 March. Mary Boone, wife of James Boone, Aged 22. Died of the Plague.'

'19 March. James Boone. Aged 26. Died of the Plague.'

EXPIATION

E.F. Benson

Philip Stuart and I, unattached and middle-aged persons, had for the last four or five years been accustomed to spend a month or six weeks together in the summer, taking a furnished house in some part of the country, which by an absence of attractive pursuits, was not likely to be overrun by gregarious holiday-makers. When, as the season for getting out of London draws near, and we scan the advertisement columns which set forth the charms and the cheapness of residences to be let for August, and see the mention of tennis clubs and esplanades and admirable golf links within a stone's throw of the proposed front door, our offended and disgusted eyes instantly wander to the next item.

For the point of a holiday, according to our private heresy, is not to be entertained and occupied and jostled by glad crowds, but to have nothing to do, and no temptation which might lead to any unseasonable activity. London had held employments and diversion enough; we want to be without both. But vicinity to the sea is desirable, because it is easier to do nothing by the sea than anywhere else, and because bathing and basking on the shore cannot be considered an employment but only an apotheosis of loafing. A garden also is a requisite, for that tranquillizes any fidgety notion of going for a walk.

In pursuance of this sensible policy we had this year taken a house on the south coast of Cornwall, for a relaxing climate conduces to laziness. It was too far off for us to make any personal inspection of it, but a perusal of the modestly worded advertisement carried conviction. It was close to the sea; the village Polwithy, outside which it was situated, was remote and, as far as we knew, unknown; it had a garden; and there was attached to it a cook-housekeeper who made for simplification. No mention of golf links or attractive resorts in the neighbourhood defiled the bald and terse specification, and though there was a tennis-court in the garden, there was no clause that bound the tenants to use it. The owner was a Mrs Hearne, who had been living abroad, and our business was transacted with a house agent in Falmouth.

To make our household complete, Philip sent down a parlour-maid and I a housemaid, and after leaving them a day in which to settle in, we followed. There was a six mile drive from the station across high uplands, and at the end a long steady descent into a narrow valley, cloven between the hills, that grew ever more luxuriant in verdure as we descended. Great trees of fuchsia spread up to the eaves of the thatched cottages which stood by the wayside, and a stream, embowered in green thickets, ran babbling through the centre of it. Presently we came to the village, no more than a dozen houses, built of the grey stone of the district, and on a shelf just above it a tiny church with parsonage adjoining. High above us now flamed the gorse-clad slopes of the hills on each side, and now the valley opened out at its lower end, and the still warm air was spiced and renovated by the breeze that drew up it from the sea. Then round a sharp angle of the road we came alongside a stretch of brick wall, and stopped at an iron gate above which flowed a riot of rambler rose.

It seemed hardly credible that it was this of which that terse and laconic advertisement had spoken. I had pictured something of villa-ish kind, yellow bricked, perhaps, with a roof of purplish slate, a sitting-room one side of the entrance, a dining-room the other; with a tiled hall and a pitch-pine staircase, and instead, here was this little gem of an early Georgian manor house, mellow and gracious, with mullioned windows and a roof of stone slabs. In front of it was a paved terrace, below which blossomed a herbaceous border, tangled and tropical, with no inch of earth visible through its luxuriance. Inside, too, was fulfilment of this fair exterior: a broad-balustered staircase led up from the odiously entitled 'lounge hall', which I had pictured as a medley of Benares ware and saddle-bagged sofas, but which proved to be cool, broad, and panelled, with a door opposite that through which we entered, leading on to the farther area of garden at the back.

There was the advertised but innocuous tennis court, bordered on the length of its far side by a steep grass bank, along which was planted a row of limes, once pollarded, but now allowed to develop at will. Thick boughs, some fourteen or fifteen feet from the ground, interlaced with one another, forming an arcaded row; above them, where Nature had been permitted to go her own way, the trees broke into feathered and honey-scented branches. Beyond lay a small orchard climbing upwards, above that the hillside rose more steeply, in broad spaces of short-cropped turf and ablaze with gorse, the Cornish gorse that flowers all the year round, and spreads its sunshine from January to December.

There was time for a stroll through this perfect little domain before dinner, and for a short interview with the housekeeper, a quiet, capable-looking woman, slightly aloof—as is the habit of her race—from strangers and foreigners, for so the Cornish account the English, but who proved herself at the repast that followed to be as capable as she appeared. The evening closed in hot and still, and after dinner we took chairs out on the terrace in front of the house.

'Far the best place we've struck yet,' observed Philip. 'Why did no one say Polwithy before?'

'Because nobody had ever heard of it, luckily,' said I.

'Well, I'm a Polwithian. At least I am in spirit. But how aware Mrs —Mrs Criddle made me feel that I wasn't really.'

Philip's profession, a doctor of obscure nervous diseases, has made him preternaturally acute in the diagnosis of what other people feel, and for some reason, quite undefined, I wanted to know what exactly he meant by this. I was in sympathy with his feeling, but could not analyse it.

'Describe your symptoms,' I said.

'I have. When she came up and talked to us, and hoped we should be comfortable, and told us that she would do her best, she was just gossiping. Probably it was perfectly true gossip. But it wasn't she. However, as that's all that matters, there's no reason why we should probe further.'

'Which means that you have,' I said.

'No; it means that I tried to and couldn't. She gave me an extraordinary sense of her being aware of something which we knew nothing of; of being on a plane which we couldn't imagine. I constantly meet such people; they aren't very rare. I don't mean that there's anything the least uncanny about them, or that they know things that are uncanny. They are simply aloof, as hard to understand as your dog or your cat. She would find us equally aloof if she succeeded in analysing her sensations about us, but like a sensible woman she probably feels not the smallest interest in us. She is there to bake and to boil, and we are there to eat her bakings and appreciate her boilings.'

The subject dropped, and we sat on in the dusk that was rapidly deepening into night. The door into the hall was open at our backs, and a panel of light from the lamps within was cast out to the terrace. Wandering moths, invisible in the darkness, suddenly became manifest as they fluttered into this illumination, and vanished again as they passed out of it. One moment they were there, living things with life and motion of their own, the next they quite disappeared. How inexplicable that would be, I thought, if one did not know from long familiarity, that light of the appropriate sort and strength is needed to make material objects visible.

Philip must have been following precisely the same train of thought, for his voice broke in, carrying it a little further.

'Look at that moth,' he said, 'and even while you look it has gone like a ghost, even as like a ghost it appeared. Light made it visible. And there are other sorts of light, interior psychical light which similarly makes visible the beings which people the darkness of our blindness.'

Just as he spoke I thought for the moment that I heard the tinkle of a telephone bell. It sounded very faintly, and I could not have sworn that I had actually heard it. At the most it gave one staccato little summons and was silent again.

'Is there a telephone in the house?' I asked. 'I haven't noticed one.'

'Yes, by the door into the back garden,' said he. 'Do you want to telephone?'

'No, but I thought I heard it ring. Didn't you?'

He shook his head; then smiled.

'Ah, that was it,' he said.

Certainly now there was the clink of glass, rather bell-like, as the parlour-maid came out of the dining-room with a tray of siphon and decanter, and my reasonable mind was quite content to accept this very probable explanation. But behind that, quite unreasonably, some little obstinate denizen of my consciousness rejected it. It told me that what I had heard was like the moth that came out of darkness and went on into darkness again. . . .

My room was at the back of the house, overlooking the lawn tennis court, and presently I went up to bed. The moon had risen, and the lawn lay in bright illumination, bordered by a strip of dark shadow below the pollarded limes. Somewhere along the hillside an owl was foraging, softly hooting, and presently it swept whitely across the lawn. No sound is so intensely rural, yet none, to my mind, so suggests a signal. But it seemed to signal nothing, and, tired with the long hot journey, and soothed by the deep tranquility of the place, I was soon asleep. But often during the night I woke, though never to more than a dozing dreamy consciousness of where I was, and each time I had the notion that some slight noise had roused me, and each time I found myself listening to hear whether the tinkle of a telephone bell was the cause of my disturbance. There came no repetition of it, and again I slept, and again I woke with drowsy attention for the sound which I felt I expected, but never heard.

Daylight banished these imaginations, but though I must have slept many hours all told, for these wakings had been only brief and partial, I was aware of a certain weariness, as if though my bodily senses had been rested, some part of me had been wakeful and watching all night. This was fanciful enough to disregard, and certainly during the day I forgot it altogether.

Soon after breakfast we went down to the sea, and a short ramble along a shingly shore brought us to a sandy cove framed in promontories of rock that went down into deep water. The most fastidious connoisseur in bathing could have pictured no more ideal scene for his operations, for with hot sand to bask on and rocks to plunge from, and a limpid ocean and a cloudless sky, there was indeed no lacuna in perfection.

All morning we loafed here, swimming and sunning ourselves, and for the afternoon there was the shade of the garden, and a stroll later on up through the orchard and to the gorse-clad hillside. We came back through the churchyard, looked into the church, and coming out, Philip pointed to a tombstone which, from its newness among its dusky and moss-grown companions, easily struck the eye. It recorded, without pious or scriptural reflection, the date of the birth and death of George Hearne; the latter event had taken place close on two years ago, and we were within a week of the exact anniversary. Other tombstones near were monuments to those of the same name, and dated back for a couple of centuries and more.

'Local family,' said I, and strolling on we came to our own gate in the long brick wall. It was opened from inside just as we arrived at it, and there came out a brisk, middle-aged man in clergyman's dress, obviously our vicar.

He very civilly introduced himself.

'I heard that Mrs Hearne's house had been taken, and that the tenants had come,' he said, 'and I ventured to leave my card.'

We performed our part of the ceremony, and in answer to his inquiry professed our satisfaction with our quarters and our neighbourhood.

'That is good news,' said Mr Stephens, 'I hope you will continue to enjoy your holiday. I am Cornish myself, and like all natives think there is no place like Cornwall!'

Philip pointed with his stick towards the churchyard. 'We noticed that the Hearnes are people of the place,' he said. Quite suddenly I found myself understanding what he had meant by the aloofness of the race. Something between reserve and suspicion came into Mr Stephens's face.

'Yes, yes, an old family here,' he said; 'and large landowners. But now some remote cousin—. The house, however, belongs to Mrs Hearne for life.

He stopped, and by that reticence confirmed the impression he had made. In consequence, for there is something in the breast of the most

We met the vicar on our stroll through the churchyard.

incurious, which, when treated with reserve, becomes inquisitive, Philip proceeded to ask a direct question.

'Then I take it that the George Hearne who, as I have just seen, died two years ago, was the husband of Mrs Hearne, from whom we took the house?'

'Yes, he was buried in the churchyard,' said Mr Stephens quickly. Then, for no reason at all, he added:

'Naturally he was buried in the churchyard here.'

Now my impression at that moment was that Mr Stephens had said something he did not mean to say, and had corrected it by saying the same thing again. He went on his way, back to the vicarage, with an amiably expressed desire to do anything that was in his power for us in the way of local information, and we went in through the gate. The post had just arrived; there was the London morning paper and a letter for Philip which cost him two perusals before he folded it up and put it into his pocket. But he made no comment, and presently, as dinner time was near, I went up to my room.

Here in this deep valley, with the great westerly hill towering above us, it was already dark, and the lawn lay beneath a twilight as of deep clear water. Quite idly as I brushed my hair in front of the glass on the table in the window, of which the blinds were not yet drawn, I looked out, and saw that on the bank along which grew the pollarded limes, there was a ladder. It was just a shade odd that it should be there, but the oddity of it was quite accounted for by the supposition that the gardener had had business among the trees in the orchard, and had left it there for the completion of his labours tomorrow. It was just as odd as that, and no odder, just worth a twitch of the imagination to account for it, but now completely accounted for.

I went downstairs, and passing Philip's door heard the swish of ablutions, which implied he was not quite ready, and in the most loafer-like manner I strolled round the corner of the house. The kitchen window which looked onto the tennis court was open, and there was a good smell, I remember, coming from it. And still without thought of the ladder I had just seen, I mounted the slope of the grass onto the tennis court. Just across it was the bank where the pollarded limes grew, but there was no ladder lying there. Of course, the gardener must have remembered he had left it, and had returned to remove it exactly as I came downstairs. There was nothing singular about that, and I could not imagine why the thing interested me at all. But for some inexplicable reason I found myself saying: 'But I did see the ladder just now.'

A bell—no telephone bell, but a welcome harbinger to a hungry man —sounded from inside the house, and I went back onto the terrace, just as Philip got downstairs. At dinner our speech rambled pleasantly over the accomplishments of today, and the prospects of tomorrow, and in due course we came to the consideration of Mr Stephens. We settled that he was an aloof fellow, and then Philip said:

'I wonder why he hastened to tell us that George Hearne was buried in the churchyard, and then added that naturally he was!'

'It's the natural place to be buried in,' said I.

'Quite. That's just why it was hardly worth mentioning.'

I felt then, just momentarily, just vaguely, as if my mind was regarding stray pieces of a jig-saw puzzle. The fancied ringing of the telephone bell last night was one of them, this burial of George Hearne in the churchyard was another, and, even more inexplicably, the ladder I had seen under the trees was a third. Consciously I made nothing whatever out of them, and did not feel the least inclination to devote any ingenuity to so fortuitous a collection of pieces. Why shouldn't I add, for that matter, our morning's bathe, or the gorse on the hillside? But I had the sensation that, though my conscious brain was presently occupied with piquet, and was rapidly growing sleepy with the day of sun and sea, some sort of mole inside it was digging passages and connecting corridors below the soil.

Five eventless days succeeded, there were no more ladders, no more phantom telephone bells, and emphatically no more Mr Stephens. Once or twice we met him in the village street and got from him the curtest salutation possible short of a direct cut. And yet somehow he seemed charged with information, so we lazily concluded, and he made for us a field of imaginative speculation. I remembered that I constructed a highly fanciful romance, which postulated that George Hearne was not dead at all, but that Mr Stephens had murdered some inconvenient blackmailer, whom he had buried with the rites of the church. Or—these romances always broke down under cross-examination from Philip—Mr Stephens himself was George Hearne, who had fled from justice, and was supposed to have died. Or Mrs Hearne was really George Hearne, and our admirable housekeeper was the real Mrs Hearne. From such indications you may judge how the intoxication of the sun had overpowered us.

But there was one explanation of why Mr Stephens had so hastily assured us that George Hearne was buried in the churchyard, which never passed our lips. It was just because Philip and I really believed it to be the true one that we did not mention it. But as if it were some fever or plague, we both knew that we were sickening with it. And then these fanciful romances stopped because we knew that the Real Thing was approaching. There had been faint glimpses of it before, like distant sheet-lightning; now the noise of it, authentic and audible, began to rumble.

There came a day of hot, overclouded weather. We had bathed in the morning, and loafed in the afternoon, but Philip, after tea, had refused to come for our usual ramble, and I set out alone. That morning Mrs Criddle had rather peremptorily told me that a room in the front of the house would prove much cooler for me, for it caught the sea breeze, and though I objected that it would also catch the southerly sun, she had clearly made up her mind that I was to move from the bedroom overlooking the tennis court and the pollarded limes, and there was no resisting so polite yet determined a woman.

When I set out for my ramble after tea, the change had already been effected, and my brain nosed slowly about as I strolled sniffing for her reason; for no self-respecting brain could accept the one she gave. But in this hot, drowsy air I entirely lacked nimbleness, and when I came back, the question had become a mere silly, unanswerable riddle. I returned through the churchyard, and saw that in a couple of days we should arrive at the anniversary of George Hearne's death.

Philip was not on the terrace in front of the house, and I went in at the door of the hall, expecting to find him there or in the back garden. Exactly as I entered my eye told me that there he was, a black silhouette against the glass door at the end of the hall, which was open, and led through into the back garden. He did not turn round at the sound of my entry, but took a step or two in the direction of the far door, still framed in the oblong of it. I glanced at the table where the post lay, found letters both for me and him, and looked up again. There was no one there.

He had hastened his steps, I supposed, but simultaneously I thought how odd it was that he had not taken his letters, if he was in the hall, and that he had not turned when I entered. However, I should find him just round the corner, and with his post and mine in my hand, I went towards the far door. As I approached it I felt a sudden cold stir of air, rather unaccountable, for the day was notably sultry, and went out. He was sitting at the far end of the tennis court.

I went up to him with his letters.

'I thought I saw you just now in the hall,' I said. But I knew already that I had not seen him in the hall.

He looked up quickly.

'And have you only just come in?' he said.

'Yes; this moment. Why?'

'Because half an hour ago I went in to see if the post had come, and thought I saw you in the hall.'

'And what did I do?' I asked.

'You went out onto the terrace. But I didn't find you there.'

There was a short pause as he opened his letters.

'Damned interesting,' he observed. 'Because there's someone here who isn't you or me.'

'Anything else?' I asked.

He laughed, pointing at the row of trees.

'Yes, something too silly for words,' he said. 'Just now I saw a piece of rope dangling from the big branch of that pollarded lime. I saw it quite distinctly. And then there wasn't any rope there at all, any more than there is now.'

★   ★   ★   ★

Philosophers have argued about the strongest emotion known to man. Some say 'love', others 'hate', others 'fear', I am disposed to put 'curiosity' on a level, at least, with these august sensations, just mere, simple inquisitiveness. Certainly at the moment it rivalled fear in my mind, and there was a hint of that.

As he spoke the parlour-maid came out into the garden with a telegram in her hand. She gave it to Philip, who, without a word, scribbled a line on the reply paid form inside it, and handed it back to her.

'Dreadful nuisance,' he said, 'but there's no help for it. A few days ago I got a letter which made me think I might have to go up to town, and this telegram makes it certain. There's an operation possible on a patient of mine, which I hoped might have been avoided, but my locum tenens won't take the responsibility of deciding whether it is necessary or not.'

He looked at his watch.

'I can catch the night train,' he said, 'and I ought to be able to catch the night train back from town tomorrow. I shall be back, that is to say, the day after tomorrow in the morning. There's no help for it. Ha! That telephone of yours will come in useful. I can get a taxi from Falmouth, and needn't start till after dinner.'

He went into the house, and I heard him rattling and tapping at the telephone. Soon he called for Mrs Criddle, and presently came out again.

'We're not on the telephone service,' he said. 'It was cut off a year ago, only they haven't removed the apparatus. But I can get a trap in the village, Mrs Criddle says, and she's sent for it. If I start at once I shall easily be in time. Spicer's packing a bag for me, and I'll take a sandwich.'

He looked sharply towards the pollarded trees.

'Yes, just there,' he said. 'I saw it plainly, and equally plainly I saw it not. And then there's that telephone of yours.'

I told him now about the ladder I had seen below the tree where he saw the dangling rope.

'Interesting,' he said, 'because it's so silly and unexpected. It is really tragic that I should be called away just now, for it looks as if the— well, the matter were coming out of the darkness into a shaft of light. But I'll be back, I hope, in thirty-six hours. Meantime, do observe very carefully, and whatever you do, don't make a theory. Darwin says somewhere that you can't observe without a theory, but to make a theory is a great danger to an observer. It can't help influencing your imagination; you tend to see or hear what falls in with your hypothesis. So just observe; be as mechanical as a phonograph and a photographic lens.'

Presently the dog-cart arrived and I went down to the gate with him. 'Whatever it is that is coming through, is coming through in bits,' he said. 'You heard a telephone; I saw a rope. We both saw a figure, but not simultaneously nor in the same place. I wish I didn't have to go.'

I found myself sympathizing strongly with this wish, when after dinner I found myself with a solitary evening in front of me, and the pledge to 'observe' binding me. It was not mainly a scientific ardour that prompted this sympathy and the desire for independent combination, but, quite emphatically, fear of what might be coming out of the huge darkness which lies on all sides of human experience. I could no longer fail to connect together the fancied telephone bell, the rope, and the ladder, for what made the chain between them was the figure that both Philip and I had seen. Already my mind was seething with conjectural theory, but I would not let the ferment of it ascend to my surface consciousness; my business was not to aid but rather stifle my imagination.

I occupied myself, therefore, with the ordinary devices of a solitary man, sitting on the terrace, and subsequently coming into the house, for a few spots of rain had began to fall. But though nothing disturbed the outward tranquility of the evening, the quietness administered no opiate to that seething mixture of fear and curiosity that obsessed me. I heard the servants creep bedwards up the back stairs and presently I followed them. Then, forgetting for the moment that my room had been changed, I tried the handle of the door of that which I had previously occupied. It was locked.

Now here, beyond doubt, was the sign of a human agency, and at once I was determined to get into the room. The key, I could see, was not in the door, which must therefore have been locked from outside. I therefore searched the usual cache for keys along the top of the door-frame, found it and entered.

The room was quite empty, the blinds not drawn, and after looking round it I walked across to the window. The moon was up, and, though obscured behind clouds, gave sufficient light to enable me to see objects outside with tolerable distinctness. There was the row of pollarded limes, and then, with a sudden intake of my breath, I saw that a foot or two below one of the boughs there was suspended something whitish and oval which oscillated as it hung there. In the dimness I could see nothing more than that, but now conjecture crashed into my conscious brain. But even as I looked it was gone again; there was nothing there but deep shadow, the trees steadfast in the windless air. Simultaneously I knew that I was not alone in the room.

I turned swiftly about, but my eyes gave no endorsement of that conviction, and yet their evidence that there was no one here except myself failed to shake it. The presence, somewhere close to me, needed no such evidence; it was self-evident though invisible, and I knew that then my forehead was streaming with the abject sweat of terror. Somehow I knew that the presence was that of the figure both Philip and I had seen that evening in the hall, and credit it or not as you will, the fact that it was invisible made it infinitely the more terrible. I knew, too, that though my eyes were blind to it, it had got into closer touch with me; I knew more of its nature now, it had had tragic and awful commerce with evil and despair.

Some sort of catalepsy was on me while it thus obsessed me; presently, minutes afterwards or perhaps mere seconds, the grip and clutch of its power was relaxed, and with shaking knees I crossed the room and went out, and again locked the door. Even as I turned the key I smiled at the futility of that. With my emergence the terror completely passed; I went across the passage leading to my room, got into bed, and was soon asleep. But I had no more need to question myself as to why Mrs Criddle made the change. Another guest, she knew, would come to occupy it as the season arrived when George Hearne died and was buried in the churchyard.

The night passed quietly and then succeeded a day hot and still and sultry beyond belief. The very sea had lost its coolness and vitality, and I came in from my swim tired and enervated instead of refreshed. No breeze stirred; the trees stood motionless as if cast in iron, and from horizon to horizon the sky was overlaid by an ever-thickening pall of cloud. The cohorts of storm and thunder were gathering in the stillness, and all day I felt that power, other than that of these natural forces, was being stored for some imminent manifestation.

As I came near to the house the horror deepened, and after dinner I had a mind to drop into the vicarage, according to Mr Stephens's general invitation, and get through an hour or two with other company than my own. But I delayed till it was past any reasonable time for such an informal visit, and ten o'clock still saw me on the terrace in front of the house. My nerves were all on edge, a stir or step in the house was sufficient to make me turn round in apprehension of seeing I knew not what; but presently it grew still. One lamp burned in the hall behind me; by it stood the candle which would light me to bed.

I went indoors soon after, meaning to go up to bed, then, suddenly ashamed of this craven imbecility of mind, took the fancy to walk round the house for the purpose of convincing myself that all was tranquil and normal, and that my fear, that nameless, indefinable load of my spirit, was but a product of this close thundery night. The tension of the weather could not last much longer; soon the storm must break and the relief come, but it would be something to know that there was nothing more than that. Accordingly I went out again onto the terrace, traversed it and turned the corner of the house where lay the tennis lawn.

Tonight the moon had not yet risen, and the darkness was such that I could barely distinguish the outline of the house, and that of the pollarded limes, but through the glass door that led from this side of the house into the hall, there shone the light of the lamp that stood there. All was absolutely quiet, and half reassured I traversed the lawn, and turned to go back. Just as I came opposite the lit door, I heard a sound very close at hand from under the deep shadow of the pollarded limes. It was as if some heavy object had fallen with a thump and rebound on the grass, and with it there came the noise of a creaking bough suddenly strained by some weight. Then interpretation came upon me with the unreasoning force of conviction, though in the blackness I could see nothing. But at the sound a horror such as I have never felt laid hold on me. It was scarcely physical at all, it came from some deep-seated region of the soul.

The heavens were rent, a stream of blinding light shot forth, and straight in front of my eyes, a few yards from where I stood, I saw. The noise had been of a ladder thrown down on the grass, and from the bough of the pollarded lime, there was a figure of a man, white-faced against the blackness, oscillating and twisting on the rope that strangled him. Just that I saw before the stillness was torn to atoms by the roar of thunder, and, as from a hose, the rain descended. Once again, even before that first appalling riot had died, the clouds were shredded again by the lightning, and my eyes which had not moved from the place saw only the framed shadow of the trees and their upper branches bowed by the pelting rain. All night the storm raged and bellowed making sleep impossible, and for an hour at least, between the peals of thunder, I heard the ringing of the telephone bell.

★   ★   ★   ★

Next morning Philip returned, to whom I told exactly what is written here, but watch and observe as we might, neither of us, in the three further weeks which we spent at Polwithy, heard or saw anything that could interest the student of the occult. Pleasant lazy days succeeded one another, we bathed and rambled and played piquet of an evening, and incidentally we made friends with the vicar. He was an interesting man, full of curious lore concerning local legends and superstitions, and one night, when in our ripened acquaintanceship he had dined with us, he asked Philip directly whether either of us had experienced anything unusual during our tenancy.

Philip nodded towards me.

'My friend saw most,' he said.

'May I hear it?' asked the vicar.

When I had finished, he was silent awhile.

'I think the—shall we call it explanation?—is yours by right,' he said. 'I will give it to you if you care to hear it.'

Our silence, I suppose, answered him.

'I remember meeting you two on the day after your arrival here,' he said, 'and you inquired about the tombstone in the churchyard erected to the memory of George Hearne. I did not want to say more of him then, for a reason that you will presently know. I told you, I recollect, perhaps rather hurriedly, that it was Mrs Hearne's husband who was buried there. Already, I imagine, you guess that I concealed something. You may even have guessed it at the time.'

He did not wait for any confirmation or repudiation of this. Sitting out on the terrace in the deep dusk, his communication was very impersonal. It was just a narrating voice, without identity: an anonymous chronicle.

'George Hearne succeeded to the property here, which is considerable, only two years before his death. He was married shortly after he succeeded. According to any decent standard, his life both before and after his marriage was vile. I think—God forgive me if I wrong him —he made evil his god; he liked evil for its own sake. But out of the middle of the mire of his own soul there sprang a flower: he was devoted to his wife. And he was capable of shame.

'A fortnight before his—his death, she got to know what his life was like, and what he was in himself. I need not tell you about the particular disclosure that came to her knowledge; it is sufficient to say that it was revolting. She was here at the time; he was coming down from London that night. When he arrived he found a note from her saying that she had left him and could never come back. She told him that he must give her opportunity for her to divorce him, and threatened him with exposure if he did not.

'He and I had been friends, and that night he came to me with her letter, acknowledged the justice of it, but asked me to intervene. He said that the only thing that could save him from utter damnation was she, and I believe that there he spoke sincerely. But, speaking as a clergyman, I should not have called him penitent. He did not hate his sin, but only the consequences of it. But it seemed to me that if she came back to him, he might have a chance, and next day I went to her. Nothing that I could say moved her one atom, and after a fruitless day I came back, and told him of the uselessness of my mission.

Now, according to my view, no man who deliberately prefers evil to good just for the sake of wickedness is sane, and this refusal of hers to have anything more to do with him, I fully believe, upset the unstable balance of his soul altogether. There was just his devotion to her which might conceivably have restored it, but she refused—and I can quite understand her refusal—to come near him. If you knew what I know, you could not blame her. But the effect of it on him was portentous and disastrous, and three days afterwards I wrote to her again, saying quite simply that the damnation of his soul would be on her head unless, leaving her personal feelings altogether out of the question, she came back. She got that letter the next evening, and already it was too late.

'That afternoon, two years ago, on the 15th of August, there was washed up in the harbour here a dead body, and that night George

Hearne took a ladder from the fruit-wall in the kitchen garden and hanged himself. He climbed into one of the pollarded limes, tied the rope to a bough, and made a slip-knot at the other end of it. Then he kicked the ladder away.

'Mrs Hearne meantime had received my letter. For a couple of hours she wrestled with her own repugnance and then decided to come to him. She rang him up on the telephone, but the housekeeper here, Mrs Criddle, could only tell her that he had gone out after dinner. She continued ringing him up for a couple of hours, but there was always the same reply.

'Eventually she decided to waste no more time, and motored over from her mother's house where she was staying at the north end of the county. By then the moon had risen, and looking out from his window she saw him.'

He paused.

'There was an inquest,' he said, 'and I could truthfully testify that I believed him to be insane. The verdict of suicide during temporary insanity was brought in, and he was buried in the churchyard. The rope was burned, and the ladder was burned.'

The parlour-maid brought out drinks, and we sat in silence till she had gone again.

'And what about the telephone my friend heard?' asked Philip.

He thought for a moment.

'Don't you think that great emotion like that of Mrs Hearne's may make some sort of record,' he asked, 'so that if the needle of a sensitive temperament comes in contact with it, a reproduction takes place? And it is the same, perhaps, about that poor fellow who hanged himself. One can hardly believe that his spirit is bound to visit and revisit the scene of his follies and his crimes year by year.'

'Year by year?' I asked.

'Apparently. I saw him myself last year, Mrs Criddle did also.'

He got up.

'How can one tell?' he said. 'Expiation, perhaps. Who knows?'

KROGER'S CHOICE

John Gordon

Mr Kroger moved very slowly. He was obliged to, for the transparent plastic suit he wore over his other clothes gave him an extra, cloud-like dimension which made him clumsy, and he was already large enough. Too large, maybe. At least that's what they said. It was his bulk, they insisted, that had caused the problem which brought him here.

Good, thought Mr Kroger; damned good. Now they can put things right. And, by God, they'd better do it as I want it.

He shifted his helmet slightly as it rested on his shoulders. It was light enough to be no discomfort but he moved it so that the tubes from the little air-purifying pack at his waist blew a gentle draught of coolness on his hot cheeks. There was a long walk ahead between the rows of cages, and Mr Kroger was going to inspect every one. It was his money they were taking, and he was going to have the best.

'It is not like the old days, Mr Kroger.'

The voice was within the helmet bubble, quacking from the tiny radio speaker an inch from his ear. It invaded his intimate space, and Mr Kroger frowned. It was one of the indignities he was forced to endure despite the money he was spending.

'What old days?'

His voice, angry and loud, echoed within the helmet, startling even himself and making him glance swiftly at his companion. But Dr Bertram Goodman appeared to have noticed nothing.

'I mean the old days of bio-transfer.' Dr Bertram, as he preferred to be addressed by his staff at the Institute, let a smile sit on the prominent lips in his long face. 'But it was not so much life-transfer in those days; it was more correctly death-transfer. Used-up parts of corpses transplanted into the flesh of the living. Things were very crude and cruel in the sixties and seventies, Mr Kroger. Small wonder that the end was usually death—sooner, rather than later.'

Dr Bertram was tall and young-looking, his handsomeness increased by the tiny wrinkles that ageing had given to his waxen skin. He had been several times married, seeming to burn up young brides who, unable to keep his pace, became haggard and fell away.

'We are wasting time.' Mr Kroger allowed his impatience to show. 'I want to see everything.'

Light from the louvred windows in the long building fell evenly on the long corridors of shining steel bars. The cages were tall and broad—airy was the word Dr Bertram would often use, very airy cages, and he would get a laugh from patients less ill-natured than Mr Kroger—and they had tiled floors, all spotless thanks to good training, and had rest areas where synthetic, hygienic straw was piled for bedding.

'What's happening down there?' Mr Kroger pointed. Halfway along the corridor, some distance away, a cage door stood open and two attendants, their plastic suits winking like water in a shaft of sunlight, were bringing out a smaller cage, no bigger than a barred box, on a trolley. Behind its bars there was a glimpse of white fur.

'She has been purchased,' Dr Bertram's voice quacked beside Mr Kroger's ear. 'The bio-transfer will be going ahead this afternoon.'

'You will be there?'

'Whenever it is a heart I am there, Mr Kroger.'

Which accounted for the price—the whole world knew that there was only one Dr Bertram.

Mr Kroger watched the backs of the men as, in the strange silence caused by his helmet, they dwindled into the distance, turned a corner and were gone. It was a vast hall, and it would take him a long time to see everything.

Mr Kroger shambled forwards and leant his belly against the shining railing in front of the nearest cage. The creature inside had long, fair hair, so silky that it floated whenever the creature moved and settled around it like thistledown when it was still. As it was now. It was the size of a chimpanzee, taller, perhaps, when it stood upright, but its face, though black, had a smoothness and lack of wrinkles that made it unlike a monkey. Yet it was an ape. From the black mask fringed with the creamy hair, a pair of brown, almost unseeing, drunkard's eyes looked at Mr Kroger with an animal's indifference. It was an apish near-attempt at humanity.

'A young male,' said Dr Bertram.

'Quality?'

'Exceptionally high.' Dr Bertram glanced down at the screen of the little computer in his gloved hand. 'And the somatic considerations, blood and so on, are well within the tolerances for your particular group.' He turned his handsome face towards Mr Kroger and raised his heavy, black eyebrows as he smiled. 'But don't make up your mind immediately. There are plenty more; a wide choice.'

From behind bars the brown, watery eyes watched them vaguely. Under the fleshy flair of the nostrils the lips of the mouth, like the rim of a large bowl, were tight shut.

'Why white hair?' said Mr Kroger.

The slightest hint of white or black, the tinge of a racial argument, and Dr Bertram was ready. Nobody could accuse him of bias. 'You might as well ask: Why long haired?' He answered his own question. 'Merely an outcome of cross-breeding—the woolly monkey, the gibbon, the chimp; these little fellows come with black faces and long fair hair bearing us gifts.'

Mr Kroger saw the humour. 'Hearts and lungs,' he said. His laugh was cut short by the gift-bearer in the cage. Leathery black fingers were probing wantonly into the silky hair of its groin. 'I want its hide,' said Mr Kroger, 'whichever I choose.'

'They make beautiful rugs,' said Dr Bertram.

Mr Kroger slid his belly along the railing to the next cage. A seemingly identical creature was walking on all fours across the tiles, using the knuckles of its hands. It ignored them.

'Female,' said Dr Bertram, 'but that makes no difference.' He pressed buttons on the computer in his hand and studied the tiny screen. 'This one would suit you almost as well as the male.'

'Would it!' Mr Kroger let his contempt show. What he wanted was the skin of a male, an arrogant, self-assured male cut down and flayed. For himself. The beautiful doctor was too blind. The beautiful doctor, Director of the Institute, must be made to see that it was Mr Kroger who was the master.

He moved on, walking much slower than he need, almost shuffling, and frequently stopping to rest against the rail. In spite of the cooling draught inside his helmet, sweat occasionally trickled down his bald dome to lodge in the corner of his eye, but the little eyes themselves, very blue and clear, glistened with boyish pleasure as they detected the impatience in Dr Bertram. My belly, he thought, is responsible for all this. And he laughed.

The Director turned his head and gazed from his glass dome down into Mr Kroger's. The blue eyes twinkled at him, the one unspoiled feature in what Dr Bertram knew was a corrupt, failing frame; the eyes and perhaps the tufts of red hair around his ears were all that were left of health. Unless wealth counted, and if one were to consider achievement as part of the whole man, then wealth did count. Dr Bertram respected tangible achievement.

'Your brochure,' said Mr Kroger, and suddenly began to quote it, sending the words like a stream of bullets from his turret towards Dr Bertram, 'speaks of freshly-matured animals of the highest quality; bred and housed in a scrupulously germ-free environment they never leave.'

Dr Bertram was aware of the brain that had made a fortune many times over, and answered carefully. 'I think you can see, Mr Kroger, our standards are high.'

Dr Bertram saw the disgust cross his face and knew he had an advantage. 'We have a breeding wing,' he said. 'It is carefully controlled.'

'I will see it.' The order was peremptory.

Dr Bertram thought for a moment before he replied, and then he spoke blandly. 'I am afraid that is out of the question. They must not be disturbed.' It was not strictly true, but it was necessary to show that there was something out of Mr Kroger's reach. He was determined, and Mr Kroger saw it.

Anger leapt in the little blue eyes but was quickly pushed aside. Mr Kroger was descending into his belly, the real refuge when events went against him. He stood where he was, pressed against the rail, and gradually slid his gloved hands along the metal bar until they just touched the swell of his flesh. He had money in many banks in the world, abstract money, figures on paper in ledgers, columns of figures; and deposited in vaults he had valuables of every kind growing in value in the dark like glittering mushrooms; and there were shipyards, factories, office blocks which he could exchange like counters to make his money thrive. But every time his money moved it was attacked. Predators cut and skimmed, took away the beauty of its growing, burrowed into him with taxes and dues, maggots of envy, greedy skeleton fingers. There was not a bank deep or dark enough to evade their sniffing out, their disgusting fingering. Except one. Mr Kroger let his precious weight fold over the rail. This was the bank no alien fingers could probe. It was his, from its outward smoothness to its dark interior, its shape and substance. Whatever he chose to put into it he kept. And if it cost a new heart to keep it functioning, then a new heart he would have.

After a full minute Mr Kroger returned to the surface. He wasted no time over regrets.

'And this one?' He nodded towards the next animal in the line.

'Unsuitable.'

Dr Bertram was about to move on but Mr Kroger lingered, watching the creature climb and swing elegantly from the bars across the top of its cage.

'Yes,' he said, as though speaking to himself, 'I would, in any case, have rejected this one.'

'You would?' Dr Bertram was curious.

'It does not have what I am looking for.'

'Which is?'

Mr Kroger shrugged. 'I shall know when I see it.' The young male, the first they had seen, had seemed to be what he needed. The urge for life was there—but young males were notorious for self-sacrifice, risking all, going out in a spark of glory, and perhaps even monkeys got satisfaction from that. It would not have been getting full value to buy what might be freely given.

Dr Bertram said nothing. He was suddenly disappointed in his client; Mr Kroger was going to make his decision on sentiment. He strode ahead with the millionaire waddling behind.

They looked at a large, rather shaggy female, and the Director deliberately refrained from giving his own findings, waiting for the subjective, unscientific verdict of his companion, but Mr Kroger surprised him.

'You are a newly married man, doctor. I hope you are happy.'

Dr Bertram bowed slightly.

'She is very beautiful.' Mr Kroger had never seen her but pictures of the famous surgeon's glamorous bride had been impossible to avoid. 'Your children will be magnificent.'

'Thank you.' Dr Bertram was startled.

'You *will* have children?' The hot blue eyes looked up sharply.

'Yes, yes.' Dr Bertram had been caught off-guard, and it was an unusual enough occurrence to make his tan a richer colour. But it was true; his wife was already pregnant. He awaited the results of this mating, as of his others, with interest.

'Children,' said Mr Kroger, 'are expensive.' It was he who now moved them on. Cage followed cage quickly and he rejected them all without waiting for the doctor's opinion.

'You have other families to provide for.' Mr Kroger switched back to the intimacies of Dr Bertram's life without apology. 'Even with all this,' he let his eyes indicate the huge hall, 'it must be difficult.'

Dr Bertram's notable charm reasserted itself. He smiled. 'All of this,' he said, 'makes it more expensive. They see my accounts, and their demands get larger and larger.'

Their eyes met and a genuine sympathy, like an electric flicker, leapt between helmet and helmet.

The millionaire waddled on at the side of the tall scientist. Their radios gave out nothing but breathing. They reached the end of the corridor and were about to turn to walk back along a parallel row of cages when Mr Kroger stopped.

'Where does that lead?' He pointed to a door.

'The breeding quarters,' said Dr Bertram, about to move on, but the millionaire stood where he was.

'We could help each other, doctor.'

The Director knew what was on his mind but he had already forbidden entrance, and now, even though they recognized in each other the strong flow of avarice, he sought gently to direct their steps away. 'Breeding is a delicate business,' he said.

'We are wearing these suits. No infection can spread from me.'

'No.' Dr Bertram shook his head inside the glass dome. 'It is more delicate than that; a question of the emotions. These are intelligent creatures, and must not be disturbed at this very critical time. I am sorry.'

'I would double your fee.'

Dr Bertram smiled ruefully.

'It need never appear in your books. It would be a gift. Cash or property.'

Dr Bertram looked at the floor, his eyebrows a single dark line.

'I would treble it.'

Dr Bertram looked around him. Their radios had a limited range and there were no attendants in the hall. Their eyes searched each other, silently bargaining.

'I have a house on a hillside in Wales,' said the voice in Dr Bertram's helmet. 'It is yours.'

Their eyes settled the deal. Abruptly Dr Bertram swung away and opened the door, and Mr Kroger followed him into an airlock.

Dr Bertram paused and looked at his watch. There should at this hour be no attendants present, but to make sure he stepped alone out of the airlock before turning and permitting Mr Kroger to follow.

It was a circular building with a high, domed roof, but it was not its shape alone that made it different to the clinical corridors they had just left. There was colour. The dome was of coloured glass, and light filtered down in faint columns of red and orange, blue and green to a floor that was soft to walk on. After the white radiance they had just left it was like stepping into a forest glade at drowsy noonday. But even here there were cages. They were ranged around the circular wall, larger than the cages outside and each with an inner compartment within which there was a fructifying dimness. There was noise also; not the occasional jungle shriek that had echoed in the hall, but a murmuring that entered Mr Kroger's helmet like the whispering within a seashell.

They walked out onto the coloured patches of the floor and as they did so Mr Kroger could see pale forms flicker behind bars and vanish into dark recesses.

'You are a stranger,' said Dr Bertram. 'They are suspicious.'

Mr Kroger did not answer. He was filled with triumph. Once again he had conquered, bought his way into a secret sanctum. There was a pulse here. He knew that in this place he would find what he sought.

Dr Bertram's voice quacked in his ear. 'The conditions have to be right or they will not breed.'

'*Will* not? You mean they choose whether to breed or not? You have no control?'

Dr Bertram shrugged. 'Some control, yes. But total control does not bring the best results. They are individuals, Mr Kroger, and gentle persuasion is the key to healthy procreation and upbringing. It works with human beings, so why not with these?'

His client did not bother to answer. Like smoke driven before a wind, the fair-haired creatures had all now vanished, but Dr Bertram chose a particular cage and walked towards it, talking as he went.

'They are all females in here, either pregnant or with their young. The males are separated after mating. It is more convenient for us; the males are not too easy to handle.' He laughed shortly. 'The ladies, however, are much more compliant.'

They stood before what appeared to be a quite empty cage. There was a little bracket attached to the bars in which, as in the corridors outside, the animal's number was displayed, but here there was an addition: the animal had a name. The placard, putting the unscientific word in quotation marks, said 'Mimi'.

Dr Bertram leant forward to tap the bars and at the same time called out the name. 'She can hear what I say despite the helmet,' he said. 'Their hearing is very acute.'

He called her again. 'Here, Mimi. Here.'

There was a stirring behind a low archway at the back.

'Here, Mimi. Bring him out and let us see him.' Dr Bertram motioned to Mr Kroger to stand back, half behind him. 'There's nothing to be afraid of, Mimi.' And then to Mr Kroger. 'She's just had her first. She's very proud of it.' He called again, coaxing, and she came into the open. Very gradually, knuckling her way across

Mr Kroger knew his search had ended.

the floor, her silky hair almost hiding her black hands and feet, Mimi approached the bars. She stopped three feet short and tilted her head sideways so that she looked directly towards Mr Kroger where he stood shielded by the Director.

Dr Bertram laughed. 'Don't worry, Mimi, it's a friend. Come and show us, there's a good girl.'

She seemed to understand. The suspicion, which had begun to wrinkle her nostrils and make her lip begin to curl, vanished and she sat back on her haunches. There was an expression on her face that was not as crude as suspicion or fear. It was more complex. It was very close to pride.

'Closer, Mimi. Let us see.'

She shuffled forward, almost to the bars. She was not a large animal, no more than of middle height, and her long hair made a cape over her shoulders under which she had now concealed both arms.

'You've got the little fellow hidden away, haven't you?' Dr Bertram's voice was soft. 'Aren't you going to let Mr Kroger see him?'

There was a pause. Very slowly, Mr Kroger came into the open. Mimi hardly glanced at him. She was parting her long hair with a delicate paw. Underneath there was a patch of darkness to which she tilted her muzzle and then, very gradually, advanced whatever it was she was looking at so they could see it. Mr Kroger gazed at a little, wizzened face. It screwed up its eyes then opened them wide. They were without expression, simply absorbing what was presented to them. And close by, clinging to the silken, fair hair, a black fist, a miniature, too small to be real, like a cunningly-made brooch, attached Mimi's baby to her.

'Clever girl,' said Dr Bertram. 'Clever girl.'

And Mimi lifted her head.

It was at that moment that Mr Kroger knew his search had ended. The pulse of life overflowed her own body into her baby and outwards towards Dr Bertram. This was infinitely superior to the mere conquering of a male. This would be to pluck at the core of existence itself. Mr Kroger had found the full, ripe heart his body needed.

He turned and walked away before Dr Bertram knew he had gone. The Director caught him up in the airlock. They looked at each other, and Mr Kroger did not insult the Director by indulging in any preamble. He permitted himself the thinnest of smiles and a slight nod of the head.

'That one,' he said.

Dr Bertram had lost some of his colour. His tan merely made him look ill. 'There's the baby,' he said.

The millionaire made no reply. He did nothing. He did not look at the Director. He did not look away. He stood as though the Director did not exist and he was alone in the cramped airlock.

And Dr Bertram, already committed to a conspiracy, felt himself standing on sand that slid from under his feet. He licked his lips.

It was then that Mr Kroger named a figure on top of all that he had already promised, and began to smile as he became aware of his own generosity.

★   ★   ★   ★

The curtains blew gently into the room as Dr Bertram raised himself on one elbow and looked down at his sleeping wife. It was a warm night and enough moonlight came through the curtains to show her head on the pillow, her blonde hair snaking over her cheek.

He had only that day told her about Mr Kroger's choice. Maybe he should not have mentioned the baby monkey—but it also had had to go; the millionaire had bought it. But, for God's sake, she knew the sort of place he ran—and anyway it had been quite painless for the little thing. Slightly worse for its mother, but only for a moment when she had seen the trolley wheeled up to the bars. Then the men had gone in quickly and she would have felt nothing, almost nothing before the drug began to work. She clung to the baby, though; even dying.

Dr Bertram was an honest man. He did not pretend to himself to feel much regret. His qualms were over that moment in the airlock when he had known he was in the other man's stronger will.

He eased himself out of bed and walked, soft-footed to the window. He wore only pyjama trousers and he enjoyed the breeze against his skin as he looked out over the valley. It was a lovely spot, full of shadows under the moon. His wife had cried before she slept but he had told her about the house on the hill and the money, and that had helped.

So who in the end had won the battle of wills? It had been expedient to bend one of his own rules, and that only slightly. Given the chance, he would do the same again. And it was he who, during the operation, had had the power of life or death over Mr Kroger. A coward would have found a way to let the millionaire die. So, thought Dr Bertram, by letting him live I have conquered him.

He leant out of the window. The whole Institute slept quietly in its grounds, no sound coming even from the animal house higher up the hill. Below him were the hospital and the scattered white bungalows of the private wards.

Mr Kroger was almost ready to leave. He had lost some weight before the operation, and now his new heart was giving him energy he had not known in years. And the deeds of the house in Wales and the money had been handed over and lay in secret places. Dr Bertram yawned, and went back to the bed to look down at his sleeping wife. Even in the faint light of the moon her beauty was obvious. And she had years of beauty ahead of her. She would not fade; not quickly. There was no doubt about it; she was the best of all. There could never be another like her, and the child she bore him would be perfect.

It was very quiet; not even a monkey crying out as they often did when the moon was high. Dr Bertram yawned and slid into bed beside his wife. She moved slightly and he put his arm across her waist, as he always did. All was well. He closed his eyes and slid into sleep.

Mr Kroger's eyes opened. He searched his mind for what it could be that had disturbed his sleep but discovered nothing. There was no pain. There was no longer even a dressing on the wound, and the scar was surprisingly small. The stitches were coming out in the morning. A complete success. How wise to have taken over at the crest of that other life. And if it ever came to be necessary he would do it again, and again.

The curtains fluttered annoyingly. That's what had woken him. He put out his hand, reaching for the cord with the bell push that would summon the nurse, but the breeze pushed the curtains inwards in a sudden flurry that made the cord swing out of reach. Far out of reach. The cord looped itself over his bedside lamp and stayed there, a yard from him.

Mr Kroger grunted and began to push himself up. But it was not easy, not even now when he was fitter and thinner than he had been in years. He pushed again, but nothing more than his head lifted from the bed. He felt leaden, heavy. He got both elbows to his sides and heaved. He knew he had the strength, yet no matter how hard he pushed his back would not leave the mattress. For one moment of panic he thought the heart in his chest, the new heart, had failed.

He closed his eyes and lay still. Gradually he felt his pulse become steady and strong. He was half asleep, dreaming; that was it. And small wonder after what he had been through.

He moved his feet and then his legs. He was wide awake now; quite certain of it. He opened his eyes.

She sat on his chest. Her fair cape was over her shoulders, and her black face was looking down at him. In the moonlight he could see the glint of her eyes in the black mask.

Mr Kroger tried to cry out. He was conscious of his mouth opening, but no sound came. And he was conscious of trying to move his arms to beat her off, but his hands, although his mind screamed at them, would not raise themselves from the sheets. Yet there were sensations in his body. He could feel the coldness of her feet on his skin, and he could choose where his eyes looked. He watched her hands. He saw them move. With a colossal effort he raised his head, to look down at his chest where the hands were busy. The black fingers began very delicately to pluck at the stitches.

The scream that eventually came woke the whole hospital. The nurse, who was first into Mr Kroger's room was used to blood, but never so much of it, everywhere. But then she saw his chest, the gaping hole. . . .

The sound of someone beating at his door woke Dr Bertram from a very deep sleep. He rolled away from his wife, but as he turned towards her, reaching for the lamp switch, he felt something warm and wet against his face. He tried to push it away but it was still there when the light came on and woke his wife. The heart lay on the pillow between their heads, still alive. It quivered, and they saw its final pulse push the last red gobbet from the torn tube, making it spread out between them.

She lost her child that night.

LAURA

Saki

'You aren't really dying, are you?' asked Amanda.

'I have the doctor's permission to live till Tuesday,' said Laura.

'But today is Saturday; this is serious!' gasped Amanda.

'I don't know about it being serious; it is certainly Saturday,' said Laura.

'Death is always serious,' said Amanda.

'I never said I was going to die. I am presumably going to leave off being, Laura, but I shall go on being something. An animal of some kind, I suppose. You see, when one hasn't been very good in the life one has just lived, one reincarnates in some lower organism. And I haven't been very good, when one comes to think of it. I've been cruel and mean and vindictive and all that sort of thing when circumstances seemed to warrant it.'

'Circumstances never warrant that sort of thing,' said Amanda.

'If you don't mind my saying so,' observed Laura, 'Egbert is a circumstance that would warrant any amount of that sort of thing. You're married to him—that's different; you've sworn to love, honour and endure him: I haven't.'

'I don't see what's wrong with Egbert,' protested Amanda.

'Oh, I dare say the wrongness has been on my part,' admitted Laura dispassionately; 'he has merely been the extenuating circumstance. He made a thin, peevish kind of fuss for instance, when I took the collie puppies from the farm out for a run the other day.'

They chased his young broods of speckled Sussex and drove two sitting hens off their nest, besides running all over the flower beds. You know how devoted he is to his poultry and garden.'

'Anyway, he needn't have gone on about it for the entire evening and then have said, "Let's say no more about it", just when I was beginning to enjoy the discussion. That's where one of my petty vindictive revenges came in,' added Laura with an unrepentant chuckle; 'I turned the entire family of speckled Sussex into his seedling shed the day after the puppy episode.'

'How could you?' exclaimed Amanda.

'It came quite easy,' said Laura; 'two of the hens pretended to be laying at the same time, but I was firm.'

'And we thought it was an accident!'

'You see,' resumed Laura, 'I really *have* some grounds for supposing that my next incarnation will be in a lower organism. I shall be an animal of some kind. On the other hand, I haven't been a bad sort in my way, so I think I may count on being a nice animal, something elegant and lively, with a love of fun. An otter, perhaps.'

'I can't imagine you as an otter,' said Amanda.

'Well, I don't suppose you can imagine me as an angel, if it comes to that,' said Laura.

Amanda was silent. She couldn't.

'Personally I think an otter life would be rather enjoyable,' continued Laura; 'salmon to eat all year round, and the satisfaction of being able to fetch the trout in their own homes without having to wait for hours till they condescend to rise to the fly you've been dangling before them; and an elegant svelte figure—'

'Think of the otter hounds,' interposed Amanda; 'how dreadful to be hunted and harried and finally worried to death!'

'Rather fun with half the neighbourhood looking on, and anyhow not worse than this Saturday-to-Tuesday business of dying by inches; and then I should go on into something else. If I had been a moderately good otter I suppose I should get back into human shape of some sort; probably something primitive—a little brown, unclothed Nubian boy, I should think.'

'I wish you would be serious,' sighed Amanda; 'you really ought to be if you're only going to live till Tuesday.'

As a matter of fact Laura died on Monday.

'So dreadfully upsetting,' Amanda complained to her uncle-in-law, Sir Lulworth Quayne. 'I've asked quite a lot of people down for golf and fishing, and the rhododendrons are just looking their best.'

'Laura always was inconsiderate,' said Sir Lulworth; 'she was born during Goodwood week, with an Ambassador staying in the house who hated babies.'

'She had the maddest kind of ideas,' said Amanda; 'do you know if there was any insanity in her family?'

'Insanity? No, I never heard of any. Her father lives in West Kensington, but I believe he's sane on all other subjects.'

'She had an idea that she was going to be reincarnated as an otter,' said Amanda.

'One meets with those ideas of reincarnation so frequently, even in the West,' said Sir Lulworth, 'that one can hardly set them down as being mad. And Laura was such an unaccountable person in this life that I should not like to lay down definite rules as to what she might be doing in an after state.'

'You think she really might have passed into some animal form? asked Amanda. She was one of those who shape their opinions rather readily from the standpoint of those around them.

Just then Egbert entered the breakfast-room, wearing an air of bereavement that Laura's demise would have been insufficient, in itself, to account for.

'Four of my speckled Sussex have been killed,' he exclaimed; 'the very four that were to go to the show on Friday. One of them was dragged away and eaten right in the middle of that new carnation bed that I've been to such trouble and expense over. My best flower bed and my best fowls singled out for destruction; it almost seems as if the brute that did the deed had special knowledge how to be as devastating as possible in a short space of time.'

'Was it a fox, do you think?' asked Amanda.

'Sounds more like a polecat,' said Sir Lulwroth.

'No,' said Egbert, 'there were marks of webbed feet all over the place, and we followed the tracks down to the stream at the bottom of the garden; evidently an otter.'

Amanda looked quickly and furtively across at Sir Lulworth.

Egbert was too agitated to eat any breakfast, and went out to superintend the strengthening of the poultry yard defences.

'I think she might at least have waited till the funeral was over,' said Amanda in a scandalized voice.

'It's her own funeral, you know,' said Sir Lulworth; 'it's a nice point in etiquette how far one ought to show respect to one's own mortal remains.'

Disregard for mortuary convention was carried to further lengths next day; during the absence of the family at the funeral ceremony the remaining survivors of the speckled Sussex were massacred. The marauder's line of retreat seemed to have embraced most of the flower beds on the lawn, but the strawberry beds in the lower garden had also suffered.

'I shall get the otter hounds to come here at the earliest possible moment,' said Egbert savagely.

'On no account! You can't dream of such a thing!' exclaimed Amanda. 'I mean, it wouldn't do, so soon after a funeral in the house.'

'It's a case of necessity,' said Egbert; 'once an otter takes to that sort of thing it won't stop.' 'Perhaps it will go elsewhere now that there are no more fowls left,' suggested Amanda.

'One would think you wanted to shield the beast,' said Egbert.

'There's been so little water in the stream lately,' objected Amanda; 'it seems hardly sporting to hunt an animal when it has so little chance of taking refuge anywhere.'

'Good gracious!' fumed Egbert, 'I'm not thinking about sport. I want to have the animal killed as soon as possible.'

Even Amanda's opposition weakened when, during church time on the following Sunday, the otter made its way into the house, raided half a salmon from the larder and worried it into scaly fragments on the Persian rug in Egbert's studio.

'We shall have it hiding under our beds and biting pieces out of our feet before long,' said Egbert, and from what Amanda knew of this particular otter she felt that the possibility was not a remote one.

On the evening preceeding the day fixed for the hunt Amanda

'I shall go on being something.'

spent a solitary hour walking by the banks of the stream, making what she imagined to be hound noises. It was charitably supposed by those who overheard her performance, that she was practising for farmyard imitations at the forthcoming village entertainment.

It was her friend and neighbour, Aurora Burret, who brought her news of the day's sport.

'Pity you weren't out; we had a quite good day. We found it at once, in the pool just below your garden.'

'Did you—kill?' asked Amanda.

'Rather. A fine she-otter. Your husband got rather badly bitten in trying to "tail it". Poor beast, I felt quite sorry for it, it had such a human look in its eyes when it was killed. You'll call me silly, but do you know who the look reminded me of? My dear woman, what is the matter?'

When Amanda had recovered to a certain extent from her attack of nervous prostration Egbert took her to the Nile Valley to recuperate. Change of scene speedily brought about the desired recovery of health and mental balance. The escapades of an adventurous otter in search of a variation of diet were viewed in their proper light. Amanda's normally placid temperament reasserted itself. Even a hurricane of shouted curses, coming from her husband's dressing-room, in her husband voice, but hardly in his usual vocabulary, failed to disturb her serenity as she made a leisurely toilet one evening in a Cairo hotel.

'What is the matter? What has happened?' she asked in amused curiosity.

'The little beast has thrown all my clean shirts into the bath! Wait till I catch you, you little—'

'What little beast?' asked Amanda, suppressing a desire to laugh; Egbert's language was so hoplessly inadequate to express his outraged feelings.

'A little beast of a naked brown Nubian boy,' spluttered Egbert.

And now Amanda is seriously ill.

TEA AND EMPATHY

Paul Dorrell

'Oh, come on now!' laughed Nick. 'You don't really believe you saw a ghost?'

'But I *did*,' insisted Kate. 'Out there in the garden, near the oak tree.'

Alison put forward a practical argument. 'I thought ghosts only went around at night.'

'And I suppose you think that they're all transparent and white as well,' Kate retorted, her cheeks red now. 'How on earth can you say whether it's true or not, when you don't know the first thing about ghosts?'

The argument went on for some considerable time, until, finally, Nick became bored by the topic and turned back to his books on business studies—dreary stuff, as far as Kate was concerned. Alison went out of the sitting room and into the hall to telephone Robin Cartwright.

At least, thought Kate, *she* won't be bothering me for a while yet.

It was raining outside, and Kate felt trapped inside the old house. She had disliked it from the day of their arrival; it seemed impossible to her that she would ever come to feel differently. Try as she might, she could not become interested in the *Teen Rock* magazine which lay on the floor in front of her. She turned the pages languidly, looking at the faces of the singers and players; all of them seemed empty and lifeless. Plastic dolls, she thought.

She must find something more absorbing. Looking up at their father's well-stocked bookshelves, her attention was caught by something else, just to one side.

Out there, only a foot or so from the window, stood the ghost. It was a woman, dressed all in black from head to toe; the face was hidden by a thick veil. And, although the rain was falling even more furiously than before, none of it seemed to touch the woman. At least, it did not seem to cling to her. Solid as she appeared, she remained as dry under this rain as she would have done under the full blaze of the sun.

Kate became aware that Nick was looking at her, and she looked up at him. He, in turn, glanced through the window at which she had been staring. When she looked at it again, the ghost was gone. But she still felt the frightful, cold thrill of fear which the figure had provoked. Whatever caused it to linger in the world of the living, this was no friendly spectre. Malice seemed to ooze from it, like poison from a festering wound; and, even though Kate had not been able to see the face through the thick black veil, she knew that the eyes must burn with hatred.

Why can't you leave me alone? she thought. What harm have I done you? Why can't you go down to Hell where you belong?

She jumped, her skin crawling with the most unspeakable sensation. She felt sure that, as she had let these thoughts slip into her mind, she had heard the swish of the long dress on the ground behind her, felt the slight disturbance which it caused in the air.

Nick had not stopped watching her, and now he was quite alarmed at her expression. He had never seen her like this before; she had always been so well-balanced, even if she did have a few strange ideas. Therefore, whatever it was that she had imagined had become very real and menacing for her. Perhaps it was fortunate at that moment that he could not see what now presented itself to Kate.

The figure had materialized once more, this time in one corner of the room, opposite the corner where Nick sat. It was clawing at its throat with horrible hook-like, crab-like hands which were encased in

The figure was clawing at its throat with horrible hook-like hands.

tight black leather gloves which seemed almost as much a part of the body as the flesh which they covered. For a moment the ghost was still, ceasing in its awful scrabblings. Kate watched in absolute terror as those claws moved once more, slowly this time. She could not scream; nor did she hear Nick call across the room to her. Slowly, the thing in black started to raise the veil. Its neck was partially revealed, a loathsome white, its skin withered and marked by the most terrible bruising.

If the spectre had intended to reveal its face to her, it was cheated, for Kate saw nothing. She fainted.

When she recovered consciousness, Kate was stretched out on the sofa, her feet resting on one of the arms, so that the blood should flow back to her head. Her mother and father stood nearby, looking down at her anxiously. Nick and Alison sat at the table where he had been working only a few minutes before. Kate's head felt heavy now, and she could feel beads of perspiration just below the hair-line. Her mouth was dry, and her brain felt as though it were made of cotton wool. The awful threatening memory of the woman in black seemed strangely remote. The bell rang, and Nick went to answer. In the hallway she could hear the lowered voices of her brother and the doctor. There was little of what they said that she could make out, but one thing which came through clearly to her caused her to feel a brief surge of anger.

'. . . her age, I expect. . . . You know, girls at that stage.'

Nick of course. At nineteen, nearly four years older than Kate, and two years older than Alison, he was very conscious of his 'adult' superiority. Not that he meant anything wrong by this. Still, it was irksome at the best of times, and at the moment she would gladly have hit him, had she had the strength.

The doctor diagnosed 'flu. A particularly nasty strain which had been spreading through the area for the past couple of weeks, particularly in the schools. One peculiarity of it was that it induced hallucinations.

Kate was sure that Nick must be nodding sagely, even though she could not see him. But then, perhaps he was right. After all, ghosts are a rather unlikely phenomenon. She was really too tired to worry about it at the moment. Her head was so heavy. When her father picked her up, to carry her upstairs, she felt a momentary panic as the whole world seemed to slip and fragment around her. Then, at last, she was safely in bed, and able to drift off to sleep once more.

When next she looked across her bedroom, it was night outside. But in the room it was mid afternoon! In a heavily upholstered armchair, which was placed so that it faced almost directly towards the bed, sat an elderly lady, not the same ghost who had so terrified Kate earlier; this time the face was perfectly visible, pale-skinned and wrinkled, with a thin, mean mouth which had set in a permanent expression of ill temper. Beneath the mob cap which she wore, the woman's thin, wispy white hair was visible. In one hand she held a heavy ebony walking cane, and in the other a sheaf of papers.

Staring towards the door, the apparition struck on the floor several times with the cane. The mean mouth opened slightly, and the eyes lit with a disgusting glee. Then she called out, quite softly at first, then very loud and with a sharp tone.

'Bolding! Bolding! Come here. I've something I'm sure you'd want to see.' She laughed harshly and looked towards the door which Kate now heard opening—a door which was not where it should be if this were the present—and then the footsteps which Kate had expected started across the room. She knew that *this* was the woman in black, and that she was going to pass right through where the bed stood. Kate turned her head, as in a dream, to face the horror which approached, but now the room had reverted to its normal state. Night darkness filled it, a darkness which should have terrified her in the circumstances, but which, Kate knew, meant that there would be no more manifestations tonight. It was only as she laid her head back on the pillow that she noticed how much she had been perspiring.

Her sleep was untroubled for the rest of the night.

It was Nick who brought her her breakfast in the morning. Despite his mocking attitude towards her, he was genuinely concerned for her. The truth was that he was exceptionally proud of his clever, artistic sister. He sat on the edge of her bed, watching her seriously, insisting that she eat, even though she protested that she could not stomach any food. Kate ate to please him, and, in fact, found that she felt much better for having done so.

'I told you so,' he said, beaming with satisfaction. 'You won't get any better if you don't take care of yourself.'

There was a period during which they said nothing, and then Kate spoke, her voice and face quite composed.

'I did see it, Nick. I saw her.'

'What was she like, this ghost?' There was no trace of mockery in his voice now. He might not yet believe her, but, after reflection, it was obvious that he was more willing to admit to such possibilities.

'I couldn't see *her* face. . . .'

'You mean there are other ghosts here?'

'Only one other, as far as I know. She was sitting over there last night.' Kate pointed to where the chair had stood. 'Only, it was afternoon in here.'

'You say the chair was . . . here?' Nick asked as he walked over to the spot.

Kate nodded.

'It's like ice, the air, just here.' When he turned to look her full in the face, she could see that he was disturbed now. Afraid? He bent towards the floor. 'Funny! For a moment I could have sworn that I could see the marks where a chair had been. But then, the pattern wasn't the same.'

It was only after a few moments that he realized what he had said, but now Kate's attention was focused on the horribly contorted face which had appeared in the twirling blackness in the far corner. A face which lolled to one side like a broken doll, the skin darkening to an almost sickening blue-black. The eyes seemed almost to spring from their sockets, and the mouth opened slightly to let the blackened tongue slide out. The eyes glazed over, and the apparition vanished almost as rapidly as it had manifested itself.

'What was. . . .' Nick faltered for a moment, as though stopping himself saying too much. 'What was it like? The ghost. . . .' His voice trailed off in a strange expectancy.

'It was a woman. They're both women. But the main one—the one that frightened me—was younger than the other one.' Kate was surprised to find herself talking about the affair so calmly, especially to Nick. 'I only saw her face for the first time just now.' She nodded towards the corner. 'Before that, she has been wearing a veil, and when

I fainted she was just starting to lift it. But I don't think she meant me to see her face just then.'

'What do you mean by that?' Nick was insistent now. Kate found this more disturbing than his previous total incredulity. If he were willing to believe even a part of it, some of that thin thread of self-assurance to which she had been clinging, an unconscious rejection of the unfamiliar and unacceptable, that slipped even further from her, leaving her more threatened.

'I think she wanted me to see her neck. It was horribly bruised. And just now, when I saw her face, it was as if she were strangling.'

Nick seemed to stiffen right through his body as she said this. He reached into his jacket pocket.

'Is that her?' She had not been prepared for this question. Nor for the photograph which Nick now held before her. She nodded. 'Alison got it from Robin Cartwright—well, from his uncle actually. She told Robin about it, and he *knew* about the ghost in this house. It's been well known for years, and his uncle—he's a ghost man, a psychic investigator—has been trying to see it for himself, for years now. But no *no one* has actually seen it in ages. Just heard things, seen signs like curtains moving when there was no breeze.'

Kate could only nod sleepily. The release of tension had brought with it a simultaneous lethargy, a reaction to the incredible strain which her mind had undergone. Nick would have pressed her further, but he could leave that to Robin's uncle, who was an expert in such things. He only needed to make one telephone call, and he was sure that the man would come round immediately.

'Not such an expert, more of a dabbler, I'm afraid,' said James Tyler when Nick introduced him to his parents.

'Expert or dabbler, we don't want to know, thank you, Mr Tyler,' said Adam Hale. 'Nick had no right to go and call you in. Kate has merely been suffering from a rather bad bout of 'flu.' He modified his tone somewhat when he saw Tyler's apologetic expression, the expression of a man who is used to ridicule. 'I'm sorry, but we don't want her upset any further.'

'Don't you think I'm disturbed enough as it is, Dad? If what I've been seeing is real or unreal, it doesn't make much difference at the moment. I'm scared, and I want it to stop.'

Kate had entered the room, fully clothed now. She was, for the moment, quite calm.

'What are you doing up?' demanded her father. 'You know the doctor said you had to stay in bed.'

'Only because he thought I had 'flu.' Kate had never stood up to her father in this way before. She had always been obedient in most things, if rather strong-willed, but the change in her now was very striking. She was less of a young girl, more an adolescent growing towards an acceptance of her own personality.

'She certainly *looks* all right now, Adam,' said Kate's mother.

'She should still be in bed. . . . Alison, if your mother won't see sense, perhaps you will,' Adam said abruptly. 'Go upstairs with Kate at once. And make sure that she gets into bed and stays there.'

Alison moved to obey him, but Kate stood her ground and faced her father. She knew she had nothing to fear from him, since he was concerned only for her well-being. Also, Nick was committed to her side now, and he was equally ready to challenge his father.

'Do you think I could bear to stay up there in that room on my own?' she asked.

'Alison will stay with you,' said her father. 'If you're that afraid, someone can sit with you until you get over this whole stupid notion.' But his words did not carry the same conviction as before. He might not be able to accept the supernatural explanation, but he could see that Kate was determined to stay where she felt safe; no amount of persuasion or commands would induce her to obey quietly.

'I think perhaps we'd better hear Mr Tyler's story,' said Nick.

'I agree,' said Alison. 'Perhaps, if it *is* true, he'll know how to get rid of the ghost.'

'I refuse to believe in such things,' said Adam.

'And I thought you always boasted about keeping an open mind on these things,' countered his wife. 'We'll sit down and hear this story out, and then, if anything can be done—always supposing that there is some truth in it—perhaps, as Alison says, Mr Tyler can do something.'

Adam looked round at the others, perplexed and not a little put out at seeing his authority being whittled away so effectively.

'You're outnumbered, Dad,' said Nick.

They settled themselves round the fireplace to hear Tyler's story.

Only Kate was uninterested. She knew it all now. She knew how Miss Bolding had come to live with Miss Harley, the embittered old spinster, as her companion. That had been over a century ago, in the 1860s. Both women had come to loathe each other, Miss Harley because her companion was younger than she, Miss Bolding because of the other's increasing and selfish demands and lack of any sign of gratitude. It was known that the old lady was extremely rich; she made a point of reminding everyone, particularly Miss Bolding, who had turned from a once attractive and open natured soul into something almost as twisted with hate as her employer. Her once slender means made every passing year into a tightening of the trap which was pulled around her. She could not afford to leave. Daily, she must endure the old woman's taunts, must wear the unbecoming uniform of black linen which rendered her less attractive still than she had grown. Her only hope was that perhaps Miss Harley might leave her some small allowance in her will. When that hope was dashed, she had killed the evil-natured old woman, had poisoned her tea after a visit from her employer's niece and her husband. During this visit, she had finally given vent to her frustrations when she learnt that the niece was to inherit everything. Every last penny.

She had protested her innocence to the end. Even on the gallows.

'I'm sorry. I'm so tired, I must go to bed now,' said Kate. 'You were right, Dad. I should have stayed there.'

Although they were all surprised, they did not attempt to stop her. Of course, they asked if she wanted someone to sit with her, but she declared that if she left her door open, everything would be all right.

Naturally, the others could not see that fearsome, smiling, dominant figure in black who now beckoned to her. And she could see no reason to tell them about it. After all, she had to obey the ghost.

After a while, the others settled back into their discussion of the case. Was there anything that Tyler could do, if there really were a ghost? Tyler did not really know. He was only a dabbler. Even Adam seemed disappointed. The fire blazed merrily.

'Have you noticed how cold it is in here?' asked Nick.

The house was too quiet. Except for the passing to and fro of heavily-shod feet upstairs, the footsteps of a middle-aged woman!

Adam was barely ahead of Nick when they reached Kate's room.

The door was locked! It did not break easily, and when it did break it did not fall to the floor. The shattered wood seemed to drift slowly in the air, like a cork in a very slow stream.

Inside the room, Kate sat at that table from over a hundred years ago, surrounded by the furnishings of that time, and across the table she faced Miss Bolding who was calmly pouring her a cup of tea.

Elizabeth screamed and tried to force her way into the room, but it was as though some invisible wall held her back. The others tried too, but they could only look in at Kate caught now in that other time as she raised the cup to her lips.

Kate drank the tea, smiling, her eyes fixed on Miss Bolding whose hard face was now turned slightly away from them as she watched the girl drain the cup. A smile crossed the cruel, bitter face, and then gave way to an expression of triumph.

But it was not a sinister triumph. Now, the ghost was revealed as a warm person, one who had known love and affection. Her eyes lost their glassy glint. There was repose in them now as she turned to face the watchers in the doorway.

'You see,' said Miss Bolding. 'Trust is a very great thing. And one cannot know peace until one's name and honour are restored, even if that is only in *one* heart.'

Almost at once, the room was restored to its present-day aspect. Kate looked for a moment at the indistinct shape which had been the ghost of Miss Bolding, and smiled as it finally faded altogether. She smiled because she knew that the poor soul would never be back, never be forced to search for one who could save her from an eternity of despair. She, Kate, had seen into the depths of that soul, and had believed what she had seen.

Now, she would be able to recount at her own leisure the true story of how Miss Harley's niece had been the poisoner. She too had cause for bitterness. The evil old woman had intended to change her will, disinheriting everyone who had once been named as a beneficiary— this merely from spite, from anger at the thought of others enjoying what she could not. It had been a very simple murder, and it had been simple to place the blame squarely on the poor governess.

Kate paused for a moment. She could feel the spirits of Miss Harley and her niece. They were most unquiet! She would have work to do. . . .

THE HAUNTED DOLL'S HOUSE

M.R. James

'I suppose you get stuff of that kind through your hands pretty often?' said Mr Dillet, as he pointed with his stick to an object which shall be described when the time comes: and when he said it, he lied in his throat, and knew that he lied. Not once in twenty years—perhaps not once in a lifetime—could Mr Chittenden, skilled as he was in ferreting out the forgotten treasures of half-a-dozen counties, expect to handle such a specimen. It was a collector's' palaver, and Mr Chittenden recognized it as such.

'Stuff of that kind, Mr Dillet! It's a museum piece, that is.'

'Well, I suppose there are museums that'll take anything.'

'I've seen one, not as good as that, years back,' said Mr Chittenden, thoughtfully. 'But that's not likely to come into the market: and I'm told they 'ave some fine ones of the period over the water. No: I'm only telling you the truth, Mr Dillet, when I say that if you was to place an unlimited order with me for the very best that could be got—and you know I 'ave facilities for getting to know of such things, and a reputation to maintain—well, all I can say is, I should lead you straight up to that one and say, "I can't do no better for you than that, Sir."'

'Hear, hear!' said Mr Dillet, applauding ironically with the end of his stick on the floor of the shop. 'How much are you sticking the innocent American buyer for it, eh?'

158

'Oh, I shan't be over hard on the buyer, American or otherwise. You see, it stands this way, Mr Dillet—if I knew just a bit more about the pedigree—'

'Or just a bit less,' Mr Dillet put in.

'Ha, ha! you will have your joke, Sir. No, but as I was saying, if I knew just a little more than what I do about the piece—though anyone can see for themselves it's a genuine thing, every last corner of it, and there's not been one of my men allowed to so much as touch it since it came into the shop—there'd be another figure in the price I'm asking.'

'And what's that: five and twenty?'

'Multiply that by three and you've got it, Sir. Seventy-five's my price.'

'And fifty's mine,' said Mr Dillet.

The point of agreement was, of course, somewhere between the two, it does not matter exactly where—I think sixty guineas. But half an hour later the object was being packed, and within an hour Mr Dillet had called for it in his car and driven away. Mr Chittenden, holding the cheque in his hand, saw him off from the door with smiles, and returned, still smiling, into the parlour where his wife was making the tea. He stopped at the door.

'It's gone,' he said.

'Thank God for that!' said Mrs Chittenden, putting down the teapot. 'Mr Dillet, was it?'

'Yes, it was.'

'Well, I'd sooner it was him than another.'

'Oh, I don't know, he ain't a bad fellow, my dear.'

'May be not, but in my opinion he'd be none the worse for a bit of a shake up.'

'Well, if that's your opinion, it's my opinion he's put himself into the way of getting one. Anyhow, we shan't have no more of it, and that's something to be thankful for.'

And so Mr and Mrs Chittenden sat down to tea.

And what of Mr Dillet and of his new acquisition? What it was, the title of this story will have told you. What it was like, I shall have to indicate as well as I can.

There was only just room enough for it in the car, and Mr Dillet had to sit with the driver: he had also to go slow, for though the rooms of the Doll's House had all been stuffed carefully with soft cotton wool, jolting was to be avoided, in view of the immense number of small objects which thronged them; and the ten-mile drive was an anxious time for him, in spite of all the precautions he insisted upon. At last his front door was reached, and Collins, the butler, came out.

'Look here, Collins, you must help me with this thing—it's a delicate job. We must get it out upright, see? It's full of little things that mustn't be displaced more than we can help. Let's see, where shall we have it? (After a pause for consideration.) Really, I think I shall have to put it in my own room, to begin with at any rate. On the big table—that's it.'

It was conveyed—with much talking—to Mr Dillet's spacious room on the first floor, looking out on the drive. The sheeting was unwound from it, and the front thrown open, and for the next hour or two Mr Dillet was fully occupied in extracting the padding and setting in order the contents of the rooms.

When this thoroughly congenial task was finished, I must say that it would have been difficult to find a more perfect and attractive specimen of a Doll's House in Strawberry Hill Gothic than that which now stood on Mr Dillet's large kneehole table, lighted up by the evening sun which came slanting through three tall sash-windows.

It was quite six feet long, including the Chapel or Oretory which flanked the front on the left as you faced it, and the stable on the right. The main block of the house was, as I have said, in the Gothic manner; that is to say, the windows had pointed arches and were surmounted by what are called ogival hoods, with crockets and finials such as we see on the canopies of tombs built into church walls. At the angles were absurd turrets covered with arched panels. The Chapel had pinnacles and buttresses and a bell in the turret and coloured glass in the windows. When the front of the house was open you saw four large rooms, bedroom, dining room, drawing-room and kitchen, each with its appropriate furniture in a very complete state.

The stable on the right was in two storeys, with its proper complement of horses, coaches and grooms, and with its clock and Gothic cupola for the clock bell.

Pages, of course, might be written on the outfit of the mansion

—how many frying pans, how many gilt chairs, what pictures, carpets, chandeliers, four-posters, table linen, glass, crockery and plate it possessed; but all this must be left to the imagination. I will only say that the base or plinth on which the house stood (for it was fitted with one of some depth which allowed of a flight of steps to the front door and a terrace, partly balustraded) contained a shallow drawer or drawers in which were neatly stored sets of embroidered curtains, changes of raiment for the inmates, and, in short, all the materials for an infinite series of variations and refittings of the most absorbing and delightful kind.

'Quintessence of Horace Walpole, that's what it is: he must have had something to do with the making of it.' Such was Mr Dillet's murmured reflection as he knelt before it in a reverent ecstasy. 'Simply wonderful; this is my day and no mistake. Five hundred pound coming in this morning for that cabinet which I never cared about, and now this tumbling into my hands for a tenth, at the very most, of what it would fetch in town. Well, well! It almost makes one afraid something'll happen to counter it. Let's have a look at the population, anyhow.'

Accordingly, he set them before him in a row. Again, here is an opportunity, which some would snatch at, of making an inventory of costume: I am incapable of it.

There were a gentleman and lady, in blue satin and brocade respectively. There were two children, a boy and a girl. There was a cook, a nurse, a footman, and there were the stable servants, two postillions, a coachman, two grooms.

'Anyone else? Yes, possibly.'

The curtains of the four-poster in the bedroom were closely drawn round four sides of it, and he put his finger in between them and felt in the bed. He drew the finger back hastily, for it almost seemed to him as if something had—not stirred, perhaps, but yielded—in an old live way as he pressed it. Then he put back the curtains, which ran on rods in the proper manner, and extracted from the bed a white-haired old gentleman in a long linen nightdress and cap, and laid him down by the rest. The tale was complete.

Dinner time was now near, so Mr Dillet spent but five minutes in putting the lady and children into the drawing-room, the gentleman into the dining-room, the servants into the kitchen and stables, and the old man back into his bed. He retired into his dressing-room next door, and we see or hear no more of him until something like eleven o'clock at night.

His whim was to sleep surrounded by some of the gems of his collection. The big room in which we have seen him contained his bed: bath, wardrobe, and all the appliances of dressing were in a commodious room adjoining: but his four-poster, which itself was a valued treasure, stood in the large room where he sometimes wrote, and often sat, and even received visitors. Tonight he repaired to it in a highly complacent frame of mind.

There was no striking clock within earshot—none on the staircase, none in the stable, none in the distant church tower. Yet it is indubitable that Mr Dillet was startled out of a very pleasant slumber by a bell tolling one.

He was so much startled that he did not merely lie breathlessly with wide-open eyes, but actually sat up in his bed.

He never asked himself, till the morning hours, how it was that, though there was no light at all in the room, the Doll's House on the kneehole table, stood out with complete clearness. But it was so. The effect was that of a bright harvest moon shining full on the front of a big white stone mansion—a quarter of a mile away it might be, and yet every detail was photographically sharp. There were trees about it, too—trees rising behind the chapel and the house. He seemed to be conscious of the scent of a cool still September night. He thought he could hear an occasional stamp and clink from the stables, as of horses stirring. And with another shock he realized that, above the house, he was looking, not at the wall of his room with its pictures, but into the profound blue of a night sky.

There were lights, more than one, in the windows, and he quickly saw that this was no four-roomed house with a movable front, but one of many rooms, and staircases—a real house, but seen as if through the wrong end of a telescope. 'You mean to show me something,' he muttered to himself, and he gazed earnestly on the lighted windows. They would in real life have been shuttered or curtained, no doubt, he thought; but as it was there was nothing to intercept his view of what was being transacted inside the rooms.

A few moments later a coach with flambeaux drove up to the door.

Two rooms were lighted—one on the ground floor to the right of the door, one upstairs, on the left—the first brightly enough, the other rather dimly. The lower room was the dining-room: a table was laid, but the meal was over, and only wine and glasses were left on the table. The man of the blue satin and the woman of the brocade were alone in the room, and they were talking very earnestly, seated close together at the table, their elbows on it: every now and again stopping to listen, as it seemed. Once *he* rose, came to the window and opened it and put his head out and his hand to his ear. There was a lighted taper in a silver candlestick on a sideboard. When the man left the window he seemed to leave the room also; and the lady, taper in hand, remained standing and listening. The expression on her face was that of one striving her utmost to keep down a fear that threatened to master her—and succeeding. It was a hateful face, too; broad, flat and sly. Now the man came back and she took some small thing from him and hurried out of the room. He, too, disappeared, but only for a moment or two. The front door slowly opened and he stepped out and stood on the top of the *perron*, looking this way and that; then turned towards the upper window that was lighted, and shook his fist.

It was time to look at that upper window. Through it was seen a four-post bed: a nurse or other servant in an armchair, evidently sound asleep; in the bed an old man lying: awake, and, one would say, anxious, from the way in which he shifted about and moved his fingers, beating tunes on the coverlet. Beyond the bed a door opened. Light was seen on the ceiling, and the lady came in: she set down her candle on a table, came to the fireside and roused the nurse. In her hand she had an old fashioned wine bottle, ready uncorked. The nurse took it, poured some of the contents into a little silver saucepan, added some spice and sugar from casters on the table, and set it to warm on the fire. Meanwhile the old man in the bed beckoned feebly to the lady, who came to him, smiling, took his wrist as if to feel his pulse, and bit her lip as if in consternation. He looked at her anxiously, and then pointed to the window, and spoke. She nodded, and did as the man below had done; opened the casement and listened—perhaps rather ostentatiously; then drew her head and shook it, looking at the old man, who seemed to sigh.

By this time the posset on the fire was steaming, and the nurse poured it into a small two-handled silver bowl and brought it to the bedside. The old man seemed disinclined for it and was waving it away, but the lady and the nurse together bent over him and evidently pressed it upon him. He must have yielded, for they supported him into a sitting position, and put it to his lips. He drank most of it, in several draughts, and they laid him down. The lady left the room, smiling goodnight to him, and took the bowl, the bottle and the silver saucepan with her. The nurse returned to the chair, and there was an interval of complete quiet.

Suddenly the old man started up in his bed—and he must have uttered some cry, for the nurse started out of her chair and made but one step of it to the bedside. He was a sad and terrible sight—flushed in the face, almost to blackness, the eyes glaring whitely, both hands clutching at his heart, foam at his lips.

For a moment the nurse left him, ran to the door, flung it wide open, and one supposes, screamed aloud for help, then darted back to the bed and seemed to try feverishly to soothe him—to lay him down—anything. But as the lady, her husband, and several servants, rushed into the room with horrified faces, the old man collapsed under the nurse's hands and lay back, and the features, contorted with agony and rage, relaxed slowly into calm.

A few moments later, lights showed out to the left of the house, and a coach with flambeaux drove up to the door. A white-wigged man in black got nimbly out and ran up the steps, carrying a small leather trunk-shaped box. He was met in the doorway by the man and his wife, she with her handkerchief clutched between her hands, he with a tragic face, but retaining his self-control. They led the newcomer into the dining-room, where he set his box of papers on the table, and, turning to them, listened with a face of consternation at what they had to tell. He nodded his head again and again, threw out his hands slightly, declined, it seemed, offers of refreshment and lodging for the night, and within a few minutes came slowly down the steps, entering the coach and driving off the way he had come. As the man in blue watched him from the top of the steps, a smile not pleasant to see stole slowly over his fat white face. Darkness fell over the whole scene as the lights of the coach disappeared.

But Mr Dillet remained sitting up in the bed: he had rightly guessed that there would be a sequel. The house front glimmered out again before long. But now there was a difference. The lights were in other windows, one at the top of the house, the other illuminating the range of coloured windows of the chapel. How he saw through these is not quite obvious, but he did. The interior was as carefully furnished as the rest of the establishment, with its minute red cushions on the desks, its Gothic stall-canopies, and its western gallery and pinnacled organ with gold pipes. On the centre of the black and white pavement was a bier: four tall candles burned at the corners. On the bier was a coffin covered with a pall of black velvet.

As he looked the folds of the pall stirred. It seemed to rise at one end: it slid downwards: it fell away, exposing the black coffin with its silver handles and nameplate. One of the tall candlesticks swayed and toppled over. Ask no more, but turn, as Mr Dillet hastily did, and look in at the lighted window at the top of the house, where a boy and girl lay in two truckle-beds, and a four-poster for the nurse rose above them. The nurse was not visible for the moment; but the father and mother were there, now in mourning, but with very little sign of mourning in their demeanour. Indeed, they were laughing and talking with a good deal of animation, sometimes to each other, and sometimes throwing a remark to one or other of the children, and again laughing at the answers. Then the father was seen to go on tiptoe out of the room, taking with him as he went a white garment that hung on a peg near the door. He shut the door after him. A minute or two later it was slowly opened again, and a muffled head poked round it. A bent form of sinister shape stepped across to the truckle-beds, and suddenly stopped, threw up its arms and revealed, of course, the father, laughing. The children were in agonies of terror, the boy with the bedclothes over his head, the girl throwing herself out of bed into her mother's arms. Attempts at consolation followed—the parents took the children on their laps, patted them, picked up the white gown and showed there was no harm in it, and so forth; and at last putting the children back into bed, left the room with encouraging waves of the hand. As they left it, the nurse came in, and soon the light died down.

Still Mr Dillet watched immovable.

A new sort of light—not of lamp or candle—a pale ugly light, began to dawn around the door-case at the back of the room. The door was opening again. The seer does not like to dwell upon what he saw entering the room: he says it might be described as a frog—the size of a man—but it had scanty white hair about its head. It was busy about the truckle-beds, but not for long. The sound of cries—faint, as if coming out of a vast distance—but, even so, infinitely appalling, reached the ear.

There were signs of a hideous commotion all over the house: lights passed along and up, and doors opened and shut, and running figures passed within the windows. The clock in the stable turret tolled one, and darkness fell again.

It was only dispelled once more, to show the house front. At the bottom of the steps dark figures were drawn up in two lines, holding flaming torches. More dark figures came down the steps, bearing, first one, then another small coffin. And the lines of torch-bearers with the coffins between them moved silently onward to the left.

The hours of night passed on—never so slowly, Mr Dillet thought. Gradually he sank down from sitting to lying in his bed—but he did not close an eye: and early next morning he sent for the doctor.

The doctor found him in a disquieting state of nerves, and recommended sea air. To a quiet place on the East Coast he accordingly repaired by easy stages in his car.

One of the first people he met on the sea front was Mr Chittenden, who, it appeared, had likewise been advised to take his wife away for a bit of a change.

Mr Chittenden looked somewhat askance upon him when they met: and not without cause.

'Well, I don't wonder at you being a bit upset, Mr Dillet. What? Yes, well, I might say 'orrible upset, to be sure, seeing what me and my poor wife went through ourselves. But I put it to you, Mr Dillet, one of two things: was I going to scrap a lovely piece like that on the one 'and, or was I going to tell customers: "I'm selling you a regular picture-palace-dramar in reel life of the olden time, billed to perform regular at one o'clock a.m."? Why, what would you 'ave said yourself? And next thing you know, two Justices of the Peace in the back parlour, and pore Mr and Mrs Chittenden off in a spring cart to the County Asylum and everyone in the street saying, "Ah, I thought it 'ud come to that. Look at the way the man drank!"—and me next door, or next door but one, to a total abstainer, as you know. Well, there was my position. What? Me 'ave it back in the shop? Well, what do *you* think? No, but I'll tell you what I will do. You shall have your money back bar the ten pound I paid for it, and you make what you can.'

Later in the day, in what is offensively called the 'smoke-room' of the hotel, a murmured conversation between the two went on for some time.

'How much do you really know about that thing, and where it came from?'

'Honest, Mr Dillet, I don't know the 'ouse. Of course, it came out of the lumber room of a country 'ouse—that anyone could guess. But I'll go as far as say this, that I believe it's not a hundred miles from this place. Which direction and how far I've no notion. I'm only judging by guesswork. The man as I actually paid the cheque to ain't one of my regular men, and I've lost sight of him; but I 'ave the idea that this part of the country was his beat, and that's every word I can tell you. But now, Mr Dillet, there's one thing that rather physicks me—that old chap—I suppose you saw him drive up to the door—I thought so: now, would he have been the medical man, do you take it? My wife would have it so, but I stuck to it that was the lawyer, because he had papers with him, and one he took out was folded up.'

'I agree,' said Mr Dillet. 'Thinking it over, I came to the conclusion that was the old man's will, ready to be signed.'

'Just what I thought,' said Mr Chittenden, 'and I took it that will would have cut out the young people, eh? Well, well! It's been a lesson to me, I know that. I shan't buy no more dolls' houses, nor waste no more money on the pictures—and as to this business of poisonin' grandpa, well, if I know myself, I never 'ad much of a turn for that. Live and let live: that's bin my motto throughout life, and I ain't found it a bad one.'

Filled with these elevated sentiments, Mr Chittenden retired to his lodgings. Mr Dillet next day repaired to the local institute, where he hoped to find some clue to the riddle that absorbed him. He gazed in despair at a long file of the Canterbury and York Society's publications of the Parish Registers of the district. No print resembling the house of his nightmare was among those that hung on the staircase and in the passages. Disconsolate, he found himself in a derelict room, staring at a dusty model of a church in a dusty glass case: *Model of St Stephen's Church, Coxham. Presented by J. Merewether, Esq., of Ilbridge House, 1877. The work of his ancestor James Merewether, d. 1786.* There was something in the fashion of it that reminded him dimly of his horror. He retraced his steps to a wall map he had noticed, and made out that Ilbridge House was in Coxham Parish. Coxham was, as it happened, one of the parishes of which he had retained the name when he glanced over the file of printed registers, and it was not long before he found in them the record of the burial of Roger Milford, aged 76, on the 11th September, 1757, and of Roger and Elizabeth Merewether, aged 9 and 7, on the 19th of the same month. It seemed worthwhile to follow up this clue, frail as it was; and in the afternoon he drove out to Coxham. The east end of the north aisle of the church is a Milford chapel, and on its north wall are tablets to the same persons; Roger, the elder, it seems, was distinguished by all the qualities which adorn 'the Father, the Magistrate, and the Man': the memorial was erected by his detached daughter Elizabeth, 'who did not long survive the loss of a parent ever solicitous for her welfare, and of two amiable children'. The last sentence was plainly an addition to the original inscription.

A yet later slab told of James Merewether, husband of Elizabeth, 'who in the dawn of life practised, not without success, those arts which, had he continued their exercise, might in the opinion of the most competent judges have earned for him the name of the British Vitruvius: but who, overwhelmed by the visitation which deprived him of an affectionate partner and a blooming offspring, passed his Prime and Age in a secluded yet elegant Retirement: his grateful Nephew and Heir indulges a pious sorrow by this too brief recital of his excellences.'

The children were more simply commemorated. Both died on the night of the 12th of September.

Mr Dillet felt sure that in Ilbridge House he had found the scene of his drama. In some old sketch book, possibly in some old print, he may yet find convincing evidence that he is right. But the Ilbridge House of today is not that which he sought; it is an Elizabethan erection of the forties, in red brick, with stone quoins and dressings.

A quarter of a mile from it, in a low part of the park, backed by ancient, stag-horned, ivy-strangled trees and thick undergrowth, are marks of a terraced platform overgrown with rough grass. A few stone balusters lie here and there, and a heap or two, covered with nettles and ivy, of wrought stones with badly carved crockets. This, someone told Mr Dillet, was the site of an older house.

As he drove out of the village, the hall clock struck four, and Mr Dillet started up and clapped his hands to his ears. It was not the first time he had heard that bell.

Awaiting an offer from the other side of the Atlantic, the doll's house still reposes, carefully sheeted, in a loft over Mr Dillet's stables, whither Collins conveyed it on the day when Mr Dillet started for the sea coast.

THE BROWN HAND

Sir Arthur Conan Doyle

Everyone knows that Sir Dominick Holden, the famous Indian surgeon, made me his heir, and that his death changed me in an hour from a hard-working and impecunious medical man to a well-to-do landed proprietor. Many know also that there were at least five people between the inheritance and me, and that Sir Dominick's selection appeared to be altogether arbitrary and whimsical. I can assure them, however, that they are quite mistaken, and that, although I only knew Sir Dominick in the closing years of his life, there were, none the less, very real reasons why he should show his goodwill towards me. As a matter of fact, though I say it myself, no man ever did more for another than I did for my Indian uncle. I cannot expect the story to be believed, but it is so singular that I should feel that it was a breach of duty if I did not put it upon record—so here it is, and your belief or incredulity is your own affair.

Sir Dominick Holden, CB, KCSI, and I don't know what besides, was the most distinguished Indian surgeon of his day. In the Army originally, he afterwards settled down into civil practice in Bombay, and visited, as a consultant, every part of India. His name is best remembered in connection with the Oriental Hospital which he founded and supported. The time came, however, when his iron

171

constitution began to show signs of the long strain to which he had subjected it, and his brother practitioners (who were not, perhaps, entirely disinterested upon the point) were unanimous in recommending him to return to England. He held on so long as he could, but at last he developed nervous symptoms of a very pronounced character, and so came back, a broken man, to his native county of Wiltshire. He bought a considerable estate with an ancient manor-house upon the edge of Salisbury Plain, and devoted his old age to the study of Comparative Pathology, which had been his learned hobby all his life, and in which he was a foremost authority.

We of the family were, as may be imagined, much excited by the news of the return of this rich and childless uncle to England. On his part, although by no means exuberant in his hospitality, he showed some sense of his duty to his relations, and each of us in turn had an invitation to visit him. From the accounts of my cousins it appeared to be a melancholy business, and it was with mixed feelings that I at last received my own summons to appear at Rodenhurst. My wife was so carefully excluded in the invitation that my first impulse was to refuse it, but the interests of the children had to be considered, and so, with her consent, I set out one October afternoon upon my visit to Wiltshire, with little thought of what that visit was to entail.

My uncle's estate was situated where the arable land of the plains begins to swell upwards into the rounded chalk hills which are characteristic of the county. As I drove from Dinton Station in the waning light of that autumn day, I was impressed by the weird nature of the scenery. The few scattered cottages of the peasants were so dwarfed by the huge evidences of prehistoric life, that the present appeared to be a dream and the past to be the obtrusive and masterful reality. The road wound through the valleys, formed by a succession of grassy hills, and the summit of each was cut and carved into the most elaborate fortifications, some circular, and some square, but all on a scale which has defied the winds and the rains of many centuries. Some call them Roman and some British, but their true origin and the reason for this particular tract of country being so interlaced with entrench-ments have never been finally made clear. Here and there on the long, smooth, olive-coloured slopes there rose small, rounded barrows or tumuli. Beneath them lie the cremated ashes of the race which cut so deeply into the hills, but their graves tell us nothing save that a jar full of dust represents the man who once laboured under the sun.

It was through this weird country that I approached my uncle's residence of Rodenhurst, and the house was, as I found, in due keeping with its surroundings. Two broken and weather-stained pillars, each surmounted by a mutilated heraldic emblem, flanked the entrance to a neglected drive. A cold wind whistled through the elms which lined it, and the air was full of the drifting leaves. At the far end, under the gloomy arch of trees, a single yellow lamp burned steadily. In the dim half-light of the coming night I saw a long, low building stretching out two irregular wings, with deep eaves, a sloping gambrel roof, and walls which were crisscrossed with timber balks in the fashion of the Tudors. The cheery light of a fire flickered in the broad, latticed window to the left of the low-porched door, and this, as it proved, marked the study of my uncle, for it was thither that I was led by his butler in order to make my host's acquaintance.

He was cowering over his fire, for the moist chill of an English autumn had set him shivering. His lamp was unlit, and I only saw the red glow of the embers beating upon a huge, craggy face, with a Red Indian nose and cheek, and deep furrows and seams from eye to chin, the sinister marks of hidden volcanic fires. He sprang up at my entrance with something of an old-world courtesy and welcomed me warmly to Rodenhurst. At the same time I was conscious, as the lamp was carried in, that it was a very critical pair of light-blue eyes which looked out at me from under shaggy eyebrows, like scouts beneath a bush, and that this outlandish uncle of mine was carefully reading off my character with all the ease of a practised observer and an experienced man of the world.

For my part I looked at him, and looked again, for I had never seen a man whose appearance was more fitted to hold one's attention. His figure was the framework of a giant, but he had fallen away until his coat dangled straight down in a shocking fashion from a pair of broad and bony shoulders. All his limbs were huge and yet emaciated, and I could not take my gaze from his knobby wrists, and long, gnarled hands. But his eyes—those peering, light-blue eyes—they were the most arrestive of any of his peculiarities. It was not their colour alone, nor was it the ambush of hair in which they lurked; but it was the expression which I read in them. For the appearance and bearing of the man were masterful, and one expected a certain corresponding arrogance in his eyes, but instead of that I read the look which tells of a spirit cowed and crushed, the furtive, expectant look of the dog whose master has taken the whip from the rack. I formed my own medical diagnosis upon one glance at those critical and yet appealing eyes. I believed that he was stricken with some mortal ailment, that he knew himself to be exposed to sudden death, and that he lived in terror of it. Such was my judgement—a false one, as the event showed; but I mention it that it may help you to realize the look which I read in his eyes.

My uncle's welcome was, as I have said, a courteous one, and in an hour or so I found myself seated between him and his wife at a comfortable dinner, with curious, pungent delicacies upon the table, and a stealthy, quick-eyed Oriental waiter behind his chair. The old couple had come round to that tragic imitation of the dawn of life when husband and wife, having lost or scattered all those who were their intimates, find themselves face to face and alone once more, their work done, and the end nearing fast. Those who have reached that stage in sweetness and love, who can change their winter into a gentle, Indian summer, have come as victors through the ordeal of life. Lady Holden was a small, alert woman with a kindly eye, and her expression as she glanced at him was a certificate of character to her husband. And yet, though I read a mutual love in their glances, I read also mutual horror, and recognized in her face some reflection of that stealthy fear which I had detected in his. Their talk was sometimes merry and sometimes sad, but there was a forced note in their merriment and a naturalness in their sadness which told me that a heavy heart beat upon either side of me.

We were sitting over our first glass of wine, and the servants had left the room, when the conversation took a turn which produced a remarkable effect upon my host and hostess. I cannot recall what it was which started the topic of the supernatural, but it ended in my showing them that the abnormal in psychical experiences was a subject to which, I had, like many neurologists, devoted a great deal of attention. I concluded by narrating my experiences when, as a member of the Psychical Research Society, I had formed one of a committee of three who spent the night in a haunted house. Our adventures were neither exciting nor convincing, but, such as it was, the story appeared to interest my auditors in a remarkable degree. They listened with an eager silence, and I caught a look of intelligence between them which I could not understand. Lady Holden immediately afterwards rose and left the room.

Sir Dominick pushed the cigar-box over to me, and we smoked for some little time in silence. That huge, bony hand of his was twitching as he raised it with his cheroot to his lips, and I felt that the man's nerves were vibrating like fiddle-strings. My instincts told me that he was on the verge of some intimate confidence, and I feared to speak lest I should interrupt it. At last he turned towards me with a spasmodic gesture like a man who throws his last scruple to the winds.

'From the little that I have seen of you it appears to me, Dr Hardacre,' said he, 'that you are the very man I have wanted to meet.'

'I am delighted to hear it, sir.'

'Your head seems to be cool and steady. You will acquit me of any desire to flatter you, for the circumstances are too serious to permit of insincerities. You have some special knowledge upon these subjects, and you evidently view them from that philosophical standpoint which robs them of all vulgar terror. I presume that the sight of an apparition would not seriously discompose you?'

'I think not, sir.'

'Would even interest you, perhaps?'

'Most intensely.'

'As a psychical observer, you would probably investigate it in as impersonal a fashion as an astronomer investigates a wandering comet?'

'Precisely.'

He gave a heavy sigh.

'Believe me, Dr Hardacre, there was a time when I could have spoken as you do now. My nerve was a byword in India. Even the Mutiny never shook it for an instant. And yet you see what I am reduced to—the most timorous man, perhaps, in all this county of Wiltshire. Do not speak too bravely upon this subject, or you may find yourself subjected to as long-drawn a test as I am—a test which can only end in the madhouse or the grave.'

I waited patiently until he should see fit to go farther in his confidence. His preamble had, I need not say, filled me with interest and expectation.

'For some years, Dr Hardacre,' he continued, 'my life and that of my wife have been made miserable by a cause which is so grotesque that it borders upon the ludicrous. And yet familiarity has never made it more easy to bear—on the contrary, as time passes my nerves became more worn and shattered by the constant attrition. If you have no physical fears, Dr Hardacre, I should very much value your opinion upon this phenomenon which troubles us so.'

'For what it is worth my opinion is entirely at your service. May I ask the nature of the phenomenon?'

'I think that your experiences will have a higher evidential value if you are not told in advance what you may expect to encounter. You are yourself aware of the quibbles of unconscious cerebration and subjective impressions with which a scientific sceptic may throw a doubt upon your statement. It would be as well to guard against them in advance.'

'What shall I do, then?'

'I will tell you. Would you mind following me this way?' He led me out of the dining-room and down a long passage until we came to a terminal door. Inside there was a large bare room fitted as a laboratory, with numerous scientific instruments and bottles. A shelf ran along one side, upon which there stood a long line of glass jars containing pathological and anatomical specimens.

'You see that I still dabble in some of my old studies,' said Sir Dominick. 'These jars are the remains of what was once a most excellent collection, but unfortunately I lost the greater part of them when my house was burned down in Bombay in '92. It was a most unfortunate affair for me—in more ways than one. I had examples of many rare conditions, and my splenic collection was probably unique. These are the survivors.'

I glanced over them, and saw that they really were of a very great value and rarity from a pathological point of view: bloated organs, gaping cysts, distorted bones, odious parasites—a singular exhibition of the products of India.

'There is, as you see, a small settee here,' said my host. 'It was far from our intention to offer a guest so meagre an accommodation, but since affairs have taken this turn, it would be a great kindness upon your part if you would consent to spend the night in this apartment. I beg that you will not hesitate to let me know if the idea should be at all repugnant to you.'

'On the contrary,' I said, 'it is most acceptable.'

'My own room is the second on the left, so that if you should feel that you are in need of company a call would always bring me to your side.'

'I trust that I shall not be compelled to disturb you.'

'It is unlikely that I shall be asleep. I do not sleep much. Do not hesitate to summon me.'

And so with this agreement we joined Lady Holden in the drawing room and talked of lighter things.

It was no affection upon my part to say that the prospect of my night's adventure was an agreeable one. I have no pretence to greater physical courage than my neighbours, but familiarity with a subject robs it of those vague and undefined terrors which are the most appalling to the imaginative mind. The human brain is capable of only one strong emotion at a time, and if it be filled with curiosity or scientific enthusiasm, there is no room for fear. It is true that I had my uncle's assurance that he had himself originally taken this point of view, but I reflected that the breakdown of his nervous system might be due to his forty years in India as much as to any physical experiences which had befallen him. I at least was sound in nerve and brain, and it was with something of the pleasurable thrill of anticipation with which the sportsman takes his position beside the haunt of his game that I shut the laboratory door behind me, and partially undressing, lay down upon the rug-covered settee.

It was not an ideal atmosphere for a bedroom. The air was heavy with many chemical odours, that of methylated spirit predominating. Nor were the decorations of my chamber very sedative. The odious line of glass jars with their relics of disease and suffering stretched in front of my very eyes. There was no blind to the window, and a three-quarter moon streamed its white light into the room, tracing a silver square with filigree lattices upon the opposite wall. When I had extinguished my candle this one bright patch in the midst of the general gloom had certainly an eerie and discomposing aspect. A rigid and absolute silence reigned throughout the old house, so that the low swish of the branches in the garden came softly and smoothly to my ears. It may have been the hypnotic lullaby of this gentle susurrus, or it may have been the result of my tiring day, but after many dozings and many efforts to regain my clearness of perception, I fell at last into a deep and dreamless sleep.

I was awakened by some sound in the room, and I instantly raised myself upon my elbow on the couch. Some hours had passed, for the square patch upon the wall had slid downwards and sideways until it lay obliquely at the end of my bed. The rest of the room was in deep shadow. At first I could see nothing. Presently, as my eyes became accustomed to the faint light, I was aware, with a thrill which all my scientific absorption could not entirely prevent, that something was moving slowly along the line of the wall. A gentle, shuffling sound, as of soft slippers, came to my ears, and I dimly discerned a human figure walking stealthily from the direction of the door. As it emerged into the patch of moonlight I saw very clearly what it was and how it was employed. It was a man, short and squat, dressed in some sort of dark-grey gown, which hung straight from his shoulders to his feet. The moon shone upon the side of his face, and I saw that it was a chocolate-brown in colour, with a ball of black hair like a woman's at the back of his head. He walked slowly, and his eyes were cast upwards towards the line of bottles which contained those gruesome remnants of humanity. He seemed to examine each jar with attention, and then to pass on to the next. When he had come to the end of the line, immediately opposite my bed, he stopped, faced me, threw up his hands with a gesture of despair, and vanished from my sight.

I have said that he threw up his hands, but I should have said his arms, for as he assumed that attitude of despair I observed a singular peculiarity about his appearance. He had only one hand! As the sleeves drooped down from the upflung arms I saw the left plainly, but the right ended in a knobby and unsightly stump. In every other way his appearance was so natural, and I had both seen and heard him so clearly, that I could easily have believed that he was an Indian servant of Sir Dominick's who had come into my room in search of

His eyes were cast upwards towards the line of bottles.

something. It was only his sudden disappearance which suggested anything more sinister to me. As it was I sprang from my couch, lit a candle, and examined the whole room carefully. There were no signs of my visitor, and I was forced to conclude that there had really been something outside the normal laws of Nature in his appearance. I lay awake for the remainder of the night, but nothing else occurred to disturb me.

I am an early riser, but my uncle was an even earlier one, for I found him pacing up and down the lawn at the side of the house. He ran towards me in his eagerness when he saw me come out from the door.

'Well, well!' he cried. 'Did you see him?'

'An Indian with one hand?'

'Precisely.'

'Yes, I saw him'—and I told him all that occurred. When I had finished, he led the way into his study.

'We have a little time before breakfast,' said he. 'It will suffice to give you an explanation of this extraordinary affair—so far as I can explain that which is essentially inexplicable. In the first place, when I tell you that for four years I have never passed one single night, either in Bombay, aboard ship, or here in England without my sleep being broken by this fellow, you will understand why it is that I am a wreck of my former self. His programme is always the same. He appears by my bedside, shakes me roughly by the shoulder, passes from my room into the laboratory, walks slowly along the line of my bottles, and then vanishes. For more than a thousand times he has gone through the same routine.'

'What does he want?'

'He wants his hand.'

'His hand?'

'Yes, it came about in this way. I was summoned to Peshawar for a consultation some ten years ago, and while there I was asked to look at the hand of a native who was passing through with an Afghan caravan. The fellow came from some mountain tribe living away at the back of beyond somewhere on the other side of Kaffiristan. He talked a bastard Pushtoo, and it was all I could do to understand him. He was suffering from a soft sarcomatous swelling of one of the metacarpal joints, and I made him realize that it was only by losing his hand that he could hope to save his life. After much persuasion he consented to the operation, and he asked me, when it was over, what fee I demanded. The poor fellow was almost a beggar, so that the idea of a fee was absurd, but I answered in jest that my fee should be his hand, and that I proposed to add it to my pathological collection.

'To my surprise he demurred very much to the suggestion, and he explained that according to his religion it was an all-important matter that the body should be reunited after death, and so make a perfect dwelling for the spirit. The belief is, of course, an old one, and the mummies of the Egyptians arose from an analogous superstition. I answered him that his hand was already off, and asked him how he intended to preserve it. He replied that he would pickle it in salt and carry it about with him. I suggested that it might be safer in my keeping than his, and that I had better means than salt for preserving it. On realizing that I really intended to carefully keep it, his opposition vanished instantly. 'But remember, sahib,' said he, 'I shall want it back when I am dead.' I laughed at the remark, and so the matter ended. I returned to my practice, and he no doubt in the course of time was able to continue his journey to Afghanistan.

'Well, as I told you last night, I had a bad fire in my house at Bombay. Half of it was burned down, and, among other things, my pathological collection was largely destroyed. What you see are the poor remains of it. The hand of the hillman went with the rest, but I gave the matter no particular thought at the time. That was six years ago.

'Four years ago—two years after the fire—I was awakened one night by a furious tugging at my sleeve. I sat up under the impression that my favourite mastiff was trying to arouse me. Instead of this, I saw my Indian patient of long ago, dressed in the long, grey gown which was the badge of his people. He was holding up his stump and looking reproachfully at me. He then went over to my bottles, which at that time I kept in my room, and he examined them carefully, after which he gave a gesture of anger and vanished. I realized that he had just died, and that he had come to claim my promise that I should keep his limb in safety for him.

'Well, there you have it all, Dr Hardacre. Every night at the same hour for four years this performance has been repeated. It is a simple thing in itself, but it has worn me out like water dropping on a stone. It has brought a vile insomnia with it, for I cannot sleep now for the expectation of his coming. It has poisoned my old age and that of my wife, who has been the sharer in this great trouble. But there is the breakfast gong, and she will be waiting impatiently to know how it fared with you last night. We are both much indebted to you for your gallantry, for it takes something from the weight of our misfortune when we share it, even for a single night, with a friend, and it reassures us to our sanity, which we are sometimes driven to question.'

This was the curious narrative which Sir Dominick confided to me—a story which to many would have appeared to be a grotesque impossibility, but which, after my experience of the night before, and my previous knowledge of such things, I was prepared to accept as an absolute fact. I thought deeply over the matter, and brought the whole range of my reading and experience to bear upon it. After breakfast, I surprised my host and hostess by announcing that I was returning to London by the next train.

'My dear doctor,' cried Sir Dominick in great distress, 'you make me feel that I have been guilty of a gross breach of hospitality in intruding this unfortunate matter upon you. I should have borne my own burden.'

'It is, indeed, that matter which is taking me to London,' I answered; 'but you are mistaken, I assure you, if you think that my experience of last night was an unpleasant one to me. On the contrary, I am about to ask your permission to return in the evening and spend one more night in your laboratory. I am very eager to see this visitor once again.'

My uncle was exceedingly anxious to know what I was about to do, but my fears of raising false hopes prevented me from telling him. I was back in my own consulting-room a little after luncheon, and was confirming my memory of a passage in a recent book upon occultism which had arrested my attention when I read it.

'In the case of earth-bound spirits,' said my authority, 'some one dominant idea obsessing them at the hour of death is sufficient to hold them in this material world. They are the amphibia of this life and of the next, capable of passing from one to the other as the turtle passes from land to water. The causes which may bind a soul so strongly to a life which its body has abandoned are any violent emotion. Avarice, revenge, anxiety, love and pity have all been known to have this effect. As a rule it springs from some unfulfilled wish, and when the wish has been fulfilled the material bond relaxes. There are many cases upon record which show the singular persistence of these visitors, and also their disappearance when their wishes have been fulfilled, or in some cases when a reasonable compromise has been effected.'

'*A reasonable compromise effected*'—those were the words which I had brooded over all the morning, and which I now verified in the original. No actual atonement could be made here—but a reasonable compromise! I made my way as fast as a train could take me to the Shadwell Seamen's Hospital, where my old friend Jack Hewett was house-surgeon. Without explaining the situation I made him understand what it was that I wanted.

'A brown man's hand!' said he, in amazement. 'What in the world do you want that for?'

'Never mind. I'll tell you some day. I know that your wards are full of Indians.'

'I should think so. But a hand—' He thought a little and then struck a bell.

'Travers,' said he to a student-dresser, 'what became of the hands of the Lascar which we took off yesterday? I mean the fellow from the East India Dock who got caught in the steam winch.'

'They are in the *post-mortem* room, sir.'

'Just pack one of them in antiseptics and give it to Dr Hardacre.'

And so I found myself back at Rodenhurst before dinner with this curious outcome of my day in town. I still said nothing to Sir Dominick, but I slept that night in the laboratory, and I placed the Lascar's hand in one of the glass jars at the end of my couch.

So interested was I in the result of my experiment that sleep was out of the question. I sat with a shaded lamp beside me and waited patiently for my visitor. This time I saw him clearly from the first. He appeared beside the door, nebulous for an instant, and then hardening into as distinct an outline as any living man. The slippers beneath his grey gown were red and heelless, which accounted for the low, shuffling sound which he made as he walked. As on the previous night he passed slowly along the line of bottles until he paused before that which contained the hand. He reached up to it, his whole figure quivering with expectation, took it down, examined it eagerly, and then, with a face which was convulsed with fury and disappointment, he hurled it down on the floor. There was a crash which resounded through the house, and when I looked up the mutilated Indian had disappeared. A moment later my door flew open and Sir Dominick rushed in.

'You are not hurt?' he cried.

'No—but deeply disappointed.'

He looked in astonishment at the splinters of glass, and the brown hand lying upon the floor.

'Good God!' he cried. 'What is this?'

I told him my idea and its wretched sequel. He listened intently, but shook his head.

'It is well thought of,' said he, 'but I fear that there is no such easy end to my sufferings. But one thing I now insist upon. It is that you shall never again upon any pretext occupy this room. My fears that something might have happened to you—when I heard that crash—have been the most acute of all the agonies which I have undergone. I will not expose myself to a repetition of it.'

He allowed me, however, to spend the remainder of that night where I was, and I lay there worrying over the problem and lamenting my own failure. With the first light of morning there was the Lascar's hand still lying upon the floor to remind me of my fiasco. I lay looking at it—and as I lay suddenly an idea flew like a bullet through my head and brought me quivering with excitement out of my couch. I raised the grim relic from where it had fallen. Yes, it was indeed so. The hand was the *left* hand of the Lascar.

By the first train I was on my way to town, and hurried at once to the Seamen's Hospital. I remembered that both hands of the Lascar had been amputated, but I was terrified lest the precious organ which I was in search of might have been already consumed in the crematory. My suspense was soon ended. It had still been preserved in the *post-mortem* room. And so I returned to Rodenhurst in the evening with my mission accomplished and the material for a fresh experiment.

But Sir Dominick Holden would not hear of my occupying the

laboratory again. To all my entreaties he turned a deaf ear. It offended his sense of hospitality, and he could no longer permit it. I left the hand, therefore, as I had done its fellow the night before, and I occupied a comfortable bedroom in another portion of the house, some distance from the scene of my adventures.

But in spite of that my sleep was not destined to be uninterrupted. In the dead of night my host burst into my room, a lamp in his hand. His huge, gaunt figure was enveloped in a loose dressing-gown, and his whole appearance might certainly have seemed more formidable to a weak-nerved man than that of the Indian of the night before. But it was not his entrance so much as his expression which amazed me. He had turned suddenly younger by twenty years at the least. His eyes were shining, his features radiant, and he waved one hand in triumph over his head. I sat up astounded, staring sleepily at this extraordinary visitor. But his words soon drove the sleep from my eyes.

'We have done it! We have succeeded!' he shouted. 'My dear Hardacre, how can I ever in this world repay you?'

'You don't mean to say that it is all right?'

'Indeed I do. I was sure that you would not mind being awakened to hear such blessed news.'

'Mind! I should think not indeed. But is it really certain?'

'I have no doubt whatever upon the point. I owe you such a debt, my dear nephew, as I have never owed a man before, and never expected to. What can I possibly do for you that is commensurate? Providence must have sent you to my rescue. You have saved both my reason and my life, for another six months of this must have seen me either in a cell or a coffin. And my wife—it was wearing her out before my eyes. Never could I have believed that any human being could have lifted this burden off me.' He seized my hand and wrung it in his bony grip.

'It was only an experiment—a forlorn hope—but I am delighted from my heart that it has succeeded. But how do you know that it is all right? Have you seen something?'

He seated himself at the foot of my bed.

'I have seen enough,' said he. 'It satisfies me that I shall be troubled no more. What has passed is easily told. You know that at a certain hour this creature always comes to me. Tonight he arrived at the usual time, and aroused me with even more violence than is his custom. I can only surmise that his disappointment of last night increased the bitterness of his anger against me. He looked angrily at me, and then went on his usual round. But in a few minutes I saw him, for the first time since this persecution began, return to my chamber. He was smiling. I saw the gleam of his white teeth through the dim light. He stood facing me at the end of my bed, and three times he made the low, Eastern salaam which is their solemn leave-taking. And the third time that he bowed he raised his arms over his head, and I saw his *two* hands outstretched in the air. So he vanished, and, as I believe, for ever.'

So that is the curious experience which won me the affection and the gratitude of my celebrated uncle, the famous Indian surgeon. His anticipations were realized, and never again was he disturbed by the visits of the restless hillman in search of his lost member. Sir Dominick and Lady Holden spent a very happy old age, unclouded, so far as I know, by any trouble, and they finally died during the great influenza epidemic within a few weeks of each other. In his lifetime he always turned to me for advice in everything which concerned that English life of which he knew so little; and I aided him also in the purchase and development of his estates. It was no great surprise to me, therefore, that I found myself eventually promoted over the heads of five exasperated cousins, and changed in a single day from a hard-working country doctor into the head of an important Wiltshire family. I, at least, have reason to bless the memory of the man with the brown hand, and the day when I was fortunate enough to relieve Rodenhurst of his unwelcome presence.

THE WELL

W.W. Jacobs

Two men stood in the billiard-room of an old country house, talking. Play, which had been of a half-hearted nature, was over, and they sat at the open window, looking out over the park stretching away beneath them, conversing idly.

'Your time's nearly up, Jem,' said one at length, 'this time six weeks you'll be yawning out the honeymoon and cursing the man—woman I mean—who invented them.'

Jem Benson stretched his long limbs in the chair and grunted in dissent.

'I've never understood it,' continued Wilfred Carr, yawning. 'It's not in my line at all; I never had enough money for my own wants, let alone for two. Perhaps if I were as rich as you or Croesus I might regard it differently.'

There was just sufficient meaning in the latter part of the remark for his cousin to forbear to reply to it. He continued to gaze out of the window and to smoke slowly.

'Not being as rich as Croesus—or you,' resumed Carr, regarding him from beneath lowered lids, 'I paddle my own canoe down the stream of Time, and, tying it to my friends' doorposts, go in to eat their dinners.'

'Quite Venetian,' said Jem Benson, still looking out of the window. 'It's not a bad thing for you, Wilfred, that friends' doorposts, go in to eat their dinners.'

Carr grunted in his turn. 'Seriously though, Jem,' he said, slowly, 'you're a lucky fellow, a very lucky fellow. If there is a better girl above ground than Olive, I should like to see her.'

'Yes,' said the other, quietly.

'She's such an exceptional girl,' continued Carr, staring out of the window. 'She's so good and gentle. She thinks you are a bundle of all the virtues.'

He laughed frankly and joyously, but the other man did not join him.

'Strong sense of right and wrong, though,' continued Carr, musingly. 'Do you know, I believe that if she found out that you were not—'

'Not what?' demanded Benson, turning upon him fiercely. 'Not what?'

'Everything that you are,' returned his cousin, with a grin that belied his words, 'I believe she'd drop you.'

'Talk about something else,' said Benson, slowly; 'your pleasantries are not always in the best taste.'

Wilfred Carr rose and taking a cue from the rack, bent over the board and practised one or two favourite shots. 'The only other subject I can talk about just at present is my own financial affairs,' he said slowly, as he walked round the table.

'Talk about something else,' said Benson again, bluntly.

'And the two things are connected,' said Carr, and dropping his cue he half sat on the table and eyed his cousin.

There was a long silence. Benson pitched the end of his cigar out of the window, and leaning back closed his eyes.

'Do you follow me?' inquired Carr at length.

Benson opened his eyes and nodded at the window.

'Do you want to follow my cigar?' he demanded.

'I should prefer to depart by the usual way for your sake,' returned the other, unabashed. 'If I left by the window all sorts of questions would be asked, and you know what a talkative chap I am.'

'So long as you don't talk about my affairs,' returned the other, restraining himself by an obvious effort. You can talk yourself hoarse.'

'I'm in a mess,' said Carr, slowly, 'a devil of a mess. If I don't raise fifteen hundred by this day fortnight, I may be getting my board and lodging free.'

'Would that be any change?' questioned Benson.

'The quality would,' retorted the other. 'The address also would not be good. Seriously, Jem, will you let me have the fifteen hundred?'

'No,' said the other, simply.

Carr went white. 'It's to save me from ruin,' he said, thickly.

'I've helped you till I'm tired,' said Benson, turning and regarding him, 'and it is all to no good. If you've got into a mess, get out of it. You should not be so fond of giving autographs away.'

'It's foolish, I admit,' said Carr, deliberately. 'I won't do so any more. By the way, I've got some to sell. You needn't sneer. They're not my own.'

'Whose are they?' inquired the other.

'Yours.'

Benson got up from his chair and crossed over to him. 'What is this?' he asked, quietly. 'Blackmail?'

'Call it what you like,' said Carr. 'I've got some letters for sale, price fifteen hundred. And I know a man who would buy them at that price for the mere chance of getting Olive from you. I'll give you first offer.'

'If you have got any letters bearing my signature, you will be good enough to give them to me,' said Benson, very slowly.

'They're mine,' said Carr, lightly; 'given to me by the lady you wrote them to. I must say that they are not all in the best possible taste.'

His cousin reached forward suddenly, and catching him by the collar of his coat, pinned him down on the table.

'Give me those letters.'

'They're not here,' said Carr, struggling. 'I'm not a fool. Let me go, or I'll raise the price.'

The other man raised him from the table in his powerful hands, apparently with the intention of dashing his head against it. Then suddenly his hold relaxed as an astonished-looking maid-servant entered the room with letters. Carr sat up hastily.

'That's how it was done,' said Benson, for the girl's benefit as he took the letters.

'I don't wonder at the other man making him pay for it, then,' said Carr blandly.

'You will give me those letters,' said Benson, suggestively, as the girl left the room.

'At the price I mentioned, yes,' said Carr; 'but so sure as I am a living man, if you lay your clumsy hands on me again, I'll double it. Now, I'll leave you for a time while you think it over.'

He took a cigar from the box and lighting it carefully quitted the room. His cousin waited until the door had closed behind him, and then turning to the window sat there in a fit of fury as silent as it was terrible.

The air was fresh and sweet from the park, heavy with the scent of new-mown grass. The fragrance of a cigar was now added to it, and glancing out he saw his cousin pacing slowly by. He rose and went to the door, and then, apparently altering his mind, he returned to the window and watched the figure of his cousin as it moved slowly away into the moonlight. Then he rose again, and, for a long time, the room was empty.

It was empty when Mrs Benson came in some time later to say goodnight to her son on her way to bed. She walked slowly round the table, and pausing at the window gazed from it in idle thought, until she saw the figure of her son advancing with rapid strides towards the house. He looked up at the window.

'Goodnight,' said she.

'Goodnight,' said Benson, in a deep voice.

'Where is Wilfred?'

'Oh, he has gone,' said Benson.

'Gone?'

'We had a few words; he was wanting money again, and I gave him a piece of my mind. I don't think we shall see him again.'

'Poor Wilfred!' sighed Mrs Benson. 'He is always in trouble of some sort. I hope that you were not too hard upon him.'

'No more than he deserved,' said her son, sternly. 'Goodnight.'

★   ★   ★   ★

The well, which had long ago fallen into disuse, was almost hidden by the thick tangle of undergrowth which ran riot at that corner of the old park. It was partly covered by the shrunken half of a lid, above which a rusty windlass creaked in company with the music of the pines when the wind blew strongly. The full light of the sun never reached it, and the ground surrounding it was moist and green when other parts of the park were gaping with the heat.

Two people walking slowly round the park in the fragrant stillness of a summer evening strayed in the direction of the well.

'No use going through this wilderness, Olive,' said Benson, pausing on the outskirts of the pines and eyeing with some disfavour the gloom beyond.

'Best part of the park,' said the girl briskly; 'you know it's my favourite spot.'

'I know you're very fond of sitting on the coping,' said the man slowly, 'and I wish you wouldn't. One day you will lean back too far and fall in.'

'And make the acquaintance of Truth,' said Olive lightly. 'Come along.'

She ran from him and was lost in the shadow of the pines, the bracken crackling beneath her feet as she ran. Her companion followed slowly, and emerging from the gloom saw her poised daintily on the edge of the well with her feet hidden in the rank grass and nettles which surrounded it. She motioned her companion to take a seat by her side, and smiled softly as she felt a strong arm passed about her waist.

'I like this place,' said she, breaking a long silence, 'it is so dismal —so uncanny. Do you know I wouldn't dare to sit here alone, Jem. I should imagine that all sorts of dreadful things were hidden behind the bushes and trees, waiting to spring out on me. Ugh!'

'You'd better let me take you in,' said her companion tenderly; 'the well isn't always wholesome, especially in the hot weather. Let's make a move.'

The girl gave an obstinate little shake, and settled herself more securely on her seat.

'Smoke your cigar in peace,' she said quietly. 'I am settled here for a quiet talk. Has anything been heard of Wilfred yet?'

'Nothing.'

'Quite a dramatic disappearance, isn't it?' she continued. 'Another

scrape, I suppose, and another letter for you in the same old strain;
"Dear Jem, help me out."'

Jem Benson blew a cloud of fragrant smoke into the air, and
holding his cigar between his teeth brushed away the ash from his coat
sleeves.

'I wonder what he would have done without you,' said the girl,
pressing his arm affectionately. 'Gone under long ago, I suppose. When
we are married, Jem, I shall presume upon the relationship to lecture
him. He is very wild, but he has his good points, poor fellow.'

'I never saw them,' said Benson, with startling bitterness. 'God
knows I never saw them.'

'He is nobody's enemy but his own,' said the girl, startled by this
outburst.

'You don't know much about him,' said the other, sharply. 'He was
not above blackmail; not above ruining the life of a friend to do
himself a benefit. A loafer, a cur, and a liar!'

The girl looked up at him soberly but timidly and took his arm
without a word, and they both sat silent while evening deepened
into night and the beams of the moon, filtering through the
branches, surrounded them with a silver network. Her head sank
upon his shoulder, till suddenly with a sharp cry she sprang to her
feet.

'What was that?' she cried breathlessly.

'What was what?' demanded Benson, springing up and clutching
her fast by the arm.

She caught her breath and tried to laugh. 'You're hurting me, Jem.'
His hold relaxed.

'What is the matter?' he asked gently. 'What was it startled you?'

'I was startled,' she said, slowly, putting her hands on his shoulder.
'I suppose the words I used just now are ringing in my ears, but I
fancied that somebody behind us whispered *"Jem, help me out."*'

'Fancy,' repeated Benson, and his voice shook; 'but these fancies are
not good for you. You—are frightened—at the dark and gloom of
these trees. Let me take you back to the house.'

'No, I am not frightened,' said the girl, reseating herself. 'I should be
never be really frightened of anything when you were with me, Jem.
I'm surprised at myself for being so silly.'

They both sat silent while evening deepened into night.

The man made no reply but stood, a strong, dark figure, a yard or two from the well, as though waiting for her to join him.

'Come and sit down, sir,' cried Olive, patting the brickwork with her small, white hand, 'one would think that you did not like my company.'

He obeyed slowly and took a seat by her side, drawing so hard at his cigar that the light of it shone upon his face at every breath. He passed his arm, firm and rigid as steel, behind her, with his hand resting on the brickwork, beyond.

'Are you warm enough?' he asked tenderly, as she made a little movement.

'Pretty fair,' she shivered; 'one oughtn't to be cold at this time of the year, but there's a cold, damp air comes up from the well.'

As she spoke a faint splash sounded from the depths below, and for her the second time that evening, she sprang from the well with a little cry of dismay.

'What is it now?' he asked in a fearful voice. He stood by her side and gazed at the well, as though half expecting to see the cause of her alarm emerge from it.

'Oh, my bracelet,' she cried in distress, 'my poor mother's bracelet. I've dropped it down the well.'

'Your bracelet!' repeated Benson, dully. 'Your bracelet? The diamond one?'

'The one that was my mother's,' said Olive. 'Oh, we can get it back surely. We must have the water drained off.'

'Your bracelet!' repeated Benson, stupidly.

'Jem,' said the girl in terrified tones, 'dear Jem, what is the matter?'

For the man she loved was standing regarding her with horror. The moon which touched it was not responsible for all the whiteness of the distorted face, and she shrank back in fear to the edge of the well. He saw her fear and by a mighty effort regained his composure and took her hand.

'Poor little girl,' he murmured, 'you frightened me. I was not looking when you cried, and I thought that you were slipping from my arms, down—down—'

His voice broke, and the girl throwing herself into his arms clung to him convulsively.

'There, there,' said Benson, fondly, 'don't cry, don't cry.'

'Tomorrow,' said Olive, half-laughing, half-crying, 'we will all come round the well with hook and line and fish for it. It will be quite a new sport.'

'No, we must try some other way,' said Benson. 'You shall have it back.'

'How?' asked the girl.

'You shall see,' said Benson. 'Tomorrow morning at latest you shall have it back. Till then promise me that you will not mention your loss to anyone. Promise.'

'I promise,' said Olive, wonderingly. 'But why not?'

'It is of great value, for one thing, and—But there—there are many reasons. For one thing it is my duty to get it for you.'

'Wouldn't you like to jump down for it? she asked mischievously. 'Listen.'

She stooped for a stone and dropped it down.

'Fancy being where that is now,' she said, peering into the blackness; 'fancy going round and round like a mouse in a pail, clutching at the slimy sides, with the water filling your mouth, and looking up to the little patch of sky above.'

'You had better come in,' said Benson, very quietly. 'You are developing a taste for the morbid and horrible.'

The girl turned, and taking his arm walked slowly in the direction of the house; Mrs Benson, who was sitting in the porch, rose to receive them.

'You shouldn't have kept her out so long,' she said chidingly. 'Where have you been?'

'Sitting on the well,' said Olive, smiling, 'discussing our future.'

'I don't believe that place is healthy,' said Mrs Benson, emphatically. 'I really think it might be filled in, Jem.'

'All right,' said her son, slowly. 'Pity it wasn't filled in long ago.'

He took the chair vacated by his mother as she entered the house with Olive, and with his hands hanging limply over the sides sat in deep thought. After a time he rose, and going upstairs to a room which was set apart for sporting requisites selected a sea fishing line and some books and stole softly downstairs again. He walked swiftly across the park in the direction of the well, turning before he entered the shadow of the trees to look back at the lighted windows of the house. Then having arranged his line he sat on the edge of the well and cautiously lowered it.

He sat with his lips compressed, occasionally looking about him in a startled fashion, as though he half expected to see something peering at him from the belt of trees. Time after time he lowered his line until at length in pulling it up he heard a little metallic tinkle against the side of the well.

He held his breath then, and forgetting his fears drew the line in inch by inch, so as not to lose its precious burden. His pulse beat rapidly, and his eyes were bright. As the line came slowly in he saw the catch hanging to the hook, and with a steady hand drew the last few feet in. Then he saw that instead of the bracelet he had hooked a bunch of keys.

With a faint cry he shook them from the hook into the water below, and stood breathing heavily. Not a sound broke the stillness of the night. He walked up and down a bit and stretched his great muscles; then he came back to the well and resumed his task.

For an hour or more the line was lowered without result. In his eagerness he forgot his fears, and with eyes bent down the well fished slowly and carefully. Twice the hook became entangled in something and was with difficulty released. It caught a third time, and all his efforts failed to free it. Then he dropped the line down the well, and with head bent walked toward the house.

He went first to the stables at the rear, and then retiring to his room for some time time paced restlessly up and down. Then without removing his clothes he flung himself upon the bed and fell into a troubled sleep.

★   ★   ★   ★

Long before anybody else was astir he arose and stole softly downstairs. The sunlight was stealing in at every crevice, and flashing in long streaks across the darkened rooms. The dining-room into which he looked struck chill and cheerless in the dark yellow light which came through the lowered blinds. He remembered that it had the same appearance when his father lay dead in the house; now, as then, everything seemed ghastly and unreal; the very chairs standing as their occupants had left them the night before seemed to be indulging in some dark communication of ideas.

Slowly and noisessly he opened the hall door and passed into the fragrant air beyond. The sun was shining on the drenched grass and trees, and a slowly vanishing white mist rolled like smoke about the grounds. For a moment he stood, breathing deeply the sweet air of the morning, and then walked slowly in the direction of the stables.

The rusty creaking of a pump-handle and a spatter of water upon the red-tiled courtyard showed that somebody else was astir, and a few steps farther he beheld a brawny, sandy-haired man gasping wildly under severe self-infliction at the pump.

'Everything ready, George?' he asked quietly.

'Yes, sir,' said the man, straightening up suddenly and touching his forehead. 'Bob's just finishing the arrangements inside. It's a lovely morning for a dip. The water in the well must be just icy.'

'Be as quick as you can,' said Benson, impatiently.

'Very good, sir,' said George, burnishing his face harshly with a very small towel which had been hanging up over the top of the pump. 'Hurry up, Bob.'

In answer to his summons a man appeared at the door of the stable with a coil of stout rope over his arm and a large metal candlestick in his hand.

'Just to try the air, sir,' said George, following his master's glance, 'a well gets rather foul sometimes, but if a candle can live down it, a man can.'

His master nodded, and the man, hastily pulling up the neck of his shirt and thrusting his arms into his coat, followed him as he led the way slowly to the well.

'Beg pardon, sir,' said George, drawing up his side, 'but you are not looking over and above well this morning. If you'll let me go down I'd enjoy the bath.'

'No, no,' said Benson, peremptorily.

'You ain't fit to go down, sir,' persisted his follower. 'I've never seen you look, so before. Now if—'

'Mind your business,' said his master curtly.

George became silent and the three walked with swinging strides through the long wet grass to the well. Bob flung the rope on the ground and at a sign from his master handed him the candlestick.

'Here's the line for it, sir,' said Bob, fumbling in his pockets.

Benson took it from him and slowly tied it to the candlestick. Then he placed it on the edge of the well, and striking a match, lit the candle and began slowly to lower it.

'Hold hard, sir,' said George, quickly, laying his hand on his arm, 'you must tilt it or the string'll burn through.'

Even as he spoke the string parted and the candlestick fell into the water below.

Benson swore quietly.

'I'll soon get another,' said George, starting up.

'Never mind, the well's all right,' said Benson.

'It won't take a moment, sir,' said the other over his shoulder.

'Are you master here, or am I?' said Benson hoarsely.

George came back slowly, a glance at his master's face stopping the protest upon his tongue, and he stood by watching him sulkily as he sat on the well and removed his outer garments. Both men watched him curiously, as having completed his preparations he stood grim and silent with his hands by his sides.

'I wish you'd let me go, sir,' said George, plucking up courage to address him. 'You ain't fit to go, you've got a chill or something. I shouldn't wonder it's the typhoid. They've got it in the village bad.'

For a moment Benson looked at him angrily, then his gaze softened. 'Not this time, George,' he said, quietly. He took the looped end of the rope and placed it under his arms, and sitting down threw one leg over the side of the well.

'How are you going about it, sir?' queried George, laying hold of the rope and signing to Bob to do the same.

'I'll call out when I reach the water,' said Benson; 'then pay out three yards more quickly so that I can get to the bottom.'

'Very good, sir,' answered both.

Their master threw the other leg over the coping and sat motionless. His back was turned towards the men as he sat with his head bent, looking down the shaft. He sat for so long that George became uneasy.

'All right, sir?' he inquired.

'Yes,' said Benson, slowly. 'If I tug at the rope, George, pull up at once. Lower away.'

The rope passed steadily through their hands until a hollow cry from the darkness below and a faint splashing warned them that he had reached the water. They gave him three yards more and stood with relaxed grasp and strained ears, waiting.

'He's gone under,' said Bob in a low voice.

The other nodded, and moistening his huge palms took a firmer grip of the rope.

Fully a minute passed, and the men began to exchange uneasy glances. Then a sudden tremendous jerk followed by a series of feebler ones nearly tore the rope from their grasp.

'Pull!' shouted George, placing one foot on the side and hauling desperately. 'Pull! pull! He's stuck fast; he's not coming; P—U—LL!'

In response to their terrific exertions the rope came slowly in, inch by inch, until at length a violent splashing was heard, and at the same moment a scream of unutterable horror came echoing up the shaft.

'What a weight he is!' panted Bob. 'He's stuck fast or something. Keep still, sir, for heaven's sake, keep still.'

For the taut rope was being jerked violently by the struggles of the weight at the end of it. Both men with grunts and sighs hauled it in foot by foot.

'All right, sir,' cried George, cheerfully.

He had one foot against the well, and was pulling manfully; the burden was nearing the top. A long pull and a strong pull, and the face of a dead man with mud in his eyes and nostrils came peering over the edge. Behind it was the ghastly face of his master; but this he saw too late, for with a great cry he let go his hold of the rope and stepped back. The suddenness overthrew his assistant, and the rope tore through his hands. There was a frightful splash.

'You fool!' stammered Bob, and ran to the well helplessly.

'Run!' cried George. 'Run for another line.'

He bent over the coping and called eagerly down as his assistant sped back to the stables shouting wildly. His voice re-echoed down the shaft, but all else was silence.

THE HAUNTED TRAILER

Robert Arthur

It was incredible, of course. Bound to happen some day. But why did it have to happen to me? What did *I* do to deserve the grief? And I was going to be married, too. I sank my last thousand dollars into that trailer, almost. In it Monica and I were going on a honeymoon tour of the United States. We were going to see the country. I was going to write, and we were going to be happy as two turtle-doves.

Ha!

Ha ha!

If you detect bitterness in that laughter, I'll tell you why I'm bitter.

Because it had to be me, Mel—for Melvin—Mason who became the first person in the world to own a haunted trailer!

Now, a haunted castle is one thing. Even an ordinary haunted house can be livable. In a castle, or a house, if there's a ghost around, you can lock yourself in the bedroom and get a little sleep. A nuisance, yes. But nothing a man couldn't put up with.

In a trailer, though! What are you going to do when you're sharing a trailer, even a super-de-luxe model with four built-in bunks, a breakfast nook, a complete bathroom, a radio, electric range, and easy chair, with a ghost? Where can you go to get away from it?

Ha!

Ha ha!

I've heard so much ghostly laughter the last week that I'm laughing myself that way now.

There I was. I had the trailer. I had the car to pull it, naturally. I was on my way to meet Monica in Hollywood, where she was living with an aunt from Iowa. And twelve miles west of Albany, the first night out, my brand-new, spic-and-span trailer picks up a hitch-hiking haunt!

But maybe I'd better start at the beginning. It happened this way. I bought the trailer in New England—a Custom Clipper, with chrome and tan outside trim, for $2,998. I hitched it on behind my car and headed westwards, happier than a lark when the dew's on the thorn. I'd been saving up for this day for two years, and I felt wonderful.

I took it easy, getting the feel of the trailer, and so I didn't make very good time. I crossed the Hudson river just after dark, trundled through Albany in a rainstorm, and half an hour later pulled off the road into an old path between two big rocks to spend the night.

The thunder was rolling back and forth overhead, and the lightning was having target practice with the trees. But I'd picked out a nice secluded spot and I made myself comfortable. I cooked up a tasty plate of beans, some coffee, and fried potatoes. When I had eaten I took off my shoes, slumped down in the easy chair, lit a cigarette, and leaned back.

'Ah!' I said aloud. 'Solid comfort. If only Monica were here, how happy we would be.'

But she wasn't, so I picked up a book.

It wasn't a very good book. I must have dozed off. Maybe I slept for a couple of hours. Maybe three. Anyway, I woke with a start, the echo of a buster of thunderbolt still rattling the willow pattern tea-set in the china cupboard. My hair was standing on end from the electricity in the air.

Then the door banged open, a swirl of rain swept in, and the wind —anyway, I thought it was the wind—slammed the door to. I heard a sound like a ghost—there's no other way to describe it—of a sigh.

'Now this,' said the voice, 'is something like!'

I had jumped up to shut the door, and I stood there with my unread book in my hand, gaping. The wind had blown a wisp of mist into my trailer and the mist, instead of evaporating, remained there, seeming to turn slowly and to settle into shape. It got more and more solid until. . . .

Well, you know. It was a spectre. A haunt. A homeless ghost.

The creature remained there, regarding me in a decidedly cool manner.

'Sit down, chum,' it said, 'and don't look so pop-eyed. You make me nervous. This is my first night indoors in fifteen years and I wanta enjoy it.'

'Who—' I stammered—'who—'

'I'm not,' the spectre retorted, 'a brother owl, so don't who-who at me. What do I look like?'

'You look like a ghost,' I told him.

'Now you're getting smart, chum. I *am* a ghost. What *kind* of a ghost do I look like?'

I inspected it more closely. Now that the air inside my trailer had stopped eddying, it was reasonably firm of outline. It was a squat, heavy-set ghost, attired in ghostly garments that certainly never had come to it new. He wore the battered ghost of a felt hat, and a stubble of ghostly beard showed on his jowls.

'You look like a tramp ghost,' I answered with distaste, and my uninvited visitor nodded.

'Just what I am, chum,' he told me. 'Call me Spike Higgins. Spike for short. That was my name before it happened.'

'Before what happened?' I demanded. The ghost wafted across the trailer to settle down on a bunk, where he lay down and crossed his legs, hoisting one foot encased in a battered ghost of a shoe into the air.

'Before I was amachoor enough to fall asleep riding on top of a truck, and fall off right here fifteen years ago,' he told me. 'Ever since I had been forced to haunt this place. I wasn't no Boy Scout, so I got punished by bein' made to stay here in one spot. Me, who never stayed in one spot two nights running before!

'I been gettin' kind of tired of it the last couple of years. They wouldn't even lemme haunt a house. No, I hadda do all my haunting out in th' open, where th' wind an' rain could get at me, and every dog that went by could bark at me. Chum, you don't know what it means to me that you've picked this place to stop.'

'Listen,' I said firmly, 'you've got to get out of here!'

The apparition yawned.

'Chum,' he said, 'you're the one that's trespassin', not me. This is my happy hunting ground. Did I ask you to stop here?'

'You mean,' I asked between clenched teeth, 'that you won't go? You're going to stay here all night?'

'Right, chum,' the ghost grunted. 'Gimme a call for 6 a.m.' He closed his eyes, and began snoring in an artificial and highly insulting manner.

Then I got sore. I threw the book at him, and it bounced off the bunk without bothering him in the least. Spike Higgins opened an eye and leered at me.

'Went right through me,' he chortled. 'Instead of me goin' through it. Ha ha! Ha ha ha! Joke.'

'You—' I yelled, in a rage. 'You—stuff!'

And I slammed him with the chair cushions, which likewise went through him without doing any damage. Spike Higgins opened both eyes and stuck out his tongue at me.

Obviously I couldn't hurt him, so I got control of myself.

'Listen,' I said craftily. 'You say you are doomed to haunt this spot for ever? You can't leave?'

'Forbidden to leave,' Spike answered. 'Why?'

'Never mind,' I grinned. 'You'll find out.'

I snatched up my raincoat and hat and scrambled out into the storm. If that ghost was doomed to remain in that spot forever, I wasn't. I got into the car, got the motor going, and backed out of there. It took a lot of manoeuvring in the rain, with mud underwheel, but I made it. I got straightened out on the concrete and headed westwards.

I didn't stop until I'd covered twenty miles. Then, beginning to grin as I thought of the shock of the ghost of Spike Higgins must have felt when I yanked the trailer from underneath him, I parked on a stretch of old, unused road and then crawled back into the trailer again.

Inside, I slammed the door and. . . .

Ha!

Ha ha!

Ha ha ha!

Yes, more bitter laughter. Spike Higgins was still there, sound asleep and snoring.

I muttered something under my breath. Spike Higgins opened his eyes sleepily.

'Hello,' he yawned. 'Been having fun?'

'Listen,' I finally got it out. 'I—thought—you—were—doomed—to—stay—back—where—I—found—you—for ever!'

The apparition yawned again.

'Your mistake, chum. I didn't say I was doomed to stay. I said I was forbidden to leave. I didn't leave. You hauled me away. It's all your responsibility and I'm a free agent now.'

'You're a what?'

'I'm a free agent. I can ramble as far as I please. I can take up hoboing again. You've freed me. Thanks, chum. I won't forget.'

'Then—then—' I spluttered. Spike Higgins nodded.

'That's right. I've adopted you. I'm going to stick with you. We'll travel together.'

'But you can't!' I cried out, aghast. 'Ghosts don't travel around! They haunt houses—or cemeteries—or maybe woods. But—'

'What do you know about ghosts?' Spike Higgins's voice held sarcasm. 'There's all kinds of ghosts, chum. Includin' hobo ghosts, tramp ghosts with itchin' feet who can't stay put in one spot. Let me tell you, chum, a 'bo ghost like me ain't never had no easy time of it.

'Suppose they do give him a house to haunt? All right, he's got a roof over his head, but there he is, stuck. Houses don't move around. They don't go places. They stay in one spot till they rot.

'But things are different now. You've helped bring in a new age for the brotherhood of spooks. Now a fellow can haunt a house and be on the move at the same time. He can work at his job and still see the country. These trailers are the answer to a problem that's been bafflin' the best minds in the spirit world for thousands of years. It's the newest thing, the latest and best. Haunted trailers. I tell, you, we'll probably erect a monument to you at our next meeting. The ghosts of a monument, anyway.'

Spike Higgins had raised up on an elbow to make his speech. Now, grimacing, he lay back.

'That's enough, chum,' he muttered. 'Talking uses up my essence. I'm going to merge for a while. See you in the morning.'

'Merge with what?' I asked. Spike Higgins was already so dim I could hardly see him.

'Merge with the otherwhere,' a faint, distant voice told me, and Spike Higgins was gone.

I waited a minute to make sure. Then I breathed a big sigh of relief. I looked at my raincoat, at my wet feet, at the book on the floor, and knew it had all been a dream. I'd been walking in my sleep. Driving in it too. Having a nightmare.

I hung up the raincoat, slid out of my clothes, and got into a bunk.

I woke up late, and for a moment felt panic. Then I breathed easily again. The other bunk was untenanted. Whistling, I jumped up, showered, dressed, ate, and got under way.

It was a lovely day. Blue sky, wind, sunshine, birds singing. Thinking of Monica, I almost sang with them as I rolled down the road. In a week I'd be pulling up in front of Monica's aunt's place in Hollywood and tooting the horn. . . .

That was the moment when a cold draught of air sighed along the back of my neck, and the short hairs rose.

I turned, almost driving into a hay wagon. Beside me was a misty figure.

'I got tired of riding back there alone,' Spike Higgins told me. 'I'm gonna ride up front a while an' look at th' scenery.'

'You—you—' I shook with rage so that we nearly ran off the road. Spike Higgins reached out, grabbed the wheel in tenuous fingers, and jerked us back onto our course again.

'Take it easy, chum,' he said. 'There's enough competition in this world I'm in, without you hornin' into th' racket.'

I didn't say anything, but my thoughts must have been written on my face. I'd thought he was just a nightmare. But he was real. A ghost had moved in with me, and I hadn't the faintest idea how to move him out.

Spike Higgins grinned with a trace of malice.

'Sure, chum,' he said. 'It's perfectly logical. There's haunted castles, haunted palaces, and haunted houses. Why not a haunted trailer?'

'Why not haunted ferry-boats?' I demanded with bitterness. 'Why not haunted Pullmans? Why not haunted trucks?'

'You think there ain't?' Spike Higgins's misty countenance registered surprise at my ignorance. 'Could I tell you tales! There's a haunted ferry-boat makes the crossing at Poughkeepsie every stormy night at midnight. There's a haunted private train on the Atchinson, Sante Fé. Pal of mine haunts it. He always jumped trains, but he was a square dealer, and they gave him the private train for a reward.

'Then there's a truck on the New York Central that never gets where it's going. Never has yet. No matter where it starts out for, it winds up some place else. Bunch of my buddies haunt it. And another truck on the Southern Pacific that never has a train to pull it. Runs by itself. It's driven I dunno how many signalmen crazy, when they saw it go past right ahead of a whole train. I could tell you—'

'Don't!' I ordered. 'I forbid you to. I don't want to hear.'

'Why, sure, chum,' Spike Higgins agreed. 'But you'll get used to it. You'll be seein' a lot of me. Because where thou ghost, I ghost. Pun.' He gave a ghostly chuckle and relapsed into silence. I drove along, mind churning. I had that to get rid of him. *Had* to. Before we reached California, at the very latest. But I didn't have the faintest idea in the world how I was going to.

Then, abruptly, Spike Higgins's ghost sat up straight.

'Stop!' he ordered. 'Stop, I say!'

We were on a lonely stretch of road, bordered by old cypresses, with weed-grown marshland beyond. I didn't see any reason for stopping. But Spike Higgins reached out and switched off the ignition. Then he slammed on the emergency brake. We came squealing to a stop, and just missed going up into a ditch.

'What did you do that for?' I yelled. 'You almost ditched us! Confound you, you ectoplasmic, hitch-hiking nuisance! If I ever find a way to lay hands on you—'

'Quiet, chum!' the apparition told me rudely. 'I just seen an old pal of mine. Slippery Samuels. I ain't seen him since he dropped a bottle of nitro just as he was gonna break into a bank in Mobile sixteen years ago. We're gonna give him a ride.'

'We certainly are not!' I cried. 'This is my car, and I'm not picking up any more—'

'It may be your car,' Spike Higgins sneered, 'but I'm the resident haunt, and I got full powers to extend hospitality to any buddy ghosts I want, see? Rule 11, sub-division c. Look it up. Hey Slippery, climb in!'

A finger of fog pushed through the partly open window of the car at his hail, enlarged, and there was a second apparition on the front seat with me.

The newcomer was long and lean, just as shabbily dressed as Spike Higgins, with a ghostly countenance as mournful as a Sunday School picnic on a rainy day.

'Spike, you old son of a gun,' the second spook murmured, in hollow tones that would have brought gooseflesh to a statue. 'How've you been? What're you doing here? Who's he?'—nodding at me.

'Never mind him,' Spike said disdainfully. 'I'm haunting his trailer. Listen, whatever became of the old gang?'

'Still hoboing it,' the long, lean apparition sighed. 'Nitro Nelson is somewhere around. Pacific Pete and Buffalo Benny are lying over in a haunted jungle somewhere near Toledo. I had a date to join 'em, but a storm blew me back to Wheeling a couple of days ago.'

'Mmm,' Spike Higgins's ghost muttered. 'Maybe we'll run into 'em. Let's go back in my trailer and do a little chinning. As for you, chum, make camp any time you want. Ta ta.'

The two apparitions oozed through the back of the car and were gone. I was boiling inside, but there was nothing I could do.

I drove on for another hour, went through Toledo, then stopped at a wayside camp. I paid my dollar, picked out a spot, and parked.

But when I entered the trailer, the ghosts of Spike Higgins and Slippery Samuels, the bank robber, weren't there. Nor had they shown up by the time I finished dinner. In fact I ate, washed, and got into bed with no sign of them.

Breathing a prayer that maybe Higgins had abandoned me to go back to 'boing it in the spirit world, I fell asleep. And began to dream. About Monica. . . .

When I awoke, there was a sickly smell in the air, and the heavy staleness of old tobacco smoke.

I opened my eyes. Luckily, I opened them prepared for the worst. Even so, I wasn't prepared well enough.

Spike Higgins was back. Ha! Ha ha! Ha ha ha! I'll say he was back. He lay on the opposite bunk, his eyes shut, his mouth open, snoring. Just the ghost of a snore, but quite loud enough. On the bunk above him lay his bank-robber companion. In the easy chair was slumped a third apparition, short and stoud, with a round, whiskered face. A tramp spirit too.

So was the ghost stretched out on the floor, gaunt and cadaverous. So was the small, mournful spook in the bunk above me, his ectoplasmic hand swinging over the side, almost in my face. Tramps, all of them. Hobo spooks. Five hobo phantoms asleep in my trailer!

And there were cigarette butts in all the ash trays, and burns on my built-in writing desk. The cigarettes apparently had just been lit and let burn. The air was choking with stale smoke, and I had a headache I could have sold for a fire alarm, it was ringing so loudly in my skull.

I knew what had happened. During the night Spike Higgins and his pal had rounded up some more of their ex-hobo companions. Brought them back. To *my* trailer. Now—I was so angry I saw all five of them through a red haze that gave their ectoplasm a ruby tinge. Then I got hold of myself. I couldn't throw them out. I couldn't harm them. I couldn't touch them.

No, there was only one thing I could do. Admit I was beaten. Take my loss and quit while I could. It was a bitter pill to swallow. But if I wanted to reach Monica, if I wanted to enjoy the honeymoon we'd planned, I'd have to give up the fight.

I got into my clothes. Quietly I sneaked out, locking the trailer behind me. Then I hunted for the owner of the trailer camp, a lanky man, hard-eyed, but well dressed. I guessed he must have money.

'Had a sort of a party last night, hey?' he asked me, with a leering wink. 'I seen lights, an' heard singing, long after midnight. Not loud, though, so I didn't bother you. But it looked like somebody was havin' a high old time.'

I gritted my teeth.

'That was me,' I said, 'I couldn't sleep. I got up and turned on the radio. Truth is, I haven't slept a single night in that trailer. I guess I wasn't built for trailer life. That job cost me $2,998 new, just three days ago. I've got the bill-of-sale. How'd you like to buy it for fifteen hundred, and make two hundred easy profit on it?'

He gnawed his lip, but knew the trailer was a bargain. We settled for thirteen-fifty. I gave him the bill-of-sale, took the money, uncoupled, got into the car, and left there.

As I turned the bend in the road, heading westwards, there was no sign that Spike Higgins's ghost was aware of what had happened.

I even managed to grin as I thought of his rage when he woke up to find I had abandoned him. It was almost worth the money I'd lost to think of it.

Beginning to feel better, I stepped on the accelerator, piling up miles between me and that trailer. At least I was rid of Spike Higgins and his friends.

Ha!

Ha ha!

Ha ha ha!

That's what I thought.

About the middle of the afternoon I was well into Illinois. It was open country, and monotonous, so I turned on my radio. And the first thing I got was a police broadcast.

'All police, Indiana and Illinois! Be on the watch for a tan-and-chrome trailer, stolen about noon from a camp near Toledo. The thieves are believed heading west in it. That is all.'

I gulped. It couldn't be! But—it sounded like my trailer, all right. I looked in my rear-vision mirror, apprehensively. The road behind was empty. I breathed a small sigh of relief. I breathed it too soon. For at that moment, round a curve half a mile behind me, something swung into sight and came racing down the road after me.

The trailer.

Ha!

Ha ha!

There it came, a tan streak that zipped round the curve and came streaking after me, zigzagging wildly from side to side of the road, doing at least sixty—without a car pulling it.

My flesh crawled, and my hair stood on end. I stepped on the accelerator. Hard. And I picked up speed in a hurry. In half a minute

I was doing seventy, and the trailer was still gaining. Then I hit eighty —and passed a motor-cycle cop parked beside the road.

I had just a glimpse of his pop-eyed astonishment as I whizzed past, with the trailer chasing me fifty yards behind. Then, kicking on his starter, he slammed after us.

Meanwhile, in spite of everything the car would do, the trailer pulled up behind me and I heard the coupling clank as it was hitched on. At once my speed dropped. The trailer was swerving dangerously, and I had to slow. Behind me the cop was coming, siren open wide, I didn't worry about him because Spike Higgins was materializing beside me.

'Whew!' he said, grinning at me. 'My essence feels all used up. Thought you could give Spike Higgins and his pals the slip, huh? You'll learn, chum, you'll learn. That trooper looks like a tough baby. You'll have fun trying to talk yourself out of this.'

'Yes, but see what it'll get *you*, you ectoplasmic excrescence!' I raged at him. 'The trailer will be stored away in some county garage for months as evidence while I'm being held for trial on the charge of stealing it. And how'll you like haunting a garage?'

Higgins's face changed.

'Say, that's right,' he muttered. 'My first trip for fifteen years, too.'

He put his fingers to his lips, and blew the shrill ghost of a whistle. In a moment the car was filled with cold, clammy draughts as Slippery Samuels and the other three apparitions appeared in the seat beside Higgins.

Twisting and turning and seeming to intermingle a lot, they peered out at the cop, who was beside the car now, one hand on his gun butt, trying to crowd me over to the shoulder.

'All right, boys!' Higgins finished explaining. 'You know what we gotta do. Me an' Slippery'll take the car. You guys take the trailer!'

They slipped through the open windows like smoke. Then I saw Slippery Samuels holding on to the left front bumper, and Spike Higgins holding on to the right, their ectoplasm streaming out horizontal to the road, stretched and thinned by the air rush. And an instant later we began to move with a speed I had never dreamed of reaching.

We zipped ahead of the astonished cop, and the speedometer needle began to climb again. It took the trooper an instant to believe his eyes. Then with a yell he yanked out his gun and fired. A bullet bumbled past; then he was too busy trying to overtake us again to shoot.

The speedometer said ninety now, and was still climbing. It touched a hundred and stuck there. I was trying to pray when down the road a mile away I saw a sharp curve, a bridge, and a deep river. I froze. I couldn't even yell.

We came up to the curve so fast that I was still trying to move my lips when we hit it. I hit it. I didn't make any effort to take it. Instead I slammed on the brakes and prepared to plough straight ahead into a fence, a stand of young poplars, and the river.

But just as I braked, I heard Spike Higgins's ghostly scream, 'Allay-OOP!'

And before we reached the ditch, car and trailer swooped up in the air. An instant later at a height of a hundred and fifty feet, we hurtled straight westwards over the river and the town beyond.

I'd like to have seen the expression on the face of the motor-cycle cop then. As far as that goes, I'd like to have seen my own.

Then the river was behind us, and the town, and we were swooping down towards a dank, gloomy-looking patch of woods through which ran an abandoned railway line. A moment later we struck earth with a jouncing shock and came to rest.

Spike Higgins and Slippery Samuels let go of the bumpers and straightened themselves up. Spike Higgins dusted ghostly dust off his palms and leered at me.

'How was that, chum?' he asked. 'Neat, hey?'

'How—' I stuttered—'how—'

'Simple,' Spike Higgins answered. 'Anybody that can tip tables can do it. Just levitation, 'at's all. Hey, meet the boys. You ain't been introduced yet. This is Buffalo Benny, this one is Toledo Ike, this one Pacific Pete.'

The fat spook, the cadaverous one, and the melancholy little one appeared from behind the car, and smirked as Higgins introduced them. Then Higgins waved a hand impatiently.

'C'm on, chum,' he said. 'There's a road there that takes us out of these woods. Let's get going. It's almost dark, and we don't wanna spend the night here. This used to be in Dan Bracer's territory.'

'Who's Dan Bracer?' I demanded, getting the motor going because I was as anxious to get away from there as Spike Higgins's spook seemed to be.

'Just a railway dick,' Spike Higgins said, with a distinctly uneasy grin. 'Toughest bull that ever kicked a poor 'bo off a freight.'

'So he means he always drank black coffee,' Slippery Samuels put in, in a mournful voice. 'Cream turned sour when he picked up the jug.'

'Not that we was afraid of him—' Buffalo Benny, the fat apparition, squeaked. 'But—'

'We just never liked him,' Toledo Ike croaked, a sickly look on his ghostly features. 'O' course, he ain't active now. He was retired a couple of years back, an' jes' lately I got a rumour he was sick.'

'Dyin',' Pacific Pete murmured hollowly.

'Dyin'.' They all sighed the word, looking apprehensive. Then Spike Higgins's ghost scowled truculently at me.

'Never mind about Dan Bracer,' he snapped. 'Let's just get goin' out of here. And don't give that cop no more thought. You think a cop is gonna turn in a report that a car and trailer he was chasin' suddenly sailed up in the air an' flew away like an aeroplane? Not on your sweet life. He isn't gonna say nothing to nobody about it.'

Apparently he was right, because after I had driven out of the woods, with some difficulty, and onto a secondary highway, there was no further sign of pursuit. I headed westwards again, and Spike Higgins and his pals moved back to the trailer, where they lolled about, letting my cigarettes burn and threatening to call the attention of the police to me when I complained.

I grew steadily more morose and desperate as the Pacific Coast, and Monica, came nearer. I was behind schedule, due to Spike Higgins's insistence on my taking a roundabout route so they could see the Grand Canyon, and no way to rid myself of the obnoxious haunts appeared. I couldn't even abandon the trailer. Spike Higgins had been definite on that point. It was better to haul a haunted trailer around than to have one chasing you, he pointed out, and shuddering at the thought of being pursued by a trailer full of ghosts wherever I went, I agreed.

But if I couldn't get rid of them, it meant no Monica, no marriage, no honeymoon. And I was determined that nothing as insubstantial as a spirit was going to interfere with my life's happiness.

Just the same, by the time I had driven over the mountains and into California, I was almost on the point of doing something desperate. Apparently sensing this, Spike Higgins and the others had been on their good behaviour. But I could still see no way to get rid of them.

It was early afternoon when I finally rolled into Hollywood, haggard and unshaven, and found a trailer camp, where I parked. Heavy-hearted, I bathed and shaved and put on clean clothes. I didn't know what I was going to say to Monica, but I was already several days behind schedule, and I couldn't put off ringing her.

There was a telephone in the camp office. I looked up Ida Bracer—her aunt's name—in the book, then put through the call.

Monica herself answered. Her voice sounded distraught.

'Oh, Mel,' she exclaimed, as soon as I announced myself, 'where have you been? I've been expecting you for days.'

'I was delayed,' I told her, bitterly. 'Spirits. I'll explain later.'

'Spirits?' Her tone seemed cold. 'Well, anyway, now that you're here at last, I must see you at once. Mel, Uncle Dan is dying.'

'Uncle Dan?' I echoed.

'Yes, Aunt Ida's brother. He used to live in Iowa, but a few months ago he was taken ill, and he came out to be with Aunt and me. Now he's dying. The doctor says it's only a matter of hours.'

'Dying?' I repeated again. 'Your Uncle Dan, from Iowa, dying?'

Then it came to me. I began to laugh. Exultantly.

'I'll be right over!' I said, and hung up.

Still chuckling, I hurried out and unhitched my car. Spike Higgins stared at me suspiciously.

'Just got an errand to do,' I said airily. 'Be back soon.'

'You better be,' Spike Higgins's ghost said. 'We wanta drive round and see those movie stars' houses later on.'

Ten minutes later Monica herself, trim and lovely, was opening the door for me. In high spirits, I grabbed her round the waist, and kissed her. She turned her cheek to me, then, releasing herself, looked at me strangely.

'Mel,' she frowned, 'what in the world is wrong with you?'

'Nothing,' I carolled. 'Monica darling, I've got to talk to your uncle.'

'But he's too sick to see anyone. He's sinking fast, the doctor says.'

'All the more reason why I must see him,' I told her, and pushed into the house. 'Where is he, upstairs?'

I hurried up, and into the sickroom. Monica's uncle, a big man with a rugged face and a chin like the prow of a battleship, was in bed, breathing stertorously.

'Mr Bracer!' I said, breathless, and his eyes opened slowly.

'Who're you?' a voice as raspy as a shovel scraping a concrete floor growled.

'I'm going to marry Monica,' I told him. 'Mr Bracer, have you ever heard of Spike Higgins? Or Slippery Samuels? Or Buffalo Benny, Pacific Pete, Toledo Ike?'

'Heard of 'em?' A bright glow came into the sick man's eyes. 'Ha! I'll say I have. And laid hands on 'em, too, more'n once. But they're dead now.'

'I know they are,' I told him. 'But they're still around. Mr Bracer, how'd you like to meet up with them again?'

'Would I!' Dan Bracer murmured, and his hands clenched in unconscious anticipation. 'Ha!'

'Then,' I said, 'if you'll wait for me in the cemetery the first night after—after—well, anyway, wait for me, and I'll put you in touch with them.'

The ex-railway detective nodded. He grinned broadly, like a tiger viewing its prey and eager to be after it. Then he lay back, his eyes closed, and Monica, running in, gave a little gasp.

'He's gone!' she said.

'Ha ha!' I chuckled. 'Ha ha ha! What a surprise this is going to be to certain parties.'

The funeral was held in the afternoon, two days later. I didn't see Monica much in the interim. In the first place, though she hadn't known her uncle well, and wasn't particularly grieved, there were a lot of details to be attended to. In the second place, Spike Higgins and his pals kept me on the jump. I had to drive around Hollywood, to all the stars' houses, to Malibou Beach, Santa Monica, Laurel Canyon, and the various studios, so they could sightsee.

Then, too, Monica rather seemed to be avoiding me, when I did have time free. But I was too inwardly gleeful at the prospect of getting rid of the ghosts of Higgins and his pals to notice.

I managed to slip away from Higgins to attend the funeral of Dan Bracer, but could not help grinning broadly, and even at times chuckling, as I thought of his happy anticipation of meeting Spike Higgins and the others again. Monica eyed me oddly, but I could explain later. It wasn't quite the right moment to go into details.

After the funeral, Monica said she had a headache, so I promised to come round later in the evening. I returned to the trailer to find Spike Higgins and the others sprawled out, smoking my cigarettes again. Higgins looked at me with dark suspicion.

'Chum,' he said, 'we wanta be hitting the road again. We leave tomorrow, get me?'

'Tonight, Spike,' I said cheerfully. 'Why wait? Right after sunset you'll be on your way. To distant parts. Tra la, tra le, tum te tum.'

He scowled, but could think of no objection. I waited impatiently for sunset. As soon as it was thoroughly dark, I hitched up and drove out of the trailer camp, heading for the cemetery where Dan Bracer had been buried that afternoon.

Spike Higgins was still surly, but unsuspicious until I drew up and parked by the low stone wall at the nearest point to Monica's uncle's grave. Then, gazing out at the darkness-shadowed cemetery, he looked uneasy.

'Say,' he snarled, 'watcha stoppin' here for? Come on, let's be movin'.'

'In a minute, Spike,' I said. 'I have some business here.' I slid out and hopped over the low wall.

'Mr Bracer!' I called. 'Mr Bracer!'

I listened, but a long freight rumbling by half a block distant, where the Union Pacific lines entered the city, drowned out any sound. For a moment I could see nothing. Then a misty figure came into view among the headstones.

'Mr Bracer!' I called as it approached. 'This way!'

The figure headed towards me. Behind me Spike Higgins, Slippery Samuels and the rest of the ghostly crew were pressed against the wall, staring apprehensively into the darkness. And they were able to recognize the dim figure approaching before I could be sure of it.

'Dan Bracer!' Spike Higgins choked, in a high, ghostly squeal.

'It's him!' Slippery Samuels groaned.

'In the spirit!' Pacific Pete wailed. 'Oh oh oh oh OH!'

They tumbled backwards, with shrill squeaks of dismay. Dan Bracer's spirit came forward faster. Paying no attention to me, he took off after the retreating five.

Higgins turned and fled, wildly, with the others at his heels. They were heading towards the railway line, over which the freight was still rumbling, and Dan Bracer was now at their heels. Crowding each other, Higgins and Slippery Samuels and Buffalo Benny swung on to a passing truck, with Pacific Pete and Toledo Ike catching wildly at the rungs of the next.

They drew themselves up to the top of the trucks, and stared back. Dan Bracer's ghost seemed, for an instant, about to be left behind. But one long ectoplasmic arm shot out. A ghostly hand caught the rail of the guard's van, and Dan Bracer swung aboard. A moment later, he was running forward along the tops of the trucks, and up ahead of him, Spike Higgins and his pals were racing towards the engine.

That was the last I saw of them—five phantom figures fleeing, the sixth pursuing in happy anticipation. Then they were gone out of my life, heading east.

Still laughing to myself at the manner in which I had rid myself of Spike Higgins's ghost, and so made it possible for Monica and me to be married and enjoy our honeymoon trailer trip after all, I drove to Monica's aunt's house.

'Melvin!' Monica said sharply, as she answered my ring. 'What are you laughing about now?'

'Your uncle,' I chuckled. 'He—'

'My uncle!' Monica gasped. 'You—you fiend! You laughed when he died! You laughed all during his funeral! Now you're laughing because he's dead!'

'No, Monica!' I said. 'Let me explain. About the spirits, and how I—'

Her voice broke.

'Forcing your way into the house—laughing at my poor Uncle Dean—laughing at his funeral—'

'But, Monica!' I cried. 'It isn't that way at all. I've just been to the cemetery, and—'

Five phantom figures fleeing, the sixth pursuing in happy anticipation.

'And you came back laughing,' Monica retorted. 'I never want to see you again. Our engagement is broken. And worst of all is the *way* you laugh. It's so—so ghostly! So spooky. Blood-chilling. Even if you hadn't done the other things, I could never marry a man who laughs like that. So here's your ring. And goodbye.'

Leaving me staring at the ring in my hand, she slammed the door. And that was that. Monica is very strongminded, and what she says, she means. I couldn't even try to explain. About Spike Higgins. And how I'd unconsciously come to laugh that way through associating with five phantoms. After all, I'd just rid myself of them for good. And the only way Monica would ever have believed my story would have been from my showing her Spike Higgins's ghost himself.

Ha!

Ha ha!

Ha ha ha ha!

If you know anyone who wants to buy a practically unused trailer, cheap, let them get in touch with me.

BAD COMPANY

Walter de la Mare

It is very seldom that one encounters what would appear to be sheer unadulterated evil in a human face; an evil, I mean, active, deliberate, deadly, dangerous. Folly, heedlessness, vanity, pride, craft, meanness, stupidity—yes. But even Iagos in this world are few, and devilry is as rare as witchcraft.

One winter's evening some little time ago, bound on a visit to a friend in London, I found myself on the platform of one of its many subterranean railway stations. It is an ordeal that one may undergo as seldom as one can. The glare and glitter, the noise, the very air one breathes affect nerves and spirits. One expects vaguely strange meetings in such surroundings. On this occasion, the expectation was justified. The mind is at times more attentive than the eye. Already tired, and troubled with personal cares and problems, which a little wisdom and enterprise should have refused to entertain, I had seated myself on one of the low, wooden benches to the left of the entrance to the platform, when, for no conscious reason, I was prompted to turn my head in the direction of a fellow traveller, seated across the gangway on the fellow to my bench some few yards away.

What was wrong with him? He was enveloped in a loose cape or cloak, sombre and motionless. He appeared to be wholly unaware of my abrupt scrutiny. And yet I doubt it; for the next moment, although the door of the nearest coach gaped immediately opposite him, he had shuffled into the compartment I had entered myself, and now in its corner, confronted me, all but knee to knee. I could have touched him with my hand. We had, too, come at once into an even more intimate contact than that of touch. Our eyes—his own fixed in a dwelling and lethargic stare—had instantly met, and no less rapidly mine had uncharitably recoiled, not only in misgiving, but in something little short of disgust. The effect resembled that of an acid on milk, and for the time being cast my thoughts into confusion. Yet that one glance had taken him in.

He was old—over seventy. A wide-brimmed rusty and dusty black hat concealed his head—a head fringed with wisps of hair, lank and paper-grey. His loose, jaded cheeks were of the colour of putty; the thin lips above the wide unshaven and dimpled chin showing scarcely a trace of red. The cloak suspended from his shoulders mantled him to his shins. One knuckled, cadaverous, mittened hand clasped a thick ash stick, its handle black and polished with long usage. The only sign of life in his countenance was secreted in his eyes—fixed on mine—hazed and dully glistening, as a snail in winter is fixed to a wall. There was a dull deliberate challenge in them, and, as I fancied, something more than that. They suggested that he had been in wait for me; that for him, it was almost 'well met!'

For minutes together I endeavoured to accept their challenge, to make sure. Yet I realized, fascinated the while, that he was well aware of the futility of this attempt, as a snake is of the restless, fated bird in the branches above its head.

Such a statement, I am aware, must appear wildly exaggerated, but I can only record my impression. It was already lateish—much later than I had intended. The passengers came and went, and, whether intentionally or not, none consented to occupy the seat vacant beside him. I fixed my eyes on an advertisement—that of a Friendly Society I remember!—immediately above his head, with the intention of watching him in the field of an eye that I could not persuade to meet his own in full focus again.

He had instantly detected this ingenuous device. By a fraction of an inch he had shifted his grasp upon his stick. So intolerable, at length,

The only sign of life in his countenance was secreted in his eyes.

became the physical—and psychical—effect of his presence on me that I determined to leave the train at the next station, and there to await the next. And at this precise moment, I was conscious that he had not only withdrawn his eyes but closed them.

I was not so easily to free myself of his company. A glance over my shoulder as, after leaving the train, I turned towards the lift, showed him hastily groping his way out of the carriage. The metal gate clanged. The lift slid upwards and, such is the contrariness of human nature, a faint disappointment followed. One may, for example, be appalled and yet engrossed in reading an account of some act of infamous cruelty.

Concealing myself as best I could at the bookstall, I awaited the next lift-load. Its few passengers having dispersed, he himself followed. In spite of age and infirmity, he *had*, then, ascended alone the spiral staircase. Glancing, it appeared, neither to right nor left, he passed rapidly through the barrier. And yet—*had* he not seen me?

The Collector raised his head, opened his mouth, watched his retreating figure, but made no attempt to retrieve his ticket. It was dark now—the dark of London. In my absence underground, minute frozen pellets of snow had fallen, whitening the streets and lulling the sound of the traffic. On emerging into the street, he turned in the direction of the next station—my own. Yet again—had he, or had he not, been aware that he was being watched? However that might be, my journey lay his way, and that way my feet directed me; although I was already later than I intended. I followed him, led on no doubt in part merely by the effect he had had on me. Some twenty or thirty yards ahead, his dark shapelessness showed—distinct against the whitening pavement.

The waters of the Thames, I was aware, lay on my left. A muffled blast from the siren of a tug announced its presence. Keeping my distance, I followed him on. One lamp-post—two—three. At that, he seemed to pause for a moment, as if to listen, momentarily glanced back (as I fancied) and vanished.

When I came up with it, I found that this third lamp-post vaguely illuminated the mouth of a narrow, lightless alley between highish walls. It led me, after a while, into another alley, yet dingier. The wall on the left of this was evidently that of a large garden; on the right came a row of nondescript houses, looming up in their neglect against a starless sky.

The first of these houses *appeared* to be occupied. The next two were vacant. Dingy curtains, soot-grey against their snowy window-sills, hung over the next. A litter of paper and refuse—abandoned by the last long gust of wind that must have come whistling round the nearer angle of the house—lay under the broken flight of steps up to a mid-Victorian porch. The small snow clinging to the bricks and to the worn and weathered cement of the wall only added to its gaunt lifelessness.

In the faint hope of other company coming my way, and vowing that I would follow no farther than to the outlet of yet another pitch-black and uninviting alley or court—which might indeed prove a dead end—I turned into it. It was then that I observed, in the rays of the lamp over my head, that in spite of the fineness of the snow and the brief time that had elapsed, there seemed to be no trace on its surface of recent footsteps.

A faintly thudding echo accompanied me on my way. I have found it very useful—in the country—always to carry a small electric torch in my greatcoat pocket; but for the time being I refrained from using it. This alley proved not to be blind. Beyond a patch of waste ground, a nebulous, leaden-grey vacancy marked a loop here of the Thames— I decided to go no farther; and then perceived a garden gate in the wall to my right. It was ajar, but could not long have been so because no more than an instant's flash of my torch showed marks in the snow of its recent shifting. And yet there was little wind. On the other hand, here was the open river; just a breath of a breeze across its surface might account for this. The cracked and blistered paint was shimmering with a thin coat of rime—of hoarfrost, and as if a finger had but just now scrawled it there, a clumsy arrow showed, its 'V' pointing inward. A tramp, an errand-boy, mere accident might have accounted for this. It may indeed have been a mark made some time before on the paint.

I paused in an absurd debate with myself, chiefly I think because I felt some little alarm at the thought of what might follow; yet led on also by the conviction that I had been intended, decoyed to follow. I pushed the gate a little wider open, peered in, and made my way up a woody path beneath ragged unpruned and leafless fruit trees towards

223

the house. The snow's own light revealed a ramshackle flight of steps up to a poor, frenchified sort of canopy above french windows, one-half of their glazed doors ajar. I ascended, and peered into the intense gloom beyond it. And thus and then prepared to retrace my steps as quickly as possible, I called (in tones as near those of a London policeman as I could manage):

'Hello there! Is anything wrong? Is anyone wanted?' After all, I could at least explain to my fellow passenger if he appeared that I found both his gate and his window open; and the house was hardly pleasantly situated.

No answer was returned to me. In doubt and disquietude, but with a conviction that all was not well, I flashed my torch over the walls and furniture of the room and its heavily framed pictures. How could anything be well—with unseen company such as this besieging one's senses! Ease and pleasant companionship, the room may once have been capable of giving; in its dirt, cold and neglect it showed nothing of that now. I crossed it, paused again in the passage beyond it, and listened. I then entered the room beyond. Venetian blinds, many of the slats of which had outworn their webbing and heavy, crimson chenille side-curtains concealed its windows. The ashes of a fire showed beyond rusty bars of the grate under a black marble mantelpiece. An oil lamp on the table, with a green shade, exuded a stink of paraffin; beyond was a table littered with books and papers, and an overturned chair. There I could see the bent-up old legs, perceptibly lean beneath the trousers, of the occupant of the room. In no doubt of whose remains these were, I drew near, and with bared teeth and icy, trembling fingers, drew back the fold of the cloak that lay over the face. Death has a strange sorcery. A shuddering revulsion of feeling took possession of me. This cold, once genteel, hideous, malignant room—and this!

The skin of the blue loose cheek was drawn tight over the bone; the mouth lay a little open, showing the dislodged false teeth beneath; the dull unspeculative eyes stared out from beneath lowered lids towards the black mouth of the chimney above the fireplace. Vileness and iniquity had left their marks on the lifeless features, and yet it was rather with compassion than with horror and disgust that I stood regarding them. What desolate solitude, what misery must this old man, abandoned to himself, have experienced during the last years of his life; encountering nothing but enmity and the apprehension of his fellow creatures. I am not intending to excuse or even commiserate what I cannot understand, but the almost complete absence of any goodness in the human spirit cannot but condemn the heart to an appalling isolation. Had he been murdered, or had he come to a violent but natural end? In either case, horror and terror must have supervened. That I had been enticed, deliberately led on, to this discovery I hadn't the least doubt, extravagant though this, too, may seem. Why? What for?

I could not bring myself to attempt to light the lamp. Besides, in that last vigil, it must have burnt itself out. My torch revealed a stub of candle on the mantelpiece. I lit that. He seemed to have been engaged in writing when the enemy of us all had approached him in silence and had struck him down. A long and unsealed envelope lay on the table. I drew out the contents—a letter and a Will, which had been witnessed some few weeks before, apparently by a tradesman's boy and, possibly, by some derelict charwoman, Eliza Hinks. I knew enough about such things to be sure that the Will was valid and complete. This old man had been evidently more than fairly rich in this world's goods, and reluctant to surrender them. The letter was addressed to his two sisters: 'To my two Sisters, Amelia and Maude.' Standing there in the cold and the silence, and utterly alone—for, if any occupant of the other world had decoyed me there, there was not the faintest hint in consciousness that he or his influence was any longer present with me—I read the vilest letter that has ever come my way. Even in print. It stated that he knew the circumstances of these two remaining relatives—that he was well aware of their poverty and physical conditions. One of them, it seemed, was afflicted with Cancer. He then proceeded to explain that, although they should by the intention of their mother have had a due share in her property and in the money she had left, it rejoiced him to think that his withholding of this knowledge must continually have added to their wretchedness. Why he so hated them was only vaguely suggested.

The Will he had enclosed with the letter left all that he died possessed of to—of all human establishments that need it least—the authorities of Scotland Yard. It was to be devoted, it ran, to the detection of such evil-doers as are ignorant or imbecile enough to leave their misdemeanours and crimes detectable.

It is said that confession is good for the soul. Well then, as publicly as possible, I take this opportunity of announcing that, there and then, I made a little heap of envelope, letter and Will on the hearth and put a match to them. When every vestige of the paper had been consumed, I stamped the ashes down. I had touched nothing else. I would leave the vile, jaded, forsaken house to reveal its own secret; and I might ensure that that would not be long delayed.

What continues to perplex me is that so far as I can see no other agency but that of this evil old recluse himself had led me to my discovery. Why? Can it have been with this very intention? I stooped down and peeped and peered narrowly in under the lowered lids in the light of my torch, but not the feeblest flicker, remotest signal—or faintest syllabling echo of any message rewarded me. Dead fish are less unseemly.

And yet. Well—we are all of us, I suppose, at any extreme *capable* of remorse and not utterly shut against repentance. Is it possible that this priceless blessing is not denied us even when all that's earthly else appears to have come to an end?

MANY COLOURED GLASS

Lucy M. Boston

The Mayor's ball was to be held in the Costume wing of the Museum. This was occasionally used for concerts of Chamber Music, and as the Mayor was also a director, it had been found possible to allow its use for a private dance to celebrate an unusual occasion. The Mayor's only son was not merely coming of age, but had recently returned with an Olympic medal. A crowd of local enthusiasts had surrounded the station for his arrival, and newspaper photographs of his smiling response to the town's welcome were pinned up in every girl's office or bedroom.

Only a minority could hope for an invitation to the ball. The Mayor, Sir Joshua Waters, was fanatical about having public functions well done. He dreamed of being remembered as a mayor who had style. His invitations therefore were sent chiefly to those who could afford a real costume, or if their name made an invitation essential he would tactfully suggest the use of costumes 'not included in the showcases', which in fact he had himself bought for the occasion. He let it leak out that he hoped guests would pay proper attention to the period of their dress. Everyone was to come as a character out of Jane Austen's books. He had bad dreams about important people in scruffy rag-bag get-up. Important people should look important.

Jane Austen's period had been chosen because the largest of the Costume Museum's many rooms was given to the period 1750–1830, also because in the attics of family mansions round about some relics— wedding dresses, uniforms or riding coats—might still be found. Sir Joshua was to appear stern but benign as Sir Thomas Bertram of Mansfield Park, his son Philip as Mr Darcy, both specially tailored. As he looked at his son with pride, he congratulated himself that a desirable engagement would almost certainly be settled on the night. He had given his son a hint that the opportunity should be used.

As the hour approached Sir Joshua took a tour round the Museum to see that everything was in order. The main room faced the terrace and beyond that, the road. The tall Georgian windows were uncurtained, so that the people outside could watch the show. All round the walls were glass-fronted cases, each containing a period scene—a morning call, a christening, a family dinner, a stolen rendezvous, the sailor's farewell. Each scene had the furniture proper to it, with looking-glasses on the wall to show the other side of the costumes. There all the dummies sat or stood, in their best clothes and with their best manners, fixed forever as if waiting for the last trump. Normally they were lit by concealed electricity, but for this occasion candlesticks and candelabra had been put in the cases, adding more animation that one would expect, and chandeliers hung at intervals down the main room. The custodian was going round lighting everything up. The buffet was in the next room and the previous century, and there the inappropriate dummies had been hidden by screens. Sir Joshua tasted the food and wine and gave his last instructions, which included a strict warning to the doorman to admit no one without an invitation card. He took a last look of surprised pleasure at his own face graced by a discreet period wig, and prepared to receive his guests.

Crowds of the uninvited began to gather outside before the first guests arrived. Usually the majority of such onlookers are staid housewives come to have a free look and good matter for gossip, but this time, because of the fame of Philip Waters, there were packed ranks of youths and girls. The police had difficulty in keeping a way open for the arriving cars.

Sir Joshua could be satisfied with his guests. Their arrival was a real pageant. The less-young ladies in the excitement of their vast bonnets with ostrich plumes, their pelisses, empire busts and trailing skirts, by behaving according to their natures while forced to a different stance and movement by the altered balance of their rig, and chattering the more from this slight physical frustration, showed how truly Jane Austen had observed the species. The local Repertory Theatre had contributed a contingent of curled and dandified soldiers, sailors and clerics with young ladies on their arms. The local beauty was cheered when, as Emma, she was handed out by Mr Knightley.

Meanwhile Ann, the as-yet-not-quite official girl-friend of the hero of the evening, was sitting in her taxi as it inched along towards the entrance. She had not seen Philip since his victorious return, and was surprised by the disturbance in her feeling—a pounding excitement which was not wholly delight. A sudden volley from part of the crowd of WE WANT PHILIP was taken up and grew to an enveloping roar, which filled her with near terror. She hated publicity, and caught herself thinking that however wonderful it was that Philip was such a star, she almost wished he had been unsuccessful and that they were going somewhere together quietly as before. The stamping chant of the young men was broken by the thin screams of girls, and Ann realized that Philip must have come to the top of the steps to wait for her. At this her panic redoubled, and also her excitement, suddenly indivisible from the hypnosis of the mob.

From somewhere near came counter shouts: 'Down with heroes! Down with snobs!' The Commissionaire opened her door, letting her out at close quarters in front of a crush of typical students, dishevelled, unwashed, buttonless, bold-eyed or shifty, defying every human tradition. After all, savages, she thought, are as clean as cats. She half rose to begin the tricky business of stepping out of a taxi with shawl, fan and reticule, the invitation card and the fare ready in her hand. With one foot projecting, her glance lit on a slight, very young man who seemed the animating centre of the student group. His face was surrounded by long frizzy chestnut hair such as Leonardo's angels have—though less celestially ordered; this was a wild halo, and his expression was to match, being of such seraphic freedom and gaiety that at sight of it everything else went out of her mind. There was a second's pause—long enough for the gaiety to evaporate and for eyes

229

suddenly grave with joy to look into hers, which must have met them with the same expression.

The surprise was so great that she tripped on her long skirt, and was saved from falling by a delicate but grubby hand. Then the gaiety came back, but Philip was there, proprietary.

No wonder the girls had shrieked as for a matador. Philip was really a figure to stun. Starting from the top, his hair had been drilled by the barber to fall in casual manly sweeps. It was fair and it shone. His face was held rigidly high by his built-up coat-collar and his stock, so that it was presented like something by Phidias on a stand. His shoulders were not too wide for grace, his chest and ribs so well adapted for holding and controlling breath that it was fascinating to watch the easy inflation and deflation under a coat that fitted like a second skin. The coat was cut away in front, as was then the fashion, well above the waistline and so exposed his hips and the whole line of his faultless Olympic legs in close-fitting cream jersey cloth.

If Mr Darcy was thought arrogant because of his long tradition of eminence and responsibility, Philip Waters was arrogant unconsciously by virtue of his superlative physique and the qualities needed for successful competition. These, after all, he knew to be admirable things.

As he stood now at the top of the steps waving his acknowledgement to the crowd, he felt it was good to be able to offer a girl a part in his glory, even if only a walking-on part. He ran down the steps to meet Ann, and falling into the staginess of the occasion, bowed to kiss her hand.

'Go on, give her a proper one!' they yelled.

'All in good time,' he called back good-humouredly, and led her up on his arm, very well pleased with their entry. He would have been less pleased if he had known that she had hardly been aware of their progress from the taxi to the big swinging doors. She could find no place, in the course and expectation of her life till now, for the experience of that timeless mutual look, too accidental to be given a meaning yet it vibrated among her thoughts like a spring wind in an unawakened wood. How was she to orientate her actions now?

Inside it was a brilliant scene. The idea of acting up to the period was taking hold of the guests. They bowed and curtsied to the Mayor and also to each other as they gathered in groups along the side of the room, where the impression of numbers was doubled by the dummies entertaining each other behind the glass of their cases, and indeed seeming to entertain the Mayor's guests too, since these were reflected in the looking glasses in their sets and must therefore be supposed to be present with them. The sailor's farewell, for instance, gained poignancy from a group of his mates waiting for him outside the display case.

Philip took Ann round with him on his arm as he went to do his duty to his father's guests and to receive from them the congratulations due to him.

'Aren't you lucky!' said the girls to Ann, rolling up their eyes. 'Isn't he absolute heaven! You needn't blush, Ann, you're not the only person who thinks so.'

The ball was to be opened by the old dance, Sir Roger de Coverley, followed by a waltz, which, though never stated to have been danced by Jane Austen's characters, was, nevertheless, growing in popularity during her lifetime.

For Sir Roger, two long lines were formed up the centre of the room. Philip led Ann to her position at the end and the innocent stylized flirtation began—the long solo journey down the centre to circle round one's opposite number without touching, with nothing but breathless smiles and the play of eyes, approaching and retreating several times, to achieve in the end a hand-in-hand gallop down the whole length and a parting bow. Such childish fun! Any booby could learn the steps, but Philip's hand was cool and hard, his look correctly genial, almost royal, and he moved with economy where other men romped or charged. Ann was glad of the formality of the dance, for she still had no idea what she might, in the course of the evening, let herself in for.

When later she and Philip were waltzing, her indecisions were far more acute, for he waltzed of course, as he well knew, divinely, travelling faster than any of the weaving, circling couples. Ann was swirled through the no-space of the crowd, guided by those inimitable shoulders and hips, feeling the pressure of his long light legs. She began to be intoxicated by the masterly movement and her own perfect submission to it. The dancers that passed across the mirrors in the cased sets imparted now a sense of movement to the lay figures,

The ball was opened by the old dance, Sir Roger de Coverley.

since they also had reflections which shifted to the dancers' eyes as they turned. If the figures themselves did not move, at least they seemed deep in thought, dreaming or remembering. In the overmantel behind the bent head of a girl reading a letter Ann saw for a moment Philip's face bent over her own with an expression of deep satisfaction. With her, or with himself? And what was that girl remembering? But questions were left behind as they moved and swung together, while in the plate-glass front of the imitation world a swirl of much thinner, broken, half-recognized dreams flickered as they passed.

Every perfect waltz should end with a kiss. It is written into the last note. Philip drew her into the recess of one of the big windows. Because of the dark beyond it, the window seemed to those inside more like a huge pierglass in which they saw only their bright selves like transfers on the surface, behind which a few wandering and irrelevant lights were passing through space. Philip's back was against the glass as he drew Ann's waist close to his, but she became aware that there was an outside world and tried to penetrate beyond the festive bubble in which she was enclosed, to the shadowy colourless movements out there, where the dark bulk of the trees only made the reflected chandeliers hang more brilliantly as if on the boughs. As Philip's hold tightened, suddenly she found and interpreted that crowded limbo, and what might have been the misty blur round a dim light was the Leonardo hair round a white face at a few yards distance, watching what to him was ultra clear.

'What are you looking at?' said Philip. 'Attend to me!'

'It's too public here. All your admirers are still out there.'

'Good luck to them.'

'No, Philip, not now. Not here. *Oh dear*, that was a lovely waltz.'

'Why *Oh dear,* in that tone? Why not "You dear!", or "my dear", my dear?'

'I don't know what I'm saying or doing,' she answered.

'Then you want a few more drinks and you'll be saying what you really mean and won't know you've done it. I shall like that. There'll be more waltzes and I shall want them all. But I shall have to leave you once or twice to dance with Father's old ladies. My father's position depends largely on the proper observances. My manager's a bit of a bully about public relations too. But I can't leave you now—let's dance this.'

This time it was a popular tune of the moment, and very strange and improper indeed did the dancing look in these most mannered costumes, as if Dionysus had got into the Assembly Rooms at Bath. The high bonnets with ostrich plumes and flying ribbons tossed and jigged, the bundles of curls flew up and down, the bosoms in front and sashes behind, the coat-tails and fobs and seals all jigged and swung, fichus slipped awry, trailing skirts were trodden on and ultimately had to be held knee high in mittened hands. Sir Thomas Bertram would not have approved at all, and indeed Sir Joshua shook his head, though this was not a giddy teenage dance and the stateliness of the Museum had a sobering effect.

'I must go now,' said Philip. 'Forgive me. There's my manager—I'll bring him to look after you till I come back. You needn't be jealous. I'm going to be horribly bored. Wait here by the door so that we can find you.'

Ann leant thankfully in the comparative coolness of the doorway, which gave on to the entrance lobby. In spite of the drumming from the ballroom her ear caught the aggressive distaste in the doorman's voice saying, 'Can I see your invitation card?' No 'Sir' she noticed.

The reply came with airy irreverent authority.

'Afraid I haven't one with me.'

'I can't admit anyone without it. And fancy dress was specified.'

'What do you suppose this is? Every banquet presupposes a beggar.'

The accent undermined the doorman's confidence. You never could tell.

'Well, Sir, shall I bring Sir Joshua to speak to you?'

'Don't bother.'

Ann had come into the lobby, sure of whom she would see. She now came forward trading—with a pang of shame—on her being known as Philip's partner.

The boy bounded in and took her hand.

'Aren't we in luck,' he said as he led her in.

In a moment they were dancing to the latest, most rhythmic hit, and from the start it was an inspired partnership. Their eyes never left each other, but their responding movements were as free as thought, as unexpected and as playful. They were two separate and equal people showing an immense exhilarating Now-ness. This was laughter, this was delight, this was—most surprisingly—a flowering tenderness, and the rhythm was simply their lively young blood racing on its circuit.

If the other dancers noticed the infiltration of something not on the programme, it was only as an increase in their own acceptance of pleasure, but Sir Joshua had seen instantly that the style of his dance was ruined. He had devastated the doorman, who pleaded that Mr Philip's young lady had over-ruled him.

'Torn jeans, no shirt under his sweater, beach shoes—no socks—it's an outrage! Spoils the whole show.'

'His rags are clean,' the Mayor's partner replied soothingly. 'Admittedly only from being washed by him in his own hand-basin. And he has an eerie charm.'

'Where's Philip's manager? He ought to be able to deal with this. The press photographer is here, and you can be sure they'll make more out of Ann dancing with that layabout than of Philip. Ah, there he is —excuse me.'

Meanwhile the dance had ended. In the recess where Ann had evaded Philip's kiss she received the lips of the stranger, and knew that he was now the magnet of her life, no other consideration whatsoever had either weight or pull.

'I shan't be able to stay here,' he said. 'Meet me in the garden behind the Museum as soon as you can. Here comes the irate Sir Joshua with a bodyguard—I must make my obeisance to him, and leave with dignity.'

Ann laughed with delight at this picture, but Philip was disentangling himself from the beautiful Emma on the other side of the room. A waltz was beginning, and from Philip's face it was going to be a furious one. Oh, *no,* thought Ann, as for the first time her predicament fully dawned on her. She began to slip away through the crowd, looking in her white and silver dress like a darting fish, and the other guests with unexpected sympathy moved to let her pass.

She fled through the empty rooms of the Museum opening one out of the other. She did not know where the door into the garden was, but if locked that would be on the inside. How long, she wondered, would it take her Romeo to go round and climb the garden wall, or however he meant to get in after he had been turned out?

The sound of the waltz grew fainter behind her. In a corridor that she judged must lead to the back she stopped to collect her thoughts. Her heart was choking her. She sat down on a bench and hid her hot face in her hands, in confusion but not in doubt.

When she opened her eyes they were confronted by a musical box against the opposite wall—one of those early Bavarian toys where mechanical figures perform to the tune.

'How odd,' she thought. The little stage showed a group of fiddlers, two couples in costumes like those of the ball she had just quitted, and in a doorway at the side, a gypsy or beggarman.

Very faintly the distant waltz came to her ears, but no footsteps ringing in the abandoned halls.

With her hand pressed to her unsteady heart, acting under a sudden compulsion, she pushed down the lever. Delicate plucked music started up; the fiddlers sawed with their clumsy arms in time to an ethereal waltz. The couples moved jerkily out and each raised an arm to clasp its partner. To various clicks and rumbles from under the floor they began to revolve with each other and to orbit round the room. Their movements were sinister because of· being both reluctant and predestined. Here they were and this was what they must do. Almost at once however, there was a whirring sound, a hesitation while the tiny figures stood quivering, then with a click and a jerk their motion was resumed. A moment later it was clear that something was going wrong. The fiddlers fiddled and the tinny music continued but there were sounds of misengagement, of metals in opposition, so that Ann was afraid she ought never to have set it in motion; the machine was out of order and might churn itself up. One of the couples divided— the lady flung off in an orbit of her own while her partner revolved on the spot, holding out his arms. To continued protest from the machinery the driven doll circled near the door. The beggarman had till now stood motionless except for an arm that jerked up and down, hat in hand, but now he was propelled forward, and after they had each twirled with arms outstretched, they met face to face and proceeded as partners. The whirring quickened as they sped round, while the abandoned partner revolved helplessly in the centre, wrenching against his imprisoning connection. He swayed this way and that as they passed him in apparently smooth working order. They passed the second couple, now ominously stationary. The beggarman seemed to have charmed his weird little stage, until they came again to the faulty point where she had first broken away. Inevitably she did so again, leaving him in the grip of the cogs near his enemy. These two then revolved round each other till they were face to face when the box gave a screech and the legitimate partner fell upon the beggar-man. The music stopped, and the last sounds were repeated metallic thuds as the beggarman's head was knocked against the floor.

And now Ann saw her own spectral face filling up the glass front of the box like a transparent stage-curtain. It wavered. She leant against the wall, appalled.

When she again began to consider where she was and what she was doing, she heard a confused murmur from the ballroom. It was like the sound in a sea-shell, not a party noise at all, and no music. From far away, but growing nearer and nearer and nearer, as in a nightmare, came the horrible toxin of an ambulance. At the peak of sound it stopped, and there followed an interval of a silence more suggestive and heart-stopping than even the terror of its approach, before it set off again with its burden.

Ann leapt to her feet and began to run as if she could run after it. Then the band in the ballroom struck up with compelling desperation, as obviously taking action to avoid calamity as the ambulance itself.

THE STRANGER

Ambrose Bierce

A man stepped out of the darkness into the little illuminated circle about our failing camp-fire and seated himself upon a rock.

'You are not the first to explore this region,' he said gravely.

Nobody controverted his statement; he was himself proof of its truth, for he was not of our party and must have been somewhere near when we camped. Moreover, he must have companions not far away; it was not a place where one would be living or travelling alone. For more than a week we had seen, besides ourselves and our animals, only such living things as rattlesnakes and horned toads. In an Arizona desert one does not long coexist with only such creatures as these; one must have pack animals, supplies, arms—'an outfit'. And all these imply comrades. It was, perhaps, a doubt as to what manner of men this unceremonious stranger's comrades might be, together with something in his words interpretable as a challenge, that caused every man of our half-dozen 'gentlemen adventurers' to rise to a sitting posture and lay his hand upon a weapon—an act signifying, in that time and place, a policy of expectation. The stranger gave the matter no attention, and began again to speak in the same deliberate, uninflected monotone in which he had delivered his first sentence:

'Thirty years ago Ramon Gallegos, William Shaw, George W. Kent and Berry Davis, all of Tucson, crossed the Santa Catalina Mountains and travelled due west, as nearly as the configuration of the country permitted. We were prospecting and it was our intention, if we found nothing, to push through to the Gila river at some point near Big Bend, where we understood there was a settlement. We had a good outfit but no guide—just Ramon Gallegos, William Shaw, George W. Kent and Berry Davis.'

The man repeated the names slowly and distinctly, as if to fix them in the memories of his audience, every member of which was now attentively observing him, but with a slackened apprehension regarding his possible companions somewhere in the darkness which seemed to enclose us like a black wall, for in the manner of this volunteer historian was no suggestion of an unfriendly purpose. His act was rather that of a harmless lunatic than an enemy. We were not so new to the country as not to know that the solitary life of many a plainsman had a tendency to develop eccentricities of conduct and character not always easily distinguishable from mental aberration. A man is like a tree: in a forest of his fellows he will grow as straight as his generic and individual nature permits; alone, in the open, he yields to the deforming stresses and tortions that environ him. Some such thoughts were in my mind as I watched the man from the shadow of my hat, pulled low to shut out the fire-light. A witless fellow, no doubt, but what could he be doing there in the heart of a desert?

Nobody having broken the silence, the visitor went on to say:

'This country was not then what it is now. There was not a ranch between the Gila and the Gulf. There was a little game here and there in the mountains, and near the infrequent water-holes grass enough to keep our animals from starvation. If we should be so fortunate as to encounter no Indians we might get through. But within a week the purpose of the expedition had altered from discovery of wealth to preservation of life. We had gone too far to go back, for what was ahead could be no worse than what was behind; so we pushed on, riding by night to avoid Indians and the intolerable heat, and concealing ourselves by day as best we could. Sometimes, having exhausted our supply of wild meat and emptied

A man stepped out of the darkness into the illuminated circle.

our casks, we were days without food and drink; then a water-hole or a shallow pool in the bottom of an arroyo so restored our strength and sanity that we were able to shoot some of the wild animals that sought it also. Sometimes it was a bear, sometimes an antelope, a coyote, a cougar—that was as God pleased; all were food.

'One morning as we skirted a mountain range, seeking a practicable pass, we were attacked by a band of Apaches who had followed our trail up a gulch—it is not far from here. Knowing that they outnumbered us ten to one, they took none of their usual cowardly precautions, but dashed upon us at a gallop, firing and yelling. Fighting was out of the question. We urged our feeble animals up the gulch as far as there was footing for a hoof, then threw ourselves out of our saddles and took to the chaparral on one of the slopes, abandoning our entire outfit to the enemy. But we retained our rifles, every man—Ramon Gallegos, William Shaw, George W. Kent and Berry Davis.'

'Same old crowd,' said the humorist of the party. A gesture of disapproval from our leader silenced him, and the stranger proceeded with his tale:

'The savages dismounted also, and some of them ran up the gulch beyond the point at which we had left it, cutting off further retreat in that direction and forcing us on up the side. Unfortunately the chaparrel extended only a short distance up the slope, and as we came into the open ground above we took the fire of a dozen rifles; but Apaches shoot badly when in a hurry, and God so willed it that none of us fell. Twenty yards up the slope, beyond the edge of the brush, were vertical cliffs, in which, directly in front of us, was a narrow opening. Into that we ran, finding ourselves in a cavern about as large as an ordinary room. Here for a time we were safe. A single man with a repeating rifle could defend the entrance against all the Apaches in the land. But against hunger and thirst we had no defence. Courage we still had, but hope was a memory.

'Not one of those Indians did we afterwards see, but by the smoke and glare of their fires in the gulch we knew that by day and by night they watched with ready rifles in the edge of the bush— knew that if we made a sortie not a man of us would live to take three steps into the open. For three days, watching in turn, we held out, before our suffering became insupportable. Then—it was the morning of the fourth day—Ramon Gallegos said:

'"Señores, I know not well of the good God and what please him. I have lived without religion, and I am not acquaint with that of you. Pardon, señores, if I shock you, but for me the time is come to beat the game of the Apache."

'He knelt upon the rock floor of the cave and pressed his pistol against his temple. "Madre de Dios," he said, "comes now the soul of Ramon Gallegos."

'And so he left us—William Shaw, George W. Kent and Berry Davis.

'I was the leader. It was for me to speak.

'"He was a brave man," I said. "He knew when to die, and how. It is foolish to go mad from thirst and fall by Apache bullets, or be skinned alive—it is in bad taste. Let us join Ramon Gallegos."

'"That is right," said William Shaw.

'"That is right," said George W. Kent.

'I straightened the limbs of Ramon Gallegos and put a handkerchief over his face. Then William Shaw said: "I should like to look like that a little while."

'And George W. Kent said that he felt that way too.

'"It shall be so," I said. "The red devils will wait a week. William Shaw and George W. Kent, draw and kneel,"

'They did so and I stood before them.

'"Almighty God, our Father," said I.

'"Almighty God, our Father," said William Shaw.

'"Almighty God, our Father," said George W. Kent.

'"Forgive us our sins," said I.

'"Forgive us our sins," said they.

'"And receive our souls."

'"And receive our souls."

'"Amen!"

'"Amen!"

'I laid them beside Ramon Gallegos and covered their faces.'

There was a quick commotion on the opposite side of the camp-fire. One of our party had sprung to his feet, pistol in hand.

'And you!' he shouted, 'you dared to escape?—you dare to be alive? You cowardly hound, I'll send you to join them if I hang for it!'

But with the leap of a panther the captain was upon him, grasping his wrist. 'Hold it in, Sam Yountsey, hold it in!'

We were now all upon our feet—except the stranger, who sat motionless and apparently inattentive. Someone seized Yountsey's other arm.

'Captain,' I said, 'there is something wrong here. This fellow is either a lunatic or merely a liar—just plain, everyday liar that Yountsey has no call to kill. If this man was of that party it had five members, one of whom—probably himself—he has not named.'

'Yes,' said the captain, releasing the insurgent, who sat down, 'there is something—unusual. Years ago four dead bodies of white men, scalped and shamefully mutilated, were found about the mouth of that cave. They are buried there; I have seen the graves—we shall all see them tomorrow.'

The stranger rose, standing tall in the light of the expiring fire, which in our breathless attention to his story we had neglected to keep going.

'There were four,' he said. 'Ramon Gallegos, William Shaw, George W. Kent and Berry Davis.'

With this reiterated roll-call of the dead he walked into the darkness and we saw him no more.

At that moment one of our party, who had been on guard, strode in among us, rifle in hand and somewhat excited.

'Captain,' he said, 'for the last half-hour three men have been standing out there on the *mesa*.' He pointed in the direction taken by the stranger. 'I could see them distinctly, for the moon is up, but as they had no guns and I had them covered with mine, I thought it was their move. They have made none, but, damn it! they have got on my nerves.'

'Go back to your post, and stay till you see them again,' said the captain. 'The rest of you lie down again, or I'll kick you all into the fire.'

The sentinel obediently withdrew, swearing, and did not return. As we were arranging our blankets, the fiery Yountsey said: 'I beg your pardon, Captain, but who the devil do you take them to be?'

'Ramon Gallegos, William Shaw and George W. Kent.'

'But how about Berry Davis? I ought to have shot him.'

'Quite needless; you couldn't have made him any deader. Go to sleep.'

THE TELL-TALE HEART

Edgar Allan Poe

True! Nervous, very, very dreadfully nervous I had been and am; but why *will* you say that I am mad? The disease had sharpened my senses, not destroyed, not dulled them. Above all was the sense of hearing acute. I heard all things in the heaven and in the earth. I heard many things in hell. How then am I mad? Hearken! and observe how healthily, how calmly, I can tell you the whole story.

It is impossible to say how first the idea entered my brain, but, once conceived, it haunted me day and night. Object there was none. Passion there was none. I loved the old man. He had never wronged me. He had never given me insult. For his gold I had no desire. I think it was his eye! Yes, it was this! One of his eyes resembled that of a vulture—a pale blue eye with a film over it. Whenever it fell upon me my blood ran cold, and so by degrees, very gradually, I made up my mind to take the life of the old man, and thus rid myself of the eye for ever.

Now this is the point. You fancy me mad. Madmen know nothing. But you should have seen *me*. You should have seen how wisely I proceeded—with what caution—with what foresight, with what dissimulation, I went to work! I was never kinder to the old man than during the whole week before I killed him. And every night about midnight I turned the latch of his door and opened it—oh, so gently!

And then when I had made an opening sufficient for my head I put in a dark lantern all closed, closed so that no light shone out, and then I thrust in my head. Oh, you would have laughed to see how cunningly I thrust it in! I moved it slowly, very, very slowly, so that I might not disturb the old man's sleep. It took me an hour to place my whole head in the opening so far that I could see him lay upon his bed. Ha! would a madman have been so wise as this? And then when my head was well in the room I undid the lantern cautiously—oh, so cautiously—cautiously (for the hinges creaked), I undid it just so much that a single thin ray fell upon the vulture eye. And this I did for seven long hours, every night just at midnight, but I found the eye always closed, and so it was impossible to do the work, for it was not the old man who vexed me but his Evil Eye. And every morning, when the day broke, I went boldly into the chamber and spoke courageously to him, calling him by name in a hearty tone, and inquiring how he had passed the night. So you see he would have been a very profound old man, indeed, to suspect that every night, just at twelve, I looked in upon him while he slept.

Upon the eighth night I was more than usually cautious in opening the door. A watch's minute hand moves more quickly than did mine. Never before that night had I *felt* the extent of my own powers, of my sagacity. I could scarcely contain my feelings of triumph. To think that there I was opening the door little by little, and he not even to dream of my secret deeds or thoughts. I fairly chuckled at the idea, and perhaps he heard me, for he moved on the bed suddenly as if startled. Now you may think that I drew back—but no. His room was as black as pitch with the thick darkness (for the shutters were close fastened through fear of robbers), and so I knew that he could not see the opening of the door, and I kept pushing it on steadily, steadily.

I had my head in, and was about to open the lantern, when my thumb slipped upon the tin fastening, and the old man sprang up in the bed, crying out, 'Who's there?'

I kept quite still and said nothing. For a whole hour I did not move a muscle, and in the meantime I did not hear him lie down. He was still sitting up in the bed, listening; just as I have done night after night hearkening to the death watches in the wall.

Presently I heard a slight groan, and I knew it was the groan of mortal terror. It was not a groan of pain or of grief—oh, no! it was the low stifled sound that arises from the bottom of the soul when over-charged with awe. I knew the sound well. Many a night, just at midnight, when all the world slept, it has welled up from my own bosom, deepening, with its dreadful echo, the terrors that distracted me. I say I knew it well. I knew what the old man felt, and pitied him although I chuckled at heart. I knew that he had been lying awake ever since the first slight noise when he had turned in his bed. His fears had been ever since growing upon him. He had been trying to fancy them causeless, but could not. He had been saying to himself, 'It is nothing but the wind in the chimney, it is only a mouse crossing the floor', or 'It is merely a cricket which has made a single chirp'. Yes, he has been trying to comfort himself with these suppositions; but he had found all in vain. *All in vain*, because Death in approaching him had stalked with his black shadow before him and enveloped the victim. And it was the mournful influence of the unperceived shadow that caused him to feel, although he neither saw nor heard, to *feel* the presence of my head within the room.

When I had waited a long time very patiently without hearing him lie down, I resolved to open a little—a very, very little, crevice in the lantern. So I opened it—you cannot imagine how stealthily, stealthily—until at length a single dim ray like the thread of the spider shot out from the crevice and fell upon the vulture eye.

It was open, wide, wide open, and I grew furious as I gazed upon it. I saw it with perfect distinctness—all a dull blue with a hideous veil over it that chilled the very marrow in my bones, but I could see nothing else of the old man's face or person, for I had directed the ray as if by instinct precisely upon the damned spot.

And now have I not told you that what you mistake for madness is but over-acuteness of the senses? now, I say, there came to my ears a low, dull, quick sound, such as a watch makes when enveloped in cotton. I knew *that* sound well, too. It was the beating of the old man's heart. It increased my fury, as the beating of a drum stimulates the soldier into courage.

But even yet I refrained and kept still. I scarcely breathed. I held the lantern motionless. I tried how steadily I could maintain the ray upon

A single dim ray fell upon the vulture eye.

the eye. Meantime the hellish tattoo of the heart increased. It grew quicker and quicker, and louder and louder, every instant. The old man's terror *must* have been extreme! It grew louder, I say, louder every moment!—do you mark me well? I have told you that I am nervous: so I am. And now at the dead hour of the night, amid the dreadful silence of the old house, so strange a noise as this excited me to uncontrollable terror. Yet, for some minutes longer I refrained and stood still. But the beating grew louder, louder! I thought the heart must burst. And now a new anxiety seized me—the sound would be heard by a neighbour! The old man's hour had come! With a loud yell, I threw open the lantern and leaped into the room. He shrieked once—once only. In an instant I dragged him to the floor, and pulled the heavy bed over him. I then smiled gaily to find the deed so far done. But for many minutes the heart beat on with a muffled sound. This, however, did not vex me; it would not be heard through the wall. At length it ceased. The old man was dead. I removed the bed and examined the corpse. Yes, he was stone, stone dead. I placed my hand upon the heart and held it there many minutes. There was no pulsation. He was stone dead. His eye would trouble me no more.

If still you think me mad, you will think so no longer when I describe the wise precautions I took for the concealment of the body. The night waned, and I worked hastily, but in silence.

I took up three planks from the flooring of the chamber, and deposited all between the scantlings. I then replaced the boards so cleverly, so cunningly, that no human eye—not even *his*—could have detected anything wrong. There was nothing to wash out—no stain of any kind—no bloodspot whatever. I had been too wary for that.

When I had made an end of these labours, it was four o'clock—still dark as midnight. As the bell sounded the hour, there came a knocking at the street door. I went down to open it with a light heart,—for what had I *now* to fear? There entered three men, who introduced themselves with perfect suavity, as officers of the police. A shriek had been heard by a neighbour during the night; suspicion of foul play had been aroused; information had been lodged at the police office, and they (the officers) had been deputed to search the premises.

I smiled,—for *what* had I to fear? I bade the gentlemen welcome.

The shriek, I said, was my own in a dream. The old man, I mentioned, was absent in the country. I took my visitors all over the house; bade them search—search *well*. I led them, at length, to *his* chamber. I showed them his treasures, secure, undisturbed. In the enthusiasm of my confidence, I brought chairs into the room, and desired them *here* to rest from their fatigues, while I myself, in the wild audacity of my perfect triumph, placed my own seat upon the very spot beneath which reposed the corpse of the victim.

The officers were satisfied. My *manner* had convinced them. I was singularly at ease. They sat, and while I answered cheerily, they chatted of familiar things. But, ere long, I felt myself getting pale and wished them gone. My head ached, and I fancied a ringing in my ears; but still they sat, and still they chatted. The ringing became more distinct;—it continued and became more distinct: I talked more freely to get rid of the feeling: but it continued and gained definitiveness—until, at length, I found that the noise was *not* within my ears.

No doubt I now grew *very* pale;—but I talked more fluently, and with a heightened voice. Yet the sound increased—and what could I do? It was *a low, dull, quick sound—and much a sound as a watch makes when enveloped in cotton*. I gasped for breath—and yet the officers heard it not. I talked more quickly—more vehemently; but the noise steadily increased. I arose and argued about trifles, in a high key and with violent gesticulations; but the noise steadily increased. Why *would* they not be gone? I paced the floor to and fro with heavy strides, as if excited to fury by the observations of the men—but the noise steadily increased. O God! what *could* I do? I foamed—I raved—I swore! I swung the chair upon which I had been sitting, and grated it upon the boards, but the noise arose over all and continually increased. It grew louder—louder—*louder!* And still the men chatted pleasantly, and smiled. Was it possible they heard not? Almighty God!—no, no! They heard!—they suspected!—they *knew!*—they were making a mockery of my horror!—this I thought, and this I think. But anything was better than this agony! Anything was more tolerable than this derision! I could bear those hypocritical smiles no longer! I felt that I must scream or die!—and now—again!—hark! louder! louder! louder! *louder!*—

'Villains!' I shrieked, 'dissemble no more! I admit the deed!—tear up the planks!—here, here!—it is the beating of his hideous heart!'

THE GORGE OF THE CHURELS

H. Russell Wakefield

'Mr Sen,' said the Reverend Aloysius Prinkle, 'I am going to take a holiday tomorrow. I'm feeling a bit jaded. I thought we'd have a picnic, if it's fine. You must come with us, of course.'

'A pleasant idea, certainly,' smiled Mr Sen. He was a Bengali babu, aged about thirty, who acted as Secretary and general factotum to the incumbents of the Mission Station. Mr Prinkle had taken him over from his predecessor three months before. He was a slightly enigmatic young man, habitually smiling and obliging, but not quite as 'open' as he might be, was Mr Prinkle's verdict. His enemies called him a 'Rice Christian', meaning he had found the Christian side of the bread the better buttered. His friends replied, 'Very sensible of Mr Sen, if he is right about the rice.' His English was fluent and personally idiomatic. His intonation pedantically precise with a wavy melody line.

'Have you yet decided on a site for the occasion?' he added. 'Possibly my advice may be welcome; possibly not.'

'Well, Mrs Prinkle and I passed what we considered an ideal spot the other day. It's a little gorge off the Kulan Valley. It's known, I understand, as The Gorge of the Churels. You know where I mean?'

Mr Sen didn't reply for a moment. He continued to wear that smile, but it contracted somewhat as though he were moved by some not entirely pleasant reflections. At length he remarked, 'Yes, I am familiar with the locality you mention, but is it not rather a long way to go? Just a suggestion, of course.'

'Not a bit of it!' laughed Mr Prinkle; 'just three-quarters of an hour in the car and a beautiful drive into the bargain.'

'Did you consider taking the youngster with you?' asked Mr Sen slowly.

'Why, naturally! He'll love it; and it'll give his Ayah the day off.'

'It is not perhaps a very satisfactory place for young children,' said Mr Sen.

'Why ever not! Snakes?'

'No, I was not thinking so much of snakes,' replied Mr Sen aloofly; 'those are, in a way, everywhere and easily avoided, terrified, or destroyed.'

'Then what *are* you thinking about?' asked Mr Prinkle. His voice was benignly patronizing.

'There is a good deal of water there; a stream and a pool, and so on. All this may be dangerous for the tender-yeared, of course.'

'Of course *not!*' laughed Mr Prinkle. 'We shall see Nikky doesn't come to a premature and watery end! It is not good, you know, Mr Sen, to be too nervous about children. It makes *them* nervous, too. "Fear and be slain!" There's a lot of truth in that, you know!'

'There is, also, of course,' smiled Mr Sen, 'the Heavenly Father on guard.'

Mr Prinkle glanced at him sharply. Was he being a shade sarcastic? One could never be quite sure with Mr Sen. A pity he couldn't be more *open*!

'Now, Mr Sen,' he said, 'I don't think you're being quite candid with me. I don't think those are your real reasons. Now tell me quite frankly, please, why you dislike going to this place, for I can see you do.'

'Oh, I don't mind really,' said Mr Sen with a quick little giggle. 'I was perhaps reverting to type, if you know what I mean, just being foolish, a silly primitive Indian.'

'I *suppose* I know what you're getting at,' said Mr Prinkle quizzingly, 'the place has some sort of evil repute; is that what you mean?'

'Since you press me on the matter, that is so. Quite absurd, of course!'

Mr Prinkle saw fit to issue a rather roguish reprimand.

'You mean, Mr Sen, it is thought to be haunted by spirits of some kind?'

'That is what I may term the rough idea,' replied Mr Sen. 'I do not desire to discuss the matter at further length, if you do not mind.'

'But I do *mind*, Mr Sen. I have instructed you that the only evil spirits are in the hearts of men. To suppose they can materialize themselves and infest certain localities is a childish superstition, primitive, as you say. Such ideas distract and confuse men's minds; they must be eradicated. I am rather surprised at you, Mr Sen, after all you've been taught. It doesn't seem to have sunk in, for in spite of your protestations, I can see that you still, in some ways, share these barbarous notions. We *will* go to this gorge and enjoy ourselves thoroughly—*all* of us! Come now to my bungalow and give me my Urdu lesson, and let's have no more reversion to type!'

Mr Sen smiled and did as he was told, but behind the mask he was charged with a great anger almost perfectly controlled. So during the next hour he delicately permitted Mr Prinkle to realize he considered him a person of lethargic wits and quite devoid of linguistic ability; that instructing him was a considerable strain on the patience and by no means a labour of love. And later he quite refused to obey the pious injunction not to let the sun go down upon his wrath, for he lay long awake that night, his fury festering, because he had been ridiculed, humiliated, and reproved, and it was like a rodent ulcer in his spirit.

Mr Prinkle was very young, earnest, pink-and-white and naively self-confident. Though he had landed at Bombay but fourteen weeks before, he felt he already knew India and the Indian mind pretty well, and the chapter headings of a book dealing with the Missionary problems of the Sub-Continent were already in his notebook. His wife, Nancy, was very young and earnest too, but much more pleasing to the eye and by no means so confident. In her heart she thought India a frightening place, and that she and her husband were really strangers in a very strange land, unwelcome strangers to ninety percent of its inhabitants, at any rate those of the Northern Punjab. She was an intelligent girl and her little boy Nicholas was an intelligent child. He was a charming, small blond boy, much too young for the climate, pronounced the pundits. He was inclined to solemnity, too, and it seemed the genes of earnestness were already busy within him.

The next morning, 13 September, was spotlessly fine and not wickedly hot, for the scimitar edge of the summer sun was by now mercifully blunted.

Punctually at eleven the four of them packed into the V-8, and Mr Prinkle facetiously exclaimed, 'Chai! Chai!' as though urging on an elephant, for he was very proud of his few words of the lingo. So, soon they were speeding through the tea-gardens and raising a dense, low-lying, light ochre dust.

At length they reached the chotal, or head of the little pass, and there below them was the Kulan Valley, the river like a sapphire necklace in an emerald case, and above it the glossy, sparkling silver of the gods of the Hindu Kush stroked the sky. They paused a moment to revel in this view, though only · Nancy really recognized how flabbergastingly well composed it was, and how brilliantly it just escaped the obvious. Then they began coasting down to the vale.

'What is the meaning of the word Churel, Mr Sen?' asked Nancy, turning round in the front seat to face that person.

Mr Sen paused before replying. He was still angry and indignant, and this was a very dangerous question, of which he'd have preferred to have received notice. He decided it was a moment for the exercise of that gift for sarcasm on which he prided himself, and which was often a good defensive dialectical weapon. With him sarcasm and verbosity went arm in arm.

'The word Churel,' he remarked in his most sing-song tone, 'is a typical example of the poor superstitious Indians' ineradicable tendency to charge vague and fearful notions with materialistic implications.'

'Very likely,' said Nancy, trying not to laugh, 'but what does it mean?'

'The poor primitive Indians,' replied Mr Sen, 'cherish fearful ideas about women who pass over in giving birth to their young. They fondly imagine that the spirits or ghosts of such unfortunate females continue to haunt the earth, with a view of seizing the soul of some living child and carrying it off to the void to comfort them. Then, if they are successful in this morbid ambition, they are content, and roam their favourite places no more. Such ghosts are called "Churels", and this gorge we are visiting is one of such favoured places. It is all very absurd, of course.'

'I think it's a strange and sad idea,' said Nancy; 'the child dies, I suppose?'

'Oh yes, naturally,' smiled Mr Sen; 'it's vital principle has been removed.'

'*You* don't believe such stuff, I hope,' said Mr Prinkle insinuatingly.

Mr Sen who believed it with fearful intensity, replied, 'Naturally, since my conversion to the true faith and the instruction of two reverends, I regard the concept as wholly fatuous.'

'It is queer,' said Nancy, frowning, 'how such ideas ever get into people's heads. I mean someone must have *started* the Churel idea. Why? Does the word mean anything else, Mr Sen? Has it any secondary meaning?'

'Oh no, indeed. Just what I have informed you. Just a silly Indian notion, altogether.'

'Then I can't quite understand it,' said Nancy.

Mr Prinkle decided it was time a superior intellect was brought to bear on the topic. Pulling out the vox parsonica stop, he proclaimed authoritatively, 'My dear girl, it is one of a myriad such phantasies connected in some way with procreation, which is always a kinetic mystery to the primitive mind. Once formed, the phantasy is *named*, inevitably. These encapsuled animistic relics in the human mind are very hard to eradicate, but I'm going to do my best to cleanse the midden; I regard it as an essential part of my mission to India.'

Mr Sen maintained his bland grin, but behind it a formidable seethe of emotions was writhing: contempt, rage, hate, a growing fear and a horrid hope. He glanced at Nikky, who was regarding him in a steady, searching way. Mr Sen wriggled uneasily; for some complex reason he was perturbed by that appraising stare.

'What are you talking about, Mummy?' asked the small one.

'Oh nothing,' replied Nancy. 'We shall soon be there.'

The Gorge of the Churels ran up from the eastern flank of the valley. It was a re-entrant from the low, limestone cliff which lined the vale. It had been burrowed out during countless aeons by a hard-running little stream, which rose somewhere in the foothills and fed the Kulan half a mile away. The entrance to it was narrow and stark, but it widened out to a breadth of some five hundred yards and was a mile or so in depth. At its eastern ending the burn fell over a steep bank, died for a moment in a deep circular basin, and poured out again from its western rim. The gorge was full of deodars, peepuls and kikars, and a few great dominating teaks. The surface was thick grass interspersed with bamboo. It was a very shady, aloof place, death-quiet, save for the splash of the fall, the murmur of the burn, and the occasional cry of a bird.

They parked the car just inside it and then strolled about for a while.

'It *is* rather a sombre spot,' said Nancy, 'though,' she added hurriedly, 'quite lovely of course.'

Mr Sen grinned.

Mr Prinkle said: 'Now *you're* getting fanciful, my dear. I don't find it sombre in the least; quite charming. Remote, no doubt, and cut off from the busy world of men; but what a relief that is! If it were in England, it would be coated with orange peel and old newspapers, and cacophonous with gramophones and loud speakers. Let's have lunch.'

They spread out the cloth in the shade of a mighty deodar. Little Nikky was very quiet during meal and not as hungry as usual. His eyes kept wandering in the direction of the pool.

'You'd like to fish in there, wouldn't you, darling?' said Nancy.

'Yes, Mummy,' he replied listlessly.

'Before we come again we must get a little rod for you,' said Nancy.

Nikky just smiled in a perfunctory way.

After the feast they smoked a cigarette, chatted for a while, and then Mr Prinkle yawned and said, 'I feel like a nap. Most unusual for me, the reaction from a very hard week I suppose.'

'I do, too,' said Nancy. 'Would you like forty winks, Nikky?'

'No, thank you, Mummy.'

'Well, what would you like to do?'

'Just play about.'

'Then don't go near the pond! What about you, Mr Sen?'

'I do not wish to sleep, thank you,' grinned that person. 'I will watch over the young shaver, if that is what you imply.'

'That's very kind of you. Just see he doesn't get into mischief. Now remember, darling, be good and *don't* go near the pond!'

'All right, Mummy.'

Mr and Mrs Prinkle then stretched themselves under a long branch of the deodar, hung out like the groping arm of a blind man. They put handkerchiefs over their faces, wriggled into comfortable positions and soon slept.

Mr Sen squatted down in the open whence he could keep Nikky in view, and began to think in his own tongue. He didn't like this place; it stirred ancestral forebodings. These callow, impercipient Europeans were fools to have come here—with a child. Because they were blind they thought there was nothing to see. Yes, he really hated them, despised them from the bottom of his heart. Let him be open with himself for once—wide open! Of course it paid him—not well, but enough—to pretend to like and respect them and their idiotic gods, but they were blind and insolent and conceited fools. If they were not, they would worship Brahma, the greatest of all god-ideas. Not, he thought to himself, that I am really greatly impressed even by Brahma, for what does he *do*? Now that I am being open, I will confess he seems to *do* nothing, and evil spirits freely defy him.

He would like to see these people punished for their vanity and stupidity. What would be the worst punishment they could suffer? The loss of the child, of course, and this was a fearful death-trap for children. No woman would bring her child near the gorge by night, and not even by day unless protected by some appropriate powerful charm. He ran his tongue across his lips. What was little Nikky doing? He was kneeling down and staring across towards the pool, an oddly intent look on his face. Mr Sen watched him for a few moments and then followed the direction of his gaze. He leaned forward, peered hard, and drew in his breath with a quick hiss. His face became set and rigid with terror. Just to the left of the basin was a circular grove of mulberry trees, and at the centre of this circle was something which had no business to be there; at least so it seemed to Mr Sen. The sun's rays coiling between the leaves, dappled and, as it were, camouflaged this intruder, so that it appeared just a thing of light and shade; like every other visible entity in the world, of course, yet somehow this was essentially incorporeal, not linked to earth, but painted thinly on the freckled air. It was this appearance which little Nikky seemed to be observing so intently, yet intermittently.

Sometimes he would look down and pretend to be playing with the grass and flowers, and then he would glance up swiftly and stealthily and become quite still and taut. He was, Mr Sen decided, trying in an innocent way to deceive anyone who might be watching him. And Mr Sen knew why he was doing this, and trembled. He pulled up the sleeve of his right arm where, round the biceps, was what resembled a large leather wrist-watch strap, but in the container was a piece of narrow scroll on which a very sacred text was inscribed. For this was a charm, idolatrously obtained, by Mr Sen, from an extremely ancient and holy Sadhu, and, though not a protection against the full power of certain demons, a great shield for sure against most dangers and evils. His possession of it he kept a close dark secret, especially from his reverend employers. He touched this charm and muttered to himself.

Presently little Nikky toddled slowly forward in the direction of the grove. Then he knelt again and nervously plucked up some blades of grass. The fretted and dubious shape remained motionless.

After a while the child glanced up and moved forward again. He was now about fifteen yards from the grove. Mr Sen began to tremble violently, not only with fear, but from some subtle emotion, atavistic and nameless. His teeth clattered and he clutched the charm. Again little Nikky glanced up from his feigned play and stared hard in front of him. Mr Sen could see he was smiling in a vague, rapt way. It was very quiet, the light toss of the fall, the stir of the brook seemed but to join the stillness and intensify it. But Mr Sen was aware of a horrid tension in the air, like the swelling potential before the lightning stroke.

Suddenly Nikky uttered a happy little cry and ran forward as fast as his chubby legs would carry him. As he reached the verge of the grove, it seemed to the entranced and quivering Mr Sen as though the thing of light and shadow moved forward to meet and greet him. The little boy threw out his arms and in another moment the two would have mingled.

And then Mr Sen, as the odd and pregnant saying has it, 'came to himself'. He leapt to his feet and ran headlong towards the grove

257

Mr Sen leapt to his feet and ran headlong towards the grove.

fiercely clutching the charm and uttering repeatedly, loudly, and hoarsely some words of warning or incantation. Little Nikky paused, glanced round and fell on his face, and the thing of light and shade seemed to lose its form and pass into the stippled air.

Mr and Mrs Prinkle came running out, dishevelled and heavy with sleep.

'What's the matter?' they cried in unison to Mr Sen, who had taken Nikky in his arms.

'The little chap fell down,' he said shrilly. 'Perhaps a touch of the sun; I do not know!'

Nancy seized the child, who had fallen into a deep sleep.

'We'd better get him home,' said Mr Prinkle urgently. And soon they had packed up and were hurrying on their way.

Presently little Nikky stirred from his deep doze, opened his round blue eyes, smiled and said, 'Pretty lady!' and went to sleep again.

'He's quite all right,' laughed Nancy in relief; 'when he smiles like that he's always well and happy.'

'Just a little tired perhaps,' said her husband resignedly. Just a false alarm. Rather spoilt our day!'

'Why did you shout, Mr Sen?' asked Nancy.

'Ah!' grinned that person, 'I am ashamed to confess it, but *I* had a snooze too. Very negligent of me, but I was properly punished, for I had a very bad dream, I assure you.'

'What did you dream about?' asked Mr Prinkle mockingly, 'those bereft and acquisitive Churels!'

'Ah no,' replied Mr Sen with a protesting smile, and slipping his left arm up his right sleeve; 'it is not fair of you, Mr Prinkle, to pull my legs so, and remind me of the ridiculous superstitions of us poor, ignorant, primitive Indians!'

MAN-SIZE IN MARBLE

E. Nesbit

Although every word of this story is as true as despair, I do not expect people to believe it. Nowadays a 'rational explanation' is required before belief is possible. Let me, then, at once offer the 'rational explanation' which finds most favour among those who have heard the tale of my life's tragedy. It is held that we were 'under a delusion', Laura and I, on that 31st of October; and that this supposition places the whole matter on a satisfactory and believable basis. The reader can judge, when he, too, has heard my story, how far this is an 'explanation', and in what sense it is 'rational'. There were three who took part in this: Laura and I and another man. The other man still lives, and can speak to the truth of the least credible part of my story.

I never in my life knew what it was to have as much money as I required to supply the most ordinary needs—good colours, books, and cab-fares—and when we were married we knew quite well that we should only be able to live at all by 'strict punctuality and attention to business'. I used to paint in those days, and Laura used to write, and we felt sure we could keep the pot at least simmering. Living in town was out of the question, so we went to look for a cottage in the country, which should be at once sanitary and picturesque. So rarely do these two qualities meet in one cottage that our search was for some time quite fruitless. But when we got away from friends and house-agents, on our honeymoon, our wits grew clear again, and we knew a pretty cottage when at last we saw one.

It was at Brenzett—a little village set on a hill over against the southern marshes. We had gone there, from the seaside village where we were staying, to see the church, and two fields from the church we found this cottage. It stood quite by itself, about two miles from the village. It was a long, low building, with rooms sticking out in unexpected places. There was a bit of stonework—ivy-covered and moss-grown, just two old rooms, all that was left of a big house that had once stood there—and round this stonework the house had grown up. Stripped of its roses and jasmine it would have been hideous. As it stood it was charming, and after a brief examination we took it. It was absurdly cheap. There was a jolly old-fashioned garden, with grass paths, and no end of hollyhocks and sunflowers, and big lilies. From the window you could see the marsh-pastures, and beyond them the blue, thin line of the sea.

We got a tall old peasant woman to do for us. Her face and figure were good, though her cooking was of the homeliest; but she understood all about gardening, and told us all the old names of the coppices and cornfields, and the stories of the smugglers and highway-men, and, better still, of the 'things that walked', and of the 'sights' which met one in lonely glens of a starlight night. We soon came to leave all the domestic business to Mrs Dorman, and to use her legends in little magazine stories which brought in the jingling guinea.

We had three months of married happiness, and did not have a single quarrel. One October evening I had been down to smoke a pipe with the doctor—our only neighbour—a pleasant young Irishman. Laura had stayed at home to finish a comic sketch. I left her laughing over her own jokes, and came in to find her a crumpled heap of pale muslin, weeping on the window seat.

'Good heavens, my darling, what's the matter?' I cried, taking her in my arms.

'What is the matter? Do speak.'

'It's Mrs Dorman,' she sobbed.

'What has she done?' I inquired, immensely relieved.

'She says she must go before the end of the month, and she says her niece is ill; she's gone down to see her now, but I don't believe that's the reason, because her niece is always ill. I believe someone has been setting her against us. Her manner was so queer—'

'Never mind, Pussy,' I said; 'whatever you do, don't cry, or I shall have to cry to keep you in countenance, and then you'll never respect your man again.'

'But you see,' she went on, 'it is really serious, because these village people are so sheepy, and if one won't do a thing you may be quite sure none of the others will. And I shall have to cook the dinners and wash up the hateful greasy plates; and you'll have to carry cans of water about and clean the boots and knives—and we shall never have any time for work or earn any money or anything.'

I represented to her that even if we had to perform these duties the day would still present some margin for other toils and recreations. But she refused to see the matter in any but the greyest light.

'I'll speak to Mrs Dorman when she comes back, and see if I can't come to terms with her,' I said. 'Perhaps she wants a rise in her screw. It will be all right. Let's walk up to the church.'

The church was a large and lonely one, and we loved to go there, especially upon bright nights. The path skirted a wood, cut through it once, and ran along the crest of the hill through two meadows, and round the churchyard wall, over which the old yews loomed in black masses of shadow.

This path, which was partly paved, was called 'the bier-walk', for it had long been the way by which the corpses had been carried to burial. The churchyard was richly treed, and was shaded by great elms which stood just outside and stretched their majestic arms in benediction of the happy dead. A large, low porch let one into the building by a Norman doorway and a heavy oak door studded with iron. Inside, the arches rose into darkness, and between them the reticulated windows, which stood out white in the moonlight. In the chancel, the windows were of rich glass, which showed in faint light their noble colouring, and made the black oak of the choir pews hardly more solid than the shadows. But on each side of the altar lay a grey marble figure of a knight in full plate armour lying upon a low slab, with hands held up in everlasting prayer, and these figures, oddly

262

enough, were always to be seen if there was any glimmer of light in the church. Their names were lost, but the peasants told of them that they had been fierce and wicked men, marauders by land and sea, who had been the scourge of their time, and had been guilty of deeds so foul that the house they had lived in—the big house, by the way, that had stood on the site of our cottage—had been stricken by lightning and the vengeance of Heaven. But for all that, the gold of their heirs had brought them a place in the church. Looking at the bad, hard faces reproduced in the marble, this story was easily believed.

The church looked at its best and weirdest on that night, for the shadows of the yew tree fell through the windows upon the floor of the nave and touched the pillars with tattered shade. We sat down together without speaking, and watched the solemn beauty of the old church with some of that awe which inspired its early builders. We walked to the chancel and looked at the sleeping warriors. Then we rested some time on the stone seat in the porch, looking out over the stretch of quiet moonlit meadows, feeling in every fibre of our being the peace of the night and of our happy love; and came away at last with a sense that even scrubbing and black-leading were but small troubles at their worst.

Mrs Dorman had come back from the village, and I at once invited her to a tête-à-tête.

'Now, Mrs Dorman,' I said, when I had got her into my painting room, 'what's all this about your not staying with us?'

'I should be glad to get away, sir, before the end of the month,' she answered, with her usual placid dignity.

'Have you any fault to find, Mrs Dorman?'

'None at all, sir: you and your lady have always been most kind I'm sure—'

'Well, what is it? Are your wages not high enough?'

'No, sir, I gets quite enough.'

'Then why not stay?'

'I'd rather not—with some hesitation—'my niece is ill.'

'But your niece has been ill ever since we came. Can't you stay for another month?'

'No, sir, I'm bound to go by Thursday.'

And this was Monday!

'Well, I must say, I think you might have let us know before. There's no time now to get anyone else, and your mistress is not fit to do heavy housework. Can't you stay till next week?'

'I might be able to come back next week.'

'But why must you go this week?' I persisted. 'Come, out with it.'

Mrs Dorman drew the little shawl, which she always wore, tightly across her bosom, as though she were cold. Then she said, with a sort of effort:

'They say, sir, as this was a big house in Catholic times, and there was a many deeds done here.'

The nature of the 'deeds' might be vaguely inferred from the inflection of Mrs Dorman's voice—which was enough to make one's blood run cold. I was glad that Laura was not in the room. She was always nervous, as highly-strung natures are, and I felt that these tales about our house, told by this old peasant woman, with her impressive manner and contagious credulity, might have made our home less dear to my wife.

'Tell me all about it, Mrs Dorman,' I said; 'you needn't mind about telling me. I'm not like the young people who make fun of such things.'

Which was partly true.

'Well, sir'—she sank her voice—'you may have seen in the church, beside the altar, two shapes.'

'You mean the effigies of the knights in armour,' I said cheerfully.

'I mean them two bodies, drawed out man-size in marble,' she returned, and I had to admit that her description was a thousand times more graphic than mine, to say nothing of a certain weird force and uncanniness about the phrase 'drawed out man-size in marble.'

'They do say, as on All Saints' Eve them two bodies sits up on their slabs, and gets off them, and then walks down the aisle, *in their marble'* —another good phrase, Mrs Dorman)—'and as the church clock strikes eleven they walks out of the church door, and over the graves, and along the bier-walk, and if it's a wet night there's the marks of their feet in the morning.'

'And where do they go?' I asked, rather fascinated.

'They comes back here to their home, sir, and if anyone meets them—'

'Well, what then?' I asked.

But no—not another word could I get from her, save that her niece was ill and she must go.

'Whatever you do, sir, lock the door early on All Saints' Eve, and make the cross-sign over the doorstep and on the windows.'

'But has anyone ever seen these things?' I persisted. 'Who was here last year?'

'No one, sir; the lady as owned the house only stayed here in summer, and she always went to London a full month afore *the* night. And I'm sorry to inconvenience you and your lady, but my niece is ill and I must go on Thursday.'

I could have shaken her for her absurd reiteration of that obvious fiction, after she had told me her real reasons.

I did not tell Laura the legend of the shapes that 'walked in their marble', partly because a legend concerning our house might perhaps trouble my wife, and partly, I think, from some more occult reason. This was not quite the same to me as any other story, and I did not want to talk about it till the day it was over. I had very soon ceased to think of the legend, however. I was painting a portrait of Laura, against the lattice window, and I could not think of much else. I had got a splendid background of yellow and grey sunset, and was working away with enthusiasm at her face. On Thursday Mrs Dorman went. She relented, at parting, so far as too say:

'Don't you put yourself about too much, ma'am, and if there's any little thing I can do next week I'm sure I shan't mind.'

Thursday passed off pretty well. Friday came. It is about what happened on that Friday that this is written.

I got up early, I remember, and lighted the kitchen fire, and had just achieved a smoky success when my little wife came running down as sunny and sweet as the clear October morning itself. We prepared breakfast together, and found it very good fun. The housework was soon done, and when brushes and brooms and pails were quiet again the house was still indeed. Is it wonderful what a difference one makes in a house. We really missed Mrs Dorman, quite apart from considerations concerning pots and pans. We spent the day in dusting our books and putting them straight, and dined gaily on cold steak and coffee. Laura was, if possible, brighter and gayer and sweeter than usual, and I began to think that a little domestic toil was really good for her. We had never been so merry since we were married, and the walk we had that afternoon was, I think, the happiest time of all my life. When we had watched the deep scarlet clouds slowly pale into leaden grey against a pale green sky and saw the white mists curl up along the hedgerows in the distant marsh we came back to the house hand in hand.

'You are sad, my darling,' I said, half-jestingly, as we sat down together in our little parlour. I expected a disclaimer, for my own silence had been the silence of complete happiness. To my surprise she said:

'Yes, I think I am sad, or, rather, I am uneasy. I don't think I'm very well. I have shivered three or four times since we came in; and it is not cold, is it?

'No,' I said, and hoped it was not a chill caught from the treacherous mists that roll up from the marshes in the dying night. No —she said, she did not think so. Then, after a silence, she spoke suddenly:

'Do you ever have presentiments of evil?'

'No,' I said, smiling, 'and I shouldn't believe in them if I had.'

'I do,' she went on; 'the night my father died I knew it, though he was right away in the North of Scotland.' I did not answer in words.

She sat looking at the fire for some time in silence, gently stroking my hand. At last she sprang up, came behind me, and, drawing my head back, kissed me.

'There, it's over now,' she said. 'What a baby I am! Come, light the candles, and we'll have some of these new Rubenstein duets.'

And we spent a happy hour or two at the piano.

At about half-past ten I began to long for the goodnight pipe, but Laura looked so white that I felt it would be brutal of me to fill our sitting-room with the fumes of strong cavendish.

'I'll take my pipe outside,' I said.

'Let me come, too.'

'No, sweetheart, not tonight; you're much too tired. I shan't be long. Go to bed, or I shall have an invalid to nurse tomorrow as well as the boots to clean.'

I kissed her and was turning to go when she flung her arms round my neck and held me as if she would never let me go again. I stroked her hair.

'Come, Pussy, you're over-tired. The housework has been too much for you.'

She loosened her clasp a little and drew a deep breath.

'No. We've been very happy today, Jack, haven't we? Don't stay out too long.'

'I won't, my dearie.'

I strolled out of the front door, leaving it unlatched. What a night it was! The jagged masses of heavy dark cloud were rolling at intervals from horizon to horizon, and thin white wreaths covered the stars. Through all the rush of the cloud river the moon swam, breasting the waves and disappearing again in the darkness.

I walked up and down, drinking in the beauty of the quiet earth and the changing sky. The night was absolutely silent. Nothing seemed to be abroad. There was no skurrying of rabbits, or twitter of the half-asleep birds. And though the clouds went sailing across the sky, the wind that drove them never came low enough to rustle the dead leaves in the woodland paths. Across the meadows I could see the church tower standing out black and grey against the sky. I walked there thinking over our three months of happiness.

I heard a bell-beat from the church. Eleven already! I turned to go in, but the night held me. I could not go back into our little warm rooms yet. I would go up to the church.

I looked in at the low window as I went by. Laura was half-lying on her chair in front of the fire. I could not see her face, only her little head showed dark against the pale blue wall. She was quite still. Asleep, no doubt.

I walked slowly along the edge of the wood. A sound broke the stillness of the night, it was a rustling in the wood. I stopped and listened. The sound stopped too. I went on, and now distinctly heard another step than mine answer mine like an echo. It was a poacher or a wood-stealer, most likely, for these were not unknown in our Arcadian neighbourhood. But whoever it was, he was a fool not to step more lightly. I turned into the wood and now the footstep seemed to come from the path I had just left. It must be an echo, I thought. The wood looked perfect in the moonlight. The large dying ferns and the brushwood showed where through thinning foliage the pale light came down. The tree trunks stood up like Gothic columns all around me.

They reminded me of the church, and I turned into the bier-walk, and passed through the corpse-gate between the graves to the low porch.

I paused for a moment on the stone seat where Laura and I had watched the fading landscape. Then I noticed that the door of the church was open, and I blamed myself for having left it unlatched the other night. We were the only people who ever cared to come to the church except on Sundays, and I was vexed to think that through our carelessness the damp autumn airs had had a chance of getting in and injuring the old fabric. I went in. It will seem strange, perhaps, that I should have gone halfway up the aisle before I remembered—with a sudden chill, followed by as sudden a rush of self-contempt—that this was the very day and hour when, according to tradition, the 'shapes drawed out man-size in marble' began to walk.

Having thus remembered the legend, and remembered it with a shiver, of which I was ashamed, I could not do otherwise than walk up towards the altar, just to look at the figures—as I said to myself; really what I wanted was to assure myself, first, that I did not believe the legend, and, secondly, that it was not true. I was rather glad that I had come. I thought now I could tell Mrs Dorman how vain her fancies were, and how peacefully the marble figures slept on through the ghastly hour. With my hands in my pockets I passed up the aisle. In the grey dim light the eastern end of the church looked larger than usual, and the arches above the two tombs looked larger too. The moon came out and showed me the reason. I stopped short, my heart gave a leap that nearly choked me, and then sank sickeningly.

The 'bodies drawed out man-size' *were gone*! and their marble slabs lay wide and bare in the vague moonlight that slanted through the east window.

Were they really gone, or was I mad? Clenching my nerves, I stooped and passed my hand over the smooth slabs, and felt their flat unbroken surface. Had someone taken the things away? Was it some vile practical joke? I would make sure, anyway. In an instant I had made a torch of a newspaper, which happened to be in my pocket, and, lighting it, held it high above my head. Its yellow glare illumined the dark arches and those slabs. The figures *were* gone. And I was alone in the church; or was I alone?

Each side of the altar lay a grey marble figure of a knight.

And then a horror seized me, a horror indefinable and indescribable—an overwhelming certainty of supreme and accomplished calamity. I flung down the torch and tore along the aisle and out through the porch, biting my lips as I ran to keep myself from shrieking aloud. Oh, was I mad—or what was this that possessed me? I leaped the churchyard wall and took the straight cut across the fields, led by the light from our windows. Just as I got over the first stile a dark figure seemed to spring out of the ground. Mad still with that certainty of misfortune, I made for the thing that stood in my path, shouting, 'Get out of the way, can't you!'

But my push met with a more vigorous resistance than I had expected. My arms were caught just above the elbow and held as in a vice, and the raw-boned Irish doctor actually shook me.

'Let me go, you fool,' I gasped. 'The marble figures have gone from the church; I tell you they've gone.'

He broke into a ringing laugh. 'I'll have to give ye a draught to-morrow, I see. Ye've been smoking too much and listening to old wives' tales.'

'I tell you I've seen he bare slabs.'

'Well, come back with me. I'm going up to old Palmer's—his daughter's ill; we'll look in at the church and let me see the bare slabs.'

'You go, if you like,' I said, a little less frantic for his laughter; 'I'm going home to my wife.'

'Rubbish man,' said he; 'd'ye think I'll permit that? Are ye to go saying all yer life that ye've seen solid marble endowed with vitality, and me to go all me life saying ye were a coward? No, sir—ye shan't do ut.'

The night air—a human voice—and I think also the physical contact with this six feet of solid common sense, brought me back a little to my ordinary self, and the word 'coward' was a mental shower-bath.

'Come on, then,' I said sullenly; 'perhaps you're right.'

He still held my arm tightly. We got over the stile and back to the church. All was still as death. The place smelt very damp and earthy. We walked up the aisle. I am not ashamed to confess that I shut my eyes: I knew the figures would not be there. I heard Kelly strike a match.

'Here they are, ye see, right enough; ye've been dreaming or drinking, asking yer pardon for the imputation.'

I opened my eyes. By Kelly's expiring vesta I saw two shapes lying 'in their marble' on their slabs. I drew a deep breath.

'I'm awfully indebted to you,' I said. 'It must have been some trick of light, or I have been working rather hard, perhaps that's it. I was quite convinced they were gone.'

'I'm aware of that,' he answered rather grimly; 'ye'll have to be careful of that brain of yours, my friend, I assure ye.'

He was leaning over and looking at the right-hand figure, whose stony face was the most villainous and deadly in expression.

'By jove,' he said, 'something has been afoot here—this hand is broken.'

And so it was. I was certain that it had been perfect the last time Laura and I had been there.

'Perhaps someone has *tried* to remove them,' said the young doctor.

'Come along,' I said, 'or my wife will be getting anxious. You'll come in and have a drop of whisky and drink confusion to ghosts and better sense to me.'

'I ought to go up to Palmer's, but it's so late now I'd best leave it till the morning,' he replied.

I think he fancied I needed him more than did Palmer's girl, so, discussing how such an illusion could have been possible, and deducing from this experience large generalities concerning ghostly apparitions, we walked up to our cottage. We saw, as we walked up the garden path, that bright light streamed out of the front door, and presently saw that the parlour door was open, too. Had she gone out?

'Come in,' I said, and Dr Kelly followed me into the parlour. It was all ablaze with candles, not only the wax ones, but at least a dozen guttering, glaring tallow dips, stuck in vases and ornaments in unlikely places. Light, I knew, was Laura's remedy for nervousness. Poor child! Why had I left her? Brute that I was.

We glanced round the room, and at first we did not see her. The window was open, and the draught set all the candles flaring one way. Her chair was empty and her handkerchief and book lay on the floor. I turned to the window. There, in the recess of the window, I saw her. Oh, my child, my love, had she gone to that window to watch

271

for me? And what had come into the room behind her? To what had she turned with that look of frantic fear and horror? Oh, my little one, had she thought that it was I whose step she heard, and turned to meet—what?

She had fallen back across a table in the window, and her body lay half on it and half on the window-seat, and her head hung down over the table, the brown hair loosened and fallen to the carpet. Her lips were drawn back, and here eyes wide, wide open. They saw nothing now. What had they seen last?

The doctor moved towards her, but I pushed him aside and sprang to her; caught her in my arms and cried:

'It's all right, Laura! I've got you safe, wifie.'

She fell into my arms in a heap. I clasped her and kissed her, and called her by all her pet names, but I think I knew all the time that she was dead. Her hands were tightly clenched. In one of them she held something fast. When I was quite sure that she was dead, and that nothing mattered at all any more, I let him open her hand to see what she held.

It was a grey marble finger.

THE WOOING OF CHERRY BASNETT

Brian Alderson

A long while back, five, or maybe six generations—catastrophe came upon the family of Michaelsons up at their farm on the fell over C—dale. God alone knows what really happened, because the passing of long time and the to-ing and fro-ing of old rumours have quite obscured whatever facts came to light. All that's known today is that a Michaelson daughter, Alice Michaelson, killed the man she was to marry, was tried for it at York Assizes and hanged.

For sure that might have been the end of the family so far as C—dale was concerned. Most people, I suppose, after a calamity like that, would have upped and offed and no more heard of them after. But the Michaelsons were a tenacious lot—hard and chill, like the land they farmed; and the father, Will Michaelson, hung on and brought up the rest of his clan as though nothing had happened. They went on working their holding, year in year out, but from that time on they lost all comradeliness in the Dale. People would avoid them, look askance, when they came to market or the Sheep Fair, and the family kept to their farms like pariahs, seeming to welcome it. When the children of a generation grew up they'd go off across country to one big town or another and they'd set up for themselves there, but always at least one Michaelson would come back to the Dale and keep the family place going.

A few years back, at the time I'm really talking about—the Michaelson patch was run by old Jacob Michaelson, who was as knotty a chip off the old block as you could ask for. He was a dark, closed, bull of a man, with nothing to say to anyone, and he seemed to tackle everything—house, land, family, the very sheep on the pasture —as though they'd done him a personal affront. It was all the more surprising therefore that he should have a girl like Nan Michaelson, who differed from him every way possible. True, those of us living down in the valley never saw much of her—old Jacob wasn't the man to flaunt anything around the Dale, let alone his daughter. Even so, for the year or two that she went to the parish school, and at the rare times when she'd come down to the village, everyone marked her as a bonny creature—dark, like all her family, perhaps, but warm-dark, demure and sweet-tempered.

Well, I don't know what plans old Jacob had for his daughter Nan, but whatever they were they had to accommodate themselves to something unexpected on the day she encountered Cherry Basnett. He was an old friend of mine was Cherry. We'd been mates at school, we were fellow drinkers at 'The Ram's Head' afterwards, and he was the debonairest fellow you could ever hope to meet. There's no doubt at all that his taking up with Nan Michaelson, if it wasn't ordained by Heaven, at least, once it happened, looked to be the most natural thing on earth.

It all came about, like most natural seeming things, by accident. I suppose Cherry had seen the girl before, and certainly he must have known about her peculiar family, but it was only by chance that he came face-to-face with her that evening in late March when everything began. Apparently he'd been up to his Dad's high pastures where there'd been some trouble over lambs, and on the way down he'd decided to cut across a patch of Michaelson's land and take the plank bridge over the river to make sure of at least an hour or two's drinking time at 'The Ram' (going round by the road we most of us used was twice as far). Anyway it seems that Michaelson had been mucking about with some of the old gates and stiles, blocking them across with drums or barbed-wire, and Cherry was blundering about trying to find a way down to the bridge when who should he meet coming out of a shippon but young Nan

Michaelson, who'd been tending a calf there. The half light of the evening was on her, mussed and draggled as she was at the end of the day, but young Cherry was smitten to the bottom of his boots and from that moment on, he decided, there was to be no other girl for him.

Instead of plunging on down to the bridge he offered to give Nan a hand with the bag and the pail that she'd got—explaining how it was that he'd sprung out of one of her Dad's fields like a moss-trooper. Nan, though, seemed reluctant for him to go back with her up to the house, and instead she left her stuff by the byre and showed him the best way there was now down to the plank bridge along a new path that skirted the edge of a bit of old timber that Michaelson had on his land. They parted that night good friends and it wasn't long before Cherry started taking his way up to Michaelson's place, banging on the door and paying his best addresses to the daughter of the house.

For most of us this all looked straight enough and in places like C—dale it bids fair to have but one consequence; a fact that was not lost on old Jacob. It doesn't seem likely that, for all his black ways, he could have had any objection to Cherry, or the Basnett family; after all, he hardly had anything to do with them from one year's end to the next. But for some reason or other he took against the whole affair. Night after night when Cherry walked up to the farm he got surlier and surlier and Cherry Basnett's springtime wooing began to seem more like a contention against the elements.

The storm broke after a week or two. Sick of the lowering temper of old man Michaelson, sick of not being able to talk or move in the house without being weighed down by the burden of his stare, Cherry decided on a ploy which, at that time, and in that place, was not altogether regular.

'Get your bonnet,' he says to Nan, 'and we'll take a turn down the road.'

'You'll do no such thing,' says old man Michaelson, 'I'll not have any daughter of mine traipsing out this time of night.'

'I should have thought that was for Nan to say,' says Cherry, 'she's of an age now to know what she's about.'

'She's of an age nothing,' says her Dad, 'she's the daughter of this house and she'll bide when I say bide and go when I say go—and that goes for you too, and you can clear out now!'

Well Cherry Basnett was not one for letting anyone shout him down and he was all set for a dust-up when he glanced a moment at Nan. She'd not moved while he and her dad had been glaring at each other, and she didn't move now, but she very gently nodded her head towards the open door and she looked him full in the eyes, loving, hoping, but still, imploring him to go.

So Cherry Basnett left the house, raging as much as ever a chap like him *could* rage, and he took the quick path again down across Michaelson's fields towards the plank bridge. By this time he'd got to know the track quite well and as he skirted the plantation below the shippon he was startled to hear footsteps pacing him among the trees to his left and then to discover Nan waiting for him at the corner of the wood above the field that led down to the river. For all that she must have come a longer way round than he had, and through some of old man Michaelson's blocked stiles too. She seemed suddenly calm and she looked at him again in a way that turned his heart over with sadness and longing.

'I love you, Cherry,' she said to him. 'I know it's not my place to say, but I love you. You mustn't let me go,' and she looked down at the ground.

Well Cherry was all for taking her off with him there and then, but they talked a bit and she made out that her dad was not perhaps the ogre he tried to be and that maybe Cherry might see him again before long, after she'd tried to tidy things up a bit. Meanwhile, though, perhaps they could go on meeting here, at the corner of the wood. It was a place well hidden from the house, and one she could easily get to.

So that's how things went. Every evening after his tea Cherry would cross the plank bridge, walk up Low Field, and meet his Nan at the corner of the wood, and every evening they'd talk of their plans for the future. At first Cherry had thought to get only a few rushed words before Nan should go back to her father, and he'd cling to her hand like a man about to be swept away on a torrent. But Nan was always calm and wonderfully unworried and she'd draw him to her, and as they talked they'd kiss and as they kissed so too they'd move

276

Her wasted body scarcely raised the sheets that covered her.

deeper into the little plantation that shielded them from the world. It was almost as though Nan needed the warmth and ardour of this meeting to protect her against whatever bitterness she had to endure once they were parted, and as the days lengthened and the spring ripened towards hay-time and summer she too seemed to fill and flourish. 'Oh, how I love you!' she'd say to Cherry, kissing him as though to draw the soul out of his body, gorging herself with him as they lay together, evening by evening under the bushes in the little wood.

Just what Cherry thought of all this at the time I don't know. He left off drinking with us at 'The Ram' and what word we got of him was that he was so daft in love with Nan Michaelson that he'd forgotten which end of a pitchfork was which. It wasn't altogether with surprise therefore, knowing what the man's reputation was, that I came upon old Jacob Michaelson storming up the high road one evening as I was setting home from 'The Ram'.

'Where's that young Cherry Basnett!' he was shouting. 'Bring me to him! Bring me to him!'

Well, for a moment I thought that was the least wise thing to do. It looked to me as though old Jacob had uncovered some hanky-panky and was out for vengeance, swift and sure. But after listening to him for a moment and taking a good look at his features I could tell that the man wasn't so much wild with anger as distress and only Cherry Basnett would do to calm him. So I grabbed him by the elbows and gave him a bit of a shake and took him down to Cherry's place to see that we could do.

As you may guess, of course, Cherry wasn't in, but since I knew a bit about his comings and goings I realized that he must be on the hill path to Michaelson's and off we set down to the river and that old plank bridge. Sure enough we'd hardly crossed it when we saw young Cherry in the gloaming, swinging his way down the field towards where we were standing. (It looked to me—with the dew shining to show up the lie of the land—that Cherry had worn something of a private path for himself down old man Michaelson's field.)

'Cherry! Cherry!' shouted Jacob as soon as he spotted him. 'Hey, lad, come here quick!'—and he rushed towards him up the path.

For a moment I fancy Cherry thought his time had come and that now he was to pay for all those secret meetings with old Jacob's daughter. But then he spotted me running towards him close behind Michaelson and then (as I'd done before) he realized that rage was no part of the man's trouble. Michaelson grabbed him by his coat and began to drag him and cajole him back up the path that he'd just descended, babbling all the while in a mad way about 'saving Nan' and, woe, woe, that he'd let everything go so far and not done something sooner.

So we all went up to the farm through the dew-drenched fields, with Michaelson's little wood sighing at us in the night breeze as we passed. And when we got to the house Michaelson seemed to go berserk, dragging us in and imploring us to do what we could—and he took us upstairs to a bedroom.

There, in bed, was Nan—or someone I could only suppose to be Nan, since her father assured us it was so. Her wasted body scarcely raised or ridged the sheets that covered her and on the pillow her head was shrunken to the contours of her skull. Her hair was a web of thin grey strands, matted at the temples, and her eyes were blank and lustreless. It was the carcass of a very old lady, sucked dry by life, and now waiting only for death.

★　　★　　★　　★

There was nothing to be done for Nan Michaelson. We sent to fetch the doctor, something that old Jacob should have had the sense to do weeks ago, but it was all too late and she died that night. And when the time came for the funeral the chaps who carried her coffin said it weighed no more than if she'd been a little child.

People made a great stir as to why she'd died, and Jacob gave it out that it was some kind of wasting fever. According to him all the spark seemed to go out of her the day after he'd had his row with Cherry and she just seemed to fade off. For a long time he'd thought it was nothing but a fit of the sullens because she couldn't get her own way, and he was too stubborn and left it too late to change his opinion.

As for Cherry himself he seemed to go half-mad. When he first saw Nan lying there in the bed he went out like a blown-lamp and for days after he wouldn't look at anyone or speak to anyone. Indeed, not until he left the place for good did he utter a word on the whole train of events and then he told me what had happened, daring me not to believe him. 'But who was she?' he said; 'who was she and where did she go to?' that woman he made love to through those spring nights in the dale.

They weren't questions that I or anyone else could answer, but I will tell you this. One day a few weeks back I went to N— to check out some old property deeds for our part of the world. While I was there I came across a bundle of old sheets and cuttings about the history of C—dale and there among them was an account of 'the trial and melancholy end, of Alice Michaelson.

It seems that she'd had a lover from the village who'd been unfaithful and that she'd stabbed him with the carving-knife 'in a parcel of woodland above Low Field'. Before the murderess 'was launched into eternity' (as the document quaintly put it) 'she showed no sign of repentance. Despite the good offices of the ordinary of the prison, the Rev Mr Greenacre, she went to her end cursing all mankind and swearing a vengeance on those who had blighted her love.'

A TOUGH TUSSLE

Ambrose Bierce

One night in the autumn of 1861 a man sat alone in the heart of a forest in Western Virginia. The region was then, and still is, one of the wildest on the continent—the Cheat Mountain country. There was no lack of people close at hand, however; within two miles of where the man sat was the now silent camp of a whole Federal brigade. Somewhere about—it might be still nearer—was a force of the enemy, the numbers unknown. It was this uncertainty as to its numbers and position that accounted for the man's presence in that lonely spot; he was a young officer of a Federal infantry regiment, and his business there was to guard his sleeping comrades in the camp against a surprise. He was in command of a detachment of men constituting a picket guard. These men he had stationed just at nightfall in an irregular line, determined by the nature of the ground, several hundred yards in front of where he now sat. The line ran through the forest, among the rocks and laurel thickets, the men fifteen or twenty paces apart, all in concealment and under injunction of strict silence and unremitting vigilance. In four hours, if nothing occurred, they would be relieved by a fresh detachment from the reserve now resting in care of its captain some distance away to the left and rear. Before stationing his men the young officer of whom we are speaking had pointed out to his two sergeants the spot at which he would be found in case it should be necessary to consult him, or if his presence at the front line should be required.

It was a quiet enough spot—the fork of an old wood road, on the two branches of which, prolonging themselves deviously forward in the dim moonlight, the sergeants were themselves stationed, a few paces in rear of the line. If driven sharply back by a sudden onset of the enemy—and pickets are not expected to make a stand after firing—the men would come into the converging roads, and, naturally following them to their point of intersection, could be rallied and 'formed'. In his small way the young lieutenant was something of a strategist; if Napoleon had planned as intelligently at Waterloo, he would have won the battle and been overthrown later.

Second Lieutenant Brainerd Byring was a brave and efficient officer, young and comparatively inexperienced as he was in the business of killing his fellow men. He had enlisted in the very first days of the war as a private, with no military knowledge whatever, had been made first sergeant of his company on account of his education and engaging manner, and had been lucky enough to lose his captain by a Confederate bullet; in the resulting promotions he had got a commission. He had been in several engagements, such as they were—at Philippi, Rich Mountain, Carrick's Ford and Greenbrier—and had borne himself with such gallantry as to attract the attention of his superior officers. The exhilaration of battle was agreeable to him, but the sight of the dead, with their clay faces, blank eyes, and stiff bodies, which, when not unnaturally shrunken, were unnaturally swollen, had always intolerably affected him. He felt toward them a kind of reasonless antipathy which was something more than the physical and spiritual repugnance common to us all. Doubtless this feeling was due to his unusually acute sensibilities—his keen sense of the beautiful, which these hideous things outraged. Whatever may have been the cause, he could not look upon a dead body without a loathing which had in it an element of resentment. What others have respected as the dignity of death had to him no existence—was altogether unthinkable. Death was a thing to be hated. It was not picturesque, it had no tender and solemn side—a dismal thing, hideous in all its manifestations and suggestions. Lieutenant Byring was a braver man than anybody knew, for nobody knew his horror of that which he was ever ready to encounter.

Having posted his men, instructed his sergeants, and retired to his station, he seated himself on a log, and, with senses all alert, began his vigil. For greater ease he loosened his sword belt, and, taking his heavy revolver from his holster, laid it on the log beside him. He felt very comfortable, though he hardly gave the fact a thought, so intently did he listen for any sound from the front which might have a menacing significance—a shout, a shot, or the footfall of one of his sergeants coming to apprise him of something worth knowing. From the vast, invisible ocean of moonlight overhead fell, here and there, a slender, broken stream that seemed to plash against the intercepting branches and trickle to earth, forming small white pools among the clumps of laurel. But these leaks were few and served only to accentuate the blackness of his environment, which his imagination found it easy to people with all manner of unfamiliar shapes, menacing, uncanny, or merely grotesque.

He to whom the portentous conspiracy of night and solitude and silence in the heart of a great forest is not an unknown experience needs not to be told what another world it all is—how even the most commonplace and familiar objects take on another character. The trees group themselves differently; they draw closer together, as if in fear. The very silence has another quality than the silence of the day. And it is full of half-heard whispers, whispers that startle—ghosts of sounds long dead. There are living sounds, too, such as are never heard under other conditions: notes of strange night birds, the cries of small animals in sudden encounters with stealthy foes, or in their dreams, a rustling in the dead leaves—it may be the leap of a wood rat, it may be the footstep of a panther. What caused the breaking of that twig?—what the low, alarmed twittering in that bushful of birds? There are sounds without a name, forms without substance, translations in space of objects which have not been seen to move, movements wherein nothing is observed to change its place. Ah, children of the sunlight and the gaslight, how little you know of the world in which you live!

Surrounded at a little distance by armed and watchful friends, Byring felt utterly alone. Yielding himself to the solemn and mysterious spirit of the time and place, he had forgotten the nature of his connection with the visible and audible aspects and phases of the night. The forest was boundless; men and the habitations of men did not exist. The universe was one primeval mystery of darkness, without form and void, himself the sole dumb questioner of its eternal secret. Absorbed in the thoughts born of this mood, he suffered the time to slip away unnoted. Meantime the infrequent patches of white light lying amongst the undergrowth had undergone changes of size, form, and place. In one of them near by, just at the roadside, his eye fell upon an object which he had not previously observed. It was almost before his face as he sat; he could have sworn that it had not before been there. It was partly covered in shadow, but he could see that it was a human figure. Instinctively he adjusted the clasp of his sword belt and laid hold of his pistol—again he was in a world of war, by occupation an assassin.

The figure did not move. Rising, pistol in hand, he approached. The figure lay upon its back, its upper part in shadow, but standing above it and looking down upon the face, he saw that it was a dead body. He shuddered and turned from it with a feeling of sickness and disgust, resumed his seat upon the log, and, forgetting military prudence, struck a match and lit a cigar. In the sudden blackness that followed the extinction of the flame he felt a sense of relief; he could no longer see the object of his aversion. Nevertheless, he kept his eyes set in that direction until it appeared again with growing distinctness. It seemed to have moved a trifle nearer.

'Damn the thing!' he muttered. 'What does it want?'

It did not appear to be in need of anything but a soul.

Byring turned away his eyes and began humming a tune, but he broke off in the middle of a bar and looked at the dead man. Its presence annoyed him, though he could hardly have had a quieter neighbour. He was conscious, too, of a vague, indefinable feeling which was new to him. It was not fear, but rather a sense of the supernatural—in which he did not at all believe.

'I have inherited it,' he said to himself. 'I suppose it will require a thousand years—perhaps ten thousand—for humanity to outgrow this feeling. Where and when did it originate? Away back, probably, in what is called the cradle of the human race—the plains of Central

Asia. What we inherit as a superstition our barbarous ancestors must have held as a reasonable conviction. Doubtless they believed themselves justified by facts whose nature we cannot even conjecture in thinking a dead body a malign thing endowed with some strange power of mischief, with perhaps a will and a purpose to exert it. Possibly they had some awful form of religion of which that was one of the chief doctrines, sedulously taught by their priesthood, just as ours teach the immortality of the soul. As the Aryan moved westward to and through the Caucasus passes and spread over Europe, new conditions of life must have resulted in the formulation of new religions. The old belief in the malevolence of the dead body was lost from the creeds, and even perished from tradition, but it left its heritage of terror, which is transmitted from generation to generation—is as much a part of us as our blood and bones.'

In following out his thoughts he had forgotten that which suggested it; but now his eye fell again upon the corpse. The shadow had now altogether uncovered it. He saw the sharp profile, the chin in the air, the whole face, ghastly white in the moonlight. The clothing was grey, the uniform of a Confederate soldier. The coat and waistcoat, unbuttoned, had fallen away on each side, exposing the white shirt. The chest seemed unnaturally prominent, but the abdomen had sunk in, leaving a sharp projection at the line of the lower ribs. The arms were extended, the left knee was thrust upward. The whole posture impressed Byring as having been studied with a view to the horrible.

'Bah!' he exclaimed; 'he was an actor—he knows how to be dead.'

He drew away his eyes, directing them resolutely along one of the roads leading to the front, and resumed his philosophizing where he had left off.

'It may be that our Central Asian ancestors had not the custom of burial. In that case it is easy to understand their fear of the dead, who really were a menace and an evil. They bred pestilences. Children were taught to avoid the places where they lay, and to run away if by inadvertence they came near a corpse. I think, indeed, I'd better go away from this chap.'

He half rose to do so, then remembered that he told his men in front, and the officer in the rear who was to relieve him, that he could at any time be found at that spot. It was a matter of pride, too. If he abandoned his post, he feared they would think he feared the corpse. He was no coward, and he was not going to incur anybody's ridicule. So he again seated himself, and, to prove his courage, looked boldly at the body. The right arm—the one farthest from him—was now in shadow. He could barely see the hand which, he had before observed, lay at the root of a clump of laurel. There had been no change, a fact which gave him a certain comfort, he could not have said why. He did not at once remove his eyes; that which we do not wish to see has a strange fascination, sometimes irresistible. Of the woman who covers her face with her hands, and looks between the fingers, let it be said that the wits have dealt with her not altogether justly.

Byring suddenly became conscious of a pain in his right hand. He withdrew his eyes from his enemy and looked at it. He was grasping the tilt of his drawn sword so tightly that it hurt him. He observed, too, that he was leaning forward in a strained attitude—crouching like a gladiator ready to spring at the throat of an antagonist. His teeth were clenched, and he was breathing hard. This matter was soon set right, and as his muscles relaxed and he drew a long breath, he felt keenly enough the ludicrousness of the incident. It affected him to laughter. Heavens! what sound was that?—what mindless devil was uttering an unholy glee in mockery of human merriment? He sprang to his feet and looked about him, not recognizing his own laugh.

He could no longer conceal from himself the horrible fact of his cowardice; he was thoroughly frightened! He would have run from the spot, but his legs refused their office; they gave way beneath him, and he sat again upon the log, violently trembling. His face was wet, his whole body bathed in a chill perspiration. He could not even cry out. Distinctly he heard behind him a stealthy tread, as of some wild animal, and dared not look over his shoulder. Had the soulless living joined forces with the soulless dead?—was it an animal? Ah, if he could but be assured of that! But by no effort of will could he now unfix his gaze from the face of the dead man.

I repeat that Lieutenant Byring was a brave and intelligent man. But what would you have? Shall a man cope, single-handed, with so monstrous an alliance as that of night and solitude and silence and

He was crouching like a gladiator ready to spring at an antagonist.

the dead?—while an incalculable host of his own ancestors shriek into the ear of his spirit their coward counsel, sing their doleful death-songs in his heart and disarm his very blood of all its iron? The odds are too great—courage was not made for such rough use as that.

One sole conviction now had the man in possession: that the body moved. It lay nearer to the edge of its plot of light—there could be no doubt of it. It had also moved its arms, for, look, they are both in the shadow! A breath of cold air struck Byring full in the face; the branches of trees above him stirred and moaned. A strongly defined shadow passed across the face of the dead, left it luminous, passed back upon it and left it half obscured. The horrible thing was visibly moving. At that moment a single shot rang out upon the picket line—a lonelier and louder, though more distant, shot than ever had been heard by mortal ear! It broke the spell of that enchanted man; it slew the silence and the solitude, dispersed the hindering host from Central Asia, and released his modern manhood. With a cry like that of some great bird pouncing upon its prey, he sprang forward, hot-hearted for action!

Shot after shot now came in from the front. There were shoutings and confusion, hoof beats and desultory cheers. Away to the rear, in the sleeping camp, was a singing of bugles and a grumble of drums. Pushing through the thickets on either side the roads came the Federal pickets, in full retreat, firing backward at random as they ran. A straggling group that had followed back one of the roads, as instructed, suddenly sprang away into the bushes as half a hundred horsemen thundered by them, striking wildly with their sabres as they passed. At headlong speed these mounted madmen shot past the spot where Byring had sat, and vanished round an angle of the road, shouting and firing their pistols. A moment later there was a roar of musketry, followed by dropping shots—they had encountered the reserve guard in line; and back they came in dire confusion, with here and there an empty saddle and many a maddened horse, bullet-stung, snorting and plunging with pain. It was all over—'an affair of outposts'.

The line was re-established with fresh men, the roll called, the stragglers were reformed. The Federal commander, with a part of his staff, imperfectly clad, appeared upon the scene, asked a few questions, looked exceedingly wise, and retired. After standing at arms for an hour, the brigade in camp 'swore a prayer or two' and went to bed.

Early next morning a fatigue party, commanded by a captain and accompanied by a surgeon, searched the ground for dead and wounded. At the fork of the road, a little to one side, they found two bodies lying close together—that of a Federal officer and that of a Confederate private. The officer had died of a sword thrust through the heart, but not, apparently, until he had inflicted upon his enemy no fewer than five dreadful wounds. The dead officer lay on his face in a pool of blood, the weapon still in his breast. They turned him on his back and the surgeon removed it.

'Gad!'said the captain—'it is Byring!'—adding, with a glance at the other, 'They had a tough tussle.'

The surgeon was examining the sword. It was that of a line officer of Federal infantry—exactly like the one worn by the captain. It was, in fact, Byring's own. The only other weapon discovered was an undischarged revolver in the dead officer's belt.

The surgeon laid down the sword and approached the other body. It was frightfully gashed and stabbed, but there was no blood. He took hold of the left foot and tried to straighten the leg. In the effort the body was displaced. The dead do not wish to be moved when comfortable—it protested with a faint, sickening odour.

The surgeon looked at the captain. The captain looked at the surgeon.

THE MONKEY'S PAW

W.W. Jacobs

Without, the night was cold and wet, but in the small parlour of Laburnam Villa the blinds were drawn and the fire burned brightly. Father and son were at chess, the former, who possessed ideas about the game involving radical changes, putting his king into such sharp and unnecessary perils that it even provoked comment from the white-haired old lady knitting placidly by the fire.

'Hark at the wind,' said Mr White, who, having seen a fatal mistake after it was too late, was amiably desirous of preventing his son from seeing it.

'I'm listening,' said the latter, grimly surveying the board as he stretched out his hand. 'Check.'

'I should hardly think that he'd come tonight,' said his father, with his hand poised over the board.

'Mate,' replied the son.

'That's the worst of living so far out,' bawled Mr White, with sudden and unlooked-for violence; 'of all the beastly, slushy, out-of-the-way places to live in, this is the worst. Pathway's a bog, and the road's a torrent. I don't know what people are thinking about. I suppose because only two houses in the road are let, they think it doesn't matter.'

'Never mind, dear,' said his wife, soothingly; 'perhaps you'll win the next one.'

Mr White looked up sharply, just in time to interrupt a knowing glance between mother and son. The words died away on his lips, and he hid a guilty grin in his thin grey beard.

'There he is,' said Herbert White, as the gate banged to loudly and heavy footsteps came towards the door.

The old man rose with hospitable haste, and opening the door, was heard condoling with the new arrival. The new arrival also condoled with himself, so that Mrs White said, 'Tut, tut!' and coughed gently as her husband entered the room, followed by a tall, burly man, beady of eye and rubicund of visage.

'Sergeant-Major Morris,' he said, introducing him.

The sergeant-major shook hands, and taking the proffered seat by the fire, watched contentedly while his host got out whisky and tumblers and stood a small copper kettle on the fire.

At the third glass his eyes got brighter, and he began to talk, the little family circle regarding with eager interest this visitor from distant parts, as he squared his shoulders in the chair and spoke of wild scenes and doughty deeds; of wars and plagues and strange peoples.

'Twenty-one years of it,' said Mr White, nodding at his wife and son. 'When he went away he was a slip of a youth in the warehouse. Now look at him.'

'He don't look to have taken much harm,' said Mrs White, politely.

'I'd like to go to India myself,' said the old man, 'just to look round a bit, you know.'

'Better where you are,' said the sergeant-major, shaking his head. He put down the empty glass, and sighing softly, shook it again.

'I should like to see those old temples and fakirs and jugglers,' said the old man. 'What was that you started telling me the other day about a monkey's paw or something, Morris?'

'Nothing,' said the soldier, hastily. 'Leastways nothing worth hearing.'

'Monkey's paw?' said Mrs White, curiously.

'Well, it's just a bit of what you might call magic, perhaps,' said the sergeant-major, offhandedly.

His three listeners leaned forward eagerly. The visitor absent-mindedly put his empty glass to his lips and then set it down again. His host filled it for him.

'To look at,' said the sergeant-major, fumbling in his pocket, 'it's just an ordinary little paw, dried to a mummy.'

He took something out of his pocket and proffered it. Mrs White drew back with a grimace, but her son, taking it, examined it curiously.

'And what is there special about it?' inquired Mr White as he took it from his son, and having examined it, placed it upon the table.

'It had a spell put on it by an old fakir,' said the sergeant-major, 'a very holy man. He wanted to show that fate ruled people's lives, and that those who interfered with it did so to their sorrow. He put a spell on it so that three separate men could each have three wishes from it.'

His manner was so impressive that his bearers were conscious that their light laughter jarred somewhat.

'Well, why don't you have three, sir?' said Herbert White, cleverly.

The soldier regarded him in the way that middle age is wont to regard presumptuous youth. 'I have,' he said, quietly, and his blotchy face whitened.

'And did you really have the three wishes granted?' asked Mrs White.

'I did,' said the sergeant-major, and his glass tapped against his strong teeth.

'And has anybody else wished?' persisted the old lady.

'The first man had his three wishes. Yes,' was the reply; 'I don't know what the first two were, but the third was for death. That's how I got the paw.'

His tones were so grave that a hush fell upon the group.

'If you've had your three wishes, it's no good to you now, then, Morris,' said the old man at last. 'What do you keep it for?'

The soldier shook his head. 'Fancy, I suppose,' he said, slowly. 'I did have some idea of selling it, but I don't think I will. It has caused enough mischief already. Besides, people won't buy. They think it's a fairy tale; some of them, and those who do think anything of it want to try it first and pay me afterwards.'

292

He heard the creaking of the bolt as it came slowly back.

'If you could have another three wishes,' said the old man, eyeing him keenly, 'would you have them?'

'I don't know,' said the other. 'I don't know.'

He took the paw, and dangling it between his forefinger and thumb suddenly threw it upon the fire. White, with a slight cry, stooped down and snatched it off.

'Better let it burn,' said the soldier, solemnly.

'If you don't want it, Morris,' said the other, 'give it to me.'

'I won't,' said his friend, doggedly. 'I threw it on the fire. If you keep it, don't blame me for what happens. Pitch it on the fire again like a sensible man.'

The other shook his head and examined his new possession closely. 'How do you do it?' he inquired.

'Hold it up in your right hand and wish aloud,' said the sergeant-major, 'but I warn you of the consequences.'

'Sounds like the *Arabian Nights*,' said Mrs White, as she rose and began to set the supper. 'Don't you think you might wish for four pairs of hands for me?'

Her husband drew the talisman from pocket, and then all three burst into laughter as the sergeant-major, with a look of alarm on his face, caught him by the arm.

'If you must wish,' he said gruffly, 'wish for something sensible.'

Mr White dropped it back in his pocket, and placing chairs, motioned his friend to the table. In the business of supper the talisman was partly forgotten, and afterward the three sat listening in an enthralled fashion to a second instalment of the soldier's adventures in India.

'If the tale about the monkey's paw is not more truthful than those he has been telling us,' said Herbert, as the door closed behind their guest, just in time for him to catch the last train, 'we sha'nt make much out of it.'

'Did you give him anything for it, father?' inquired Mrs White, regarding her husband closely.

'A trifle,' said he, colouring slightly. 'He didn't want it, but I made him take it. And he pressed me again to throw it away.'

'Likely,' said Herbert, with pretended horror. 'Why, we're going to be rich, and famous and happy. Wish to be an emperor, father, to begin with; then you can't be henpecked.'

He darted round the table, pursued by the maligned Mrs White armed with an antimacassar.

Mr White took the paw from his pocket and eyed it dubiously. 'I don't know what to wish for, and that's a fact,' he said, slowly. 'It seems to me I've got all I want.'

'If you only cleared the house, you'd be quite happy, wouldn't you?' said Herbert, with his hand on his shoulder. 'Well, wish for two hundred pounds, then, that'll just do it.'

His father, smiling shamefacedly at his own credulity, held up the talisman, as his son, with a solemn face, somewhat marred by a wink at his mother, sat down at the piano and struck a few impressive chords.

'I wish for two hundred pounds,' said the old man distinctly.

A fine crash from the piano greeted the words, interrupted by a shuddering cry from the old man. His wife and son ran toward him.

'It moved,' he cried, with a glance of disgust at the object as it lay on the floor. 'As I wished, it twisted in my hand like a snake.'

'Well, I don't see the money,' said his son as he picked it up and placed it on the table, 'and I bet I never shall.'

'It must have been your fancy, father,' said his wife, regarding him anxiously.

He shook his head. 'Never mind, though; there's no harm done, but it gave me a shock all the same.'

They sat down by the fire again while the two men finished their pipes. Outside, the wind was higher than ever, and the old man started nervously at the sound of a door banging upstairs. A silence unusual and depressing settled upon all three, which lasted until the old couple rose to retire for the night.

'I expect you'll find the cash tied up in a big bag in the middle of your bed,' said Herbert, as he bade them good night, 'and something horrible squatting up on top of the wardrobe watching you as you pocket your ill-gotten gains.'

He sat alone in the darkness, gazing at the dying fire, and seeing faces in it. The last face was so horrible and so simian that he gazed at it in amazement. It got so vivid that, with a little uneasy laugh, he felt on the table for a glass containing a little water to throw over it.

His hand grasped the monkey's paw, and with a little shiver he wiped his hand on his coat and went up to bed.

★　　　★　　　★　　　★

In the brightness of the wintry sun next morning as it streamed over the breakfast table he laughed at his fears. There was an air of prosaic wholesomeness about the room which it had lacked on the previous night, and the dirty, shrivelled little paw was pitched on the sideboard with a carelessness which betokened no great belief in its virtues.

'I suppose all old soldiers are the same,' said Mrs White. 'The idea of our listening to such nonsense! How could wishes be granted in these days? And if they could, how could two hundred pounds hurt you, father?'

'Might drop on his head from the sky,' said the frivolous Herbert.'

'Morris said the things happened so naturally,' said his father, 'that you might if you so wished attribute it to coincidence.'

'Well, don't break into the money before I come back,' said Herbert as he rose from the table. 'I'm afraid it'll turn you into a mean, avaricious man, and we shall have to disown you.'

His mother laughed, and following him to the door, watched him down the road; and returning to the breakfast table, was very happy 't the expense of her husband's credulity. All of which did not prevent her from referring somewhat shortly to retired sergeant-majors of bibulous habits when she found that the post brought a tailor's bill.

'Herbert will have some more of his funny remarks, I expect, when he comes home,' she said, as they sat at dinner.

'I dare say,' said Mr White, pouring himself out some beer: 'but for all that, the thing moved in my hand; that I'll swear to.'

'You thought it did,' said the old lady soothingly.

'I say it did,' replied the other. 'There was no thought about it; I had just—What's the matter?'

His wife made no reply. She was watching the mysterious movements of a man outside, who, peering in an undecided fashion at the house, appeared to be trying to make up his mind to enter. In mental connection with the two hundred pounds, she noticed that the stranger was well dressed, and wore a silk hat of glossy newness. Three times he paused at the gate, and then walked on again. The fourth time he stood with his hand upon it, and then with sudden resolution flung it open and walked up the path. Mrs White at the same moment placed her hands behind her, and hurriedly unfastening the strings of her apron, put that useful article of apparel beneath the cushion of her chair.

She brought the stranger, who seemed ill at ease, into the room. He gazed at her furtively, and listened in a preoccupied fashion as the old lady apologized for the appearance of the room, and her husband's coat, a garment which he usually reserved for the garden. She then waited as patiently as her sex would permit, for him to broach his business, but he was at first strangely silent.

'I—was asked to call,' he said at last, and stopped and picked a piece of cotton from his trousers. 'I come from Maw and Meggins.'

The old lady started. 'Is anything the matter?' she asked, breathlessly. 'Has anything happened to Herbert? What is it? What is it?'

Her husband interposed. 'There, there, mother,' he said, hastily. 'Sit down, and don't jump to conclusions. You've not brought bad news, I'm sure, sir'; and he eyed the other wistfully.

'I'm sorry—' began the visitor.

'Is he hurt?' demanded the mother, wildly.

The visitor bowed in assent. 'Badly hurt,' he said, quietly, 'but he is not in any pain.'

'Oh, thank God!' said the old woman, clasping her hands. 'Thank God for that! Thank—'

She broke off suddenly as the sinister meaning of the assurance dawned upon her and she saw the awful confirmation of her fears in the other's averted face. She caught her breath, and turning to her slower-witted husband, laid her trembling old hand upon his. There was a long silence.

'He was caught in the machinery,' said the visitor at length in a low voice.

'Caught in the machinery,' repeated Mr White, in a dazed fashion, 'yes.'

He sat staring blankly out at the window, and taking his wife's hand between his own, pressed it as he had been wont to do in their old courting-days nearly forty years before.

'He was the only one left to us,' he said, turning gently to the visitor. 'It is hard.'

The other coughed, and rising, walked slowly to the window. 'The firm wished me to convey their sincere sympathy with you in your great loss,' he said, without looking round. 'I beg that you will understand I am only their servant and merely obeying orders.'

There was no reply; the old woman's face was white, her eyes staring and her breath inaudible; on the husband's face was a look such as his friend the sergeant might have carried into his first action.

'I was to say that Maw and Meggins discaim all responsibility,' continued the other. 'They admit no liability at all, but in consideration of your son's services, they wish to present you with a certain sum as compensation.'

Mr White dropped his wife's hand, and rising to his feet, gazed with a look of horror at his visitor. His dry lips shaped the words, 'How much?'

'Two hundred pounds,' was the answer.

Unconscious of his wife's shriek, the old man smiled faintly, put out his hands like a sightless man, and dropped, a senseless heap, to the floor.

★　　★　　★　　★

In the huge new cemetery, some two miles distant, the old people buried their dead, and came back to a house steeped in shadow and silence. It was all over so quickly that at first they could hardly realize it, and remained in a state of expectation as though of something else to happen—something else which was to lighten this load, too heavy for old hearts to bear.

But the days passed, and expectation gave place to resignation— the hopeless resignation of the old, sometimes miscalled apathy. Sometimes they hardly exchanged a word, for now they had nothing to talk about, and their days were long to weariness.

It was about a week after that the old man, waking suddenly in the night, stretched out his hand and found himself alone. The room was in darkness, and the sound of subdued weeping came from the window. He raised himself in bed and listened.

'Come back,' he said, tenderly. 'You will be cold.'

'It is colder for my son,' said the old woman, and wept afresh.

The sound of her sobs died away on his ears. The bed was warm, and his eyes heavy with sleep. He dozed fitfully, and then slept until a sudden wild cry from his wife awoke him with a start.

'*The paw!*' she cried wildly. 'The monkey's paw!'

He started up in alarm. 'Where? Where is it? What's the matter?'

She came stumbling across the room toward him. 'I want it,' she said, quietly. 'You've not destroyed it?'

'It's in the parlour, on the bracket,' he replied, marvelling. 'Why?'

She cried and laughed together, and bending over, kissed his cheek.

'I only just thought of it,' she cried, hysterically. 'Why didn't I think of it before? Why didn't you think of it?'

'Think of what?' he questioned.

'The other two wishes,' she replied, rapidly. 'We've only had one.'

'Was not that enough?' he demanded fiercely.

'No,' she cried triumphantly; 'we'll have one more. Go down and get it quickly, and wish our boy alive again.'

The man sat up in bed and flung the bedclothes from his quaking limbs. 'Good God, you are mad!' he cried, aghast.

'Get it,' she panted; 'get it quickly, and wish—Oh, my boy, my boy!'

Her husband struck a match and lit the candle. 'Get back to bed,' he said, unsteadily. 'You don't know what you are saying.'

'We had the first wish granted,' said the old woman, feverishly; 'why not the second?'

'A coincidence,' stammered the old man.

'Go and get it and wish,' cried his wife, quivering with excitement.

The old man turned and regarded her, and his voice shook. 'He has been dead ten days, and besides he—I would not tell you else, but—I could only recognize him by his clothing. If he was too horrible for you to see then, how now?'

'Bring him back?' cried the old woman, and dragged him towards the door. 'Do you think I fear the child I have nursed?'

He went down in the darkness, and felt his way to the parlour, and then to the mantlepiece. The talisman was in its place, and a horrible fear that the unspoken wish might bring his mutilated son before him ere he could escape from the room seized upon him, and he caught his breath as he found that he had lost the direction of the door. His brow cold with sweat, he felt his way round the table, and groped along the wall until he found himself in the small passage with the unwholesome thing in his hand.

Even his wife's face seemed changed as he entered the room. It was white and expectant, and to his fears seemed to have an unnatural look upon it. He was afraid of her.

'*Wish!*' she cried, in a strong voice.

'It is foolish and wicked,' he faltered.

'*Wish!*' repeated his wife.

He raised his hand. 'I wish my son alive again.'

The talisman fell to the floor, and he regarded it fearfully. Then he sank trembling into a chair as the old woman, with burning eyes, walked to the window and raised the blind.

He sat until he was chilled with the cold, glancing occasionally at the figure of the old woman peering through the window. The candle-end, which had burned below the rim of the china candlestick, was throwing pulsating shadows on the ceiling and walls, until, with a flicker larger than the rest, it expired. The old man, with an unspeakable sense of relief at the failure of the talisman, crept back to his bed, and in a minute or two afterwards the old woman came silently and apathetically beside him.

Neither spoke, but lay silently listening to the ticking of the clock. A stair creaked, and a squeaky mouse scurried noisily through the wall. The darkness was oppressive, and after lying for some time screwing up his courage, he took the box of matches, and striking one, went downstairs for a candle.

At the foot of the stairs the match went out, and he paused to strike another; and at the same moment a knock, so quiet and stealthy as to be scarcely audible, sounded on the front door.

The matches fell from his hand and spilled in the passage. He stood motionless, his breath suspended until the knock was repeated. Then he turned and fled swiftly back to his room, and closed the door behind him. A third knock sounded through the house.

'*What's that?*' cried the old woman, starting up.

'A rat,' said the old man in shaking tones—'a rat. It passed me on the stairs.'

His wife sat up in bed listening. A loud knock resounded through the house.

'It's Herbert!' she screamed. 'It's Herbert!'

She ran to the door, but her husband was before her, and catching her by the arm, held her tightly.

'What are you going to do?' he whispered hoarsely.

'It's my boy; it's Herbert!' she cried, struggling mechanically. 'I forgot it was two miles away. What are you holding me for? Let go. I must open the door.'

'For God's sake don't let it in,' cried the old man, trembling.

'You're afraid of your own son,' she cried, struggling. 'Let me go. I'm coming, Herbert; I'm coming.'

There was another knock, and another. The old woman with a sudden wrench broke free and ran from the room. Her husband followed to the landing, and called after her appealingly as she hurried downstairs. He heard the chain rattle back and the bottom bolt drawn slowly and stiffly from the socket. Then the old woman's voice, strained and panting.

'The bolt,' she cried, loudly. 'Come down. I can't reach it.'

But her husband was on his knees groping wildly on the floor in search of the paw. If he could only find it before the thing outside got in. A perfect fusilade of knocks reverberated through the house, and he heard the scraping of a chair as his wife put it down in the passage against the door. He heard the creaking of the bolt as it came slowly back, and at the same moment he found the monkey's paw, and frantically breathed his third and last wish.

The knocking ceased suddenly, although the echoes of it were still in the house. He heard the chain drawn back, and the door opened. A cold wind rushed up the staircase, and a long loud wail of disappointment and misery from his wife gave him courage to run down to her side, and then to the gate beyond. The street lamp flickering opposite shone on a quiet deserted road.

THE LATE DEPARTURE

Glenn Chandler

Mr Harrington caught the 11.45 train from Kings Cross to Hitchin ten minutes before it was due to depart. For that reason, he needn't have hurried. But there he was, red faced, his suit bedraggled, steam pouring out from somewhere, and his tie extremely crooked. It was not the way Mr Harrington liked to be seen doing business, so he tidied himself up very thoroughly in the corridor before entering the compartment. His business was over, of course; he was going home. But a businessman by habit, he disliked being seen a mess by anyone. Mr Harrington felt the need to be meticulous in his suit, starched white shirt and trilby hat, with his shoes radiating fresh black polish and a crease in his trousers that you could cut your finger on. How rarely, though, in his particular line of business, could he ever achieve it— taxiing round London at a breakneck speed, meeting lunch appointments, attending conferences, taking clients out to dinner in the evening —invariably it was an exhausting day, and he rarely had time to clean up before he was due somewhere else. Tonight he had been dining a client at a top London hotel, and had picked up the bill for sixty pounds. His company would pay that gladly, for it had been a fruitful night, with a firm contract worth sixty thousand pounds tucked cosily in Mr Harrington's briefcase.

Mr Harrington was going home. The frantic rush from Piccadilly to catch his last train had been unnecessary. There he was, sitting now in the compartment, wheezing and puffing, his heart thumping against the flab of his chest, with a nasty sweaty feeling all over that itched and fretted his skin. He tried breathing in through his nose and out again through his mouth—it was supposed to help you get your breath back. Athletes did it after a race, he'd heard. Not that Mr Harrington was athletic. Far from it, he never had the time. He was up at seven each morning, drove his car to the station, caught the train to London, taxied everywhere, caught the train back, drove home, swallowed a drink, went to bed. Exercise was for cranks, and walking simply a waste of time. He bothered with neither.

Lunch was often snatched, and dinner frequently over-indulgent. Mr Harrington liked his food, his figure amply revealed that. He was partial to a juicy steak, and had a sweet tooth—the dessert trolley seemed to arrive beside him automatically whenever he sat in a restaurant, and he'd demolish portions of strawberry trifle, cheesecake and cherry gateau all at one sitting. His doctor had warned him about overeating, but he paid little heed, seeing no pleasure whatsoever in the 'rabbit's diet' of yoghourt, lettuce and carrots that his wife was always trying to inflict on him.

Mr Harrington was looking forward to telling her of the deal he had just made. She probably wouldn't understand it—in fact she'd probably be in bed when he got home, fast asleep, and disinclined to listen. Still, he'd have a Scotch to celebrate and knock himself to sleep. He opened his briefcase, and rifled through a collection of little bottles. There were some yellow ones for indigestion, some blue ones for breathlessness, and some red ones for strain and blood pressure. His doctor was always giving him tablets, telling him to slow down, to take a holiday. He took the tablets, but never the holiday. Tonight he took a blue one and two red ones. The red ones were nearly finished. He would have to go back and get some more.

'Needn't have rushed,' he said to the other two occupants of the carriage, making a display of swallowing his tablets. 'Down the hatch, eh!'

One was a girl in her early twenties—she wore a pale blue cardigan and skirt, had shoulder length fair hair, and a pallid complexion. The other was a middle-aged woman, bossily done out in a tweed suit, with massive legs and a coat folded across her lap. They both looked at the wheezing, perspiring object in the seat by the window.

'Excuse me, but this is the 11.45 isn't it? I am on the right train?'

'Yes,' the girl replied. There was a sad, plaintive look in her eyes. Wistfully, she concealed it.

'Good! Good!' Mr Harrington exclaimed, sitting back and preparing to snooze. 'Rushed on, hardly had time to look. Needn't have though. Watch must be fast. Have you the correct time?'

She glanced at a delicate silver watch on her wrist.

'Twenty minutes to twelve,' she answered.

'Needn't have rushed. Still, I'm aboard. That's the main thing. If you miss this train, there isn't another one you know.'

Restlessly, he looked out of the compartment window. A uniformed porter, a seedy little man with hollow cheeks, was pushing a trolley of mailbags aimlessly up the platform. Another porter came rushing towards him, a more official one judging by his manner. There was an argument, lots of pointing, and gesticulating with the hands, then the porter with the trolley turned it round in a half circle and pushed it away in the opposite direction. That, thought Mr Harrington sneering, is British Rail all over. Wasted time. Time was money, in business and industry.

As businessmen do, he rummaged through his yawning briefcase and brought out a file to read. It was far more productive than dozing, and besides, it let everyone know he was a businessman. There was a list of things to do in preparation for a conference at the weekend, a set of accounts, and a document describing a new way of soundproofing walls. All intriguing stuff to Mr Harrington. He spread it out, taking up two seats, his own plus the vacant one next to him, and gazed at the print. It drifted in and out of focus alarmingly. He blinked, rubbed his eyes with a knuckle, and tried again. Still, the print was a blur. The strain of the day was probably affecting his vision. Promptly, without fuss, he put it all away, and fastened his briefcase shut. Mr Harrington yawned.

How he longed to be home. He fidgeted and sighed. Waiting for trains to depart was rather like watching a kettle and waiting for it to boil.

'Excuse me,' he said, 'but this one isn't going to be delayed, is it?'

'No one's announced a delay to my knowledge,' answered the bossy woman.

'It must be quarter to now.'

'It is,' said the girl.

'Typical!' cursed Mr Harrington. 'Ran all the way for nothing, now they can't even move the train on time. Probably they can't find the driver, or he doesn't want to drive it because his cab's dirty. That's what usually happens.'

The girl smiled thinly, not committing herself.

'The whole trouble with this country. Shifts itself at a snail's pace.'

Mr Harrington took out a packet of cigarettes, saw the NO SMOKING sign, put them away.

'You may smoke. It won't bother me,' said the woman.

'Very civil of you. Thank you very much.'

He offered her one. She refused. So did the girl. Mr Harrington stuck one between his lips, lit it, and inhaled the smoke. A moment later there was a racking pain in his chest and he bent double, coughing and choking and spluttering, but still he went on inhaling, as though his life depended on it. That was another thing his doctor had told him to cut down on. Mr Harrington smoked sixty a day, and possessed a pair of lungs which had forgotten what fresh air was like.

'Bally train. I think I'll go and find the guard. Ask him what the delay is. Mending the tracks, I suppose, they do daft things like that when people want to get home.'

He heaved himself out of his seat, kicked the girl's ankle on the way out of the compartment, and let the partition door slide shut behind him. On his weary way up the corridor, a young man in a suede jacket, and sprouting a beard, brushed by him. An arty type, thought Mr Harrington.

'Evening,' the young man said.

'Do you know what's wrong with this train?' Mr Harrington snapped at him.

'Why—nothing as far as I know.'

'It was due to start ten minutes ago.'

'I think they're doing a ticket check,' said the young man.

'A ticket check! What for?' shouted Mr Harrington. 'Can't they do that while the train's moving? Incompetent idiots. Don't they realize that people have homes to go to?'

'I'm sorry. I don't run the train,' apologized the young man profusely, and went on his way.

Mr Harrington continued up the corridor, and into the next carriage. The compartments were quite full for that time of night, but how typical of the average commuter, thought Mr Harrington, not to get up and make a fuss. If the train was an hour late in setting off, they'd probably still all sit there gazing at each other stupidly like sheep, and never once think of complaining. He would. He expected perfect service every time. If it couldn't be provided, he expected an announcement at the very least. It was just typical of British Rail not to let you know what was happening.

He came to the buffet car. He supposed he might get a cup of coffee and a sandwich at some vastly inflated price, but the car was shut up, and the glass shelves were empty and covered in dust. It was a very old carriage, with chipboard panelling and grey net curtains on the windows. Tables stood empty, their formica surfaces unmarked. An old lady leant on a stick in the corner, her eyes peering out from behind wrinkles of flesh, her fingers dry and cracked like parchment. A man had his arms folded across the bar. He was about fifty, had a glazed expression on his chubby face, and scuffed his foot noisily along the buffet car floor. Another man leant by a window, tall and willowy, with forlorn, hanging eyes.

'What's wrong? No service?' barked Mr Harrington.

'It's closed,' said the old lady.

'What did you want?'

'What did I want? I wanted to get a cup of coffee. It looks like I can't even do that now.'

'They don't serve coffee on this train,' said the willowy man.

'Isn't that just like British Rail? The very last lifeline, and they deprive you of it.'

'Lifeline?'

'Yes. Blast it, I pay enough for a season ticket, the least I can expect is a hot, stimulating drink on the way home. I suppose they can't get the staff. I suppose that's it. Nobody wants to provide a real service these days.'

'No one else is complaining,' said the chubby man with the glazed expression.

'That's the trouble with you fellows.' He glanced, momentarily, at the old lady, then carried on. 'The only way to get anywhere is if you complain. What's wrong, eh? Quarter of an hour late in departing, and not a peep from anyone in authority. Would it be too much trouble for somebody to come down the train and offer an explanation?'

'Are you in a hurry?' the old lady quizzed him.

'No. I just want to get home!'

'We all want to get home,' she told him. 'Out of the bustle, out of the race. Why must you bring it on the train? Why can't you relax, you—you irritating man!'

'I say, look here—'

'What is it? Do you know better than me? Would you argue with an old lady who's lived her life, and to the full?'

The blood drained out of Mr Harrington's cheeks. He wasn't accustomed to being lectured to by total strangers. He dropped the end of his cigarette, ground it into the floor with his shoe, then roused himself to admit,

'You look more of a positive person than some of the men I've seen on this train. Why don't *you* approach the guard. They always listen to a woman, didn't you know that?'

'But I'm in no hurry,' said the old lady in reply. 'No hurry at all.'

'Very well, I shall,' said Mr Harrington with panache. There was nothing he enjoyed more than a good complaint on behalf of his fellows. He would have the backing of the whole train, he felt sure. He elbowed his way out of the buffet car, past the willowy man who was taking up far too much room, and stormed up the corridor of the adjoining carriage. Despite the fact that the windows were all closed, the train felt very chilly—probably the heating had broken down. Every compartment he passed was filling up with pasty, blank-faced commuters. Was this what the human race was coming to, he asked himself? Apathetic idiots! But not Mr Harrington, not he. British Rail would sit up and take notice of him.

'Guard—I say, guard!'

He found himself in the guard's van. It was empty, save for a couple of chairs, and on one of them sat the guard in his black and red uniform.

'Yes. Can I help?'

'I demand to know why this train is quarter of an hour late in departing.'

'There's a ticket check, sir.'

'Well I'm sorry, but I'm not accepting that as an excuse. Ticket check indeed! Who's making it, the driver?'

'The inspector, sir.'

'It's absolutely disgraceful. I'm a businessman, I've spent a very tiring day, and I dislike being held up on trains. Why on Earth is the inspector checking tickets on the train when there is a ticket barrier on the platform?'

'There's no barrier at the other end, sir.'

'No barrier? What are you talking about? I go through it every day of my working life!'

'No barrier, sir,' the guard repeated.

'Is this, or is this not, the 11.45 to Hitchin?' Mr Harrington demanded.

'The *what*, sir?'

The guard looked puzzled, almost amused.

'I was told this *was* the right train. Is it?'

'You won't get to Hitchin on this train, sir,' the guard said glibly. 'Whoever told you that was wrong. Whether or not it is the right train—well, that very much depends on you.'

'I shall report you!' Mr Harrington waved his fat finger at the guard. 'Late departures I can understand, insurbordination I cannot. You people are employed to perform a service for the public. I am a member of that public. Are you listening to me?'

Mr Harrington was getting redder and redder, and steadily angrier. His mounting fury produced another cigarette between his lips. But the guard continued smiling in an unhurried, unflustered manner.

'The train will depart in five minutes,' he said.

'About time too. Not the right train indeed! There is only one at this time. Even I know that!'

Mr Harrington worked his way back down the seemingly endless string of carriages, through the buffet car, and took up his own seat

308

in his own compartment again. He was huffing and puffing, and just as tense and exhausted as when he'd stepped on the train. He took another red pill out of his case—let the train take the strain, indeed!—and swallowed it. There was one other person in the compartment besides the woman and the girl, and that was the arty fellow with the beard. He was sitting opposite the girl, holding her hands, and they were searching each others' eyes like reunited lovers. Sickening, thought Mr Harrington, as he wiped his hand across his brow. It was a good job he was perspiring, otherwise he would freeze on that train. His feet already felt like lumps of ice.

'Impudent guard,' he blew off steam. 'Do you know what he told me? That this wasn't the train to Hitchin!'

'It isn't,' said the woman.

Mr Harrington paused for breath. The cigarette hung smouldering between his yellowy fingers.

'What did you just say?'

'You're on the *wrong train*.'

Mr Harrington puffed out his cheeks in the direction of the girl. He was starting to think of being stranded in London overnight, of having to put up at a hotel, of the expense and inconvenience, of having to explain it to his wife.

'You told me it was the right train!' he bellowed at her.

She tore here eyes away from her lover.

'Yes,' she admitted.

'To Hitchin!'

You didn't ask that, with respect. You merely asked if this was the 11.45. That is the right train, isn't it?'

Mr Harrington seized his briefcase from the floor, and stood up.

'Excuse me!' he bawled.

There was much tripping up and kicking of ankles as he shouldered his way out of the compartment. He was about to mutter sorry when he realized that nobody had noticed it. He was positive he'd trodden on the bossy woman's foot, and expected her at least to give a flicker of annoyance. But not a sign passed across any of their faces. He had no time to question the matter. If he was on the wrong train, he would have to get off, and simply pray that his right train had been delayed also. In his head, he was already concocting his letter of complaint, when a collision with the old lady from the buffet car sent him flying.

'I'm so terribly sorry.' she apologized, unruffled by the encounter. Mr Harrington picked himself off the corridor floor.

'Stupid woman. Why can't you look where you're going?'

'Why can't you?'

And yet—and yet—it was said so unmaliciously. Mr Harrington, not accustomed to taking the blame, turned and bore down on the old lady with her stick. But no, what he saw—it could not be, it was a trick of his tired eyes. He saw straight through her head, up to the far end of the carriage!

'Let me off this train!' he cried, and turned frantically to the door. But it was jammed, and would not open.

A whistle blew, shrill and clear, up the platform. Mr Harrington tried again, pushed down the window, and attempted to open the door from the outside. Neither way would it let him out. Beads of sweat broke into rivulets, and meandered down his cheeks. He called up the platform to the porter he had seen earlier, the man with the trolley stacked with mailbags.

'You! I say—you!'

The porter just stood still, both hands on his metal trolley. He was gazing straight at Mr Harrington.

'Are you deaf? Open this door for me! I have a train to catch!'

But the porter, like the door, wasn't going to move an inch. Mr Harrington panted back to his carriage. He heard the whistle blow a second time, and felt the heaving and cranking underneath the floor. The train was leaving! He was in a quandary what to do now, his mind was fuzzed, his reactions were slow, he couldn't think clearly. The old lady leant on her stick, watching him, drifting in and out of his vision. What he needed was muscle, young muscle! He bundled his briefcase under his arm, and opening the sliding door of his compartment, said to the arty young man with the beard, 'I need help to get out of the train. I think . . . I think it's . . . jammed.'

But his voice cracked, and fell away at what he saw. A lump charged up his throat, and his spine ran cold. For the people with whom he had been sharing a compartment were only *just* there. He looked straight through their bodies to the fabric of the seats. The

He looked straight through their bodies.

woman, the young man, the girl, their eyes locked on some mysterious destination, the hands of the lovers touching, joining—they were smiling, all of them, going home . . . home.

Mr Harrington dropped his briefcase, and tried to wriggle through the open window while the train was moving, but he was much, much too fat. Not enough exercise, too much to eat and drink—this was the toll, the terrible toll. And what an ignominous sight it would make, a respectable businessman crawling through a train window head first! And yet—supposing he stayed on that train? Where would it take him? The fading bodily image of the old lady who stood next to him provided the answer, and it froze the back of his neck. It was the last train. But it wasn't going to Hitchin.

'No, I'm not ready yet!' he pleaded. 'Please hear me, somebody! I'm not ready yet!'

'Mr Harrington?'

Mr Harrington turned round. The gentleman facing him was solid flesh and blood, like himself. He was an inspector, and bore the word in gold braid on his sleeve.

'What—what do you want?' Mr Harrington asked.

'There appears to be some mistake. May I see your ticket please?'

It seemed pointless to argue or shout any more. He couldn't write a letter of dissatisfaction to the operators of this train—they were beyond his reach. He brought out his wallet, and with shaking, clammy hands dug among his membership cards and driving licence and credit cards until he found his season ticket. He handed it to the inspector.

'Ah, there has been a mistake, Mr Harrington,' said the inspector. 'I'm terribly sorry. As a matter of fact, I've been going up the train looking for you. It's a good job I spotted you when I did. There couldn't have been any turning back, you understand?'

Mr Harrington nodded. He could feel the train moving, and saw the platform slipping by through the window.

'Please—' he whined, 'Let me off.'

'Certainly sir.'

The Inspector stretched up his hand and pulled the communication cord. There was a grinding of wheels and screeching of brakes as the long train shuddered to a stop. The inspector then opened the door so that Mr Harrington could step down onto the platform.

'I'm terribly sorry for any inconvenience we've caused,' he said by way of an apology. 'Perhaps you'll just be in time to catch your proper train, if you don't rush.'

'I bally well hope so!' said Mr Harrington, grabbing his briefcase, and leaving the train with such speed that he almost fell over. The inspector wound up the window and watched him run. He waved, just a slow, lethargic elevation of his hand. Mr Harrington didn't see it. The train began moving again.

Mr Harrington was half way down the platform, when the porter with the trolley called out to him.

'Hey! You! Where are you going?'

'Which platform does the Hitchin train leave from?' Mr Harrington retaliated. 'Quickly, you idiot. I haven't got much time.'

'Number nine. What were you doing on this platform?'

'Catching a train. What do you think?'

'There are no trains on this platform. It's closed, can't you see? Track repairs. I don't know how they let you on.'

Mr Harrington didn't have time to argue. He didn't even have time to see the pulled-up tracks. But he did glance back, just once—very briefly—and what he saw made his legs go very weak indeed. The rear end of the train on which he had travelled home was disappearing into an eerie spectral mist, and a moment later had completely vanished.

He summoned strength to his legs, and belted for his train. He caught it, with minutes to spare. The odd thing was that the station clock only read 11.42, as though twenty minutes of his life had just disappeared. He flashed his season ticket, boarded a smoker, and threw himself into a seat. His heart was pounding, his nerves were in shreds, but the compartment was empty. Relieved beyond measure, he lit a cigarette, inhaled deeply, and exploded in a rasping cough. What it did to his chest was nothing compared to what he thought it did for his nerves.

Mr Harrington was going home. It had been a hard day, and he had narrowly escaped the clutches of something he wished not to think about. Yet one thing still bothered him, a niggling little detail that wouldn't, no matter how hard he tried to forget the experience, leave him alone.

It was the disconcerting fact that the inspector on the other 11.45 had known his name.

DAMP SHEETS

H. Russell Wakefield

'Exactly how much are you overdrawn, Robert?'

'Oh, I don't know; quite a bit.'

'That's *so* like you! Now, you've *got* to tell me.'

'Oh, about eight hundred.'

'Eight hundred! And how do you propose to work that off?'

'Well, I can't see any way at the moment.'

'Would Uncle Samuel help you?'

'I don't like to ask him.'

'Because he knows you're a born fool about money, and might alter his will?'

'If you like to put it in that typically courteous way.'

'How old is he? I always forget.'

'Seventy-five or six.'

'Is he strong?'

'No, his chest's groggy, but he takes very good care of himself.'

'Why not ask him to stay—he's never been here—and make a fuss of the old thing, and see if you can't get something out of him? We can't go on like this. Are you still betting?'

'Well, I've been doing better lately.'

'How much did you lose last month?'

'Look here, Agatha, I'm sick of your abuse and nagging!'

'Will you write and ask your uncle to stay?'

'Oh, all right.'

This amiable little domestic dialogue took place between Robert Stacey and his spouse, Agatha Henrietta Stacey, in the morning-room of Cardew House, near Hallocks, Sussex. It was characteristic of many such, for Robert was improvident and feeble, and Agatha despised him and was strong. When—and why—she had married him he had been a comparatively rich man, with a delightful little estate and great prospects. He still possessed the estate—mortgaged to the hilt—and the prospects—but his decadent financial condition has just been revealed. He had frittered his money away in conveniently fatuous ways. By a fatuous belief in his racing judgment, by a fatuous confidence in fundamentally unsound commercial ventures, by fatuous personal extravagance. He owned one of those long, dog-like faces sometimes described as 'aristocratic', a back-parting, a clumsy body, and stupid, loutish hands. He was forty years of age.

His prospects would be realized on the death of his uncle, Samuel— already referred to—who was leaving him £150,000 and Framley Court, in Surrey, an ugly old house, but large, lavishly furnished, and very comfortable. Uncle Samuel knew nothing of his nephew's financial incompetence and straits, and his ignorance of them was just about the tribute to Robert's intelligence that it had ever been possible to pay. The dispelling of that ignorance would have had disastrous consequences, for Uncle Samuel was very proud of the fortune he had made, and would have regarded the prospect of its improvident dispersal with an absolute lack of enthusiasm. And there was already the complication that the old man disliked Agatha. In that he was of the vast majority. Robert had married her for her looks in a vague 'time I settled down' mood. She was neither 'pretty' nor a 'beauty', but she out-pointed the majority of those who were. Her small, slanting, green eyes, which seemed always to be observing with extreme intensity, set in a face pallid but exquisitely shaped, inevitably seized and held attention. Her other features suggested strength, her red hair temperament; but those glittering, little restless eyes suggested at times frigid malignity and always insatiable egoism. Her body, of which she took the greatest care, was small, slim, but very strong. She neither smoked nor drank, but she never stopped thinking. She had married solely for money, and she had learned bitterly to blame herself for her bad judgment in choosing Robert, for he had had many prosperous rivals. She was just thirty-two.

Robert at first tried to keep his financial collapse from her, but her wits were far too keen for this, and when cross-examined ruthlessly he had collapsed. Since then he had meekly done as he was told, save for a few feeble and ineffectual revolts.

Agatha had one vulnerable spot—her daughter Elizabeth, for whom she showed a savage feline affection; when she kissed her it was as if a panther was licking her cub. She was disliked by her neighbours for her arrogance, but they feared her tongue. She was the daughter of a Polish actress and an Englishman in business in Warsaw. They had both died many years before, leaving her with £200 a year. Besides that she had nothing.

After the pleasant dialogue already related she went to her bureau and began to write, while Robert turned over in his mind the project of this invitation to his uncle to which he had pledged himself. There were difficulties—the old man's dislike of Agatha, his set ways and hypochondriacal tendencies. Then, was it wise to give him a hint of his precarious financial state? Probably not, but he'd got to get money somehow and soon, for the bank had politely intimated that they would prefer not to increase his overdraft. But he had to get some ready money.

'Look here, Agatha,' he said at length, 'there are certain difficulties about asking Uncle Samuel here.'

'One,' she replied, 'is the fact that he loathes me. Well, I can assure you I'll butter up the old fool. He's interested in pictures, isn't he?'

'Yes.'

'Well, tell him we'll ask Sir Arthur Welby to meet him.'

'Who's he?'

'He's a famous critic. I met him at the Gilbeys'.'

'But will he come?'

'Oh yes. He pretended to tell me about painting, but he gave me several languishing glances and put his hand on my knee while praising my appearance. He compared me with some woman in a picture, and said he tremendously looked forward to seeing me again.

Oh yes, he'll come when he's called! He's staying with the Gilbeys for another month. Come over here and write down what I tell you.'

Robert did so, and once again his cringing detestation of the tyrant who dominated him was combined with a grudging but deep respect for that bully's brains. It was just the letter, he knew, which might persuade Uncle Samuel to pay them a visit.

And it was so, for three days later he wrote accepting. He would arrive in his car about 5.30 on Friday, 4 January, and stay till Monday. It was clear that the prospect of meeting Sir Arthur had done the trick. He added a list of things he would require—Vichy water, Ryvita bread, and other fussy commodities. He even indicated the number of blankets he wanted on his bed.

Robert scraped together enough cash to ensure his adequate but not lavish entertainment. The atmosphere Agatha wished him to create was that of essential stability but temporary embarrassment; of an economy—not really necessary, but prudently advisable—till the stock he had bought—a purely fictitious purchase, needless to say—had completed its rise and his broker advised him to sell. This mythical holding was in a certain Talking Machine concern then having a frenetic boom.

It gave Agatha a peculiar pleasure thus to plan a coherent, rather complex, deception, but it was an exasperating labour to make Robert word-perfect in it. She'd have forced her way to success, using, breaking, exploiting, fooling other men, and women too!

Sir Arthur accepted an invitation to dine on Saturday—with a gallant postscript. Uncle Samuel arrived precisely at 5.30 on Friday. He was a fussy, frail, sharp-witted and tongued little fellow. He greeted Agatha rather over-politely, but turned quickly away from her. To Robert he was slightly condescendingly affable. He said he was tired by his journey and would lie down until it was time to dress. He appeared highly gratified that he was to meet Sir Arthur on the morrow.

Agatha had told Robert not to open the subject of his finances until she gave the word. She acted perfectly during dinner, seeming deferential and most anxious to please, fond of Robert, a contented, settled married woman. Uncle Samuel glanced at her sharply once or twice, as if not quite sure; but after some excellent light sherry, the better part of a bottle of estimable champagne, and two glasses of port,

he became mellow and loquacious. He was, however, no believer in late hours for a man of his age, and stated that he always retired at 10.30 unless there was some important cause for his staying up late —the company of Sir Arthur would certainly be such a cause. So at 10.15 Agatha went up to his room to see that his fire was all right, and that the Vichy was by his bedside. She remained there for about eight minutes, during which she kept the door locked.

Punctually at 10.30 Uncle Samuel went to bed. Next morning he had his breakfast in bed and did not appear downstairs till eleven o'clock. He hadn't slept very well and thought he had caught a slight chill. He was testy, nervous, and looked very fragile. But the prospect of meeting Sir Arthur neutralized his concern about his health, and he was more vivacious and even-tempered after luncheon. He took a short drive in the afternoon, and then went to his room to get into their proper order the photographs of his treasured pictures at Framley, and to catalogue the list of questions to put to Sir Arthur concerning them.

He greeted the great man with effusion, and during dinner insistently claimed his attention. The famous art critic did his best to appear vastly interested in Uncle Samuel's pictures. They were, for the most part, attributed to minor Flemish masters, but their authenticity was highly dubious. Sir Arthur would gladly have preferred to pay *sotto voce* and semi-senile compliments to his hostess, whose personality stirred up within him feelings which he had hoped had deserted him for ever. Agatha was at first utterly bored with all this pernickety highbrow chat, but one thing Sir Arthur said caught her attention. 'The desire to make money is at the root of all artistic endeavour. The rest is humbug!' He didn't quite mean it, but he was getting weary of Uncle Samuel's infatuation for his second-rate stuff, and how fascinated he was by Agatha's little animal green eyes! Later on he made another pronouncement: 'The old should make way for the young. And, furthermore, the old should not become critics when their creative impulse is moribund. When they have said all they have to say in paint let them keep silence, and not attempt to imprison the young and vital in the stocks of their senility.' And his right knee touched Agatha's left. She had never doubted the truth of either of these propositions, but it amused her to hear this old fool subscribing to them. 'Every-

319

one is the same,' she thought; 'money's everything, and the old must pay or go.' She became bland, sensuous, and light-hearted, and slyly tapped Sir Arthur's right knee with her left.

Robert hardly spoke a word, for he had nothing to contribute to the discussion, and he was thinking about Monday morning and the absolute necessity for cashing another cheque. He ate and drank and occasionally smoothed his back-parting. After Sir Arthur had left, Uncle Samuel stayed up for a little while longer, Agatha seizing the opportunity to run up and see that her guest was provided with everything he wanted. She remained eight minutes and kept the door locked.

'When shall I say anything?' asked Robert, after his guest had gone up to bed.

'Possibly tomorrow evening. I'll let you know,' replied Agatha. About eight o'clock the next morning a maid came to Agatha's room to say that Mr Walton complained of feeling ill and would like to see her. She dressed quickly and went to his room.

'My chill has developed, Agatha,' he said querulously. 'I cannot control my shivering, and I am convinced I have a temperature. Do you know, I'm certain my sheets have been damp on both nights.'

'Oh no, Uncle Samuel, I saw they were aired myself. Let me look at your hot-water bottle.' She put her hand in the bed and drew it out. 'Yes,' she said, 'it's been leaking—it's all wet round the top and wants a new washer. What a pity you did not let us lend you one of ours!'

'It's never leaked before,' said Uncle Samuel.

'I'll go and get you another. Do you think you ought to see a doctor?'

'I *must* have him,' replied Uncle Sam nervously and irritably. 'Chills are terribly dangerous to those with chests as weak as mine. Send for him at once, please.'

'I'll ring him up immediately.'

However, she didn't quite keep her word, for she went first to Robert's room and said. 'The old man's ill.'

'Ill! What's the matter with him?' asked Robert, a certain excitement in his voice.

'He says he has a bad chill. I'm going to ring up Dr Prichard.'

'We owe him twenty pounds.'

'Well, he'll have to come, and the old man can pay the bill.'

The doctor was unable to say anything definite about his patient's condition. 'His temperature is just over a hundred degrees, and I have detected what may be the beginning of mischief in the right lung, but it is too early to say yet.'

However, after he returned in the evening his uncertainty ended. 'He's in for an attack of pneumonia, which must be a very serious thing indeed for a man of his age and medical history. He'll have to have day and night nurses, and I'll go and arrange about them at once.'

When he had gone, Agatha and Robert exchanged glances. 'Perhaps there'll be no need for me to say anything,' suggested the latter, inadequately concealing the trend of his thoughts.

'When you're with him you'd better act better than that,' replied Agatha contemptuously. 'He's got plenty of time to make another will.'

Uncle Samuel might just, but only just, have had time, for he became unconscious on the evening following, and made but little fight. On Tuesday evening Agatha relieved the day nurse for a time. She sat by the fire reading *Vogue*, and planning a second trousseau. Uncle Samuel had not been conscious for twenty-four hours. Suddenly, hearing a rustle from the bed, she glanced towards it. Uncle Samuel was sitting up and staring at her. ('How ghastly he looks!' she thought.) He continued to stare for a moment or two, and then he said, in a horrible, harsh whisper, 'Agatha, my sheets *were* damp.' And then he fell back and died.

*   *   *   *

Two months later Agatha and Robert went into residence at Framley Court. Robert was in so exuberant a psychic state that he made the most fulsome promises concerning his future rectitude, and promised to limit his personal expenditure to an agreed sum.

Agatha was in her element, for she was a born manager and chatelaine. For a time she was almost tolerant of Robert, and a feeble imitation of matrimonial harmony was established. However, a fortnight after their arrival at Framley she was given cause to suspect that she had not finished with Uncle Samuel. She was sitting writing in her boudoir about six o'clock when slowly and insidiously she found her-

Uncle Samuel was standing in the doorway and staring at her.

self losing the thread of what she wanted to say. Her head was muddled. She put down her pen and glanced behind her, and then she gripped the sides of the desk, for Uncle Samuel was standing in the doorway and staring at her. She looked away and then looked again, and he had gone.

'Simply an illusion,' she half decided.

But on the next evening, when she was strolling in the garden at dusk, she became aware of a figure standing motionless some distance away across the flower-beds. The light was dim, but she had no doubt as to who it was. She turned and walked back to the house. The next day she again detected this curious echo of Uncle Samuel watching her from the end of the passage near her bedroom. Agatha had never known such an experience before, but her courage was absolute, and she determined to defy and, as far as possible, disregard this hallucination. No one else in the house seemed to share it. One thing she could never succeed in doing, and that was to stare back. She made the attempt, but her eyes always fell.

She and Robert had decided to give a large weekend party for their friends to celebrate their good fortune. On the Tuesday before the guests were to assemble, Agatha decided to make an inspection of the resources of her linen-room, which might be severely taxed. She went up there after dinner. It was on the top floor next to the laundry room in which one of the maids was at work. . . . The figure she knew so well came in just behind her.

Presently the maid in the laundry room heard a slight thud. She looked up, but for a few minutes went on with her work, and then she decided to see if anything had happened in the linen room. She opened the door and peeped in. A look of amazement came over her face, and she bent down and lifted something: then she screamed.

★   ★   ★   ★

The Coroner always considered it one of the most inexplicable cases into which he had ever inquired. As he pointed out at the inquest, the sheets, wrapped in paper and resting on their shelves some feet from the ground, had apparently slid from their receptacles, knocked Mrs Stacey down, and then, as it were, billowed out over her head, so stifling her. He could not see how this could possibly have happened. He closely cross-examined the maid who had first found her body, but her tale never varied.

'But there's one thing, sir,' she added, 'p'raps I should have said—them sheets was all damp.'

'What difference does that make?' said the Coroner testily.

THE BATTLE WITH THE BOGLES

Sorche Nic Leodhas

There was once a young doctor of learning who was sore troubled with bogles. He was the only son of an old couple to whom he had been born when they were getting along in years, and as they were determined to make a man of learning of him and had the brass to pay for it he had been little at home since he was a bit of a lad, being off and away at one school or another most of his days. He went to day school, and to grammar school, then to a Scottish public school. Then he went to the University of Edinboro', and after that to various universities here and there about the face of Europe. While he was away getting all this schooling his mother and father got older and older, and at last they got so old they died of it, both satisfied that they'd done their best for their son.

By that time he'd got all the knowledge he thought he needed, and he decided it was time to come home to the house his parents had left him and write a book about all the things he'd learned.

So back he came and settled into the house.

He found that it was a dreary old house in a dreary old street in the heart of the old part of Dundee, where the smoke from all the chimneys of the town had hung over it for long, long years. The Dundee Law seemed to tower over it and want to shut it in, although it was really not so near as it looked. But the house stood close by the Howff, that ancient graveyard which has held the honoured and famous dead of the town for over three hundred years.

The house was as dark and dismal inside as it was without. The walls were dark and damp and of no sort of colour you could lay a name to. There were great wooden blinds to the windows that kept the light out, for his mother had always said the light would fade the carpet.

Why he should stay there in the dank old place at an age when other young men were out enjoying themselves was a queer sort of riddle. Maybe he couldn't have told the answer to it himself, if he'd ever thought about it at all.

There was no lack of money, for he'd been left plenty. But he was a quiet, steady young man and his wants were few, and maybe he was just glad to settle down in peace after all the travelling around from one school to another. So he took the house the way it was and let it be.

His father and mother had never told him about the bogles, and maybe they never noticed them at all, but he soon found out about them for himself.

When he settled in he looked about till he found himself a cook and a lass to keep house for him. The two of them came with their boxes and took over. But after they'd been there a day or two the cook came to him and said, 'There's somewhat amiss with the garret, maister.'

'What would it be?' he asked.

'The draught is terrible,' she told him. 'Ye canna keep a door ajar, but a breeze comes by and bangs it shut. And the locks won't hold, for as soon as it's shut, the draught bangs it wide open again. What with banging and creaking all the night the lass and me can get no sleep at all!'

'Well, move down to the next storey,' said the doctor. 'I'll have in a man to look to the garret.'

The man came and looked to the garret, but he could find naught wrong, for the windows were tight and he couldn't find the sign of a place for the draught to come in.

But a few days later the doctor came down to his breakfast to find the boxes of the two women in the hall and the women beside them, white as winding sheets.

The cook spoke for both of them. 'We'll be leaving ye, maister,' said she, 'this very morning's morn!'

'Why then?' asked the astonished doctor.

'We'll not be staying in a place where there's bogles!' said the cook firmly. The serving lass shrieked a wee shriek and rolled her eyes and clutched the cook's arm.

'Bogles!' The doctor laughed. 'You mean ghosts? Oh come, come now! You are a sensible woman. You know there are no such things as ghosts!'

'I know what I know!' said the cook.

Then the two of them picked up their boxes and out of the door they went, without waiting to ask could they get their wages!

Well that was the way it was after that. The doctor would find himself a new couple of women to look after the house. They'd come with their boxes and all, but after a few days the boxes were down in the hall and the women beside them ready to go their ways, and all because of the bogles!

Two by two they came, and two by two they went, over and over again, and not even the promise of better wages would tempt them to stay.

And at last came a time when the doctor could find no one who would come at all, for the ones who left had spread the news wide and there wasn't a lass in the town of Dundee who'd step a foot into the doctor's house. No! Not even for all the money in Dundee!

Then the doctor took the ferry over the Tay to Newport, thinking maybe he could find a cook and housemaid there. But the news of the doctor's bogles had got to Newport before him, being the sort of news that travels fast. The Newport lassies who were willing to go into service would have nothing at all to do with him, after they found out who he was.

It came into his mind then that he'd heard that they had a wheen of ghosts in St Andrews. Maybe the women there'd be used to them, and wouldn't be minding a house that was said to have bogles in it.

Not that he believed in bogles himself. No indeed. Not he!

So he made the journey from Newport to St Andrews. But he had no luck there at all. There were bogles galore, 'tis true. In fact the place must have been teeming with them, for the folks at St Andrews told him proudly that there was scarcely a house in the town that hadn't a bogle or two in it—certainly not one of the older houses.

But the trouble with St Andrews was that if there were no lack of bogles, there were no lassies who weren't already in service. And they all said they were suited fine where they were, thank you, and wouldn't like to be making a change, even for the bigger wages the doctor was willing to pay.

So it looked as if he'd just have to do for himself, though he didn't know how to cook at all, and as for cleaning up and making things tidy he knew less about that.

He started back home again, for there was nothing else he could do.

When he was on the ferry going back from Newport to Dundee he saw a lass on the boat. She was the sort of lass you look twice at, for she had the reddest hair in the world, springing up in wee curls in the fresh wind from the Tay. She had the white skin that goes with that sort of hair, and a saucy nose with a sprinkle of freckles across it, and eyes of the bluest blue he'd ever seen.

She was neat as a silver pin, too, with a little flat straw hat pinned tight to her curls and a white blouse and a tidy black skirt. But what he noticed most was her smile, for it was merry and kind.

He thought she wouldn't be minding if he went and spoke to her. So he went over and stood beside her at the rail of the boat.

'Do you believe in bogles?' he asked her.

She looked at him and her eyes crinkled, and she broke into a laugh. 'Och do I not!' she cried. 'My old grannie at Blairgowrie that I'm going to stay with had a rare time with a pair of them a year or so back, till she rid them out!'

'Oh,' said he.

'Do you not believe in them?' asked the red-haired lass curiously.

'No I don't!' said he.

And that was the end of that, for if she believed in bogles there was no use asking her to come and keep house for him, because she would not stay any more than the rest of them.

When he got back home he went into the scullery to see what there was for his supper. But what was there that had to be cooked, he didn't know what to do with. He just had to make do with the heel of a loaf of bread and a bit of stale cheese that wasn't fit to bait a mousetrap with.

So when he went into his study he was hungry and he was tired and he was plain put about!

He sat down at his desk, and he banged his fist on it, and he shouted out loud! 'Tis all nonsense! THERE ARE NO BOGLES!'

'Oh, aren't there?' asked a quiet voice behind him.

He whirled around in his chair, and then his eyes bugged out and his hair stood straight up on his head.

There were three big white things standing there, *and he could see right through them.*

But the doctor was awful stubborn. 'There are no bogles,' he said again, only his voice wasn't so loud this time and he didn't sound as if he was so sure about it.

'Then what would you be calling us?' asked one of them politely.

Well, there was no two ways about it. Bogles they were, and bogles he had to call them. So he had to admit that there *were* bogles in his house.

What he didn't know yet was how many of them were there. Because they liked his house fine. It was so nice and dark and damp.

It was not so bad as far as his meals went, for he was taking them at the inn, rather than starve at home. But at home he was fair distracted, for it seemed as if there were more and more bogles all the time.

Bogles peered down at him from over the rail of the staircase, and there were always some of them lurking about in the corners of any room he was in, blinking their eyes at him and sighing at him, and they fair gave him a chill. The three first ones followed him about, and when he went up to his bed at night they came along and sat on the foot of the bed and talked to him.

They all came from the Howff, they told him.

'Och aye,' sighed one of them. ''Twas a fine graveyard, one time.'

'For the first hundred years or so,' said the second bogle.

'But after that it began to get crowded. A lot of new people got brought in, and some of them wasn't the sort we'd want to neighbour with,' said the first one again.

But since they had found his place they told the doctor, 'twas far better. They liked it fine in his house, and all the best bogles were

329

moving over there, too, so they felt much more at home than they did in the Howff.

Things being the way they were, the doctor had no peace by day or by night. He was writing away on his learned book about some sort of wisdom or other, I wouldn't know what. He was having a hard time of it, for the bogles were that curious that they hung about him and peered over his shoulder, and even took to criticizing what he wrote. One of them even got so familiar that he'd lean on the doctor's shoulder and point out places where the doctor could be doing better with his words. It annoyed the doctor a lot, because he found himself writing down what the bogle said, and he had ideas of his own that he liked better than the ones the bogle was giving him.

One day as he sat in the inn eating his dinner he made up his mind that he'd take no more of the bogles, for he had had enough!

So he went home and put on his best clothes for a journey, and off he went to Blairgowrie to find the red-haired lass and ask her what her grannie had done to rid herself of her bogles.

When he got to Blairgowrie he went about the town looking for the lass. He couldn't ask for her for he didn't know her name. By-and-by he got to the end of the town and there he saw a neat little two-storied cottage, with a low stone wall around it, and inside of the wall a big garden full of flowers. There was a bench by the door of the cottage, and on the bench sat the red-haired lass, and she was still smiling.

'Good day!' says he.

'Good day!' says she. 'I thought you'd soon be coming along.'

'You did!' said he, surprised. 'Why did you then?'

'Because you asked if I believed in bogles. So then I knew that you had some of your own and would be coming to find out what my grannie did to get rid of hers.'

He was amazed that one so bonny could be so wise. So he opened the gate and went into the garden. He sat down on the bench beside her and told her all his trouble.

'Will you come and help me get them out of the house?' he asked, when he'd finished his story.

'Of course I will!' said she.

Then she took him in to her grannie. Her grannie was just like her, only her hair was white and she wasn't so young, but her eyes were just as blue and her smile was as merry and kind.

'Grannie,' said the lass, 'I'm going with this gentleman to keep house for him, and to rid him of some bogles he has at home.'

'If anyone can, you can!' said her grannie, and the two of them laughed as if bogles were no trouble at all.

So the lass got ready and off she went with the doctor.

When he opened the door of his house and they went in, the lass wrinkled her nose and made a face. 'Faugh!' said she. 'It smells of bogle! A proper graveyard smell,' she added, looking around at the place.

'They come from the Howff,' he told her, as if that explained it.

'I'll be bound!' she said. 'And to the Howff they'll go back!'

That night the doctor ate his meal at home, instead of going to the inn. It was a good one, too, for the lass got it, and nobody had ever said that she didn't know how to cook.

There wasn't a sign of a bogle that night, but that was because they were biding their time and looking the lass over.

The next morning the lass came into the study. She had on a blue overall, the same colour as her eyes, and there was a fresh white kerchief tied to cover her hair.

'This is a proper dark old place,' said she, looking about the room. 'Why do you not throw back those big old blinds and open the windows to let a wee bit of sun and fresh air in?'

'My mother said it would let dust in and fade the carpets,' the doctor said. He remembered that from the time when he was a wee lad, before he went off to his schools.

'What if it does!' said she. 'Can you not buy new ones?'

'I never thought of that!' he said. 'Of course I can.'

So the lass pulled the curtains back and folded back the wooden blinds. Then she opened the windows wide and the sea air came pouring in from the harbour, with the sun riding on top of it.

'That's better!' the lass told him.

'It is, indeed!' said the doctor, as he took a long deep breath of the fresh cool air.

But the red-haired lass took another look at the dingy old room and frowned. 'No wonder you have bogles,' she said. 'I never saw a place they'd like better. But I can do no more for you till time for your dinner, so I'll leave you. I'm turning out the scullery.'

So the doctor worked at his book and the lass worked at the scullery, and the day went by.

That night the bogles came in a crowd and gathered around the doctor's bed.

'Who is the red-haired lass in the house?' asked the first bogle.

'She's my new housekeeper,' the doctor told them, yawning because he had worked awful hard on his learned book all day. The bogles hadn't come near him, because they didn't like all the sunlight that came into the study after the lass opened the windows.

'Is she going to stay here?' they asked.

'I hope so!' yawned the doctor. He had had a good supper, and he'd eaten a lot of it, and now he was so sleepy he couldn't keep his eyes open. Before the bogles had time to ask him anything else he'd fallen fast asleep.

They couldn't wake him for all they tried. So they gave him up and went to see could they scare the red-haired lass away, the same as they had the others. But she had worked hard and eaten well, too, so they couldn't waken her, no more than they could the doctor. They all agreed it was a bad day for the bogles when the lass came into the house. It was going to take an awful lot of hard work to get her out again.

The next day the red-haired lass was up early, and the day after that, and the next day after, too. The kitchen and the scullery were beginning to look like different places, for she swept and dusted and scrubbed and scoured and polished from morn to night. The doctor saw little of her except at mealtimes, but the meals were the best he'd ever had in his life, and she sat across the table from him and poured his tea and smiled at him.

At night he and the lass were so tired out, him with his writing and her with her turning out, that they couldn't be bothered about the bogles.

The bogles were there, nonetheless. They'd brought a lot more bogles from the Howff to help them—even some of the riffraff they'd moved to the doctor's house to get away from! There were plenty of dark old

They tried to look as grisly as they could.

rooms in the house still, for the lass was still busy with the scullery and the kitchen and hadn't come off the ground floor yet.

So at night the bogles tried all their best tricks that never had failed before. They swept through the house like a tempest, banging doors open and shut, wailing and gibbering, moaning and mowing, clanking chains and rattling bones, and the like.

It all did no good. Nobody heard them except maybe a passerby in the street, who thought it was the wind rising from the sea, and hurried home so as not to get caught in a storm.

When the end of the week came along the red-haired lass said to the doctor, 'You'd best take your pens and paper and things over to my grannie's at Blairgowrie and do your writing there. I'm through with the kitchen and the scullery, and now I'm going to turn out the rest of the house.'

He didn't want to go, but she told him he'd got to for he'd only be in her way.

'You can leave me some money to get some things I'll be needing, and to pay for help to come in, to do what I can't do myself,' she told him. 'And don't come back till I send for you, mind!'

So he packed up, and off he went to her grannie's house as she told him to.

As soon as he was gone, the red-haired lass started in again, and now she really showed what she could do. The bogles were so upset about what was going on that one night they laid in wait for her and caught her on the stairs as she was going up to her bed. They tried to look as grisly as they could, and the noises they made were something horrible.

But the red-haired lass only stared straight through them. 'Go away you nasty things!' she said.

'We won't then!' they said indignantly. 'We got here first and we've a mind to stay. Why don't you go away?'

'I like my work and I'm useful here,' said the lass. 'Which is more than you can say.'

'It was all fine till you came,' complained one of the bogles.

'It was all wrong till I came,' said the lass right back at them. 'And I wish you'd stop argy-barging and let me get to my bed. I've a big day's work ahead of me tomorrow, for the painters are coming in and the men to take away the blinds, and when they're done 'twill be all sunny and bright and a treat to see!'

All the bogles groaned like one big groan.

'Sunny!' moaned one.

'Bright!' shrieked another.

'Well anyway, we're not going away,' said they.

'Stay if you like,' said the lass. 'It's all one to me if you stay or go. But you won't like it!' she promised them. And with that she walked straight up the steps and through the lot of them, and went to bed and to sleep.

After that the battle between the bogles and the lass really began. You couldn't say they didn't put up a fight for it, but the lass was more than a match for them. She drove them from the first storey of the house to the second, and from the second to the third, and from the third to the garret, for they couldn't stand the sunlight and brightness that followed her as she went up through the house at her work.

At last they had to pack up their extra winding sheets and their chains and bones and things and go back to the graveyard they'd come from, for the house wasn't fit for a bogle to stay in, and even if the Howff was crowded it suited them better now.

Well, when the painters and carpenters and all were gone the lass found a serving maid to help her with the work. And this one stayed! But the lass didn't bother to look for a cook, for she thought her own cooking would suit the doctor best when he came back to his house.

The doctor was just as comfortable in her grannie's house and just as well fed there, and everything was fine, except that he missed the red-haired lass, for he'd begun to get used to having her around. There were no bogles to bother him at the lass's grannie's house, for she had rid herself of hers a long time ago. It came to his mind that he hadn't seen much of his own bogles lately, but he didn't miss them at all.

A week went by and then a second one and a third one. And the doctor found that instead of writing his learned book he'd be sitting and thinking how bright the red-haired lass's hair looked with the sun on it or how blue her eyes were or how the freckles looked on her saucy little nose. He was that homesick for her, he'd even have

335

put up with the bogles, just to be at home, with her pouring out his tea and smiling at him from across the table.

So when she sent word at the end of the fourth week that he was to come back he went off so fast that he almost forgot to thank her grannie for having him and to say goodbye!

When he got back to his house he had to step out into the road and look well at it, for he wasn't sure it was his.

The windows were open from ground floor to garret, and all the heavy wooden blinds had been taken away entirely. There were fresh white curtains blowing gently at all the windows and flowerpots on the sills.

Then the door opened and the red-haired lass stood in the doorway and smiled at him. It was his house after all!

'You've come then!' said she.

'I've come!' said he. And up the steps he went, two at a time. He could hardly believe 'twas the same place, when he saw what she'd done with it. Everything was light and bright, and through the whole house the fresh air blew, in one window and out another, so that the place was as sweet and fresh and wholesome as the red-haired lass herself.

'How about the bogles?' asked the doctor.

'They've gone,' said the lass.

'All of them? Where did they go?' asked the doctor.

'Back to the Howff, I suppose,' said the lass. 'This isn't the sort of place bogles would be liking to bide in.'

'No!' said the doctor, looking around. 'I can see that for myself.'

But he had one more question to ask, so he asked it. 'Will you marry me?' he said.

'Of course I will!' said the red-haired lass. And she smiled at him and said, 'Why else did you think I came here in the first place?'

So they were married, and the doctor had no more bogles in his house. But what he did have was half a dozen bairns, lads and lassies, all with red hair and blue eyes and saucy noses with freckles across them and merry smiles, just like their mother.

And bairns are better to fill a house with than bogles ever could be, so they all lived merrily ever after.

336

A PAIR OF HANDS

Sir Arthur Quiller-Couch

'Yes,' said Miss Le Petyt, gazing into the deep fireplace and letting her hands and her knitting lie for the moment idle in her lap. 'Oh, yes, I have seen a ghost. In fact I have lived in a house with one for quite a long time.'

'How you *could*—!' began one of my host's daughters; and 'You, Aunt Emily?' cried the other at the same moment.

Miss Le Petyt, gentle soul, withdrew her eyes from the fireplace and protested with a gay little smile. 'Well, my dears, I am not quite the coward you take me for. And, as it happens, mine was the most harmless ghost in the world. In fact'—and here she looked at the fire again—'I was quite sorry to lose her.'

'It was a woman, then? Now *I* think,' said Miss Blanche, 'that female ghosts are the horridest of all. They wear little shoes with high red heels, and go about *tap, tap*, wringing their hands.'

'This one wrung her hands, certainly. But I don't know about the high red heels, for I never saw her feet. Perhaps she was like the Queen of Spain, and hadn't any. And as for the hands, it all depends *how* you wring them. There's an elderly shopwalker at Knightsbridge, for instance—'

'Don't be prosy, you know that we're just dying to hear the story.'

Miss Le Petyt turned to me with a small deprecating laugh. 'It's such a little one.'

'The story, or the ghost?'

'Both.'

And this was Miss Le Petyt's story:

'It happened when I lived down in Cornwall, at Tresillack on the south coast. Tresillack was the name of the house, which stood quite alone at the head of a coombe, within sound of the sea but without sight of it; for though the coombe led down to a wide open beach, it wound and twisted half a dozen times on its way, and its overlapping sides closed the view from the house, which was advertised as 'secluded'. I was very poor in those days. Your father and all of us were poor then, as I trust, my dears, you will never be; but I was young enough to be romantic and wise enough to like independence, and this word "secluded" took my fancy.

'The misfortune was that it had taken the fancy, or just suited the requirements, of several previous tenants. You know, I dare say, the kind of person who rents a secluded house in the country? Well, yes, there are several kinds; but they seem to agree in being odious. No one knows where they come from, though they soon remove all doubt about where they're "going to", as the children say. "Shady" is the word, is it not? Well, the previous tenants of Tresillack (from first to last a bewildering series) had been shady with a vengeance.

'I knew nothing of this when I first made application to the landlord, a solid yeoman inhabiting a farm at the foot of the coombe, on a cliff overlooking the beach. To him I presented myself fearlessly as a spinster of decent family and small but assured income, intending a rural life of combined seemliness and economy. He met my advances politely enough, but with an air of suspicion which offended me. I began by disliking him for it: afterwards I set it down as an unpleasant feature in the local character. I was doubly mistaken. Farmer Hosking was slow-witted, but as honest a man as ever stood up against hard times; and a more open and hospitable race than the people on that coast I never wish to meet. It was the caution of a child who had burnt his fingers, not once but many times. Had I known what I afterwards learned of Farmer Hosking's tribulations as landlord of a "secluded country residence", I should have approached him with the bashfulness proper to my suit and faltered as I undertook to prove the bright exception in a long line of painful experiences. He had bought the Tresillack estate twenty years before—on mortgage, I fancy—because the land adjoined his own and would pay him for tillage. But the house was a nuisance, an incubus; and had been so from the beginning.

'"Well, miss," he said, "you're welcome to look over it; a pretty enough place inside and out. There's no trouble about keys, because I've put in a housekeeper, a widow-woman, and she'll show you round. With your leave I'll step up the coombe so far with you, and put you in your way." As I thanked him he paused and rubbed his chin. "There's one thing I must tell you, though. Whoever takes the house must take Mrs Carkeek along with it."

'"Mrs Carkeek?" I echoed dolefully. "Is that the housekeeper?"

'"Yes: she was wife to my late hind. I'm sorry, miss," he added, my face telling him no doubt what sort of woman I expected Mrs Carkeek to be; "but I had to make it a rule after—after some things that happened. And I dare say you won't find her so bad. Mary Carkeek's a sensible comfortable woman, and knows the place. She was in service there to Squire Kendall when he sold up and went: her first place it was."

'"I may as well see the house, anyhow," said I dejectedly. So we started to walk up the coombe. The path, which ran beside a little chattering stream, was narrow for the most part, and Farmer Hosking, with an apology, strode on ahead to beat aside the brambles. But whenever its width allowed us to walk side by side I caught him from time to time stealing a shy inquisitive glance under his rough eyebrows. Courteously though he bore himself, it was clear that he could sum me up to his satisfaction or bring me square with his notion of a tenant for his "secluded country residence".

'I don't know what foolish fancy prompted it, but about halfway up the coombe I stopped short and asked:

'"There are no ghosts, I suppose?"

'It struck me, a moment after I had uttered it, as a supremely silly question; but he took it quite seriously. "No; I never heard tell of any *ghosts*." He laid a queer sort of stress on the word. "There's always been trouble with servants, and maids' tongues will be runnin'. But Mary Carkeek lives up there alone, and she seems comfortable enough."

'We walked on. By-and-by he pointed with his stick. "It don't look like a place for ghosts, now, do it?"

'Certainly it did not. Above an untrimmed orchard rose a terrace of turf scattered with thorn-bushes, and above this a terrace of stone, upon which stood the prettiest cottage I had ever seen. It was long and low and thatched; a deep verandah ran from end to end. Clematis, Banksia roses and honeysuckle climbed the posts of this verandah, and big blooms of the Maréchal Niel were clustered along its roof, beneath the lattices of the bedroom windows. The house was small enough to be called a cottage, and rare enough in features and in situation to confer distinction on any tenant. It suggested what in those days we should have called "elegant" living. And I could have clapped my hands for joy.

'My spirits mounted still higher when Mrs Carkeek opened the door to us. I had looked for a Mrs Gummidge, and I found a healthy middle-aged woman with a thoughtful but contented face, and a smile which, without a trace of obsequiousness, quite bore out the farmer's description of her. She was a comfortable woman; and while we walked through the rooms together (for Mr Hosking waited outside) I "took to" Mrs Carkeek. Her speech was direct and practical; the rooms, in spite of their faded furniture, were bright and exquisitely clean; and somehow the very atmosphere of the house gave me a sense of well-being, of feeling at home and cared for; yes, *of being loved*. Don't laugh, my dears; for when I've done you may not think this fancy altogether foolish.

'I stepped out into the verandah, and Farmer Hosking pocketed the pruning-knife which he had been using on a bush of jasmine.

'"This is better than anything I had dreamed of," said I.

'"Well, miss, that's not a wise way of beginning a bargain, if you'll excuse me."

'He took no advantage, however, of my admission; and we struck the bargain as we returned down the coombe to his farm, where the hind chaise waited to convey me back to the market town. I had meant to engage a maid of my own, but now it occurred to me that I might do very well with Mrs Carkeek. This, too, was settled in the course of the next day or two, and within the week I had moved into my new home.

'I can hardly describe to you the happiness of my first month at Tresillack; because (as I now believe) if I take the reasons which I had for being happy, one by one, there remains over something which I cannot account for. I was moderately young, entirely healthy; I felt myself independent and adventurous; the season was high summer, the weather glorious, the garden in all the pomp of June, yet sufficiently unkempt to keep me busy, give me a sharp appetite for meals, and send me to bed in that drowsy stupor which comes of the odours of earth. I spent the most of my time out of doors, winding up the day's work as a rule with a walk down the cool valley along the beach and back.

'I soon found that all housework could be safely left to Mrs Carkeek. She did not talk much; indeed her only fault (a rare one in housekeepers) was that she talked too little, and even when I addressed her seemed at times unable to give me her attention. It was as though her mind strayed off to some small job she had forgotten, and her eyes wore a listening look, as though she waited for the neglected task to speak and remind her. But as a matter of fact she forgot nothing. Indeed, my dears, I was never so well attended to in my life.

'Well, that is what I'm coming to. That, so to say, is just *it*. The woman not only had the rooms swept and dusted, and my meals prepared to the moment. In a hundred odd little ways this orderliness, these preparations, seemed to read my desires. Did I wish the roses renewed in a bowl upon the dining-table, sure enough at the next meal they would be replaced by fresh ones. Mrs Carkeek (I told myself) must have surprised and interpreted a glance of mine. And yet I could not remember having glanced at the bowl in her presence. And how on earth had she guessed the very roses, the very shapes and colours I had lightly wished for? This is only an instance, you understand. Every day, and from morning to night, I happened on others, each slight enough, but all together bearing witness to a ministering intelligence as subtle as it was untiring.

'I am a light sleeper, as you know, with an uncomfortable knack of waking with the sun and roaming early. No matter how early I rose at Tresillack, Mrs Carkeek seemed to have prevented me. Finally I had to conclude that she arose and dusted and tidied as soon as she judged me safely a-bed. For once, finding the drawing-room (where I had been sitting late) "redded-up" at four in the morning, and no trace of a plate of raspberries which I had carried thither after dinner and left overnight, I determined to test her, and walked through to the kitchen, calling her by name. I found the kitchen as clean as a pin, and the fire laid, but no trace of Mrs Carkeek. I walked upstairs and knocked at her door. At the second knock a sleepy voice cried out, and presently the good woman stood before me in her nightgown, looking (I thought) very badly scared.

'"No," I said, "it's not a burglar. But I've found out what I wanted, that you do your morning's work over night. But you mustn't wait for me when I choose to sit up. And now go back to your bed like a good soul, whilst I take a run down to the beach."

'She stood blinking in the dawn. Her face was still white.

'"Oh, miss," she gasped, "I made sure you must have seen something!"

'"And so I have," I answered, "but it was neither burglars nor ghosts."

'"Thank God!" I heard her say as she turned her back to me in her grey bedroom—which faced the north. And I took this for a carelessly pious expression and ran downstairs, thinking no more of it.

'A few days later I began to understand.

'The plan of Tresillack house (I must explain) was simplicity itself. To the left of the hall as you entered was the dining-room; to the right the drawing-room, with a boudoir beyond. The foot of the stairs faced the front door and beside it, passing a glazed inner door, you found two others right and left, the left opening on the kitchen, the right on a passage which ran by a store-cupboard under the bend of the stairs to a neat pantry with the usual shelves and linen-press, and under the window (which faced north) a porcelain basin and brass tap. On the first morning of my tenancy I had visited this pantry and turned the tap; but no water ran. I supposed this to be accidental. Mrs Carkeek had to wash up glassware and crockery, and no doubt Mrs Carkeek would complain of any failure in the water supply.

'But the day after my surprise visit (as I called it) I had picked a basketful of roses, and carried them into the pantry as a handy place to arrange them in. I chose a china bowl and went to fill it at the tap. Again the water would not run.

'I called Mrs Carkeek. "What is wrong with this tap?" I asked. "The rest of the house is well enough supplied."

'"I don't know, miss. I never use it."

'"But there must be a reason; and you must find it a great nuisance washing up the plate and glasses in the kitchen. Come around to the back with me, and we'll have a look at the cisterns."

'"The cisterns 'll be all right, miss. I assure you I don't find it a trouble."

'But I was not to be put off. The back of the house stood ten feet from a wall which was really but a stone face built against the cliff cut away by the architect. Above the cliff rose the kitchen garden, and from its lower path we looked over the wall's parapet upon the cisterns. There were two—a very large one, supplying the kitchen and the bathroom above the kitchen; and a small one, obviously fed by the other, and as obviously leading, by a pipe which I could trace, to the pantry. Now the big cistern stood almost full, and yet the small one, though on a lower level, was empty.

'"It's as plain as daylight," said I. "The pipe between the two is choked." And I clambered onto the parapet.

'"I wouldn't, miss. The pantry tap is only cold water, and no use to me. From the kitchen boiler I gets it hot, you see."

'"But I want the pantry water for my flowers." I bent over and groped. "I thought as much!" said I, as I wrenched out a thick plug of cork and immediately the water began to flow. I turned triumphantly on Mrs Carkeek, who had grown suddenly red in the face. Her eyes were fixed on the cork in my hand. To keep it more firmly wedged in its place somebody had wrapped it round with a rag of calico print; and, discoloured though the rag was, I seemed to recall the pattern (a lilac sprig). Then, as our eyes met, it occurred to me that only two mornings before Mrs Carkeek had worn a print gown of that same sprigged pattern.

'I had the presence of mind to hide this very small discovery, sliding over it some quite trivial remark; and presently Mrs Carkeek regained her composure. But I own I felt disappointed in her. It seemed such a paltry thing to be disingenuous over. She had deliberately acted a fib before me; and why? Merely because she preferred the kitchen to the pantry tap. It was childish. "But servants are all the same," I told myself. "I must take Mrs Carkeek as she is; and, after all, she is a treasure."

'On the second night after this, and between eleven and twelve o'clock, I was lying in bed and reading myself sleepy over a novel of Lord Lytton's, when a small sound disturbed me. I listened. The sound was clearly that of water trickling; and I set it down to rain. A shower (I told myself) had filled the water pipes which drained the roof. Somehow I could not fix the sound. There was a water-pipe against the wall just outside my window. I rose and drew up the blind.

'To my astonishment no rain was falling; no rain had fallen. I felt the slate window-sill; some dew had gathered there—no more. There was no wind, no cloud: only a still moon high over the eastern slope of the coombe, the distant splash of waves, and the fragrance of many roses. I went back to bed and listened again. Yes, the trickling sound continued, quite distinct in the silence of the house, not to be confused for a moment with the dull murmur of the beach. After a while it began to grate on my nerves. I caught up my candle, flung my dressing-gown about me, and stole softly downstairs.

'Then it was simple. I traced the sound to the pantry. "Mrs Carkeek has left the tap running," said I: and, sure enough, I found it so—a thin trickle steadily running to waste in the porcelain basin. I turned off the tap, went contentedly back to bed, and slept.

'—for some hours. I opened my eyes in darkness, and at once knew what had awakened me. The tap was running again. Now it had shut easily in my hand, but not so easily that I could believe it had slipped open again of its own accord. "This is Mrs Carkeek's doing," said I; and am afraid I added "Bother Mrs Carkeek!"

'Well, there was no help for it: so I struck a light, looked at my watch, saw that the hour was just three o'clock, and descended the stairs again. At the pantry door I paused. I was not afraid—not one little bit. In fact the notion that anything might be wrong had never crossed my mind. But I remember thinking, with my hand on the door, that if Mrs Carkeek were in the pantry I might happen to give her a severe fright.

'I pushed the door open briskly. Mrs Carkeek was not there. But something *was* there, by the porcelain basin—something which might have sent me scurrying upstairs two steps at a time, but which as a matter of fact held me to the spot. My heart seemed to stand still—so still! And in the stillness I remember setting down the brass candlestick on a tall nest of drawers beside me.

'Over the porcelain basin and beneath the water trickling from the tap I saw two hands.

'That was all—two small hands, a child's hands. I cannot tell you how they ended.

'No: they were not cut off. I saw them quite distinctly: just a pair of small hands and the wrists, and after that—nothing. They were moving briskly—washing themselves clean. I saw the water trickle and splash over them—not *through* them—but just as it would on real hands. They were the hands of a little girl, too. Oh, yes, I was sure of that at once. Boys and girls wash their hands differently. I can't just tell you what the difference is, but it's unmistakable.

'I saw all this before my candle slipped and fell with a crash. I had set it down without looking—for my eyes were fixed on the basin—and had balanced it on the edge of the nest of drawers. After the crash, in the darkness there, with the water running, I suffered some bad moments. Oddly enough, the thought uppermost with me was that I *must* shut off that tap before escaping. I *had* to. And after a while I picked up all my courage, so to say, between my teeth, and with a little sob thrust out my hand and did it. Then I fled.

'The dawn was close upon me: and as soon as the sky reddened I took my bath, dressed and went downstairs. And there at the pantry door I found Mrs Carkeek, also dressed, with my candlestick in her hand.

'"Ah!" said I, "you picked it up."

'Our eyes met. Clearly Mrs Carkeek wished me to begin, and I determined at once to have it out with her.

'"And you knew all about it. That's what accounts for your plugging up the cistern."

'"You saw . . .?" she began.

'"Yes, yes. And you must tell me all about it—never mind how bad. Is—is it—murder?"

'"Law bless you, miss, whatever put such horrors in your head?"

They were the hands of a little girl.

'"She was washing her hands."

'"Ah, so she does, poor dear! But—murder! And dear little Miss Margaret, that wouldn't go to hurt a fly!"

'"Miss Margaret?"

'"Eh, she died at seven year. Squire Kendall's only daughter; and that's over twenty year ago. I was her nurse, miss, and I know—diphtheria it was; she took it down in the village."

'"But how do you know it is Margaret?"

'"Those hands—why, how could I mistake, that used to be her nurse?"

'"But why does she wash them?"

'"Well, miss, being always a dainty child—and the housework, you see—"

'I took a long breath. "Do you mean to tell me that all this tidying and dusting—" I broke off. "Is it *she* who has been taking this care of me?"

'Mrs Carkeek met my look steadily.

'"Who else, miss?"

'"Poor little soul!"

'"Well now"—Mrs Carkeek rubbed my candlestick with the edge of her apron—"I'm so glad you take it like this. For there isn't really nothing to be afraid of—is there?" She eyed me wistfully. "It's my belief she loves you, miss. But only to think what a time she must have had with the others!"

'"The others?" I echoed.

'"The other tenants, miss: the ones afore you."

'"Were they bad?"

'"They was awful. Didn't Farmer Hosking tell you? They carried on fearful—one after another, and each one worse than the last."

'"What was the matter with them? Drink?"

'"Drink, miss, with some of 'em. There was the Major—he used to go mad with it, and run about the coombe in his nightshirt. Oh, scandalous! And his wife drank too—that is, if she ever *was* his wife. Just think of that tender child washing up after their nasty doings!"

'I shivered.

'"But that wasn't the worst by a long way. There was a pair here—from the colonies, or so they gave out—with two children, a boy and gel, the eldest scarce six. Poor mites!"

' "Why, what happened?"

' "They beat those children, miss—your blood would boil!—*and* starved, *and* tortured 'em, it's my belief. You could hear their screams, I've been told, away back in the high-road, and that's the best part of half a mile. Sometimes they was locked up without food for days together. But it's my belief that little Miss Margaret managed to feed them somehow. Oh, I can see her, creeping to the door and comforting!"

' "But perhaps she never showed herself when these awful people were here, but took to flight until they left."

' "You didn't never know her, miss. The brave she was! She'd have stood up to lions. She've been here all the while: and only to think what her innocent eyes and ears must have took in! There was another couple—" Mrs Carkeek sunk her voice.

' "Oh, hush!" said I, "if I'm to have any peace of mind in this house!"

' "But you won't go, miss? She loves you, I know she do. And think what you might be leaving her to—what sort of tenant might come next. For she can't go. She've been here ever since her father sold the place. He died soon after. You mustn't go!"

"Now I had resolved to go, but all of a sudden I felt how mean this resolution was.

' "After all," said I, "there's nothing to be afraid of."

' "That's it, miss; nothing at all. I don't even believe it's so very uncommon. Why, I've heard my mother tell of farmhouses where the rooms were swept every night as regular as clockwork, and the floors sanded, and the pots and pans scoured, and all while the maids slept. They put it down to the piskies; but we know better, miss, and now we've got the secret between us we can lie easy in our beds, and if we hear anything, say 'God bless the child!' and go to sleep."

' "Mrs Carkeek," said I, "there's only one condition I have to make."

"What's that?"

' "Why, that you let me kiss you."

' "Oh, you dear!" said Mrs Carkeek as we embraced: and this was as close to familiarity as she allowed herself to go in the whole course of my acquaintance with her.

'I spent three years at Tresillack, and all that while Mrs Carkeek lived with me and shared the secret. Few women, I dare to say, were ever so completely wrapped around with love as we were during those three years. It ran through my waking life like a song: it smoothed my pillow, touched and made my table comely, in summer lifted the heads of the flowers as I passed, and in winter watched the fire with me and kept it bright.

'"Why did I ever leave Tresillack?" Because one day, at the end of five years, Farmer Hosking brought me word that he had sold the house—or was about to sell it; I forget which. There was no avoiding it, at any rate; the purchaser being a Colonel Kendall, a brother of the old Squire.'

'"A married man?" I asked.

'"Yes, miss; with a family of eight. As pretty children as ever you see, and the mother a good lady. It's the old home to Colonel Kendall."

'"I see. And that is why you feel bound to sell."

'"It's a good price, too, that he offers. You mustn't think but I'm sorry enough—"

'"To turn me out? I thank you, Mr Hosking; but you are doing the right thing."

"Since Mrs Carkeek was to stay, the arrangement lacked nothing of absolute perfection—except, perhaps, that it found no room for me.

'"*She*—Margaret—will be happy," I said; "with her cousins, you know."

'"Oh yes, miss, she will be happy, sure enough," Mrs Carkeek agreed.

'So when the time came I packed up my boxes, and tried to be cheerful. But on the last morning, when they stood corded in the hall, I sent Mrs Carkeek upstairs upon poor excuse, and stepped alone into the pantry.

'"Margaret!" I whispered.

'There was no answer at all. I had scarcely dared to hope for one. Yet I tried again, and, shutting my eyes this time, stretched out both hands and whispered:

'"Margaret!"

'And I will swear to my dying day that two little hands stole and rested—for a moment only—in mine.'

Acknowledgments

The publishers would like to extend their grateful thanks to the following authors, publishers and others for kindly granting them permission to reproduce the copyrighted extracts and stories included in this anthology.

THE RIDDLE and BAD COMPANY by Walter de la Mare. Reprinted by kind permission of the Literary Trustees of Walter de la Mare and The Society of Authors as their representative.

THE SYBARITE and A LITTLE HOUSE OF THEIR OWN by Stanley W. Fisher. © 1980 Stanley W. Fisher. Reproduced by kind permission of Mrs Muriel Fisher.

ECHOES IN THE SAND by Roger F. Dunkley. © 1980 Roger F. Dunkley.

FAME by Michelle Maurois. Reprinted by kind permission of the proprietors Flammarion.

GIOVANNI PAOLO'S LAND by Hesbia Brinsmead-Hungerford. Reprinted by kind permission of the author.

THE RED ROOM by H. G. Wells. Reprinted by kind permission of the Estate of the late H. G. Wells.

LONELY BOY and TEA AND EMPATHY by Paul Dorrell. © 1980 Paul Dorrell.

THE PHANTOM HORSES from *Uncle Gustave's Ghosts* by Colin Thiele. Reprinted by kind permission of Rigby Ltd, Adelaide, Australia. © 1974 Colin Thiele.

THE YELLOW CAT by Michael Joseph. Reprinted by kind permission of Mrs Michael Joseph.

KROGER'S CHOICE by John Gordon. © 1980 John Gordon.

THE HAUNTED DOLL'S HOUSE by M. R. James. Reprinted by kind permission of the publishers Edward Arnold.

THE BROWN HAND by Sir Arthur Conan Doyle. Reprinted by kind permission of John Murray (Publishers) Ltd and Jonathan Clowes Limited.

THE WELL and THE MONKEY'S PAW by W. W. Jacobs. Reprinted by kind permission of The Society of Authors as the literary representative of the Estate of W. W. Jacobs.

THE HAUNTED TRAILER by Robert Arthur. © 1939 by the Munsey Co.; © renewed 1966 by Robert Arthur. Reprinted by kind permission of the Regents of the University of Michigan, Ann Arbor.

MANY COLOURED GLASS from *Young Winter's Tales*. © 1970 Lucy M. Boston. Reprinted by kind permission of the author and the Macmillan Co. of London and Basingstoke.

DAMP SHEETS and THE GORGE OF THE CHURELS by H. Russell Wakefield. Reprinted by kind permission of Curtis Brown Ltd on behalf of Russell Wakefield.

THE WOOING OF CHERRY BASNETT by Brian Alderson. Reprinted by kind permission of the author.

THE LATE DEPARTURE by Glenn Chandler. © 1980 Glen Chandler.

THE BATTLE WITH THE BOGLES, originally entitled 'The Bogles from the Howff' from *Heather and Broom* by Sorche Nic Leodhas. Reprinted by kind permission of McIntosh and Otis, Inc.

A PAIR OF HANDS by Sir Arthur Quiller-Couch. Reprinted by kind permission of Miss Fay F. Quiller-Couch.

Every effort has been made to clear copyrights and the publishers trust that their apologies will be accepted for any errors or omissions.